In Memoriam. Dedicated to the memories of my two favourite authors - Jacqueline Lindauer and Antoine de Saint-Exupery for their wonderful stories

That appeal to both adults and children, *Joysanta* and *The little Prince.*

The commander of the horse archers and his lieutenants were sitting on their horses watching the long, wide, and totally disorganized column of men and wagons moving slowly toward Devon and Cornwall on the road below them. There were five of them and they were watching the road from just inside the tree line at the top of a grassy hill that stretched upwards from it. Each of the men had a longbow and several very full quivers of arrows slung over his shoulder and at least four additional fully loaded quivers hanging over his horse's back in front of his saddle. Every one of the five men was an experienced horse archer and a long-serving veteran of the company of archers based in Cornwall—and they had almost fifty similarly trained and equipped men who were waiting further back in the trees.

There was no doubt about it so far as the veteran archers watching the road were concerned; the sight of their disorganized and unprepared enemies moving slowly past them was very encouraging to men who were highly trained, superbly armed with the most modern of weapons, and willing to fight for their free company and its holdings in Cornwall—men like them and the archers they commanded.

The London Gambit

Chapter One

The tournament at Windsor.

The sun was coming through the castle's wall openings and the two de Montfort brothers were just standing there looking at each other. They each obviously had something they wanted to say to the other but they were waiting for the cleric who had been advising them to leave the room.

The French priest serving as their cleric was going off to begin preparing a list of England's barons and the number of knights each was thought to be supporting with his lands. The brothers were smiling at each other because their lice were not bothering them and they totally agreed with the priest's suggestion—that they should be the next kings of England with older of them going first.

When the list of England's barons was finished the priest and the two de Montforts planned to sit down and carefully go over it name by name to decide who amongst the barons on the list they should try to recruit to help them and who they should not approach. They intended to be highly organized and get things right this time. The stakes were too high to do anything less. The stakes, of course, being their heads and necks. But the opportunities were also high; almost every one of the twenty-four members of England's Great Council was at the tournament—and the king was not there to support his cause because he was too weak and poxed to leave his bed and prayers.

The priest's first suggestion that they both should be kings of England, with the son-less older brother going first, was a grand idea. What had not gone down so well was their cleric's second suggestion, that to receive God's favour for their efforts to obtain the crown they must swear that England would remain as a papal state and continue King Henry's practice of paying money to the Church each year for its prayers.

Agreeing to continue the king's practice of paying the Church a substantial tithe each year for its prayers was something entirely different from agreeing to be kings. Indeed, agreeing to pay anything to anybody was something to be avoided if at all possible since the English barons, and particularly the twenty-four of the most biggest and important of them who served on the Great Council, were always angry about the taxes that would have to be levied on them to make the tithing payments— and nothing angered them more than the taxes that were being collected so King Henry could send coins to Rome "so God will look favourably upon me and my kingdom when I die."

Despite their reservations and their almost certain knowledge that they would not last long as kings if they tried to collect taxes from the barons or agreed to pay anything to Rome, the brothers had nodded their heads and agreed with their cleric that continuing to send the tithe coins to Rome was a good idea.

"Sending the kingdom's overdue tithe coins is one of the very first things I will do," the older brother had earnestly assured the priest as he blessed them and left to go to his chamber to begin scribing the list. Even priest knew he was lying through his teeth.

In fact, the brothers were not at all sure about the need for England to continue as a papal state if it meant England would have to continue sending large amounts of coins to the Church, or even small amounts for that matter. Rome, after all, was far away and it would be hard for the Pope to send a papal army to force the barons to pay the necessary taxes if the next king renounced the current king's vassalage to the Pope or, even better, just ignored it entirely so there would never be a decisive break.

On the other hand, agreeing to answer to the Pope by pretending to be one of his vassal states would not be a problem. Words were only words, after all, and could be ignored or misunderstood or lost in translation. Coins on the other hand were coins and they had to come from somewhere. Even so, the brothers knew they would *promise* to continue England as a papal state if it became absolutely necessary to do so in order to attract enough of England's noble landowners who were actually religious to their cause.

Whether either of the de Monforts, or anyone else for that matter, would actually keep his promise to continue England as a papal state and *also* actually pay an annual tithe to the Pope each year was another matter entirely. The brothers knew full well that it would be hard to recruit an adequate army, let alone for either of them to be accepted as England's king, if the barons knew that they were even thinking about continuing to tax the barons' lands in order to keep sending coins to Rome.

Father Pierre, the French Franciscan priest who was their cleric, also knew in his heart of hearts that it was unlikely that either of the de Montforts would keep his promise to continue sending tithe coins to Rome. He knew they would not want to risk being overthrown by the kingdom's taxpayers. On the other hand, he also knew that *he* was likely to be greatly rewarded by the next Pope if England's next king sent *any* coins to Rome, especially if the next Pope was French as the last two had been.

He heaved a great sigh as he picked up his quill and vowed to himself to continue pushing the de Montforts to at least send something to Rome. It was important, particularly if the next Pope turned out to be French so that he himself would be properly rewarded.

On the other hand, and something he would *never* share with the two de Montforts or anyone else, he would have to rethink everything if the next Pope was an Italian such that he would be ignored no matter what he accomplished or how many coins he sent to Rome. *Hmm;*

perhaps there was some way he could get his hands on whatever coins were collected and keep them safe until there was another French Pope. It was, he decided, an interesting possibility and he decided to think about how he might accomplish it.

As their plans stood, the older brother would be the first de Montfort king; his much younger brother would be the second because he would succeed his son-less older brother and be immediately recognized as the heir. And if their fellow barons did not proclaim them as England's next kings they would, at least, likely be allowed to recover their family's earldom and the lands in Leicester which had been taken from their family when their father and oldest brother had their heads chopped off a few years earlier as a reward for their own failed efforts to replace the King Henry.

The not so minor problem the two brothers faced, of course, was that England already had a king; and that a few years earlier the king and his son Edward the crown prince, had executed their father and older brother, along with many others, the last time England's barons had risen and tried to unseat him. The titles and lands of many of the rebel families, including theirs, had been forfeited to the king and his supporters as a result. But now things had changed—King Henry was old and dying and his heir, Prince Edward, had gone off on the Ninth Crusade to help recapture Jerusalem from the Saracens. There was also the not-so-minor problem that a number of other English barons also wanted to be the next king.

******

The two brothers stood silent whilst the priest with whom they had been talking left the room. Only when they were sure Father Pierre could no longer hear them did they resume talking to each other about the matter at hand. And then, because they knew they were thinking of doing something that was dangerous to even think about, they instinctively spoke to each other in low voices even though none of their servants were in the room to overhear them.

"Father Pierre is right. King Henry is old and poxed and only has his personal guards to protect him. He depends on the barons to defend England and keep him on the throne because he has no army of his own. Without enough of the barons supporting him England is lost and so is he," the younger of the two said out loud as if to re-assure himself that they would be safe if they proceeded. He nodded his head to agree with himself as he did.

His older brother nodded his head in agreement and repeated the rest of the story they intended to use to attract supporters to their cause. He did so because he very much wanted to be England's next king or, at the very least, regain the family's title and lands for himself, and he still was not sure about his younger brother's resolve.

"Even better, the Queen's despised French relatives have surrounded the King Henry and are making his decisions and collecting his taxes. They are being allowed to do so because the prince who is the King's heir is off crusading in the Holy Land in an effort to get God's approval for him to stay out of purgatory when he dies."

Hearing their basic argument out loud encouraged them both. So the younger brother picked up the story they planned to tell. It was almost as if they each needed to hear it once again themselves and be assured that the other was on board.

"Aye, you are certainly right about that, brother. Edward is indeed unfit to return from his crusade to be England's king and everyone knows it. In any event, what really matters now is that it will not be long before England will need a new king. And Father Pierre is absolutely correct when he says we need to get ourselves ready to act quickly, very quickly, since Henry will soon be on his deathbed if he is not there already.

"So what we need to do now, before King Henry dies, is get on with putting together an army that is as big as possible and have it ready to march with a new king to Westminster Abbey and put a crown on his head as soon as Henry passes.

"The barons' big mistake in the past was to hold down the number of good men who were involved so that each of them would each get a bigger share when the lands of the king and his supporters were portioned out." That was not exactly true, of course, but they needed to have an explanation ready if someone appeared to be reluctant to join because the barons' previous efforts to replace the king had failed with such disastrous results for many of those who had been involved—including the de Montforts' father and various of their relatives including their older brother and several cousins.

The older of the two brothers agreed with the story.

"I agree with you, brother; you know I do. If there is anything to be learned from the previous efforts to get rid of the king and replace him with someone more worthy, it is that we need to bring in as many as possible of the smaller barons and fence-sitting larger ones into our army or, at the very least, get them to agree to remain neutral and not come against us when we make our move. We cannot march until we have assembled an army that is large enough to win."

The younger man agreed. He wrongly considered himself to be the driving force and his more fearful older brother to be the weak link in the family chain.

"Yes, you are right about that; you certainly are. And that means we especially need to recruit the barons with largest numbers of knights and biggest levies—and then be patient and wait until the king is in the ground and his heir has no supporters to mobilize and no time to find them. And next week's tournament at Windsor is just the place to begin doing what needs to be done."

"Aye," the older man replied with a note of warning in his voice, "and Father Pierre is also right about what we should do when we get to Windsor—we need to profess a great loyalty to King Henry and at the same begin quietly vouchsafing the rumour that Edward intends to remain as a crusader in the Holy Land in order to atone for his many sins and those of his family. Besides, it might even be true."

Chapter Two

Windsor during the tournament.

The five men had taken a break and were pissing against a nearby wall whilst one of unhorsed entrants was being tended to where he had fallen. It looked bad for the man on the ground and the crowd was very excited and pleased.

There were many "oohs" and "aahs" and much cheering and clapping for both the winner and the badly injured loser. The younger de Montfort saw his chance and took it. So did several of the entrants who had not yet ridden; they decided to drop out in order to pray for the man who had been knocked off his horse. Besides, they told themselves, there was no real need to participate and risk getting hurt or killed; King Henry would not see their bravery and favour them since he had taken to his bed and only left it to pray in his nearby chapel.

"My brother and I are with King Henry and loyal to him in all ways," the younger de Montfort said to the Earl of Westminster as he shook his dingle and dropped his tunic. "But we must be ready to act on the King's behalf if his distant relatives in France try to take advantage of the King being seriously poxed by invading England when he cannot fight back because he has neither an army in place nor an army commander to take his place.

"The latest reports have it that King Phillip intends to try to take the throne and will land his army someplace far to the west of Dover because Dover Castle is so strongly held and because the Portsmen of the Cinque Ports will almost certainly sally out to fight when they see the French fleet approaching —which the Portsmen must do or they will lose both their heads and their privileges as sea lords.

"But Phillip and his army can avoid being intercepted by the Portsmen and having to fight at sea if they sail far enough to the west and land at Exeter or Plymouth or even in Cornwall itself. And that is what our spies tell us they intend to do."

I was telling a lie when I told them that the French were coming to seize the throne, of course. And we had no spies. But convincing enough people like my fellow pissers that it was true was the necessary first step in our plan to put together a great "Loyal Army" of barons. It would be understood amongst a select few such as these men, but never said out loud or put down on parchment, that the barons of the "Loyal Army" would take the throne and install one of their own even if the French never came.

The men gathered at the pissing wall were listening intently so he continued.

"I think we all agree with the most experienced of the fighting men amongst us who say that western Devon is probably the best place for our men to muster and wait for the French. That is because Cornwall is adjacent and its lands have no lords and knights to stop us from foraging for food in its villages and monasteries whilst we wait for the Phillip and his men.

"And also, of course, and this is important, because the lands on the border between Devon and Cornwall are far enough from Windsor so the King's few remaining supporters will not think we are forming an army to start another uprising against the king—which we are certainly *not* doing and *never* will." *He smiled as he told his lie with greatest possible sincerity in his voice and the others smiled back because they knew he did not mean it.*

The younger de Montfort continued after a brief pause to smooth out his finely embroidered tunic.

"We have no choice. We must stop the French from seizing our lands and England's throne. No one else can stop them because Prince Edward is off crusading to save his soul and cannot get back in time. Even worse, Edward has no reason to come back from the Holy Land because he knows God will never approve of him being the king. That is because of his sins and his mother's sins when Henry was away fighting and now whilst he is poxed and has taken to his bed.

"Indeed, washing away his sins and those of his mother and her relatives is why Edward keeps telling everyone he will almost certainly stay in the Holy Land after Henry dies. It is God's truth that he is a good Christian, eh Edmund?" *It too was a lie; but who could say otherwise. Besides it might even be true.*

What the younger de Montfort said was intended to sway the Earl of Westminster, who was standing next to him, to join their cause. They wanted him to become actively involved because he was one of England's most powerful barons with more than a hundred knight's fees on his great landholdings around London and eleven more on his family's traditional lands in the north of Kent. It was also well known that the Earl's lands in and around London had made him England's richest man with more coins in his chests than the king. It also did not escape the de Montforts that because the Earl of Westminster was so rich he could employ entire companies of mercenaries if he so desired.

Unfortunately, at least for the two de Montforts, Westminster was also known to be as ambitious as they were to increase his wealth and position. But they felt they had to have him on their side or at least neutral; perhaps an advance of his title to Duke and more lands in the north would suffice. That is what their cleric suggested Westminster be offered. And if he did not accept, they had asked? In that case, the cleric had suggested, they should arrange for the Earl have an accident during the fighting or eat something that poxed him. Campaigning, after all, was always dangerous and everyone knew it.

What the younger de Montfort said had been carefully thought out so that he could not be accused of treason if his words got back to King Henry and his supporters. It was also carefully said so as to not put any ideas in the Earl's head about the Earl himself trying to become England's next king. *The brothers de Montfort need not have concerned themselves with that—the idea was already behind the Earl's eyes and had been there for years. He was the noble living closest to the king's London residence and had been jealous for years that it was much grander than his. The solution was simple so far as the Earl was concerned—he would become king and own them both.*

In any event, the younger de Montfort's argument about why Edward might not return was a particularly good one to make to his fellow pissers. Firstly, because Edward's mother, the Queen, was genuinely detested because she was French-born and had surrounded herself and King Henry with her French relatives instead of loyal Englishmen. And second, because James of Chichester, one of the barons standing along the pissing wall with the de Montforts and Westminster, had some years earlier deposed his crusading older brother and seized control of his family's lands using a somewhat similar argument and a few carefully placed coins to obtain the king's acceptance of him as the rightful baron ruling his family's lands around Chichester.

The other men standing next to them and listening intently were all members or the sons of members of the Great Council of twenty-four barons which periodically met to advise the king on matters of war and taxes. They nodded their heads in agreement with what they heard. Whether they actually meant it or were just being polite was still uncertain.

"If you agree that something must be done to keep the French from taking England's throne from King Henry, we can talk again tonight over a bowl of wine about how best to prepare for the arrival of the French invaders without alarming the king or turning our backs on him. The only thing that is certain is that there will *never* be another barons' war against the king—only a very just war against the French who have stolen the King's lands in France and are apparently once again coming for his lands and crown in England. We must gather our men to stand *with* the king to protect him and England from the French."

The younger de Montfort said it with greatest sincerity he could muster, and he looked intently at each of them, in turn, until they had each nodded their heads in agreement. Moments later the tournament horn was blown and the men hurried back to their seats. They were just getting to them as the horn sounded again and the next two knights were announced.

It was a good first step the younger de Montfort thought as he smiled to himself and led the men back to their seats on the benches reserved for the families of nobles and knights. The next step would be to meet with each of the barons individually and very cautiously feel them out to see where they really stood. But no matter what they said we will follow Father Pierre's advice and wait until the "Loyal Army" is already formed and under our command before we begin raising the question as to what the "Loyal Army" should do if Edward has not returned by the time the King dies.

The Church might be able to wait for a Pope, but when King Henry died the younger de Montfort was fairly sure that he and his brother could convince his fellow barons that England could not wait for a king—especially if their armies were already assembled in western Devon "waiting for the French" on the road that led directly to Windsor and London. *If Prince Edward unexpectedly returned before the king died they would weigh their chances and if they found them wanting they would slink off to their homes and pretend they were always loyal.*

****** *The de Montforts' success*

Most of England's barons and their knights were moved by "the need for you and your men to join the Loyal Army immediately so we can be fully ready to fight when the French begin landing in the west." Their enthusiasm was aided by the suggestion whispered into the ears of many of them that their taxes would be eliminated and the lands of the traitorous lords who rallied to the French would be distributed according to the size of each baron's contribution to the Loyal Army. Many of them were also encouraged to believe that the same benefits would be received if they supported whomever among them became the new king when Henry passed from the scene.

It was also helped by the fact that England's lords and their knights knew that once the tournament was over they would be once again bored out of their minds by spending their days watching their slaves and serfs plough their fields and harvest their crops. Going off to get ready to fight the French *"wink wink"*, on the other hand, would bring some excitement into their lives. And, of course, many of the barons and knights saw it as a chance to get away from their wives without having to spend the coins needed to feed their men or take the risks necessary to go crusading.

As you might imagine, the formation of the "Loyal Army" was well underway by the time the tournament was over. That the barons would be subsequently asked to select a new king if Edward had not returned by the time King Henry died was understood by many of them but never mentioned.

King Henry and the Queen's relatives, as you also might imagine, soon learned all about the formation of the

"Loyal Army." It was inevitable. Fortunately, the Church's ambassador to England, the Nuncio who had been appointed by Pope Clement before he died, was able to convince the ailing king, whilst King Henry was between his many daily prayers and barberings, that the army of loyal Englishmen being formed to fight off a French invasion was a good idea.

The Nuncio did so by making much of the fact that the "Loyal Army" would be forming up far away from the king along the border between Devon and Cornwall so there would be no mistake about its peaceful intentions toward him. It was forming up there, the Nuncio explained to the king, because the French were expected to land somewhere in the southwest in order to stay well away from Dover and the Portsmen of the Cinque Ports, and also because Cornwall had no barons and knights who would be distressed when the army foraged for food.

Moreover, and quite important, or so the Nuncio claimed, he had been present at the meeting after the tournament when each of the barons put his hand on a bible and swore an oath to protect Good King Henry from the perfidious French and *never* stand against him or try to replace him.

King Henry was greatly touched by the devotion of his barons after so many years of treachery and swayed by the Nuncio's assurances of their good intentions and his promises that with only a few more prayers and donations the king would be able to totally avoid a visit to purgatory before ascending to heaven. As a result, he ignored Queen Eleanor's warnings and agreed with the Nuncio that an army of Englishmen sworn to protect him and his kingdom was a good thing, especially since it would not cost him any coins and he would be able to keep paying his tithes to the Church and making the additional donations and prayer purchases necessary to keep himself out of purgatory.

It was, of course, all true. But what the Nuncio had somehow forgotten to mention to the King was that no such oaths were being sworn to protect his heir. The Nuncio also did not mention the substantial amount of coins and the knight's fee in Kent he had been promised by the de Montfort brothers if King Henry did not oppose the formation of the Loyal Army. *It was not that the Nuncio wanted to leave the Church and live in Kent, he told the young French priest who was his "special friend"; but only God knew what would happen to French priests like themselves if the next Pope was an Italian.*

Queen Eleanor and her relatives, on the other hand, were not sure what to think about the army that was being formed. As a result, they ended up doing nothing except complain just as Nuncio had predicted to the de Montforts' cleric. Well almost nothing; one of her dull-witted nephews foolishly took it upon himself to scribe a parchment and send it to Phillip, France's new king, asking if there was any truth to the rumour that he was sending a French army to invade England.

King Phillip did not respond immediately. But he knew of Henry's advanced age and he too had heard about Henry's decline and Edward's absence. And the more he thought about it and looked at the maps of England, the more he thought it might be a good idea.

A week or two later King Phillip sent a warm and friendly message back to the Queen's nephew swearing before God Almighty that he had no quarrel with King Henry that could possibly lead to war—and immediately began planning to gather an army and invade England as soon as he received word that Henry's death had either occurred or was imminent.

If William of Normandy could do it, so could he. Besides, it would keep his son and heir busy and could be easily accomplished. The key to success was to avoid losing a battle at sea with the Portsmen of the Cinque Ports that cost him part of his army. And that could be accomplished, he decided, by landing his army somewhere further down the coast where they would be able to get ashore unopposed and wait for his English supporters to rally to him—someplace like Exeter or Plymouth, for instance.

Chapter Three

Storm Clouds and uncertainty.

It was early in June in the year 1271 and the Commander of the Cornwall-based Company of Archers, Robert Robertson, a Company veteran who had held the position of Commander for more than ten years, had just returned from the Company's fortress on Cyprus, the hub of the Company's operations east of Gibraltar. He needed to know if anything important had happened in England during his absence and was waiting impatiently at the Company's headquarters at Cornwall's Restormel Castle for the arrival of the men who could tell him.

Commander Robertson routinely spent half of every year east of Gibraltar. He sailed from Cornwall to Cyprus each year because most of the coins the Company earned came from its operations in the east. The Company earned the coins by using its fleet of Cyprus-based war galleys and transports to carry passengers, cargos, and money orders from port to port despite the Moorish pirates who infested those waters.

Many of them, the coins earned by the Company in the east that is, were sent to Cornwall where some of them were used to pay the men of the Company who were stationed in England and to cover the Company's various and sundry other expenses including the recruiting and training of the steady stream of new archers that had to be sent east to expand the Company's operations and replace the men who had fallen. The rest of the coins were hoarded at Restormel and several other Company strongholds for when they would almost certainly be needed when Jesus returned in the near future and peace broke out everywhere. It would not be long now as the Church was already soliciting coins to help pay for the welcoming ceremonies and feasts.

Typically the Company's commander sailed to the east from Cornwall when the leaves began to fall off the trees around Restormel Castle and returned to spend the summer at Restormel when the buds of the fresh new leaves began to the spring forth from their winter-deadened branches. He returned to Cornwall each such time of leaf springing instead of staying in the east because Restormel Castle was the site of the Company's depot where it trained ambitious English men to be archers. It was also a nice place to be compared to the torturously hot summers of the east.

Restormel Castle was the site of the Company's school where likely young boys recruited from all over England, and especially from Cornwall and the families of the archers themselves, were taught to sum and scribe so they might someday become the Company's captains and commanders. They were commoners all because the sons of nobles and knights were often too full of themselves to be learnt how to get along with commoners and how to fight as a single force with modern weapons such as longbows and the bladed pikes produced by the smiths at the Company's great stronghold on Cyprus.

Commander Robertson travelled back and forth between Cornwall and Cyprus in one of the Company's war galleys and inspected the Company's shipping posts at the ports along way both coming and going. It was a hard and dangerous way for a man to earn his daily bread and particularly so for those of his men who crewed the Company's war galleys and did not have enough rank to live in the relative comfort of one of each galley's two deck castles, the small one in the bow where the ranking man aboard lived in splendid isolation and the much larger one in the stern where his lieutenants and his senior sergeants slept in extremely close proximity. Everyone else on board wrapped themselves in skins and slept wherever he could find shelter, mostly on or under their assigned rowing benches and in the unlit cargo hold if there was enough room.

On the other hand the Commander and his men were paid well, very well actually, for their efforts and privations. The Company had nine ranks and its men were paid according to the rank they held. The ranks were indicated by the number of stripes and large circles sewn on to the front and back of each man's tunic.

Importantly, each additional rank doubled an archer's pay and also his share of any prize monies or ransoms to which he might be entitled. Thus a captain of one of the Company's war galleys or shipping posts wearing four stripes was at the sixth highest rank and paid thirty-two times as many coins as an archer marching in the Company's rear ranks with one stripe on his tunic, sixteen times as many as a chosen man with two stripes, eight times as many as a sergeant with three, four times as many as a Sergeant Major with three stripes with a circle over them, and twice as many as a lieutenant with three stripes and two circles. And if a man lasted long enough to become a captain he had a chance to rise even further and become one of the Company's three five-stripe major captains, or four six-stripe lieutenant commanders, or even wear the seven stripes of the Company Commander himself.

There was no doubt about the fact that a common man *could* serve long enough and successfully enough to rise in rank and get rich serving in the Company. It was not likely in the circumstances in which they lived and fought, of course; but it was possible as every man could see. The reality, however, was that he was more likely to find himself dead or even worse before he obtained a high rank. It was an unfortunate fact that most of the Company's recruits would die or become disabled from fighting or be taken by a terrible pox or a tragedy at sea long before they could become rich and retire in England or wherever else they might want to end their days.

Fortunately for the Company, the likelihood that a man would not make it to an honourable retirement on half pay was a reality that was ignored by its recruits. To the contrary, the Company was never short of men willing to make their marks on the Company roll and go off to be trained for an archer—probably because there were few other ways for a commoner to improve his lot in Cornwall or anywhere else in England. It had always been that way and still is to this very day.

****** *The annual meeting at Restormel*

Lieutenant Commander George Courtenay was visiting Restormel Castle to meet with the Company's newly returned Commander along with the Company captains who were the constables commanding the Company's strongholds at Launceston Castle and Plymouth's Plympton Castle. George was there because he had the six stripes of a lieutenant commander on his tunic and commanded the Company of Archers' horse archers and outriders based at Okehampton Castle on the Devon side of the River Tamar. He was, in addition, the constable charged with holding Okehampton Castle for the Company.

George was the Company's highest ranking man in England when Commander Robertson was not present and the Commander's number two, the man who would automatically step into the Commander's sandals and take over the command of the Company if the Commander went down. It was probably a good indication of where the Company earned most of its coins that the Company's other three lieutenant commanders and two of its three major captains were all permanently stationed in the east.

In the interim, whilst he waited for the Commander to fall or retire, George was tasked with keeping Cornwall and the Company's school and recruit-training depot at Restormel Castle safe from interferences by outsiders. Indeed it was explicitly scribed in the Company's compact on which every man made his mark that Cornwall and the Company were to be defended against anyone who might want to interfere with what the Company was doing and attempt to share in its revenues and wealth—and that meant just about everyone from England's poxed and pious old king Henry and the power-hungry English and French nobles who attended his court to the wandering priests and bishops who might try to mislead the people of Cornwall into doing something stupid such as giving them coins in exchange for their prayers and promises.

The Company of Archers had been formed eighty years or so years earlier by King Richard to go crusading in an effort to liberate Jerusalem from the heathen Saracens. George's great-grandfather, William Courtenay, had been a runaway serf when he and his priestly brother had gone for archers with King Richard.

William and his priestly brother had made their marks to join King Richard's original Company of Archers and he had been learnt to push arrows out of a longbow. The brothers had fought in the Company's ranks in the Holy Land for some years until its handful of surviving archers had elected William to be their captain. That had happened some ten years or so later after King Richard suddenly deserted what was left of his men in order to return to England.

Desperate to survive after the king abandoned them, the archers had initially become mercenaries employed to help defend crusader castles. It was George's great-grandfather and his brother and their handful of fellow surviving archers who had begun transforming the Company of Archers from earning its men's coins and daily bread by fighting on land as mercenaries to primarily earning them at sea by safely carrying refugees and other passengers and cargos from one port to another.

Cornwall had become the site of the Company's depot and training ground for new archers for the simple reason that Cornwall was where William Courtenay, George's great-grandfather, and the last few survivors of his men had first gone ashore when they finally returned to England. How it all happened and why the Company's survivors subsequently recruited new men and led them back to the Holy Land was a very exciting story and long ago told.

Today, fortunately, at least from the Company's point of view, the Saracens once again held Jerusalem and Christians trying to win favour in the eyes of God or tired of the weather and life where they live still travelled to the east to go crusading or make pilgrimages to the Holy Land. The hostilities between them, the Saracens and Christians that is, provided many fine opportunities for the Company to earn coins and grow. The real world of the thirteenth century, in other words, was both dangerous and an absolute pangloss for the Company and its men—the best of all possible worlds.

George Courtenay was the third man with that name to serve in the Company of Archers and rise in its ranks. Doing so had become a family tradition. In fact, and despite his family name being Courtenay, George was on the Company's roll as George Young or, more precisely, as George the Younger. He had been enrolled in the Company with that name by a clerk who was trying to avoid the inevitable confusion that would occur if there were two men on the Company's roll at the same time with exactly the same name.

The potential problem had existed at the time because George's late grand uncle, also named George Courtenay, had still been on active duty as the Company's commander when George had been found to be sufficiently full of Latin, summing, and scribing such that he was passed out of the Company's school at Restormel Castle to become one of the Company's twenty or so highly-valued apprentice sergeants. How each of the apprentice sergeants advanced in the Company after he had spent a few years scribing and summing for one of the Company's illiterate captains was up to him. As you might well imagine, many of the five or six lads who joined the Company from the school each year fell along the way before reaching an honourable and prosperous retirement at half pay.

George had completed his schooling at the Company's school at the age of sixteen when he had been examined and found sufficiently full of learning and the ability to fight with the modern weapons used by the Company such as longbows and bladed pikes with long handles. He had immediately been allowed to make his mark on the Company's roll and join it as an apprentice sergeant. Simultaneously, because he had been learnt in school to scribe and babble in Latin, he had been ordained as an Angelovian priest so he could go off and earn his daily bread muttering prayers in Latin and selling indulgences if it turned out that he was not up to serving as an archer.

George's ability to babble and scribe in Latin and also to do sums, in addition to his ability to put his foot down to the beat of a drum, push arrows out of a longbow, and use one of the Company's deadly long-handled and bladed pikes, had set him apart from the Company's inevitably illiterate archers and sailors and served him well. He was also very unique in that he and many others in his family, including both of his sons, had his father's and grandfather's bright red hair.

Indeed, the clerk who had scribed George's name on the Company's roll later admitted to him over a bowl of ale in a Cyprus tavern that he had seriously considered entering George's name on the roll as George Redman or George Redhair to distinguish him from all the other Georges in the Company. His friends from school still called him "Red" and so did his men behind his back.

That was twenty-six years ago. Today in early June of 1271 George's hair was beginning to turn grey around the edges and he was one of the Company's four lieutenant commanders, the captain of the Company's highly trained horse archers, and the Commander's number two who would take over if the Commander fell. He and his wife lived at Okehampton Castle, which he also commanded as its constable, in the three rooms assigned to the Commander's number two in that very formidable stronghold on the approaches to Cornwall.

Befitting his high rank and because rank had its privileges, George and his wife lived in rooms at the very top of the castle's citadel with their own fireplace, woven carpets from the Saracen lands on its floors and walls to reduce the draughts of cold air, and a chamber pot that was all their own. Their rooms had a fine view out of their archer slits, caught the sun from every direction so that it was relatively warm and dry when the sun was shining, and was high enough to be away from the foul smells of the castle's moats that surrounded each of its three curtain walls. It also had wooden shutters that could be closed at night to keep the poisonous night airs from coming in through the archer slits.

Okehampton Castle was just inside Devon on the approaches to Cornwall and important because it effectively controlled the road that branched off from the old Roman road between London and Exeter and crossed into Cornwall at the nearby River Tamar ford. It was the only road into Cornwall and the ford was the first one a traveller would come to if he walked up the river from the ocean. It was also the only ford which was served by a ford.

The castle itself was relatively impregnable as castles go even though it did not particularly look that way from the outside. To the contrary, it looked relatively benign because only the castle's moated outermost wall and the top of its citadel where George lived with his wife could be seen by anyone standing outside the castle and looking up at it. In fact, Okehampton was anything but benign because over the years the men of the Company of Archers had surrounded the original castle and its original moated wall with two additional moated and portcullised curtain walls made of stone. At some point the archers had dug a well in the inner bailey that went down far enough to reach the water seeping into it from the stream on its north side that supplied all three of the castle's moats with water.

Moreover, and because Okehampton was owned by the Company of Archers who used it as the headquarters for the Company's horse archers and outriders, it always had enough grain and firewood in its cellars so that the relatively small number of defenders needed to prevent its capture could hold out for at least two years.

The archers stationed there were all riders and their families and horses lived inside the castle in stalls that ran all along the inside of the outer curtain wall. Somewhat uniquely, the horse archers and outriders were *not* intended to be part of the castle's defensive garrison. In the event of an attack on the Company or its lands or Cornwall their families would be evacuated to safety in western Cornwall and they would be deployed outside the castle in raiding companies to hang like roving packs of wolves upon the attackers' foragers and encampments.

George's tunic displayed the six stripes on its front and back that indicated he held the rank of a lieutenant commander in the Company of Archers and the numerous battle dots sewn on above them indicated that he was a veteran who had fought in a number of battles with the Moors and others of the Company's various enemies. He was 41 years old and had three daughters from his plague-taken first wife and two younger sons from his second. Anne, his second wife, was herself the daughter of a long-gone archer lieutenant. All three of George's daughters were married to archers stationed on Cyprus and both of his sons, Edward, 13, and Thomas, 15, were enrolled in the Company school for apprentice sergeants at Restormel Castle, the same school that George himself had attended many years earlier.

If and when George's sons were ever found sufficiently full of summing and scribing and reasonably competent in the babbling of Latin they would likely be allowed to follow in their father's footsteps and enter the Company of Archers as apprentice sergeants; if they were not they would have to settle for being priests or, perhaps, clerics who did the scribing and summing for their illiterate betters amongst England's nobles and merchants in a manner similar to the work usually done by the Company's apprentice sergeants. The difference, of course, was the Company's apprentice sergeants could distinguish themselves and rise in rank by virtue of their merit whereas a priest or cleric was doomed to stagnate unless he could find enough coins to buy a better position from his superiors.

The boys did not know it, of course, but George and his wife already had a plan about what to do if it was decided that either of their sons were not up to joining the Company—after a bit of priestly seasoning in a parish to make sure they knew how to mumble prayers and extract coins from the faithful and those pretending to be, George would use the coins he had saved from his pay to buy the prayers necessary to obtain a bishop's diocese somewhere in England for either or both of them. The sons of the lords might have titles and grand names and the useful contacts necessary to become bishops; but he, goddamn them all, had the coins and knew exactly how to spend them and who to bribe in order to get what he wanted from the Holy Father in Rome. It was something he would do only if it was absolutely necessary.

George was also second in line to be the next landless Earl of Cornwall after his older brother Robert who was himself a five-stripe major captain based at the Company's stronghold on Cypress. That was because the current Earl, his elderly uncle, Charles, had no sons and neither did his brother Robert. The most important thing about George, however, at least so far as the men of the Company were concerned, was that he had twenty-six years of experience successfully leading men in battles on both land and sea— as everyone could plainly see from his promotions and the large number of battle dots sewn on the back and back of his tunic above the six stripes of his high rank.

Ambitious commoners like George and his uncle and the other men of Cornwall's Company of Archers were never properly understood by the English kings and their nobles. They thought of the Company and its men, if they thought of them at all, as inconsequential and ignorable because the Company's captains and men were all commoners and a good number of them had been birthed as serfs and slaves. And it was certainly true that there was not a single knight or knight's son amongst them. Their enrolment as archers was forbidden by the articles of the Company as a result of their inevitable haughty behaviour towards the commoners who filled the Company's ranks and were all self-made men as a result of extensive training and having arms strong enough to push an arrow out of a longbow or wield a sword or one of the Company's newfangled bladed pikes.

The King and his nobles saw the Earl of Cornwall and his heirs as similarly unimportant. That was because, unlike all of England's other hereditary earls, the current Earl of Cornwall was *not* a knight and did *not* hold any lands that could provide him with the knights and the men of the poorly armed and badly trained village levies that England's king and its nobles valued so highly and used in their wars—until they got tired of buying food for their men and went home without them.

Actually, truth be told, England's kings and their courts had rarely, if ever, even seen an Earl of Cornwall or communicated with him. That was because, by family tradition and a very firm rule of the Company of Archers, neither the Earl nor any member of his family ever attended the king's court or a tournament. Similarly, they always quietly paid the king's required scutages such that they never had to participate when the king marched away on one of his periodic wars to see off the ever-rebellious Scots or once again attempted to regain some of his family's lost lands in France. In other words, the Earl and the Courtenay family might be famous and influential in the Mediterranean ports and states but they were effectively unknown in England outside of western Devon and Cornwall and no man's vassals; they were Company men and only Company men.

In fact, Cornwall's first Courtenay earl, George's great grandfather, William, had been a serf who ended up commanding the Company of Archers when it was down to a handful of exhausted men who had survived King Richard's crusade and Richard's treacherous abandonment of his men. He had only become the Earl of Cornwall years later when he bought the then-worthless title off Prince John when King Richard was still alive and John was his regent and needed money. And he only bought it in order to prevent someone else from buying it and trying to involve himself in what the Company had begun doing in Cornwall and in the eastern Mediterranean.

William bought the worthless earldom, or so the story went, with some of the coins he and his priestly brother had taken off a murderous bishop when William and what was left of the Company's men decided to stop crusading and return home to England. He and his brother had subsequently taken Courtenay as their family name some years later because they liked the way it sounded when they took Okehampton Castle and learned the name of the Norman lord they had killed when he was stupid enough to come out of Okehampton and attack a party of archers passing on the nearby road. He, the Norman lord William and his men had killed, had apparently attacked them because the archers had not paid him a toll for using the road.

George did not know if the stories about his ancestors and his family name were accurate; but he liked them and had told them to his sons as if they were. Boys, after all, need to know from whence they came even if it might not be altogether true.

What George also knew, and even his children and wife did not, was a much more closely guarded family secret—that there were many chests of gold and silver coins and other valuables in the windowless room next to the Earl's Restormel Castle bed chamber and also in one of the castle's secret escape tunnels that had long ago been sealed off so no one could get into it from outside the castle. Only the oldest three men in the family were allowed to know about the family hoard and the other tunnels. It was so scribed in the parchment book of instructions and rules for the family and the Company that had been laid down by William, the Company's first Courtenay, before he died.

In other words, in addition to George's savings there might well be other family coins that could be used to buy an obscure diocese and a bishop's mitre for one or both of George's sons if they were not allowed to make their marks on the Company's roll. *The source of the great and growing cache of coins, how they got to Restormel, and why there were so many of them is an exciting story and also long ago told.*

In any event, in the summer of 1271 the Courtenay family's earl held Restormel Castle and the great wealth secreted within it and both sons of George Courtenay and his wife Anne were in the Company school at Restormel

Castle. He was proud of the fact that his sons would serve in the Company's ranks if and when the school found them to be sufficiently full of learning and able to put their feet down to the beat of a marching drum. Also in 1271, and in return for the Company's use of part of the castle and its grounds, the Company of Archers was continuing to be committed to defend Restormel Castle in addition to the three Company-owned strongholds that guarded the approaches to Cornwall—Okehampton Castle near the ford over the Tamar, Launceston Castle which was near the ford on the Cornwall side of the River Tamar, and Plympton Castle on the outskirts of Plymouth.

Every man in the Company understood that the Company was committed to do whatever was necessary to defend Cornwall and the three Company strongholds that were strung out along the River Tamar that served as Cornwall's border with the rest of England.

The Company's willingness to fight to defend Cornwall and its strongholds from outsiders was thought to be necessary for several reasons: First, to keep out meddling outsiders such as nobles and priests who might interfere with the Company's activities and its good relationship with the people, mostly franklins, who worked its lands. Second, because the Company had a permanent contract with the Earls of Cornwall to protect Cornwall and it was important to maintain the Company's reputation for honouring its contracts even if meant serious fighting. The Company would have fought to defend Cornwall and its depot at Restormel Castle without the contract but its existence had long ago formalized its commitment.

Indeed the importance of the Company's doing everything possible to honour its contracts was constantly hammered into every man even before he was allowed to make his mark on the Company's roll. The reason it had to be done, or so the men were told and most of them were smart enough to understand, was quite simple— passengers and cargos and money orders fetched higher prices when the passengers and merchants believed a very determined effort, including fighting against pirates if necessary, would be made by the Company's crews to insure that they and their cargos would safely reach their destinations. It was the reason that archers rowed the Company's galleys and crewed its transports instead of the slaves used by its competitors.

Being known for being willing to fight to honour its commitments to protect its passengers and cargos was important because of the additional coins the merchants and passengers were willing to pay to reduce the risk that they would be captured or killed. The additional coins, in turn, meant the Company would not only be able to continue paying its men and retirees and providing them with food and shelter and periodic opportunities to earn prize monies, but also would be able to put some coins aside so that it could continue doing so when Jesus returned and peace broke out everywhere such that cargos and passengers no longer needed the archers' protection.

In any event, in the early summer of 1271 the Company held the three Cornwall-related strongholds on the approaches to Cornwall with its well-trained and superbly armed archers. It did so despite most of the Company's men being deployed in the east to operate its shipping posts and serve in its vast and constantly growing fleet of war galleys and ever-larger transports. In essence, and right under the upturned noses of the King of England and his nobles and the free-loaders who attended his court, the Company of Archers had become Britain's first great armed merchant company—and the King and the nobles who attended his court and aspired to take the King's place continued to know little, if anything, about either Cornwall or the Company and its men.

And not only were the King and his lords and knights barely aware of the Company, they also did not know much about Cornwall and they cared even less. As they saw Cornwall in the early days of summer in the year 1271, the only thing of value in it were its stannaries whose revenues from the mining and refining of tin all belonged to the King and had been declining for years despite one or two new discoveries and ever deeper mines.

Indeed, Cornwall had always been thought to be so poor that even the Romans had not bothered to build a road to it from London—they had, instead, turned left when they reached the River Tamar and continued along the east side of the river until they reached Exeter and Plymouth on the coast and began to build what are now known as Exeter's Rougemont Castle and Plymouth's Plympton Castle.

As a result of the ignorance of England's kings and their nobles, the men of Cornwall were rarely asked to join the King's armies or those of his baronial enemies. It would have been considered a waste of time to ask or require them to join because it was well known that the men of Cornwall who did not choose to work for the king in the stannaries had to join the Company and sail to the eastern Mediterranean as archers to earn their daily bread. They could not earn enough farming in Cornwall, or so it was constantly claimed by the Company's Commander and his captains, because all of the useful lands were owned by the monasteries such that Cornwall could not support a single knight or priest let alone a land-owning noble or two.

In other words, the men of the Company and Cornwall were not available to serve in the King's wars because they were with either serving with the Company of Archers in the east; or digging in the tin mines for the king; or chanting prayers and buggering each other in Cornwall's monasteries.

It was a sad and discouraging view of Cornwall and one that the Company's captains and commanders constantly went out of their way to spread as widely and frequently as possible. Of course they did. There were no flies on the men who made the Company's decisions. They knew they had a good thing going and they neither wanted to lose their highly trained men in the king's meaningless wars nor share their coins and prospects with anyone else. And they certainly did not want some land-oriented English noble or knight who had not been learnt to lead men in battle giving them orders or telling them how to fight.

As you might imagine, the men serving in the Company's ranks agreed with their captains. They knew it was better to go for an archer to earn their daily bread and coins than almost anything else they might do in England. That was because the Company was a place where a commoner might improve his lot and his rank with hard work and a little luck, especially when the alternative for most of them was to walk endlessly behind a plough as some lord's vassal until it was time to starve and die by following his lord into a war that had no meaning or purpose for a common man and his family.

In essence, the prospects of a man who was allowed to make his mark on the Company's roll as an archer or sailor were better than those of most commoners because the King was far away, the roads in the rest of England were always bad, and the Company went out of its way to protect its men from trouble-making priests and nobles.

Cornwall in the latter half of the thirteenth century, in other words, was a pangloss for the Company of Archers— the best of all possible worlds—an almost perfect place to recruit and train archers and send them eastward to earn coins for themselves and their fellow archers. It was also a good place to recruit sailors for the Company's fleet of galleys and transports because of the England's seafaring tradition.

The Company's main problem, of course, was that England was far away from where the Company earned its coins. And also that it rained frequently in Cornwall and archers' bowstrings do not do very well when they are wet. On the other hand, the ale in Cornwall's taverns had always been uncommonly good and its taverns and their fires warm and welcoming when the weather was bad.

In any event, a constant stream of the Company's men and their galleys and transports periodically sailed to the east where the winters were warmer and archers who knew how to push arrows out of a longbow were highly prized and carefully nurtured, at least to the extent it was possible to do so under the circumstances of constantly sailing in dangerous pirate-filled seas and periodically fighting their way aboard Moorish transports and war galleys to take them as prizes.

******

Unlike prosperous and thriving Cornwall in the year 1271, the rest of England was like a finely embroidered tunic that was fraying and coming apart at the seams. England's king, Henry III, the son of King John of Magna

Carta fame, or infamy depending upon one's point of view and position, was elderly and had been England's overly pious king for more than sixty years. Henry was poxed with various ailments and it was understood by both his friends and his foes that he was fading fast and would soon be gone.

Henry's oldest son, Prince Edward, was his heir. Unfortunately, Edward's succession was uncertain and a great problem for several reasons. One was because God was not available to recognize Edward as England's new king if his father died. That was the result of there being no Pope available to talk to God in his prayers and get God's approval to place England's crown on Edward's head. Another was that Edward had gone off crusading to the Holy Land and would not be back for years, if ever, since most crusaders ended up in unmarked graves far away from where they had been birthed.

Edward's papal problem was that the Church's last old Pope had died several years earlier and the cardinals who were supposed to elect his replacement had not been able to agree on who should replace him. The cardinals, it seems, were split between the French and Italians such that they had not been able to agree on a replacement for Pope Clement who had inconveniently died and gone to join Jesus in heaven several years earlier—to help Jesus plan for his imminent return and second resurrection according to the Church.

The dispute between the Italian and French cardinals was a serious problem for England because only a properly elected Pope could talk to God and find out who God wanted to wear England's crown and pay its taxes and tithes to the Church. The source of the apparently insurmountable problem, or so it seemed at the time, was that the Church's cardinals could not agree if God would better understand the prayers of his representative on earth if he spoke Latin with an Italian accent or with a French accent.

Moreover, and making the problem worse, was that none of the cardinals had accumulated enough coin to buy the large amount of prayers from the other cardinals that was necessary to swing God's choice toward any one particular man. The days of one particular cardinal coming from a family rich enough to be able to buy enough prayers from the other cardinals were apparently gone, at least temporarily.

As a result of the uncertainty about Henry's health, God's intentions, and Prince Edward's absence, a number of nobles and princes in both England and France had begun suggesting that they had access to enough coins to buy the agreements, soldiers, and prayers necessary for God to choose them to rule England instead of Prince Edward when Henry died. Whether that was true or not remained to be seen. Most probably did not; the likely exceptions being the King of France and the Earl of Westminster who had vast landholding in and around

London from which he collected rents from the markets, tenements, and warehouses he allowed to be built on them.

Making matters worse for the Church and its pilgrims and crusaders and the merchants who served and supplied them, and thus making things *better* for the Cornwall-based Company of Archers, the Moorish pirates were once again in ascendance in the waters east of Gibraltar despite the Moors recent losses to the Christians in northern and central Spain. At the moment, because of those losses, the Kingdom of Granada was only Moorish state left in Spain.

Fortunately for the Company of Archers, however, the Kingdom of Granada was quite large and particularly well located. It stretched all along the entire Mediterranean coast of Spain and controlled all the pirate-sheltering ports east of Gibraltar. As a result, the Company's archer-rowed and defended war galleys were still the best and safest way for pilgrims, crusaders, and cargos to run to the gauntlet of Moorish pirates and get back and forth to Europe from the Holy Land or wherever else they were visiting or trading in the east.

The Company's galleys and transports had a very good reputation. Because they were archer rowed and crewed they were considered to be the fastest and safest way to move people and cargos between the various other major Mediterranean and Holy Land ports. Moreover, and as a consequence of its galleys and transports being the preferred way to travel because they were the most likely to get safely past the Moorish pirates, the Company was able to charge prices for its services that were significantly higher than those charged by the other carriers of cargos and passengers who served the east. It also helped that the Company had a reputation for honouring its contracts and not stealing the cargos it carried or selling its passengers to the Moors for slaves.

In other words, the growing strength of the Moorish pirates in the waters east of Gibraltar and Granada's continuing control of the Spanish coast was *good* for the Company and the archers who were being constantly trained in Cornwall and sent east to fill its ranks and fuel its expansion. It was good for the Company because it meant that the Company could continue to charge very high prices for the carrying of cargos, passengers, and money orders back and forth between England and the Holy Land and between the many ports it served such as Rome, Athens, and Constantinople that were east of Gibraltar.

Cargo shippers and passengers could, of course, pay less and take their chances sailing with the Venetians and Greeks and various Italians, all of whom had weak blood and were unable or unwilling to fight to protect them as a result of being birthed where the sun shined too much and there was not enough rain to keep their skins moist and wash the colour out of their hair to whiten it if they lived long enough.

Even better for the men who were allowed to make their marks on the Company's roll, they could earn prize money for themselves over and above their regular pay by participating in the Company's taking of Moorish prizes, collecting ransoms in exchange for leaving unscathed the Moorish ports when the Company's galleys periodically "visited" them, and being contracted out by the Company to fight as mercenaries. In other words, being in the Company of Archers was truly the best of all possible worlds for an ambitious English commoner, especially since he had so few alternatives in England.

And perhaps best of all—the English King and his chamberlain were so ignorant of the Company's successes and wealth that they did not try to cut themselves in for a share or try take some of it for themselves in taxes. There was no doubt about it; danger, uncertainty, and knowing how to lead men and use modern weapons could be good for men who knew what they were doing and kept their mouths shut about their successes, particularly if they were willing to take chances and risk their lives to get ahead—men like those who made their marks and served in the Company of Archers.

Elsewhere in the Christian world early in the summer days of 1271 the Company's prospects of being able to earn enough coins to pay its men, and also set some aside for the coming lean years, were mixed but for the most part had remained highly favourable. The lean years would not start, it was widely believed, until Jesus returned and there was once again peace on earth. Then the Company would have to dip into its coin chests to pay its men and keep the Company's fleet intact until Jesus decided to leave again and the fighting and piracy resumed. The Company's problems would almost certainly begin soon; the Church was already collecting coins to pay for the big celebration.

The Company's only truly major setback in recent years had occurred ten years or so earlier when the Constantinople-based Latin Empire had somewhat peacefully fallen by trickery to a band of fanatically religious Greeks who had been able to get through one of the great city's gates by bribing its guards. Once inside they had promptly deposed the descendents of the victorious crusaders who had similarly seized the city some years earlier and restored the Constantinople-based Greek speaking Byzantine Empire. The newly installed Greek emperor had promptly cancelled the Company's most lucrative single contract—the use of some of the Company's war galleys to collect the tolls that seafarers paid to use the Dardanelles and Bosporus Straits and the Marmara Sea that lay between them.

It was one of the Company's few disasters: The new emperor had cancelled the Company's contract because the lords and princes who kicked out the Latin Empire and restored the Byzantine Empire and their new emperor were Orthodox Greeks whereas it was their predecessors in the recently fallen Latin Empire who had made the toll-collecting contract with the Company. *The Latin Empire was so called because its emperor and his nobles were descendents of crusaders who had taken city some years earlier and promptly replaced the Byzantine Empire's Greek priests with Latin babbling priests that no one could understand. Now the Latin priests and nobles were out and a Greek emperor claiming to be a descendent of the deposed emperor was back with his own nobles and priests.*

The toll-collecting contract had been lost, according to the archers, because the Greek Orthodox Patriarch, newly restored to his palace and influence in Constantinople as a result of the Greek victory, was a sore loser and still unhappy about some missing relics and the military assistance that the Company had provided many years earlier to the Empire's previous anti-Greek rulers—for which the Company had been paid by being given the exclusive right to collect the Empire's sea tolls and keep most of them.

As a result of the Orthodox Church having a long memory and still being pissed at the Company for the help it had provided to the enemies of the Orthodox Church, the Church's current Patriarch had informed the new Greek emperor that God wanted the new emperor to use his own galleys to collect the tolls and pay a tithe to the Orthodox Church instead of letting the Company's galleys continue to collect the toll coins and keep them in exchange for helping to defend the empire. *We should have moved faster and offered the Patriarch a share of the tolls. Ah well, live and learn; and I certainly cannot complain even if everyone else in the Company is still pissed about the loss of the toll coins.*

Truth be told, George was the only man in the Company who had benefited from the Company losing its most lucrative single contract; it was his older brother who had been the Company's major captain in Constantinople at the time—and he had neither stepped in fast enough to defend the city when the Greeks merely walked in through an open gate and took it nor offered a large enough share of the tolls to the Patriarch after the city had been re-taken.

As a result of his brother's two big failures, the Company had lost its biggest single source of coins and the promotion to lieutenant commander that would have gone to George's brother had gone to George instead—who had been serving at the time as the major captain commanding the Company's great fortress on Cyprus where the Company had its shipyard and also the school where the likeliest men from amongst the Company's veteran archers were learnt to scribe and sum so they could better function in the years ahead as lieutenants and captains.

On the other hand, things had *not* gone totally wrong for the Company in Constantinople and the other ports that had previously been under the control of the now-dissolved and replaced Latin Empire. That was because the restored Greek emperor had listened to his tax-paying merchants and allowed the Company's shipping post to continue operating in Constantinople to serve them.

Even more importantly, the new emperor had *also* continued the deposed Latin Emperor's policy of *not* allowing Venetian shipping posts and merchants to operate in the city or elsewhere in his empire. As a result, and because it did not have to compete with the Venetian merchants and moneylenders, the Company was more than holding its own in the sale of money orders and the earning of coins by carrying passengers and cargos to and from that great city and ports of its huge empire.

Moreover, and despite the return of the Greek-babbling Byzantine princes and priests to many of the ports in the Mediterranean, the Company's shipping posts in the once-again Orthodox ports had also continued to operate and generate a continuous flow of coins for the Company's chests. That was, it was widely believed by Company's commander and his captains, the result of a belated but generous annual gift for the prayers of the Patriarch similar to that which the Company had been giving to the Pope for his prayers before he died and went to heaven. The God of the Orthodox Church, it seems, was willing to accept galleys and transports crewed by English archers in its ports if enough coins found their way into the hands of the church's Patriarch to pay for the necessary prayers.

Nothing of real significance had changed elsewhere in the Mediterranean ports served by the Company's galleys and transports as a result of Constantinople changing hands and a Greek emperor taking the throne of that city's great empire: The Venetians continued to hold Crete and some of the Greek islands; the Moorish pirates continued to threaten the shipping lanes east of Gibraltar; and the handful of Templars who were still in the east continued to hold Acre and a couple of fortresses on the coast of the Holy Land.

Most of the Templars, however, had already abandoned the Holy Land and returned to France and the countries around it, including England, by the early summer of 1271. A few had initially returned to France some years earlier in order to raise money for their order's efforts in the Holy Land by selling pilgrims a chance to kiss and pray in front of a piece of the cross on which the Romans hung Jesus. And then more and more of the Templars had to come back from the Holy Land to protect the ever-growing patchwork of lands and manors the Templars were obtaining by using their cross-kissing coins to "temporarily" buy land from would-be crusaders. The Templars did so, temporarily buy the land of the would-be crusaders that is, because their order was sworn to do everything possible to help crusaders get to the Holy Land and join the Christian army that was fighting to take Jerusalem from the Saracens.

It seems that would-be crusaders, being the good Christians that they were or hoped to become, were not allowed to pay interest to borrow the money they needed to spend to get to the Holy Land and sustain themselves and their men while they were there. That was because somewhere in the bible there was a passage that could be interpreted as prohibiting the payment of interest in order to borrow money. As a result, would-be crusaders had to *temporarily* sell their lands to the Templars to get the coins they needed to pay for their crusades. The Templars, in turn, promised to keep the crusaders' lands safe and defend them until the crusaders returned and bought them back. The problem was that many of the crusaders fell in the Holy Land and never returned to buy them back, and also that many of the crusaders who did return did so without enough coins to reacquire their lands.

As a result, more and more of the Templars had to return from the east to protect their order's ever growing patchwork of newly acquired lands in France and England and elsewhere. And the Templars could not stop buying the would-be crusaders' lands because they were sworn to help and encourage every man who wanted to become a crusader.

In essence, the Templars finding a piece of the true cross had started a virtuous circle that ended up turning the Templars into money lenders and removing most of the Templars from the Holy Land. And that, in turn, allowed the Saracens to conquer more and more of the Holy Land such that there were more and more refugees for the Company to carry to safety. In other words, God worked in mysterious ways, Jerusalem remained in the hands of the Saracens, and the Company of Archers was greatly benefited by being able to carry the refugees who could pay to be saved from the turmoil and fighting that resulted from God's requirements and the absence of Jesus.

The Templars themselves were not hostile to the Company of Archers. That was because the Company was not earning its coins from relic-kissing and made no effort to help would-be crusaders by temporarily purchasing and protecting their lands. To the contrary, the Company was earning its coins in other ways and whenever possible was holding on to them so it could continue to pay and feed its men when Jesus returned and peace broke out.

And when the Company did acquire priceless relics, as it had when it helped some be saved and evacuated when the crusaders sacked Constantinople, it did not keep them and sell kisses and touches. To the contrary, it subsequently sold them so that they would end up in Rome instead of keeping them for pilgrims to pay to kiss. For example, all three of the right hands of John the Baptist subsequently "found" by the Company after the sacking of Constantinople by the crusaders, the very hands that had baptised Jesus, were sold by the Company to great Christian kings and princes who immediately donated them to the Latin Church in return for various recognitions, favours, and dispensations.

The Company was similarly maintaining a fragile peace with the Venetians even though the Venetians also carried passengers and cargos and sold money orders, albeit at significantly lower prices because their galleys that carried them were rowed by slaves who were unlikely to fight to defend. As a result, passengers and cargos carried by the Venetians were more likely to be lost if they encountered pirates. In other words, the Company and the Venetians were competing for different types of customers—but they viewed each other warily and at times had come to blows because there was some overlap and each wanted the other gone so it could take over the other's customers.

Another difference that allowed the Venetians and the Company to tolerate each other was the Venetians' constant efforts to take over obscure Greek islands so the sons of Venice's lords and great merchants could become the islands' lords and princes with hereditary titles that God would approve if enough prayers were bought from the Pope.

The Company was different, very different. Its commanders and their captains were primarily oriented towards earning coins. They had no interest in acquiring poor little islands because they generated very few passenger or cargo coins and because obtaining dubious titles of nobility so their sons could be the lords of little islands filled with Greek peasants was not something to which the captains of the Company aspired. Besides, and to the Company's great delight, the Venetians' constant efforts to take over one or another of the islands so pissed off the new Greek emperor who claimed the islands for himself and his fellow Greeks that he continued to keep the Venetians out of the lucrative Constantinople trade and many of his empire's other ports.

Things were similarly unchanged in England except for the growing weakness of its elderly king and the absence of his heir who had gone for a crusader: The Scots continued to raid, the Barons continued to complain about their taxes, and King Henry continued to send tithes to Rome and buy indulgences for his past sins in order to get the prayers necessary to reduce his time in purgatory when he died and for the return of his lands in France. And recently the king had begun sending Rome even more coins. His increased tithing had begun when the Nuncio, the Church's ambassador, had suggested that Jesus might descend through the clouds and land in England if his welcome and the feasts organized by the Church were grand enough.

Even the fact that King Henry's brother, Richard, had been named the Duke of Cornwall and given the revenues from the King's stannaries was of no consequence to the Company. Richard had never once visited Cornwall—and it was not likely that he ever would because he too was elderly, and poxed, and fading away like his brother, King Henry. Besides, the stannaries' revenues had become negligible because the king's mines were running out of tin to mine and refine.

Similarly unaware of the Company and its strength in England was Prince Edward, King Henry's son and heir. He was in the Holy Land as part of the 9th crusade and was not expected to return for years, and quite possibly never as an unmarked grave in a foreign land was the fate of most crusaders. *On the other hand Edward had chartered a Company galley to carry him and his retinue of priests and supporters to the Holy Land and he was bound to learn more about the Company in general whilst he was there.*

In any event, Edward was gone and that was the somewhat stable state of affairs in England and elsewhere in the Christian world when some of England's more ambitious barons once again found a reason to rise in rebellion and decided to use western Devon as a safe place to gather their forces. They did so, according to one of the de Montforts, because

"Western Devon is a safe place for us to gather our army as there will be no one of any consequence to oppose our men when they go out foraging in nearby Cornwall"

It was, as everyone understood, another way of saying "Devon is where we can gather our men without having to spend our coins to buy food for them to eat."

The Company's problem was that the Commander and his captains had not yet fully realized what was happening and were about to be blind-sided by the arrival of an invading army of English barons and their increasingly hungry men.

Chapter Four

Important traditions.

George Courtenay rode much of the way from Okehampton to Restormel with John Farmer and Freddie Hogg, the captains commanding the Company's Plympton Castle and Launceston Castle strongholds. The three castle constables met at the Company-owned *Red Bull* tavern that stood next to the River Tamar ford where the side road that branched off from the main London to Exeter road came into Cornwall. The side road was the only road into Cornwall and was badly maintained inside Devon to discourage its use by outsiders. The roads inside Cornwall were much better.

The two captains had deliberately joined up with George at the *Red Bull* so the three of them could talk amongst themselves as they rode together to Restormel Castle for the meeting with the Company's commander to which the three men had been summoned.

Their meeting with the Company Commander was an annual event that was traditionally held in the early summer of each year as soon as the Commander returned from spending the previous half of the year in the eastern Mediterranean.

More specifically, the Commander traditionally travelled from Cornwall to the Company's stronghold on Cyprus each year when leaves began to fall from England's trees, and then returned about six months later when the new leaves were beginning to spring from their winter-deadened branches.

The Commander made the trip to Cyprus each fall because the eastern Mediterranean was where the Company stationed most of its men and earned most of its coins. It was, as a result, where many important decisions had to be made each year by the Company's Commander. It was also a much nicer place for the Commander to spend the winter months because it was inevitably warmer and less windy and rainy than Cornwall. Indeed, the winters were so much warmer that many of the Company's men chose to retire there. It had not at all surprised George that Anne, George's wife, had recently begun reminding him that he had three daughters there with their archer husbands and his grandchildren and that their sons were likely to be stationed there when they finished being filled with learning at the Company school for boys at Restormel Castle.

Not at the at the meeting of the three castle constables was Richard Adams, reputed to be one of the Company's most ferocious fighting men and now the post captain of the Company's London shipping post. Richard had been expected to ride in from London and join them at the *Red Bull* on what would have been the final leg of his long overland trip; but he had not appeared. They were somewhat surprised by Richard's absence but not alarmed. Richard knew about the meeting and they were confident he was either already at Restormel or would show up there sooner or later.

Each of the three men was accompanied by one of his sergeants. In addition, they had been joined by four of the Company's elite outriders, the men who patrolled the approaches to Cornwall and its roads and villages. It was a small but sufficiently formidable force to insure they would not be molested along the way.

There were no apprentice sergeants riding with them. That was because all three of the men had been adequately filled with learning at the Company school at Restormel and could read and scribe for themselves. George had a lieutenant assigned to him as an aide and errand runner but the poor fellow had come down with a coughing pox a few weeks earlier and been ordered to stay at home so he could be tended to by his wife. She would be assisted, if necessary, by the archer who functioned as Okehampton Castle's barber in addition to his other duties as an archer who specialized in caring for horses.

Also not accompanying George was his number two, Captain Adam Merton, also a graduate of the Company's school. He had remained at Okehampton because it was a Company requirement that someone senior be available at all times to make decisions in case a problem suddenly arose on Cornwall's frontier.

It was not impossible for someone who was unable to read or scribe to reach the rank of captain or higher in the Company of Archers, and about half of the Company's captains could not. But it certainly had become more and more difficult ever since the Company opened a second school on Cyprus some years earlier.

The Cyprus school was where the more promising of the Company's veteran archers were sent to be learnt to scribe and sum so that they could better function in the years ahead as the lieutenants and captains of the Company's war galleys, transports, and shipping posts. It was not a new idea to teach veteran soldiers to read and scribe so they could send and receive written orders and reports; the Roman legions did something similar a thousand years earlier. The Romans required that only men who could read and scribe could be centurions or their lieutenants known as optios. The result was a literate army as the men banded together to teach each other to read and scribe in order to get ahead. The Company was heading to a similar requirement as fast as possible.

Each of the three high ranking archers was coming from a Company stronghold on the border between Devon and Cornwall to attend the Company's annual meeting with the Company's Commander, Robert Robertson, who had recently returned from making his annual visit to Cyprus and the Eastern Mediterranean. Also attending the meeting would be George's uncle, Charles Courtenay, the elderly Earl of Cornwall who had retired from the Company some years earlier and was now on half-pay based on his previous five-stripe rank as a major captain.

George's Uncle Charles would be participating in the meeting both because Restormel Castle belonged to him and his heirs and because whoever was the Earl was paid to be responsible for seeing that the Company's retirees and widows and orphans in England received the coins and food to which they were entitled. He was also responsible for seeing that they always had a roof over their heads to keep them out of the rain and cold.

For his services the Earl was paid an annual stipend as if he was a lieutenant commander on active duty in addition to any retirement half pay he might be due from his years on active service. In addition, the Company maintained, and defended Restormel Castle for the earl in exchange for the use of all of it except the innermost citadel where the Earl lived with his extended family. It was a mutually beneficial arrangement that had been in effect for many years and seemed to be working well.

The early summer visit of the three stronghold constables and the London shipping post captain to Restormel Castle was an annual event. It was the meeting at which the Company's captains stationed in England would report to the newly returned Company Commander and to each other as to the state of the Company's affairs for which they were responsible. They would also hear the Commander's report about the Company's operations in the east and discuss the various transfers and promotions that needed to be made throughout the Company to replace the men who had fallen or retired.

This year, although they did not know it yet, their meeting with Commander Robertson would last longer than usual both because of the uncertain and potentially dangerous situation developing in England and also because an upturn in the number of sweating pox victims in the east had created more than the usual number of vacancies in the upper ranks of the Company that had to be filled with promotions.

******

The year's annual meeting was held, as always, with the men sitting together on the wooden benches that ran along both sides the long wooden table in Restormel's great hall. It began as soon as the three travellers arrived and were properly welcomed with bowls of ale and had a chance to visit the castle's piss pot and shitting ditch in the innermost of the castle's three bailies. Richard Adams, the captain of the Company's London shipping post, was already there. He had come on a Company galley with an especially strengthened hull that was outbound from London to Cyprus and the Holy Land carrying a cargo of iron ingots and a large number of crusaders and pilgrims. As was often the case, several of the sea-poxed passengers disembarked and swore never to travel by sea again. They would attempt to return to their homes overland.

Commander Robertson sat at the head of the table at the end nearest the fireplace even though it was not lit because of the warm weather. His men sat themselves below him along either side of the table according to their ranks and seniority. Captain Harry Franklin, the Commander's senior aide, sat closest to the Commander on his right side with a pile of parchments and his quill and ink pot at the ready. He would take notes and tactfully remind the Commander if there was something on the Commander's previously prepared list that had not yet been fully discussed. George Courtenay sat to the Commander's immediate right by virtue of being the Commander' number two and his designated successor.

The Commander began the meeting by bringing the four men up to date on the Company's operations in the east. He had nothing unusual to report other than the fact that there had been an unusually high number of sweating pox casualties in some of the fleet's galleys and transports.

According to Commander Robertson, the Company had done well over the winter and he had brought back several chests of additional coins to add to the Company's reserves so that the Company's men stationed in England could continue to be paid and fed when peace broke out and the hard times arrived. The Company's only serious losses, the Commander reported, had been Captain Jack Jackson's Number Sixty-two Galley which had apparently gone down in a storm and two of the Company's transports that had been taken by Moorish pirates operating out of Algiers. Jack had been well-liked and his passing was lamented with a few soft curses.

It was immediately understood by everyone at the meeting that Algiers would be receiving a revenge-seeking visit by some of the Company's galleys in the not too distant future. Indeed, doing so, getting a right and proper revenge for every archer who was killed, wounded, or taken, was required by the Company's compact which was read out loud to the men on the first Sunday of every month and on which every man had made his mark when he joined the Company.

The Company's losses had already been made good, Commander Robertson told his captains; the galley by a new-build coming out of the Company shipyard on Cyprus and the transports by retaining two prizes from amongst the five useful transports that had been taken off the Moors during a "visit" to Algiers. The other three transports were not up to the Company's standards and had already been sold along with the cargos from all five of the prizes. The prize monies due to the crews of the galleys that took the five transports had already been paid.

It was getting dark and almost time for supper by the time the Commander finished describing the Company's affairs in the east and answering questions so that George and his captains would know about them. So they adjourned for the day and talked about all sorts of things including their personal lives and families over a splendid meal of roast duck, fresh bread and butter, pickled cabbage, and cheese. The Earl's elderly wife had supervised the preparation of the meal and claimed to be delighted that it had pleased the visitors.

No prayers preceded or followed the meal. They were not needed since all the men seated at the table were graduates of the nearby Company school located in Restormel Castle's middle bailey. As such, they had each been ordained as an Angelovian priest after being found to be sufficiently full of Latin and memorized prayers in addition to being good with a longbow and able to put his feet down to the beat of a marching drum.

Accordingly, in the Angelovian tradition, the Commander and his men would pray by themselves silently whenever they felt the need to do so. It was something an earlier Pope had approved because the archer captains and their men were automatically members of the Papal Order of Poor Landless Sailors and, as such, were often at sea where organized prayers were not possible. That was the official explanation.

In fact, the only real function of the Angelovians and the order was to bring a few "prayer coins" to Rome each year for the Pope's personal use. They were some, but certainly not all, of the coins collected from the faithful, especially the pilgrims, for the Pope's prayers for their safe arrival when they sailed on a Company galley or transport. It was a good coin earner for the Company—the passengers did not complain if they arrived alive and were not around to complain if they did not.

The Company gladly handed some of the "prayer coins" over to the Holy Father each year because they tended to keep whoever was the Pope sweet about the Company's periodic transgressions. In addition, being known to be close to the Pope greatly helped when the Company's captains had to deal with officious churchmen and influential true believers. It was a tradition that George's grandfather and his priestly brother, Thomas, established in the early days when the Company was just beginning to carry cargos and passengers.

The candles lighting the hall were blown out after the meal and the hour or so of drinking that followed it and the visitors settled down to sleep on the floor of the hall. Each of them did so using the sleeping skins he had carried into Restormel tied behind his saddle. Each man carrying his own skins was a similarly important Company tradition, this one to keep down the spread of bugs and prevent the more fastidious of the men from being forced to use the significantly foul and bug-infested skins of some of their less-caring fellow archers.

******

The meeting resumed the next morning after the visitors finished breaking their nightly fasts with a splendid meal of duck eggs scrambled with cheese, breakfast ale, cheese and apple slices, and fresh bread that was still warm from its cooking and either slathered with butter or dipped into sour wine and the juice squeezed out of olives, both of which were carried to Restormel on our galleys in big jars that had been cooked to seal them so liquids would not seep out so long as they were not cracked.

It was a meal similar to that which was served to the boys in the nearby school each morning when they broke their overnight fasts. As such it brought back fond memories and much reminiscing since every man at the meeting was a graduate of the nearby school and had at least one funny story to tell about his experiences and those of his long ago friends and monkish teachers. Most of the men present had heard the stories more than a few times in years past but they laughed and enjoyed them as if they had not. They were the school's old boys and proud of it.

George and the three captains were not the only ones who attended the two days of meals and meetings with Commander Robertson and the Earl. The Commander's assistant, a four-stripe captain by the name of Harry Franklin sat with them throughout the two days of meetings. So did the major captain in charge of the recruiting and training of the Company's new archers and the defence of Restormel Castle, Bill Brewer. Brewer was, like George, a son of the Company and George's counterpart; he was responsible for the day to day affairs of everything west of the River Tamar.

Others who periodically attended to give their reports and be closely questioned and advised included the Bishop of Cornwall who was also an archer with the rank of a four-stripe captain and a mitre and diocese that the Company had bought for him from Rome along with a nicely embroidered gown. Also attending one of the early sessions was Arthur Tinker, a former apprentice sergeant who had come before them to be informed that he was being promoted to Sergeant Major and that he would be expected to give a detailed report at a later session on the next day.

Arthur understood what that meant—he had become the Company's ranking alchemist now that his lieutenant predecessor had managed to get himself unexpectedly killed. It had happened a few months earlier, the lieutenant's death that is, when the metal tube of a ribald that had been hammered together by the castle's smiths shattered into little pieces that scattered in every direction when the flame was put to the lightning powder in it instead of making gold or throwing out the rocks that had been crammed into the tube on top of the powder. One of the pieces, unfortunately, had hit him in the head and put a hole in it that killed him.

Arthur was young for a Sergeant Major and he knew it. He was also extremely ambitious and at the moment he did not know whether he should smile because he had just been promoted and should appear grateful, or be properly sad because he had just finished explaining the death of his predecessor and why he thought it had happened. He elected to keep a straight face and do neither. He also kept a straight face and nodded dutifully and said "Aye, Commander," when he was told to select a likely lad from amongst the year's six new apprentice sergeants to be his assistant.

"And try to keep both him and yourself alive, Arthur. Use a longer candle to put fire to the lightning power, eh?" the Commander had ordered. *What Arthur did not know was that he himself had been selected by his late predecessor strictly because his name on the Company roll was Tinker; the lieutenant serving as the Company's alchemist had thought that the son of a family that earned its bread hammering and working metal might be useful in the making of ribalds, the tubes of iron and hollowed-out oak logs that sometimes threw stones great distances when fire was put to a proper mixture of the powders of charcoal, sulphur, and white bird shite.*

Initially all the other news the Commander heard was favourable. No priests or nobles had gotten across the Tamar who might interfere with the Company's operations or the prosperity of its people, Cornwall's crops were coming along nicely so that there was likely to be more than enough food for the Company to buy or receive as in-kind taxes and rents, and the recruiting of English commoners to go for archers was proceeding quite well both in Cornwall and elsewhere in England and also in Wales. There were, of course, the inevitable various and sundry local problems but they were relatively minor in nature and had either already been resolved or would be shortly.

All was reported to be normal and the problems minor and easily handled until it was the turn of Richard Adams, the four-stripe captain who commanded the Company's London shipping post, to make his presentation. His report would be about the conditions the Company faced in London and the rest of England. He was the last of the Commander's captains to speak because he was the most junior of the captains at the meeting.

London's shipping post captain usually travelled to the meeting each summer by road in order to get a sense of the conditions in the shires of England that were outside London. Not this year. Richard reported that he had listened carefully to London's merchants and money lenders and to the Company's two priestly spies at Windsor. As a result of what he had heard, he had travelled to the meeting on a Cyprus-bound Company galley from London. It had come up the Fowey to drop off Captain Adams and the forty or so new recruits who been accumulating in the stalls at the Company's London horse stable where the year's new potential amblers were housed prior to being taken under heavy guard to Okehampton.

One reason he had travelled via a Company galley, Captain Adams told the others, was because the old Roman road that ran from London to Exeter was reported to now be too dangerous for a single traveller to use as a result of armed bands of robbers that had begun infesting it. That in itself was of little consequence except for the inconvenience it would have caused to the Company's activities in London if he had taken one or two of the archers stationed at the Company's shipping post away from their regular duties to ride with him as his guards.

What caused everyone at the table to sit up and gape at Richard in disbelief was what he said next—that he had primarily come by sea because there were credible reports by London's merchants and the Company's two priestly spies at Windsor that the armies of some of England's most important barons would be gathering into one great army in the near future and might be marching on Devon and Cornwall.

Why the barons would be doing so was uncertain, according to Captain Adams. Some of the London merchants and moneylenders had suggested it was to be ready to take over control of England when old King Henry died; others that it was to be in position to stop a French invasion to put a Frenchman on England's throne, an invasion that would land in the west of England in order to avoid the strong resistance they might expect from Dover Castle and the Portsmen of the Cinque Ports. The only thing that was certain, according to Captain Adams, was that almost every merchant and money lender in London thought the barons were up to something and it was rumoured that Cornwall and Devon might somehow be involved because southwestern England was where the French were expected to land.

Captain Adams said that he had been informed by multiple sources that where and when the barons would gather their individual armies into one great "Loyal Army" would be determined by two important nobles, both of whom were de Montforts. And many of the reports suggested it would be in Devon or Cornwall. There were also rumours, he said, that two of England's richest men other than King Henry, the Earls of Sussex and Westminster, were involved and so were the de Montforts and several other ambitious noblemen who aspired to the crown.

He had travelled by sea, Captain Adams had explained to his stunned friends and the Commander, because he had no desire to meet one or more of the nobles' ill-disciplined and inevitably hungry and rapacious armies on the road without enough fighting men to protect the forty or so recent recruits who would be accompanying him on foot along with the horses that had been bought over the winter and spring to be added to the Company's horse herd.

"Besides," he said ruefully amidst an explosion of laughter, "I might have had to run for it if we met too many of the barons' men on the road, and God knows I am not much of a horseman and always get a sore arse if I have to ride hard."

Richard's explanation had gotten a good laugh from his fellow captains despite the seriousness of the situation he was describing. That was because he was one of the Company's most renowned fighting men and the new recruits from the villages around London would have been travelling with him.

They laughed because it was absolutely inconceivable that Richard, or any of the Company's other captains or anyone else who had made his mark on the Company's roll for that matter, would "run for it" and abandon the new recruits—both because he would be instantly looked down upon in disgust by his fellow captains for abandoning men under his command and also because it was in the Company compact that a "great and severe penalty," meaning a sword or rope, would fall on the neck of any man who abandoned the men serving with him or under his command in a time of danger.

******

Captain Adam's troubling report about the barons caused much discussion and ended up causing many actions to be taken. The Bishop, for example, was ordered by Commander Robertson to get confidential messages to several of the Company's spies requesting any information they might have about the king's health and the intentions of the de Montforts and the barons they were recruiting. Discreet inquiries would also be sent to a "friend" in the

French court and to a couple of Jewish merchants in London with whom the Company did much trade.

The Company's spies in England were two young archer apprentice sergeants from the nearby Company school who were on active duty as Angelovian priests and employed as scribes and clerks in the households of the King and papal Nuncio. They had gotten their positions as a result of substantial anonymous "donations" to the Keeper of the King's Wardrobe and the Nuncio.

The two archer priests would obey the bishop's order and provide whatever information they could uncover. They would do so because the bishop was a captain in the Company and because both of the priests, like the bishop, were Company men and archers first and foremost. In fact, all three of them were graduates of the Company's school who had been allowed to make their marks to join the Company as apprentice sergeants after they had been found full enough of learning to command men and serve as priests if necessary. After a few more years of being assigned to spying each of the two young priestly sergeants would be promoted and assigned to new duties in the Company.

If the past was any guide, each of the men could expect to move on from being a spy with the rank of Sergeant Major and one or both of them might very well someday return to Cornwall to be its bishop with the rank of captain or major captain or even to a similar position purchased in Rome with the rank of bishop or cardinal. That too had become a Company tradition. *At the moment we had two minor bishops in Rome. They were both lieutenants and quite helpful in knowing how much the Company needed to "give" in prayer coins to the Holy Father's personal purse each year when there was a Pope in residence and who else in the Church needed to be "supported" with coins in the event the Company needed a "special consideration."*

Following Captain Adam's report and intense grilling came an unfortunately forlorn report from the newly promoted sergeant major, Arthur Tinker, who had recently begun serving as the Company's alchemist and ribald maker. Until recently he had been a sergeant and the previous lieutenant's assistant.

Gold is made when lightning strikes lead. The newly promoted Tinker and the late and greatly lamented lieutenant had been engaged in one of the Company's longest term projects—trying to produce gold in usable amounts with man-made lightning. We had long ago learned how to make lightning by putting a flame to a mix of powdered sulphur, charcoal, and white bird shite. It was the using of the lightning to make gold and throw stones at our enemies that had proved to be difficult.

The basic problem was the need to concentrate the lightning so it hit only the lead and turned it into gold. What we had discovered is that this could only be done by placing lead and a proper mixture of various powders in a wooden or iron tube or pot called a ribald in such a way that the lead was the only thing the lightning could hit when fire was put to the powder. The sealing was done by stuffing rocks into the ribald on top of the lead so the lightning could not escape. Smooth river stones were used because it had been learnt that the jagged edges of regular rocks sometimes caught on the ribalds' uneven surfaces and tore them apart.

Unfortunately, all kinds of things can go wrong if the powder is not properly ground or properly stirred up or there are not enough stones used to hold the lightning in or if the ribald is not strong enough to hold the lightning in. As a result, sometimes gold was made when fire was put to the powder but other times the ribald came apart and the pieces hit the people standing around it. Other times it expelled the stones and threw them long distances because there were not enough of them packed into the ribald to keep the lightning from escaping instead of hitting the lead.

What it meant was that deliberately not stuffing in enough stones to hold in the lightning could be used to throw the stuffed-in stones out of the end of the ribald. Then, if the ribald was pointed properly, the stones would fly out of the end of the ribald and land on the Company's enemies with great effect.

We first used ribalds to throw stones at our enemies years ago when the Company was helping the Empress of the Latin Empire fight the Greeks that were attacking Constantinople. The problem was then, and still is, that sometimes the stones go astray and other times the ribald breaks into pieces that hit the man who put the fire to its powder mixture and the people who are standing too near it.

Over the years we have tried everything to keep the ribalds from breaking up including wrapping them in strong lines and having our smiths make the ribalds out of iron. Our efforts both to make gold and throw stones accurately had been going on for years. Some progress had been made in the throwing of stones but clearly not enough.

"Why not send Sergeant Major Tinker and a couple of keen young apprentice sergeants to Oxford to learn what they can from the alchemists and other troublemakers who are rumoured to have begun gathering there in some of the village's monastic halls?" someone suggested.

"We could even set up an Angelovian Hall, eh? And then chum in the men whose knowledge and thinking we want to search by offering them a roof over their heads and free suppers. It would be like throwing corn in the waters of the moat to attract the fish and ducks who are tired of eating shite and bugs."

The suggestion was made by the Earl. He promptly explained that he had always liked the idea of the Company making its own gold and being able to throw rocks at its enemies and kill them before they could get close enough to cause casualties amongst the archers. The problem was that the testing was always done at Restormel and the noise sometimes scared the castle's hens such that they stopped laying eggs for a day or two.

Commander Robertson was having none of it and said as much.

"The castle's hens' and their eggs are not as important to the Company's future as making gold and using our ribalds to throw stones at our enemies. So the gold-making experiments and stone-throwing tests are not to be done at Oxford or anywhere else except here at Restormel. Otherwise someone else might find out how to do it before we do."

But then, after a brief pause, he added something important.

"On the other hand, getting some new ideas would be probably useful; we have been trying to perfect the old ones for many years and they are still not working very well."

That resulted in a long exchange about the importance of chickens and eggs and a decision to recall the new alchemist Sergeant Major for further discussions.

Chapter Five

Everything appears normal.

No word had been received about any particular problems or armies on the road when the meeting was finished the next day and the visitors rode out of Restormel to return to their posts. Commander Robertson, however, had decided to take no chances. And that meant, he told his captains, that he and everyone else needed to be kept closely informed as what was happening throughout England and "we must get our men and strongholds prepared for the worst." Accordingly, amongst the many orders he immediately issued, the Commander ordered Captain Adams to ride with the captains of the three castles to Okehampton, and then continue on a scouting ride to London with a strong guard of horse archers.

More specifically, the Commander told Captain Adams that he wanted him and the men who would be riding with him to ride slowly back to London and ask a lot of questions to "try to find out what it is the barons intend to do and when and where they intend to do it." They were to do so by talking to the people and gentry they met on the road and in the markets and taverns along the way.

Later that day, with only George present, the Commander quietly told Captain Adams about the two specific places where he *must* stop and make inquiries. He also told him that he and the archers accompanying him were at all times to present themselves as mercenaries seeking employment and never under any circumstance reveal that they were archers on the rolls of the Company of Archers.

The captain and his men were not to reveal themselves as archers, the Commander explained, "Because we do not want the barons and their knights to know we will be ready and waiting for them with our gates barred, our larders full, and the points of our arrows sharpened."

Captain Adams was also to attempt to deliver the bishop's request for information verbally to each of the Company's two priestly spies when he reached Windsor, but only if he could do so without compromising them. If he could not safely meet with them he was to leave written copies of a request from their bishop with the Company's agent who would deliver them to each of the Angelovian priests—the agent being Windsor's village priest, a somewhat shady Franciscan who earned additional coins for himself from time to time by providing certain services for the Company in addition to food and lodging for visiting churchmen.

The scribed order sounded quite innocent in case it was intercepted. It merely informed each of the priests that he, the Bishop of Cornwall, a fellow Angelovian, would be in London for a few days in his usual rooms and expected the priest to join him so they could pray together about the priest's future. Each of the archer priests would understand from the message that it was important that he speak with the captain of the Company's London shipping post's as soon as possible, but not why. When he got to London he would be allowed to read the bishop's order that had been specifically scribed for him and then it was to be immediately burned whilst both men were watching.

When Captain Adams finally did get back to London he was to closely question the would-be crusaders and pilgrims who come in from England's cities and villages to buy passages to the Holy Land. He was also to spend his days prowling about in London's markets to make discreet inquiries amongst the merchants and moneylenders. "And especially talk to the Jewish moneylenders; they know everything about everything."

Commander Robertson also issued a warning before the men rode back to their posts.

"We may have to keep this year's class of recruits in England and send to Cyprus for reinforcements if the barons are really forming up armies that might try to enter Cornwall. I will let you know what I decide after we learn more about what it is that the barons intend to do and when and why."

As a result of the Company Commander's order, Captain Adams did not return to London by sea. Instead, he rode out of Restormel Castle with George and the Company's other castle captains with the intention of picking up a strong guard of horse archers at Okehampton and riding with them on the old Roman road all the way to London. *After a thousand years the old road was still the only way to travel between London and Cornwall except by sea.*

Adams and his men were to make inquiries in the markets and taverns along the way, and especially at Crediton, Oxford, and Windsor. It was just one of the many efforts the Company would make in an attempt to find out if the threat to Cornwall was real and, if it was, who was involved and what they hoped to accomplish and how and why and when.

The horse archers assigned to accompany Captain Adams to London were to remain in London temporarily to reinforce the six archers normally stationed at the Company's shipping post. They would stay with their horses in the nearby stable where the Company's newly acquired horses and recruits were accumulated for periodic shipments to Cornwall. The horse archers were to remain in London to help guard the shipping post and carry messages, the Commander decreed, until some additional foot archers could be moved to London by sea to relieve them.

******

George and his fellow captains rode out of Restormel the next morning. They expected a peaceful ride until they crossed the River Tamar that served as the border between Cornwall and Devon. It was a reasonable expectation; Cornwall's roads and villages were well known to be relatively safe and so were those along the western edge of Devon where it bordered Cornwall. They were safe due to the Company's outriders, the elite riders who constantly patrolled them, and also because of the immediately available horse archers the outriders could summon from Okehampton in the unlikely event they found themselves in need of serious reinforcements.

Indeed, it was well-known, at least in Cornwall and western Devon where the Company's outriders patrolled, that would-be robbers and ambitious nobles and priests would have very short and exciting lives in Cornwall and on the one road leading into it. An approaching army, especially a large one, the four men knew and discussed as they rode, would be something else entirely.

Without a word being spoken each of the three men with a stronghold to defend knew that the first thing he would do when he got back home would be to inspect his castle's siege supplies and water well to make sure they were adequate such that he could hold his castle for at least the eighteen month minimum that the Company required of them. Commander Robertson had already announced that his twice-yearly inspection tour and the make-believe war-fighting that accompanied it would begin almost immediately, month earlier than usual. They knew with a great deal of certainty from the way he said it that any man whose stronghold was not fully prepared to resist an extended siege would be immediately replaced.

All three of the men also knew that he had also better be able to show Commander Robertson that he had enough wagons immediately available so that the people in the surrounding villages and their livestock and personal possessions could be moved to isolated places of safety deep in Cornwall before the invaders arrived.

And merely being able to move the people to safety was not enough; they would have to be fed and sheltered whilst they were there. That would not be an impossible problem if the farmers could get their crops harvested before they fled with their livestock, because then they could carry the food with them that they would need to survive the winter. On the other hand, it would be a huge problem if some or all of the armies of the individual barons arrived before the harvest was in and took the harvest for themselves.

Unfortunately, since the invaders were English barons they would know all about farming since that was all that most of them ever did when they were not campaigning or attending tournaments. It led George to say out loud what they all knew:

"If the barons are coming they are probably already on their way and almost certainly intend to arrive before the crops of Devon and Cornwall can be harvested and the livestock driven away to safety. They would be fools not to do so."

It was a comment which resulted in much laughter when one of his travelling companions wryly finished his sentence by adding "which is encouraging because it means we only need to prepare for less than half of them arriving early."

The big problem, all four of the men agreed when they stopped laughing, would be convincing the farmers in western Devon and eastern Cornwall, almost all of whom were franklins, to move their families and livestock westward before they finished harvesting their crops. Was it even possible before the crops were harvested? And what should the Company do to encourage them to leave if the barons were coming? Those were the questions the four men talked about almost constantly as they rode.

Captain Adams listened as the three stronghold captains discussed their potential refugee and food supply problems and was glad he did not have them. He had his own special problems as a result of being so far away in London and badly out-numbered without strong walls to hide behind.

On the other hand, he certainly agreed with the recommendation each of the three castle constables said he intended to make to Commander Robertson when arrived on his inspection trip—do not wait; take the battle to the barons' armies before they arrive and keep attacking them constantly. Constant attacks and skirmishes on the road might not stop the barons but at least it *might* slow them down long enough for the crops to be harvested and give the franklins and their families more time to flee. It would also reduce their foraging efforts if their armies did get into Cornwall because the barons would surely suffer great casualties and have fewer mouths to feed.

"And we will have fewer mouths to feed ourselves," George said sourly. He was only half listening to the others whilst he once again began thinking about the various orders he should give when he reached Okehampton.

John Farmer had an additional problem at Plympton. He could hire the local fishing boats to make repeated trips to carry the local villagers and their personal possessions to safety further down the Cornwall coast. But he could do so only if the farmers left their livestock and their wagons behind and abandoned the crops that were still in their fields.

"Most of them will not abandon them in time," he said to the others with a sound of resignation in his voice as he slid off his horse to piss by the side of the road. "They will wait until it is too late. The only thing I can do is to quickly get as many of them as possible started on the road to

Okehampton with their livestock so they can cross into Cornwall at the ford whilst it is still open."

"Those with livestock might be willing to have their boys starting driving them immediately," Freddie Hogg suggested hopefully.

Freddie was secretly glad that he was assigned to Launceston Castle on the Cornwall side of the River Tamar. The people he was responsible for protecting would have more time to get their crops harvested and their families and livestock to safety. That was because the roads were such that the barons' armies would first have to reach eastern Devon near Okehampton and then force their way over the Tamar before they could get to the lands and people that were his responsibility to defend. *"Thank God," he thought to himself but did not say, "I will not have to make the decisions about the refugees and holding the ford; they will be up the Commander and George."*

In their hearts all four of the men knew the farmers, especially the franklins around Plymouth who have much further to go to get to safety, would not abandon their fields and leave for Cornwall until it was too late. And by the time the franklins knew for sure the barons' army was actually coming it would almost certainly be too late for them to escape. That was because they would have so far to go before they could get far enough north on the Devon side of the Tamar to reach the first fordable spot on the river where they could cross into Cornwall, the ford near Okehampton.

"Perhaps you could send men out to burn the crops after the villagers run for the fishing boats in order to escape," George suggested without much enthusiasm.

In fact, Lieutenant Commander Courtney was absorbed in thinking behind his eyes and only half listening to what the others were saying. He had a number of additional problems that the others did not. For one, he was not only responsible for defending Okehampton as the castle's constable, but also for both equipping and leading the Company's horse archers and for protecting the Company's large and growing horse herd at its isolated and undefendable horse farm north of Okehampton.

The horse farm was important because it provided the horse archers with the sturdy and carefully bred and gelded amblers the archers used almost exclusively. Amblers were preferred both because they were easier on a man's arse when they had to ride long distances and because pushing arrows out of a longbow was much easier when a horse was ambling smoothly than when he was bouncing its rider up or down by trotting or galloping; geldings because they did not get distracted by mares and were easier to manage.

And to further complicate George's life, Commander Robertson had ordered that all the available foot archers, even the recruits still being trained, were to be culled for potential riders so the ranks of George's elite horse archers could be expanded as much and as quickly as possible—and then frowned when an embarrassed George could not give an exact answers when he was asked "how many more archers can you provide with horses and equipment in the next month or two? And how many supply wagons do you have so your horse archers can stay out in the field without having to return for food and arrows?"

What George *did* know was that every available horse would be needed by the Company's horse archers if there was a war. That would be particularly true if the Commander's decision was what he expected—to ride out with every available man and take the war to the barons instead of waiting for them to reach Devon and Cornwall.

Unfortunately, George also knew that any additional horses taken from the Company's herd would have to be trained and equipped with saddles and bridles. And he also knew that the brood mares and principal stallions would need to be moved deep into Cornwall if there was a war. *Or should we try to use some of them as mounts? Alternately, of course, we could provide some of the horse archers with only one horse instead of one to ride and a remount to lead. Hmm. Would that work for the men who did not have to ride so far?*

George did not realize it, but he rode silently at times because he was so deep in thought about the state of Okehampton's defences and about the training the archers newly assigned to become riders would require and how many additional useful horses the Company's stud farm could provide in the coming weeks if an all-out effort was made to provide them—which, so far as he was concerned, there damn sure would be. And that was only the half of it; he also needed to decide where to intercept the barons' armies before they reached western Devon and how to fight them.

* * * * * *

The captains' ride from Restormel to the *Red Bull* tavern at the Tamar River ford went quickly. The road was well maintained and they could see the crops beginning to come up and the franklins in their fields. Even better, the people were as friendly as ever. That would helpful if the people and their beasts and their stores of food had to be moved deeper in Cornwall.

The friendliness of the people along the way was understandable; many of their sons and brothers were serving in the Company, their rents and taxes were low compared to those in the rest of England and could be paid in kind, and what the franklins produced that they did not eat themselves could be sold to the Company and used to feed their sons and brothers and their families and fellow archers.

Periodically the four captains met and overtook travelers and once they stopped to help push an overloaded hay wain out of a rut so it could get back on the road. And along the way they made a pact between themselves—they would *not* tell anyone in their strongholds that they were getting ready in case a war was coming; they would merely tell them that they were getting their castles ready because Commander Robertson was coming early for this year's readiness inspection.

"I like it," said Captain Hogg of Launceston. "That way it is less likely the nobles or whoever comes will get word that we know they are coming and are getting ready to fight them."

"It is much better than that, Freddie," was George's reply. "Because when the word of our preparations does get back to the nobles, which it sooner or later will, they might be misled into thinking that we are preparing to hide behind our walls whilst they besiege us such that they will be free to live off the land whilst they form up their various armies and get them ready to fight together as one."

George replied in that way because he was fairly sure he knew how and where Commander Robertson intended to fight. He had known as soon as the Commander ordered as many additional horse archers as possible to be mounted—and he totally agreed. He also hoped it was all a false alarm and that he would lead the horse archers into battle if it was not.

******

George and the others waved and shouted cheerful farewells as Freddie Hogg and his sergeant peeled off to ride down to Launceston on the Cornwall side of the River Tamar. Two of the outriders were amongst the six outriders permanently based there and went with them.

The remaining men stopped for a bowl of ale and some apples and cheese at the *Red Bull* and then splashed across the ford and rode together until they reached the cart path that led up to Okehampton. That was where John Farmer and his sergeant waved their farewells; they would continue on for a few more miles and then head south on the old Roman road until they reached the turnoff near Exeter that would take them to their home at the Company's Plympton Castle stronghold. The partings were optimistic. It was hard to be worried about the future when the weather was good, the crops seemed to be coming in rather nicely, and the travelers on the road had reported nothing that sounded troublesome.

There were smiles on the faces of George and Richard Adams as they turned their horses on to the cart path that led up to Okehampton. George was smiling because he was glad to be home and have his wife in his bed once again; Richard because George had just told him that one of his absent sons' string beds was available so that he would not have to sleep on the hard stone floor of Okehampton's great hall.

Richard would spend the night at Okehampton and then slowly begin making his way on to London with a band of "fellow mercenaries" that was comprised of not less than nine or ten very dependable horse archers selected by George and their horses and remounts. At least that was the plan as the outermost of Okehampton's three curtain walls came into view through the trees. They could not see the other two walls, of course, because they were no higher than the outer wall and the castle was on the highest ground around.

Hmm, George thought. I wonder if the barons know about the inner walls?

Chapter Six

The captains ride.

Captain Adams enjoyed a fine supper of mutton,
cheese, and turnips with George and his wife and had a
good night's sleep in the bed of one of their absent sons
who was attending the Company school. The next
morning George took the captain to meet Sergeant Cooper
and the eight horse archers who had been assigned to ride
to London with him. The type of news and information
they would be looking for had been explained to the
sergeant and his men; why they were seeking it was still
not exactly clear to them. It would be soon enough.

Captain Adams liked what he saw when he met the
men with whom he would be riding to London; they
looked to his professional eye like good men. And they
immediately fetched a second horse for him, a fine brown
ambler, so he would have an adequate and already
saddled remount in the event he ever needed a fresh
horse. One of the experienced horse archers would lead it
along with his own remount.

A few minutes later, just before they mounted to
leave, Sergeant Cooper also swapped out the horse the
captain had been riding for one of Okehampton's more
dependable amblers. Sergeant Cooper did so when one of

his men recognized the horse the captain had ridden in on and alerted him to the fact that it was a riding horse from Restormel's stables.

"It be one of the dogs we sent to Restormel last year for the boys to ride" was how the archer put it.

Sergeant Cooper growled his displeasure at the news and ordered the horse to be immediately replaced with something better. Of course he did; horse archers sometimes need to ride fast and sometimes they need to ride long distances—and a patrol can only go as fast and as far as its slowest and least reliable horse unless the leader of the patrol was willing to leave a horse behind when it faltered for some reason. The sergeant knew he would not be the leader of the patrol whilst they were riding for London, but he had been in the Company long enough that he damned well knew he would have the highest rank on the way back and be blamed if he and his men arrived back at Okehampton without all of their horses.

Although Captain Adams did not know it and never would, the horse archers did *not* like what they saw when they met him. It was understandable since he had innocently remarked that he had not really been on a horse since he left the Company school at Restormel where every boy was taught to ride and given a horse of his own to take care of during his last two or three years. The horse he had ridden in on had been one of those—and he had made a great mistake, at least in their eyes, by saying it was "alright." They knew it was not.

Sergeant Cooper made the best of what he and his men increasingly saw as a problem assignment from which they could not escape. Accordingly, In addition to the archer leading the captain's remount Sergeant Cooper assigned his two most dependable men to stay close to Captain Adams at all times.

"Watch yon captain like a hawk and do whatever it takes to keep him out of trouble; Red says he will be doing something important along the way and we must get him through to London after he finishes making his inquiries."

****

It was mid-morning and the sun had come out as Commander Courtenay and a dozen or so horse archers prepared to ride out of Okehampton. Captain Adams and his London-bound "band of mercenaries" were riding out at the same time. As a result the castle's outer bailey where they were assembling was full of riders and on-lookers.

The Commander and the men riding with him were riding north to visit the Company's horse herd and meet with the handful of archers and hostlers who guarded it and trained the sturdy gelded amblers that were selected to be the horse archers' mounts and remounts. They expected no trouble and were not leading remounts. They were, however, carrying their longbows and a quiver full of arrows as was required of all horse archers any time they were on their horses outside of Okehampton's walls.

Accompanying George were one of the Company's two horse barbers, all three of Okehampton's farriers, and a number of the horse archers who were thought to be particularly knowledgeable about caring for horses and getting them ready to be ridden. The horse barber and the farriers and a few of the other men were told they would be staying with the herd for a while to help get them ready; the rest of the archers would return with George in another day or two. The men did not know it yet but some of the horses at the farm would be returning with them.

Sergeant Allen, the Company's other full-time horse barber, was already at the horse farm because he lived there permanently. He and his family lived in their own hovel in the little village that sprung up next to the stables and birthing barns. They were there and he had his sergeant's stripes because he knew how to reach into the mares to grab and tug on the unborn foals to help the mares birth them.

The large number of horsemen assembling in the outermost of Okehampton's three baileys, in turn, attracted almost all the Okehampton's women and children and a good number of the archers who would be remaining behind. They watched and talked as the departing men took turns pissing one last time in one of the several jars the archers who served as the Company's tanners and saddle makers had lined up against the bailey wall and then swung into their saddles. Their horses were fresh and a little bit excited and skittish because they anticipated the coming ride.

The only thing that surprised the on-lookers and took up more than a little of the conversations was the appearance of the men who were riding for London. They were not at all dressed like archers. To the contrary, they were wearing the patched and battered tunics of farm workers and labourers and their remounts were carrying their short swords and galley shields. It was different and no one knew why, not even the men. They would be told more about the real reason they were wearing them once they were on the road.

Much of the onlookers' talk was because the longbows and quivers that every archer was required to carry appeared to be missing. It was unheard of. But just because their bows and arrows could not be seen did not mean the horse archers bound for London were leaving without their most important weapon. They were not; each archer's longbow and his quivers full of arrows were wrapped in linen and packed away out of sight, and either being carried on his remount or on one of the group's their two supply horses along with their food supplies and the tent that would shelter them at night if there was rain. In other words, the men of the patrol going to London looked like they were supposed to look—like a very dangerous band of sword-carrying robbers or mercenaries.

The appearance of Captain Adams and the men riding with him had been explained to their families and mates as being necessary to prevent the people they encountered along the way from getting upset because they thought they were seeing an invading army of archers. It was not much of an explanation but it was the only one George could think to come up with on short notice. Besides, it did not much matter what their families and mates thought about how the men looked; it was the people they encountered along the way that mattered and whether or not word as to what they were doing and why got back to the barons.

Despite the rough and unexpected dress of some of them, there was no sense of concern or worry amongst the men who getting ready to ride out. Indeed, to the contrary, there was a somewhat festive atmosphere. That was to be expected since no dangers were foreseen for any of the men and about half of them were riding out to the horse herd and were expected to be back that day or within the next few days. The other half of the riders in the bailey were looking forward to a long arse-rubbing ride to London followed by a few days in that great city to enjoy its delights followed by another long ride back. Whether the ride would be enjoyable or result in their arses being rubbed raw on wet saddles depended on the weather; that was to be expected and they all knew it.

Most of the men riding to London had never been there before and were excited by the prospect. Indeed, they were looking forward both to visiting the big city and also to gulling the people they met along the way into believing they were mercenaries newly returned from the lowlands. They had already begun asking those of their mates who had visited London previously what to do in the city and where to go. If the past was any guide, most of the questions were about where to find friendly women and bowls of strong drink.

Some of the women and children in the bailey, mainly those clustered about Sergeant Cooper and his men, seemed a bit distressed because he and his men would be gone for at least two or three weeks on their trip to London whilst others of them showed no emotion or, in one case, obvious relief.

Everything, in other words, appeared quite normal as Captain Adams lifted his hand and nodded one last thank you to Anne, George's wife, who had come to see them off. He did so as he and Sergeant Cooper led their sword-carrying "mercenaries" through the gate in Okehampton's outermost wall and on to the muddy cart path beyond its moat. George and his men were right behind them.

It was a nice partly cloudy summer day and it was already beginning to get quite warm. A fish surfaced and ducks and geese rose off the castle's foul-smelling outer moat as they clattered across it on the outer drawbridge.

****** *Farrier Sergeant Thomas Smith*

Our horses ambled slowly in single file as we rode up the cart path toward the Company's horse farm. It was about three hours ahead of us. The path started behind Okehampton's back wall and wound its way for several miles through a downward sloping and very thick stand of trees that began behind the castle's outermost wall and stretched down into the little valley behind it. It was the only cart path to the horse farm and it was always maintained in relatively good shape for that reason. The horses would have no trouble with it and I fervently prayed that their shoes would hold—they should since I had spent every hour since I heard Red and some of the lads would be riding out today checking their shoes. It would not do much for my future to have a shoe come loose and for Red to get angry about it, would it?

It was an enjoyable ride on an unexpectedly warm summer day even though the bugs were quite fierce about my face and even got into my eyes and beard where the trees were thickest or the ground marshy. Several times we splashed our way across little streams including the one that fed water into the moats that surrounded each of Okehampton's three curtain walls and were the home of the shite-eating fish and the nobbled ducks and geese we were sometimes allowed to catch and eat along with the wild birds they sometimes chummed in. After the moat stream the path began wondering haphazardly across the side of a hill and then down it and up through an even thicker stand of trees and then on around yet another hill.

An hour or so after we left Okehampton we came upon a couple of overloaded wains bringing hay to the horse farm and a horse-drawn wagon hauling what looked to be sacks of grain for use as food for the horses. The brace of oxen pulling the wains were lurching their way north around the side of a hill as we overtook them. A horse-drawn wagon was right behind them with its driver obviously hoping to find an open space where he could get it past the oxcarts. It might have been my imagination or perhaps the wind picked up, but it seemed to have gotten a bit cooler.

A little later, just before we reached the second little stream we met a little convoy of two empty hay wains coming toward us on the rough and muddy path. They were both being pulled by oxen. The men driving the oxen were two of Okehampton's tenant farmers. I recognized them both and gave them a hearty and very friendly hoy as we veered out around them and kept going. *Of course I did; my middle boy has his eye on the daughter of one of them.*

Other than meeting the wains and carts everything felt very isolated as we periodically rode though woods on both sides of the path that were so heavy with trees and full of brush as to be impassable. The cart path we were on ran from Okehampton through the forests and over the downs to the Company horse farm. It was a three hour ride for a man on a good horse and took the best part of a long summer day for a hay wain pulled by a brace of oxen that were never allowed to stop.

Overall, the cart path was in very good shape. That was no surprise since the Company constantly maintained and improved it. We had to do it ourselves because it ran between Okehampton and the Company's horse farm and there was nothing, not even a single farm or woodcutter's hovel on the hillsides in between.

Red's horse continued ambling slowly and steadily along on the cart path until in the distance we could see the little village that had sprung up over the years because of our horses. And, of course, our horses did too in order to keep up with him, amble that is. A minute or so later we could see the Company's horse farm itself. As we rode toward the buildings and pastures in the distance I got increasingly worried about what Red would find when we got there.

It suddenly crossed my mind as we got closer and closer to the horses that I had not been up here as frequently as I should have been to make sure Old Bob White, my assistant farrier, had been shoeing the horses all right and proper. I got more and more worried as we got closer. My God; what if Red was coming here and bringing the farriers from Okehampton because he had heard rumours about the horses' shoes not being right.

****** *George Courtenay*

The sun was directly above us when the Company's horse farm and its little village came into view through the trees. They sat in the middle of a big meadow on the side of a very gentle hill. A little stream of water came through the far end of the main pasture and ran just below the village. The stream ran throughout the year. It was said that there were fish in it but I had never seen any.

What we saw in front of us were six large wooden barns with fenced enclosures on either side of them and another dozen or so smaller buildings with enclosures. Some of the fences surrounding the enclosures were made of stone but more than half were wood. There was also a very large fenced pasture extending out over much of the hill with a number of mares and colts in it. Battered wains and ploughs were scattered about haphazardly but the fences and buildings looked to be well-maintained. We could see the smoke coming from the farm's smithy and could hear the hammering coming from it even before we saw the camp.

The stream that ran next to the horse farm and through the big fenced pasture meant that no water wells were needed. Even so, water had to be carried in buckets from the stream to fill water troughs in the various enclosures and for the people to cook with and drink in their homes. As we rode in we could see a couple of the farm's horse boys carrying a heavily laden wooden bucket from the stream to one of the stables. They were hurrying which probably meant the bucket was leaking badly.

Horses were in most of the larger fenced enclosures and some of them had foals. Almost all of the smaller buildings also had fenced enclosures and most of them had horses and other beasts such as mules and oxen inside them as well. Only one of the very small enclosures had a man in it, the one that held a mare with a very wobbly young foal that might have been getting its first look at the world. A man standing near them turned and began watching us we rode in.

One of the medium-sized enclosures was full of mules and a couple of oxen could be seen in another, but all the rest of the enclosures had horses in them including a number of foals and yearlings. The mules and oxen were used to pull iron ploughs in the nearby unfenced hay fields and to pull the wains. There were a few plough and wagon horses stationed at the farm but not many.

Almost a dozen archers were permanently assigned to the horse farm. They were under the command of the Company's horse captain, an elderly lieutenant by the name of Edward Smith who lived with his wife in a large thatch-roofed hovel with its own fireplace and a nearby outside kitchen. The other archers lived with their families in a somewhat straight line of smaller hovels, also with their own fireplaces to help warm them and for cooking, that ran along the north side of the cart path as it entered the farm. A well-worn cart path ran along in front of them. It was much improved with stones filling its holes and little ditches running along either side of it to carry away some of the water when it rained.

On the south side of the cart path were the thatched roof hovels of the dozen or so free families who helped the archers care for the horses and maintain the barns and the stone and wooden fences that keep the horses in and the wolves and robbers out. The commons where the farm's families kept their gardens and grazed their livestock was off to the right beyond the hovels of the free families. There also was a small log tavern with a fireplace where most of the local people spent their evenings in the middle of the little village. And at the far end of the village there was a little cemetery next to a very small church where the villagers would pray on Sunday despite there being no priest in the village and use for their weddings and funerals.

Lieutenant Smith, the horse farm's captain, must have gotten word that we were coming because he came hurrying up to the entrance gate even before we reached it and everywhere men seemed to working with an uncommon intensity including a number of the young boys who seemed to working at training the horses to be ridden under the supervision of half a dozen or so archers and free men who were standing around watching them.

The twenty or so horse boys in the camp were mostly orphans and runaways waiting to be old enough and strong enough to go for archers. They had somehow heard about the horse farm, showed up for some reason or another, and were put to work in exchange for their food and shelter. The boys lived in the sheds and hay barns and in the farm's large tack room which was full of saddles and other gear.

One of the smaller wooden buildings was the kitchen where the wife of one of the resident archers prepared the horse boys' food. Smoke was coming out through the thatch of the kitchen's roof and also from the smithy where the loud hammering noise was coming from. By tradition the lieutenant's wife acted as the boys' captain and the lieutenant sent them off to go for archers when he thought they were ready.

When the archers and the local men and the boys were not busy caring for the horses and training them they worked on building and repairing the horse farm's fences and barns. Sometimes they built new and better hovels for the men and families posted to the farm or they worked to improve or repair the cart path. And when they had nothing else to do they gathered stones and replaced the horse farms wooden fences with stone fences.

It had always been that way for as long as anyone could remember. Men and women were welcome to build hovels and stay so long as they were willing to work at whatever the horse captain told them to do. They were paid for their work with grain for their bread and allowed to have their own gardens and graze a few sheep or a cow or two on the little village's commons. Some of the wives weaved and sewed rough clothes of wool and linen to trade for whatever their families needed.

Now that I was actually looking at the horse farm and thinking seriously about it in terms of the barons' men actually finding it and taking its horses as prizes to sell or eat, I began to realize how thoughtfully the camp had been located to keep it isolated—and I began re-thinking the need to move the herd deeper into Cornwall if push came to shove and an invasion threatened, particularly since we were about to remove as many as possible of the farm's horses for the Company's immediate use.

Indeed, the more I thought about it in the hours that followed, the more I was leaning toward *not* moving the herd deeper into Cornwall if an invasion threatened. But there was a potential problem and it was painfully visible even though I had obviously seen it and ignored it as meaningless ever since I had been posted to Okehampton a few years earlier—a narrow footpath leading elsewhere had grown over the years so the camp's residents could come and go from the farm without passing near Okehampton and being seen as deserters or slackers. So where did it go?

I inquired and cursed out loud when I heard the answer. According to Lieutenant Smith, the footpath led to the little village of Hatherleigh which was a three or four hours walk back toward the south on the main road between London and Exeter. It was the same main road that subsequently passed near Okehampton—and the road the barons' armies were sure to be on because it was only road an army could use if it was marching to Cornwall.

I instantly knew that the path was a serious problem. It meant that sooner or later a party of enemy foragers, men either encamped near Hatherleigh or passing through it, would hear about the horse farm when they visited the village tavern. When they did they were likely to walk up the path to see if there was any food or loot at the other end.

It was enough of a potential problem that I decided to stay over at the horse farm for the night and in the morning take one of the farm's archers as a guide and walk the path to see for myself how dangerous the foot path might be. The rest of the current day would be spent on our more immediate need—getting more useful horses for the archers to ride.

******

The farm's horse captain was an old lieutenant by the name of Tom Smith. He was a white-bearded veteran horse archer. As soon as I arrived I had taken him aside and quietly told him why I had come—because Commander Robertson wanted to know how many useful horses the farm could immediately provide to the horse archers in the event of an absolute emergency wherein we needed every horse that a man could ride?

Tom had squinted at me in the sunlight and nibbled on a piece of grass he had plucked off the ground before he answered.

"We still have the older horses that were swapped out for the last two years because we hold them for reserves in case more horses are quickly needed due to a horse pox or heavy casualties. There are about forty of them. The mares provide us with about thirty new amblers a year and this year's are trained and ready.

"So I have about seventy good ready-to-ride ambler geldings I can give you right now today. And maybe another twenty that are almost ready such that the Company's really good riders could finish training them. That is ninety I can give you immediately.

"And then, of course, there are about twenty more likely-looking colts that we have just begun trying to train and are not yet ready to be ridden. They might come along faster and be ready in a couple of months if they could be shown what was expected of them and men who were good with horses were responsible for them. And, as usual, about half of them will turn out *not* to be amblers. But they could be useful if we are seriously short of amblers and desperately need horses to ride.

"My men and I also have a dozen or so good amblers which we have been using for our own riding and to use whilst we are training the young colts. We can give you those and begin using some of the riding horses that turned out not to be amblers, the ones we usually sell each year. I will have to do an actual count but I would guess we have about a hundred and ten useful amblers you could take right now, perhaps a few more.

"And then, of course, there are the non-amblers that are sold each year at the horse fairs along with some of the mares and stallions that produced them. We have some thirty or forty of them that we intended to send to the Exeter horse market next month. We had to begin training them to be ridden so we could see if they were natural amblers or could be trained to amble. They are rideable as non-amblers and could be useful in a pinch with more training.

I summed the numbers behind my eyes and was stunned; one hundred and forty or more additional useful horses for my horse archers? And all their remounts too. I was stunned; I had not realized we could provide mounts for so many more men. And even some young boys who knew how to ride and could serve as horse holders to free up experienced archers to fight? We could take them too, the boys that is. It changed everything.

Tom mistook my look of surprise as one of disapproval because there were so few horses. So he tried to explain the horse farm to me by telling me what I mostly already knew.

"We have about a dozen stallions and one hundred and forty or so mares for them to cover. From the mares we get about one hundred and twenty or thirty foals each year. But half of the foals are fillies and about half are colts that we geld. But only about half of the sixty or so colts turn out to natural amblers though the percentage has been slowly growing for some reason. So each year we usually produce about thirty fully trained three-year-old amblers and send them to the Company to replace those who have fallen or broken down or are aging out.

"At the moment along with our breeding stock we have about a hundred and twenty new foals and about a hundred and ten two-year-olds of whom about half or slightly more will turn out to be amblers. We also have about forty or so of the older and not quite right amblers that the archers returned when we delivered last year's new three-year old amblers. As I told you earlier, we hold the useful returns in reserve for a couple of years in case they are needed again. So all in all there is another hundred you could have fairly quickly even though they won't be as strong or ready as we usually provide.

"Also since I think I see where you are coming from and will need more riders for the additional horses, you should know that we have about twenty horse boys who know how to ride and could ride with the archers and be used as horse holders. The boys come in all the time. They fetch water and help where they can. For example, several horse archers and two or three of the horse boys ride on duty all night in the pastures to protect the herd from wolves and sound the alarm if they see horse thieves.

"Why just a couple of days ago two more young ones walked in. Half starved they were and the older boy carrying the younger. Not sure where they come from, probably Wales or from somewhere in the north since I could not understand a word they said. My wife sewed up some tunics for them, so she did. Eating like wolves they are."

When Tom finished I told him I appreciated what he was doing and began barking out orders.

"Sergeant Murphy, send a reliable man back to Okehampton with a message for Captain Merton. He is to bring one hundred and fifty riders here tomorrow. They are *not* to bring their remounts, but each man is to bring his remount's bridle and leads because each man will be leading a new horse back to Okehampton from the herd. Each of the men is also to bring hobbles for both horses.

"Also tell him that the men he leaves behind are to prepare to receive and stable as many as one hundred and fifty additional horses tomorrow evening. He will also need to provide sleeping places and make feeding arrangements for twenty or so additional men most of whom will be experienced horse boys who can stay in the stables with the new horses and help care for them. There will also be a handful of archers from the horse farm.

Tom listened as I gave the orders. He waited until Sergeant Murphy repeated his orders back to me and hurried off to carry them out. Then Tom looked at me carefully and tried to tactfully ask me what was happening.

"Commander, I have been a horse archer in the Company for almost thirty years and we have never been asked to do anything like this before. Not once. So it sounds as though there is some kind of a serious trouble and I need to do everything possible to get more horses for you and the lads to ride. Should I be doing that?" Tom spoke quietly and had a question in his voice as he looked at me intently.

I sighed and nodded my head.

"Aye, we may well be facing something very serious, Lieutenant Smith; a real threat to the Company and Cornwall. It is a secret because we are not yet sure what it means or even if the threat is actually real. We are not at all sure I am sorry to say. So you must keep your mouth shut about what I just told you because we do not want our enemies to know that we are getting ready to go against them and defeat them if they come. It is a Company secret.

"Besides, it may be a false alarm and it might cause panic and other problems for the Company if it became known that we were fearful and getting ready for a possible fight against invaders. So you are not to say anything about the possibility to anyone, not even to your wife. But do everything you can to get as many useful horses and archers to us as possible, Lieutenant, and also all the boys who can ride since they can be horse holders; there is no sense taking chances, eh?"

I had gone formal with the use of Tom's rank as was the Company's tradition when important orders were being explained and given. Tom was an old sweat; he understood immediately.

"You can count on me Commander Courtenay to provide the Company with every possible horse and rider," the lieutenant said as he stood to attention and knuckled his brow. He had a very determined look on his face as he said it.

Chapter Seven

Captain Adams begins his ride.

Sergeant Cooper and I rode side by side as we led our men and remounts out of Okehampton and on to the cart path that ran through the trees to a spur of the old Roman road that ran between London and Exeter. The path from the castle to the London road was in good condition, it was a lovely June day, and everyone's spirits were high. I was now aboard an absolutely splendid grey ambler and one of the horse archers was leading my remount in addition to leading his own.

There were ten of us in our party including me and every man including me was wearing a sheathed short sword and had a galley shield either slung over his shoulder or hanging from his saddle. And, of course, every one of us also had a longbow, an archer's tunic, and three or four quivers of arrows. Each of us had them wrapped in piece of linen and hidden away along with our tunics so no one would be able to look at us and know we were men of the Company of Archers. Mine were being carried by the supply horse that was also carrying the linen tent we would all crowd into at night in the event it rained or the bugs were bad.

As Red had explained to me and the men, we needed to conceal our tunics and bows because we would be pretending to be English mercenaries who were looking for employment. Hopefully, we looked the part and would attract inquiries from barons interested in strengthening their forces or concerned because their ambitious neighbours might be strengthening theirs.

Our main hope, as you might imagine, was that we would learn something useful as we went about the process of offering our services as mercenaries "because we heard rumours there might be something going on in the west of England involving the French and some of the English barons." What we hoped, of course, was that by asking around we would get answers that would help us learn what the barons were doing or thinking of doing. At least that was the plan and what Sergeant Cooper and I told the men during our first piss and water break after we cleared Okehampton's gate.

Commander Courtenay and some of his lads rode out of the castle right behind us. He immediately turned them to starboard as soon as they clattered across the drawbridge of the outermost moat. He did so in order to lead the men riding with him around to the back of the castle and on to the cart path that led up to the Company's horse farm. I had never been up there, to the horse farm that is, but I had been told it was about a three hour ride to the north.

No one told me exactly why George was going to visit the Company's horse farm, but it almost certainly had something to do with barons' army that was thought to be forming up and might be coming to Devon and Cornwall. It was clear to me that having as many good horses as possible would be important if the barons did come because they would enable us to meet them further out towards London with more men. And that, in turn, set me to thinking about how my shipping post could get additional useful horses to Okehampton.

Unfortunately no one was exactly sure why the barons or the French would be coming to Cornwall or even if the rumours were true. That was why I had been ordered by Commander Robertson to begin hopscotching my way back to my post in London—to try to find out what, if anything, was happening by pretending to be the leader of a mercenary band seeking employment and making inquiries along the way.

Only one thing was certain if it was true that an army of English barons or dirty-dingled Frenchies intended to invade Cornwall: They would not be getting past the approaches to Cornwall without fighting a couple of very serious battles and surviving numerous skirmishes and ambushes all along the way.

There was no question about the fact that the Company would resist and there would be fighting if the barons tried to come this way; so far as my fellow captains were concerned we and our men were like one of the songs from the old days that we sang when we were in school: The Company was like an oak tree planted near the water; we shall not be moved—at least not without a fight.

****** *Captain Richard Adams*

We rode easy the first few days until we reached the village of Crediton. We camped outside the village just off the road on the banks of the River Creedy. Sergeant Cooper left his most senior chosen men in charge of the others so that he and I could walk into the village just as the sun was going down.

Commander Robertson had instructed me to visit *The Raven* tavern and quietly talk to the tavern keeper. "He is a friendly man and tends to know what is happening in England because he talks to a lot of people. Ask him the question with *exactly* the words I told you and then say no more and do not pester him; let him come to you."

The tavern was easy to find because it was located right next to the road and had a large black raven painted above its door. It was also surprisingly large with a number of sleeping rooms both above the public room and to one side of it. There was a barn-like building that was almost certainly a stable standing about a hundred or so paces behind the tavern. It had a well-trod little footpath running down to it.

The Raven's public room was crowded and smoky because the fireplace at the far end of the room was also used for cooking—and everyone stopped talking for a few moments and stared at us when Sergeant Cooper and I walked in. It is always that way when someone walks into a tavern. Everyone turns to see who it is. In our case, probably because of our appearance, they looked away as soon as they saw us and resumed their talking with many a sideways looks to take our measure without catching our eye. There was a group of priests, some merchants, and a couple of families of gentry all of whom looked to be travelers spending the night.

The surreptitious looks we received were no surprise. Taverns along the road to London were certainly used to seeing new faces. What had caught everyone's attention, however, were the rounded galley shields slung over our backs and our sheathed short swords. We looked like rough and tough fighting men; and that, of course, was reasonable because rough and tough mercenary fighting men were exactly what Sergeant Cooper and I were pretending to be—and also ready to instantly become if anyone gave us a hard time or tried to attack us.

A cheerful and rather plump man hurried up to greet us and show us to a table. He had a big smile to show his snaggly teeth and a few wisps of white hair sticking out of the side of his otherwise bald head. He was the tavern keeper for sure.

"Be you Alec the smith from Taunton who now the runs the tavern here?" I asked the tavern keeper with as pleasant a smile as I could muster as we followed him toward some wooden stools that were set around an upside down wooden barrel. Those were the words I was told to use when I first spoke to the Raven's tavern keeper.

"We were told that you, seeing as you keep a popular tavern, might know who in these parts might be looking to hire a small company of dependable guards and swordsmen to protect his lands."

The man's eyes widened in surprise at my greeting and he looked us over carefully before he replied.

"No, I am not a smith. I be Thomas and a tavern keeper and hostler all my life and my father before me. What can I get for you two good masters? Perhaps a bowl of good ale and some bread and cheese to eat for just a piece of one of the king's good copper pennies?

"My wife brews ale and cooks bread uncommonly good for a Newcastle woman; yes she does—but only, I am sorry to have to say, if you have enough coin bits to pay for them. We also have a number of particularly fine sleeping rooms at the top of the stairs with shared beds for those who can pay and a stable with grain and good hay for your horses."

The bald man told us what his tavern had available with a great deal of friendliness and enthusiasm such that we could see he had truly found his calling when he became a tavern keeper. The men sitting around the table where we were seating ourselves were openly curious and listening intently as I nodded my head and said I agreed.

"Aye, a bowl of ale sounds good and some bread and cheese would go down well for each of us. We still have coins left from our recent contract as mercenaries in the lowlands and our throats are dry from the road."

"I will fetch them for you right away," the friendly tavern keeper said with another big smile as he hurried away. He was exceedingly friendly and clearly going out of his way to avoid any trouble from men who looked as though they knew how to use the weapons they were carrying.

"Thomas be right about that, you know," said one of the men sitting at the next table said as he turned toward us with a friendly smile. As he did he gave a wave of the bowl in his hand toward the tavern keeper who was heading toward the ale barrel in the far corner of the room. "His wife does indeed brew uncommonly good ale and his rooms and beds are the best and cleanest on this section of the road. And what brings you two masters here if I might ask most respectful?"

Our questioner's red nose, sun-browned face, and the dust and straw on his un-patched clothes suggested he might be a prosperous franklin or a reeve and that he often enjoyed more than a few bowls of the tavern's ale after a day in his fields with his serfs and slaves.

"I be Richard and this be my friend Steven. We be passing through. The two of us and some of our mates be newly returned from being mercenaries for some nobles and merchants in the lowlands and Anvers. We be on our way to London with the hope of finding employment for our little company with some lord or rich merchant along the way." *I did not want to give out that I was birthed and schooled in Cornwall so I was using my best effort to gobble like an Englishman from up north by the border. Sergeant Cooper picked up on it immediately and did the same.*

Sergeant Cooper and I ate our bread and cheese and drank a couple of bowls of ale—and we talked most friendly with the man at the next table as we ate. His name was James and he was indeed a reeve, the overseer of the serfs and slaves on a manor adjacent to the village that was assigned to an elderly knight named Sir Ranulph as a knight's fee. James introduced the man sitting with him as his friend Paul. If either of them had a family name he did not mention it. And James was right about the ale and I told him so—it was uncommonly good.

What soon became apparent was that James reeve liked to talk and that he had spent his entire life in the village and the surrounding countryside. He seemed almost desperate to hear about life beyond Crediton. We told him that we both had been birthed in villages in the north of Yorkshire and that our mothers had left their home villages to follow their husbands who had become mercenaries because it was the only way they could earn their daily bread.

"Fighting for coins and our daily bread is in our blood and all we know how to do," I told James. "We are ten in all on the road and every man both good and dependable in a fight. The rest of the lads are camped by the river just outside of the village. They elected me as the captain when we decided to leave Anvers and return to England. There are another dozen or so in our company. They are waiting with their wives in Exeter until we find an acceptable contract.

"We were in Anvers in Robert Wolf's free company. Have you heard of Robert? No? Well it does not matter because Robert got himself killed and our pay and food died with him. We heard rumours that some of the English barons would soon be recruiting for a campaign in Cornwall so we decided to return to where we could at least understand what people were saying when we talked with them.

"Have you heard anything about the barons ? Surely there must be a baron who needs some dependable Englishmen to stand with him on a campaign or to stay behind and protect his lands whilst he is away. There are twenty-one of us, if you count the eleven men waiting in Exeter, and we have our own horses and weapons." *It was the story I had been told to tell.*

James the reeve seemed quite sorrowful when he responded that he did not know of anyone. It was clear that he and his friend meant us well and would have told us if they had known of anyone who might need our services.

"No I do not," said James the reeve. "There are always rumours, of course, but I am sorry to say I have not heard of anyone who was actually looking to employ a free company for a campaign in Cornwall. And certainly not my manor's old Sir Ranulph. His campaigning days are over for sure. And I know naught of any others. Lord William holds most of the land hereabouts and would be the man most likely to know which of the barons in these parts might need men.

"But you will not find Lord William in here tonight; his keep is just to the north of Stockleigh so he mainly drinks at the *Three Bells* when he is home and wants to get away to visit with his friends. You might inquire there. Stockleigh is a three or four hours walk to the north on the road."

"Stockleigh is where to find Lord William?" I replied with a question in my voice. "That is good to know. Thank you most kindly, Master James. We have nothing better to do, unfortunately, so perhaps we will stop there in the morning and inquire. And may I buy you and Paul another bowl? It is indeed uncommonly good. Do you think the alewife uses a special recipe from Newcastle?

Sergeant Cooper and I learned more about Lord William as we ate our meal and drank with our new-found friends. When we finished we gave our new friends the most agreeable of farewells and walked out of the tavern. Thomas the tavern keeper followed us out into the moonlight a moment later. Both the London road and the village's moonlit dirt street were empty of people when he caught up with us—and when he did the tavern keeper spoke softly and with a sense of urgency in his voice.

"Tell Commander Robertson that there are rumours amongst the travelling merchants and messengers that something is definitely afoot with the English barons and it involves Devon and Cornwall. It is being much talked about but no one is exactly sure what it means. Tell him the thin man has everything ready and will keep him informed. Also tell him would be helpful if he would send a rider or even two to help the thin man since it will be suspicious if the thin man has to leave to carry a message and also that he cannot count on anyone else to do the necessary if there is additional news to be sent."

I carefully repeated his message back to him so he would know I had it correctly. And in a strange way I was glad to hear it—for it confirmed what I had heard in London and told Commander Robertson at our meeting. Actually, I breathed a great sigh of relief at getting the bad news confirmed; God only knows what would have happened to me if what I had warned the Commander about at Restormel had turned out to be false and cost the Company dearly.

Then I made a spur of the moment decision that would greatly affect both me and the Company in the days and weeks that followed.

"I think we can provide you with a rider to be your courier if you really need one. Do you want him?"

"My God, yes. It would be most helpful. The wife and I have been here alone ever since last fall when the coughing pox took our hostler. And do not worry about your man; there is a place for him to sleep in one of the stable's stalls." He said it reassuringly as if having a place to sleep in the tavern's stable was quite important—and it turned out that it certainly was.

"We will bring a rider and his horses to the stable to you tonight after the tavern closes. He can be your new hostler until you need him for a courier or we send for him."

"Thank you, thank you indeed. I am much obliged. And please do not show a light or talk loud when you bring him."

Chapter Eight

We leave a man behind.

Much later that night Sergeant Cooper and I led young one-stripe archer Martin Swindon and his two horses slowly and quietly down the road to the *Raven*'s stables. We walked silently without talking. The only noise was the distinctive clicking and clopping sound of the horses' metaled hooves as they stepped on the stones that paved the old road.

Martin was the youngest of the three unmarried horse archers in our party. He "volunteered" to stay in the village at Sergeant Cooper's request because "it is important, Martin, and requires an archer such as yourself who is good with horses and also a very good rider."

"I chose Martin because he is the most dependable of the three men riding with us who do not have wives and families back at Okehampton," Sergeant Cooper had quietly explained to me an hour or so earlier as we watched in the moonlight while the young archer hurriedly retrieved his linen-wrapped longbow and quivers from one of the supply horses.

We had no idea how long Martin would have to stay in the village and I told him as much. I also told him he should consider anything Thomas the tavern keeper wanted him to do to be an order coming out of my mouth and that he was *never* to admit to being an archer or a member of the Company.

"Not to anyone, ever; and always be where the tavern keeper and his wife can instantly find you at any time day or night. And be sure to keep your bow and quivers hidden at all times so no one can ever name you for an archer."

I also explained to Martin that the story he was *always and only* to tell the people he met was that he was just a former pike-carrying mercenary who had gotten tired of fighting in the lowlands around Anvers and did not want to talk about where he had been and what he had done. But if pressed, he was to say his company's last employment was guarding the warehouses of some Anvers merchants from their troublesome rivals and that he and his older brother and some of the men had left when their company's captain, Robert Wolf, had been killed whilst beating off an attack. He could also say that he and his brother had sailed on a Hollander cargo cog to Exeter where his brother had stayed because of a lass he had met.

Martin had nodded his head and repeated the story back to me and Sergeant Cooper several times until we were sure he had it right. It was a good story and likely to gull anyone who heard it, at least we hoped so.

What I did not tell either Martin or Sergeant Cooper was that I had it in mind to have Sergeant Cooper leave another of the unmarried men behind to provide the tavern keeper with a second rider when the horse archers rode back past Crediton in a week or two. That would be when they were riding back to Okehampton from London without me.

I had seriously thought behind my eyes about leaving two of our men in Crediton to ride back to carry the tavern keeper's messages to Commander Robertson. But I decided to wait until I talked to the tavern keeper again. I did so because it had sounded as if he had nothing to report that was pressing. It turned out to be a good decision even though I did not know it at the time.

******

We saw no one as we walked quietly in the moonlight until we reach the entrance to the stable that next to *The Raven*. Thomas the friendly tavern keeper was waiting for us. Indeed, it gave me quite a start when he and his wife stepped away from the stable's dark wall and materialized in front of me in the moonlight as by some conjurer's trick. His greeting "hoy" was whispered so soft that I barely heard it. We made no response because it was immediately followed by a similarly soft "Shh; not a word."

The door to the stable was already open and the tavern keeper and his wife led us straight into it. It smelled like a stable and was quiet except for the familiar sound of horses periodically moving about in their stalls and the familiar clip clop sound of Martin's two horses as he led into the stable.

The stable became pitch black when the creaking stable door was shut behind us. As it was being shut one of the horses already in the stable whinnied a greeting to the new arrivals and there was some moving about and huffing from the others. Almost immediately, however, the alewife pulled an already lighted candle lantern out from under an overturned crate so we could see and be seen.

There was an immediate soft "oh" of dismay from the woman as she held up the lantern just as I said "this is Martin from Swindon and two good horses. He will stay with you and do whatever you tell him to do." ... "Is something wrong?"

"It is my fault," the tavern keeper said. "I should have warned you that he should not have brought his bow. Someone might see it or come upon his bow and quivers when he is away from the stable. We do not want anyone to find it and know he is an archer, do we?"

"Not a problem. We will take his bow and his quiver with us and return them to him later." After a pause I added, "Is your message to Commander Robertson of such importance that I need to detach someone from our patrol to carry it to him immediately; or can it wait until the next time I send a message to him from further to the east?"

"It can wait. There is no desperate need for it to be sent immediately. So it can wait until you have a messenger coming this way on the road. But the Commander will want to know that the wife and I are fully ready to do what must be done if trouble comes this way.

"The Commander will know what "fully ready" means so be sure to tell him. I will keep your lad with me until I have something so serious to report that it cannot wait. Even so, please tell each of the riders you have going west on the road in the weeks ahead to stop and *privately,* very privately, ask me or my missus if there is a message to be picked up for Cornwall." He emphasized the word privately.

I nodded my agreement and started to ask what his message meant, but then I stopped; I had no need to know. Besides, from the way he said it I knew that he would not tell me.

******

Sergeant Cooper and I walked back to our patrol's camp in the darkness. We talked quietly as we walked. Neither he nor I had any idea what the tavern keeper's message meant or why it was important but not pressing.

Our camp was easy to find because our men had been told to keep their cooking fire going so we could see it from the road and find them. It was not raining and did not look as if it would that night so the men had not erected the shelter tent. It was a warm summer night and the moon was out; we would sleep in the open with our heads and hands under the archer tunics we were carrying with us in an effort to avoid the bugs.

We could see the men sitting around the fire yarning as we came off the road and walked up to them They heard us coming and stood up with various of their weapons at the ready when they heard us coming, but relaxed as soon as they saw me walking up to them with Sergeant Cooper right behind me.

"All is well. Martin is safe and has a warm berth," I quickly said it in response to their gasps of surprise and obvious concern at seeing their sergeant carrying Martin's longbow and quivers—and understandably so; archers never parted with their bows so someone carrying another man's bow and quivers usually meant that he had fallen.

"But everyone is to forget that Martin will be here for awhile and is to pretend they do not know him if they see him again," I added as the men gathered in closer to better hear what was being said. The fire was flickering behind them as they did.

That was not enough for Sergeant Cooper.

"Listen carefully to what Captain Adams just ordered, lads. Your stripes depend on it and so does Martin's life. Martin is now pretending *not* to be an archer or in the Company. He is doing something that may put him in mortal danger and cause get great harm to the Company and all our mates if anyone outside the Company even thinks that he might be one of us.

"So you will hurt the Company and endanger Martin if you see him and let on that you know him or say anything about him to anyone. In other words, lads, you are to keep your mouths shut and your faces blank if you see Martin or anyone asks about him, not even to your wives and mates back at Okehampton when we return.

"Remember, not even your wives or your mates are to know. Let Martin make the first move if you see him. As God is my witness, any man who blows Martin's cover story and endangers his life and hurts the Company by recognizing him or even hinting that he is an archer or that he might be doing something special will lose a lot more than just his stripes."

Such a serious threat, as you might expect, greatly excited the men and would no doubt result in much talking amongst them and many speculations. It turned out to be a damn good thing that such a strong warning had been given because we did see him again. It also caused the men to be more than a little jealous because it meant that Martin was doing something exciting and they were not. For the first time they realized that they were not just on a somewhat meaningless ride to London.

The men's sense of excitement rose even more when Sergeant Cooper posted *two* sentries and told everyone to sleep with their shields next to them, their swords drawn, their sandals on, and the reins of their fully packed and hobbled horses within reach. It was not that he expected trouble that night, he later confided to me, but "the lads need to take this seriously."

What Sergeant Cooper did not say was that the tavern keeper's words and behaviour had given off the smell of danger and totally changed *his* view of the ride and its importance.

****** *Captain Adams*

The men were awakened by Sergeant Cooper before the first light of dawn and told to string their bows, take the hobbles off their horses, and be ready to leap into their saddles and gallop away if we were hit with a dawn attack. Should that happen and anyone got separated, he was to ride to the east towards Crediton if possible and wait on the north side of the road five miles *beyond* the village. Cheese, cold strips of previously burnt meat, and cold flatbreads were eaten as we waited in the darkness for dawn's early light. Everyone listened intently for sounds in the night as we did. The meat and flat breads had been cooked the previous night on a piece of metal carried on one of the supply horses.

"Remember lads, it is much more important that we get away safe so we can continue our ride and inquiries. That means there is to be no stopping to fight and we will rally on the road five miles past the far side of yon village if we get separated."

Sergeant Cooper repeated this to his men at least two more times whilst we waited in the dark for the sun to arrive. He reminded me of a mother goose whose goslings were expected to follow along behind her without knowing why or where she was leading them.

Everyone was tense and ready to leap on to his horse and gallop off to safety when dawn's early light arrived; but nothing happened. Even so, having everything already loaded on our horses and ready for an instant departure was good precaution and would become our daily practice until we reached London. And starting the next night, as we waited for the arrival of dawn's early light, I decided that in the future we would put out our nightly cooking fire and then move well away from it before we actually bedded down for the night. That too smacked of the presence of danger and would help keep the lads alert— and safe if the possibility of danger turned out to be real. *It was an idea we learned about in school. Apparently it had worked well for the Company several times in the past.*

Sergeant Cooper treated my decision as a formal order when I lowered my voice and told him what I had decided.

"Aye Captain. I will see to it'" he whispered back. "It is a good idea. Moving the lads and horses to someplace new after we put out each night's cooking fire could be useful in confusing anyone who might want to attack us. I should have thought of it." *I felt good about Sergeant Cooper's response; it was obvious from the tone of his voice that he agreed with my efforts to keep us as safe as possible.*

We mounted our horses and rode out of our campsite as soon as we could begin to see the river and the shape of the trees along it. True dawn broke a few minutes later when the sun actually began to arrive on its daily trip around the world. By then we had already made our way back to London road and our horses were leisurely ambling through Crediton and past *The Raven* and its stable.

Sergeant Cooper and I were riding at the front of our little column as we rode past the stable. There was no sign of Martin. As we rode past the tavern I realized it was much larger than most roadside taverns and there was something unique and different about it; but I could not put my finger on what it was and soon forgot all about it.

We were not the only ones who were up and about and on the road. Despite the early hour there were a number of men and women and wagons coming out of the village to get to their fields. The people stared at us as we rode past them but, unlike Cornwall and western Devon, they did not smile and wave to greet us even though we nodded to them and smiled most friendly. There were also merchants' wagons and walking travelers on the road. From the looks of most of them they had been sleeping rough as we had been, even those who were well-dressed—for it was one thing to risk the lice of sharing a tavern bed with strangers if it was cold and raining; and quite a foolish thing to do if it was not.

It only took a few hours for us to reach Stockleigh and we easily found the *Three Bells* because its front door was literally only a few feet from the road. A worn and muddy dirt track was next to the tavern building and ran slightly downhill into the little village of about twenty hovels that stretched out behind it. There was a barn-like building and a fenced enclosure behind the tavern that was almost certainly the tavern's stable. The wooden enclosure next to the stable had a couple of horses in it.

Three bells were painted in red on the wall above the tavern's door and a couple of men were coming out of the tavern as we rode up. One of them hurried back inside as soon as he saw us; the other, a rather portly fellow, just stood there without moving for a few moments and watched us ride up.

"Hoy," I shouted as I began to dismount. I did so most friendly with my hand held up and open to indicate that we were peaceful. "Be you the *Three Bells* keeper?"

The man shook his head and motioned toward the door as he turned and walked rapidly around to the far side of the building. He said not a word and was out of sight and long gone by the time I pulled up my horse and dismounted.

Somewhat to my surprise since I had just seen someone go through it, the door was barred when I tried to enter. The man who had gone into the tavern as we rode up, whoever he was, must have thought we were robbers or tax collectors and barred it.

"Hello, Hello," I shouted as I pounded on the door. Nothing. I somehow had the feeling that there was no one inside even though I just seen someone use it. Perhaps he had walked through tavern and gone out the rear.

"Sergeant Cooper, please take a couple of men and ride around to the rear and see if there anyone is back there. Be friendly, eh?"

I pounded on the door and shouted several more times whilst I waited for Sergeant Cooper to return. Suddenly there was the sound of bar being lifted and the door opened. To my great surprise, Sergeant Cooper was standing in front of me.

"The back door was wide open so I walked in," he said as he held the door open so I could enter. "The place is empty; the public room, at least, Captain. I did not go up the stairs to look in the sleeping rooms or the tavern keeper's quarters. He may have gone up there. But it feels empty."

I was not worried and let the sergeant know it.

"It is early, eh? Perhaps the tavern keeper is still upstairs or has gone to the stables to care for the horses or to the village to visit or buy supplies. We will wait. Sooner or later someone will show up. Tell the lads to dismount out back but to stay alert and to give a shout if anyone shows up."

And with that I pulled up a stool and sat down to wait in the empty room with the door open. It had a low wooden ceiling, smelled of smoke and spilled ale like a tavern usually smells, and was dimly lit from the open door and the light leaking into from around edges of the wooden shutters that covered the wall openings and were closed. It was very quiet. I sensed that no one was upstairs. Its emptiness was very strange; at the very least there should have been an alewife or at least a servant on the premises.

After a while Sergeant Cooper came in and joined me—and we once again commenced speculating as to why no one was in the *Three Bells* and how it was that the Crediton tavern keeper knew Commander Robertson and the meaning of his message.

******

An hour or so later one of the archers came running in to report a company of about a dozen riders were coming in fast from the east and that they did not look like the usual travelers on the road—it looked from a distance, he said, as if they were an armed party. Sergeant Cooper and I both jumped to our feet.

"Hurry, tell the men to mount up with their bows strung but to hold them down on the far side of their horses so they cannot be seen. And then move them off into the pasture behind the stable. As soon the riders get here you are to take your men out into the field on the far side of the road where the sheep are grazing and circle around to come in behind them. Hobble my riding horse outside the back door and be ready to ride in fast and shoot them down in case a rescue is needed. Take my remount horse with you. I will wait here with my sword and shield and greet whoever is coming. Run."

Sergeant Cooper hurried out the back door and I got ready to greet the new arrivals. I did so by unsheathing my sword. I also opened the wooden shutters on the wall openings that were not already open so I could see better and also so I could dive out one of the windows and escape in the event things went terribly wrong. When I finished preparing I sat myself down on a stool and leaned back against the far wall with my bared sword resting across my knees with my hand on the handle and the shield at my feet and ready to be instantly snatched up— and waited.

Through the wall openings I could see and hear the horsemen as they trotted up to the front of the tavern. There were about a dozen of them on a variety of motley horses of which about half looked like they were normally used to pull wagons and ploughs.

Leading the new arrivals were three bearded men carrying sheathed long swords in their hands who may have been knights or soldiers of some sort. At least one of the three appeared to be wearing a chain shirt as I was. The rest looked to be a manor's levy that had been hastily summoned by their lord—farm workers and castle servants armed with spears, clubs, and rusty swords. None of the men were carrying shields or wearing helmets, not even the men who appeared to be knights. Had even one of them been carrying a shield I would have stood up and moved to the back door so I could step into the doorway and defend myself against them one at a time.

Chapter Nine

The foot path to Hatherleigh.

Two archers accompanied me as I followed a hostler from the horse farm down the "secret" footpath that by-passed Okehampton and led to the little village of Hatherleigh and its one and only public house, a relatively large one because it was on the main road from London to Exeter and Plymouth. The rest of the horse archers and all of the immediately usable horses had already been taken back to Okehampton along with some of the farm's archers and hostlers. Only the mares and fillies, six stallions that had not been ridden for years, and the colts too young to be ridden or trained had been left behind.

I had stayed behind to check out the footpath to Hatherleigh whilst I continued to wrestle with the question of whether or not to move what was left of the horses to someplace more secure, meaning deep into Cornwall where they would be hard to find. If the horses were to be moved it probably should be done before the roads and paths became clogged with people and their beasts and wagons moving west to escape the fighting and foragers. Perhaps their move could be announced as a practice and the horses returned if the invasion by the barons did not materialize?

As I walked down the narrow footpath as it weaved through the thick forest it became clear to me that the well-worn foot path had existed for many years. It was also increasingly clear to me that the Company's horse captains and everyone else at the horse farm had known about the path for years and periodically used it to quietly come and go from the horse farm without anyone at Okehampton knowing that they were doing so.

Lieutenant Smith had admitted as much and had been openly surprised to learn that *I* was surprised at hearing of the path's existence. Obviously the Company's secret location of its horse herd was not much of a secret after all. Certainly it would be well-known at the other end of the path in Hatherleigh's single tavern and, thus, throughout the entire little farming village that clustered around it on both sides of the road. Walking up the path was probably how most of the horse boys arrived at the farm after hearing about it in the village as a place where they might find food and shelter.

Normally I would have had no choice but to move what was left of the horses and hide them somewhere deeper in Cornwall. But if I did that, then even more people would see the herd as it moved and be able to pilot any invaders to it. So what should I do? It was a good question, especially now that the herd had been significantly reduced by the removal of every horse that might be useful in the weeks ahead—except, of course, as food for a hungry army.

I stopped on the path and turned around to begin walking back to the horse farm as soon as I could see Hatherleigh village and the road that ran through it. There was no need to walk all the way into the village to know that the villagers, and especially those who frequented its tavern, almost certainly all of them, would know all about the path and what was at the other end of it.

It was an hour or so after my companions and I had begun walking back toward the horse farm that a possible solution came out of nowhere and popped into my head behind my eyes. It arrived just after a brief rain when I slipped on a protruding tree root and fell on my arse for the third or fourth time. It happened as I was climbing up the wet and narrow path through a large and very heavy and virtually impassable forest of trees and heavy brush that covered the entire side of the little hill through which the path wandered.

It occurred, my fall that is, when I was sweating profusely and slipping and sliding on the damp grass and weeds that were growing on a somewhat steep portion of the path, and trying to wave my hand in front of my face to brush away the swarms of bugs that were attacking me. I was doing so, trying to wave away the bugs, because there was nowhere to go to escape them. Indeed, the trees and brush were so thick on either side of the path that we would have had trouble getting far enough off the path if we wanted to do so. Besides, the bugs were undoubtedly everywhere. All we could do was hurry forward to get away from them.

Hmm. If we are trapped on this path in the middle of a thick stand of trees and cannot get off it to get away from the bugs or even to relieve ourselves, then no one else could get off it either—no matter how desperately they were for food or how determined they were to reach the horse herd the villagers told them was at the end of the path.

What that meant, of course, was that we might successfully ambush anyone coming up the path. Two or three archers under a steady sergeant would play merry hell with any a party of foragers trying to come up such a narrow path with no way to get off it. Alternately we could do something else such as cut down the trees on either side of it so they dropped across the path and made it totally impassable. Or we could do both.

Hmm. Maybe we should consider what was left of the horse herd as bait for an opportunity to bring the barons and some of their men into a killing zone instead of a problem that needed to be solved?

******

I finally got back to the horse farm in the middle of the afternoon and immediately set off on my waiting horse to ride down the cart path to Okehampton. My wrists and arms had red bug bites all over them, my face felt swollen, and my clothes were wet and muddy from having slipped and fallen several times on the foot path—and I had the makings of a plan behind my eyes.

Chapter Ten

Captain Adams and the Baron.

Three grim-faced men with determined looks on their faces came striding into the tavern together—and were instantly quite surprised and taken aback by finding me sitting on a stool with an unsheathed short sword resting across my knees, a big smile on my face, and a rounded galley shield leaning up against my leg with my left hand on its handle. It was clearly not the welcome they expected.

Through the wall openings in the tavern's walls I could see Sergeant Cooper's men slowly spreading out in the distance in the hay field on the other side of the road. They were still far beyond the still-mounted new arrivals but slowly walking their horses toward them. It was a good move; he was bringing his men around behind them just as I had ordered him to do.

The horse archers each had a hand on the hilt of his sheathed sword in a somewhat threatening manner as he rode, but I could see from the way that they were sitting on their horses that they had their bows close at hand. They all had their quivers slung over their shoulders and were almost certainly holding their bows up against the far side of their horse's with their other hand so they could not be seen. *Placing their hands to draw attention to their swords whilst concealing the bows they would stand off and almost certainly use if there was fighting was a good deception. I should have thought of it; Sergeant Cooper is a good sergeant and I need to remember that.*

"Welcome to the *Three Bells*," I said to the new arrivals with a smile that I hoped looked sincere. "We have been waiting for you, Lord William. Did you and your men have a pleasant ride?" *Of course it was Lord William; they were clearly not travelers and who else could be hurriedly riding in from that direction with a gaggle of poorly armed supporters mounted on plough horses.*

My friendly greeting and relaxed appearance truly perplexed the three men. They had not expected it and it stopped them in their tracks. Their mouths did not gape open or anything like that, but I could see the surprise in their eyes. They had come in expecting to intimidate whomever they came upon with how ferocious and dangerous they were—and perhaps even to draw their sheathed swords and set upon us if my men and I appeared to be sufficiently cowed or vulnerable.

"Who are you?" the relatively well-dressed middle-aged man wearing the chain shirt finally demanded to know after he had looked around to assure himself that I was the only one in the room.

The question came from Lord William himself. I had instantly known it was him both from the tavern keeper's description and from his appearance and the quality of his clothes. I also knew it from the arrogance in his voice and the fact that he had been the *second* man through the door and had brought some of his village levy with him. He looked and acted, in other words, exactly as the tavern keeper had described him.

It was also apparent to me that the most immediately dangerous man of the three was the younger man who had been sent through the door first in case it was an ambush. I had seen a hundred young men like him— young and mostly un-blooded and overly anxious to prove himself in some way. It was he, not Lord William, who was likely to start any trouble that might occur. I marked him as the man I should take out first and quickly if there was fighting.

"I am a mercenary soldier riding to London with some of the men of my free company, Lord William. We are newly returned from service in the lowlands in and around Anvers and are looking for a new contract for the coming year or years. Some of us and our women are waiting in Exeter where we landed and the rest of the men are with me. It was suggested to us when we stopped in Crediton that you might need the services of a free company of experienced English fighting men, or perhaps that you might know a lord who does. Is it possible?"

What I did *not* tell him was that I was a captain in the Company of Archers or that I had fought my way up to my rank by going against much better fighting men than him and his. So far as I was concerned I was the wolf and he and his two men were three village dogs. The problem, of course, was that his lordship and his men did not know about me and even dogs have teeth.

******

Lord William stopped in the middle of the room and looked at me suspiciously. "How did you know it was me?" he finally demanded.

"Probably because I am a good judge of men," I said cheerfully.

"Impossible. We have never met," he said with a snort and a shake of his head.

"Oh. Not you, Your Lordship. Not you. I meant the people we met in *The Raven* when we stopped in Crediton. We spent last night in Crediton and the people we met in *The Raven* described you. I could tell from the way they were talking that they were telling the truth about you. They respect you; indeed they do.

"They said you were a good landlord, well-dressed, and lived with your family in a manor just east of Stockleigh. So who else could bring in the farmers of his manor's levy so quickly? It had to be you."

"Perhaps. Perhaps. But what if we had attacked you for a band of robbers instead of walking in here most peaceful?"

"Why then we would have had to cut you and your men down, of course. Or at least enough of you so that the rest of your men would either surrender or run."

The young man gave a rather arrogant snort of disbelief. So I looked at him sympathetically and tried to gently explain the facts of life with a touch of sadness in my voice.

"Of course that is what would have happened, young sir. My men and I are all experienced fighting men and his lordship and his men spend much of their time watching over his lands and farming them. Well-armed and experienced fighting men versus inexperienced farmers who are poorly armed? It would have been a slaughter and quite unnecessary."

"And that is exactly why you or one of your fellow nobles should hire us," I said to Lord William with a smile that blossomed on my face, a nod of my head to agree with myself, and a great deal of satisfaction in my voice.

It was about then that Sergeant Cooper startled everyone including me when he opened the door in the rear of the public room and walked in carrying his shield and with his sword half drawn. He promptly pushed it into the sheath hanging from his belt when he saw that Lord

William men had theirs sheathed and mine was idly lying across my lap.

"God bless all here," he said cheerfully with a smile and a shrug as he took in the scene in front of him and pushed his blade into its scabbard. "I apologize for barging in on you, Captain. I thought you might be in need of some help. I did not realize there were only three of them."

* * * * * *

Lord William was an interesting man once he got over his surprise and we began talking, especially after the tavern keeper of the *Three Bells* returned from wherever he had been hiding and began bringing us bowls of ale from the barrel in the corner and some bread and cheese. His lordship was mostly interested in hearing about where we had been and what we had done so I made up a fine story about being in Robert Wolf's mercenary company and fighting in the lowlands for some landowners near Anvers who were being threatened because of a dispute over their ownership of some their lands. Sergeant Cooper listened intently so, as he told me later, he could use the story himself if the need arose.

His lordship, in turn, told me that he and the two knights with him had been in France a few years earlier with King Henry during the king's most recent attempt to regain his French lands. The younger one was the son of a friend and had been with him as his squire. The lad had been presented to King Henry and knighted just before the king abandoned his army and returned to England. *The young man puffed up when Lord William mentioned that he had been knighted by the king; it was as if he thought that being knighted by the king somehow protected him.* His lordship also had two other knights who were not present.

What Lord William did not say was instantly obvious—that he was a very minor lord who had gone to France with the king's army because he could not afford to pay the scutage for himself and his four knights. In other words, he was not likely to be able to hire mercenaries even if he wanted to do so.

"Sir William, do you have any suggestions as to where my men and I might find employment? We heard rumours that some of the barons might be forming an army that would be foraging in Devon and Cornwall. Hopefully, one of them will want to have more good fighting men under his command and give us a contract."

"Oh, I would think that someone is very likely to give you a contract—not for foraging, of course, because they will not need help for that, but because sooner or later they will need every available man when the French invade after King Henry dies or there is fighting over who should next sit on England's throne. The French will probably land in Exeter or Plymouth in order to avoid Dover and the Portsmen of the Cinque Ports, at least that was what everyone was saying at the Windsor tournament I attended a few weeks ago."

"But why do my men and I keep hearing about Cornwall?"

"Because that is where the Great Council's Loyal Army intends to forage whilst it waits for the French to land in the west. We will make our stand on the only road into the area and trap the French between our army and the sea. It will also put us in a blocking position to prevent any English barons who rally to the French from joining up with the French army. It is said there will be good foraging in Cornwall and along the road on the Devon side of the Tamar because there are no knights or nobles to stop us from taking what we need."

"So you *will* be going to Devon's border with Cornwall and into Cornwall itself, eh? When will that be? And are you not afraid that *your* manor will be foraged when the barons marching for the southwest come this way with their men? Surely you could use some additional men to go with you or to help defend your lands whilst you and yours are gone off to Devon and Cornwall to wait for the French?"

"No because my men and I will stick around here to defend our lands and women until the Loyal Army finishes passing through. But I am sure someone will want to employ you, if only because it is said the lands of those who support the French will be allocated to the loyal

Englishmen according to the size of their contribution to the army."

"When will this happen. The loyal barons' moving their men into western Devon and Cornwall, I mean?"

"Oh, soon I should think. Indeed, it is likely that some of the barons whose armies have the greatest distances to travel are already marching. The rest will probably begin moving their men in the next few weeks now that this year's crops have all been planted and the early hay has been cut. The rumour at the Windsor tournament was that the French army was already beginning to form up because King Henry might pass away at any moment. It costs money to feed an army once it has been formed so it said by many that Louis is likely to sail as soon as his army is ready."

Sergeant Cooper and I just looked at each other. I could tell that he was greatly surprised at what he had heard. Me not so much; I had been forewarned.

But one thing was now certain—the barons were indeed coming west with an army and intended to forage in eastern Devon and in Cornwall. It was something Commander Robertson needed to know as soon as possible. It was time to get my scribing materials out of my saddle pouch and send off a warning message.

******

Lord William was a bit tipsy and still more than a little uncertain about me and my men, but outwardly friendly, when Sergeant Cooper and I made our farewells and walked to the tavern door to depart. He and his two knights followed us out and then stood in front of the tavern's door and watched as one of our horse holders rode in with our saddled horses. His men were gathered off to the side of the road nervously watching the half dozen horse archers who had spread out in a wide half circle around them on the other side of the road and were several hundred paces away. One of the archers began leading my horse and Sergeant Coopers' forward as soon as he saw us; all of our men's remounts were being held by a single rider further down the road.

Seeing the archers on their horses with their swords showing and so purposely positioned reminded me of a pack of wolves closing in on a flock of sheep. It must have had a somewhat similar impact on Lord William's men if the looks of relief that appeared on their faces when we emerged with his lordship acting friendly toward us meant anything.

"Thank you for your good advice about who might be needing good fighting men, your lordship; my men and I appreciate it," I said as I swung aboard my saddle. "And I will certainly give your warm greetings to your cousin, Lord Randolph, at Tiverton Castle if I have an opportunity to talk to him."

******

"I need to stop as soon as we get clear of the village and scribe an important message to warn Commander Robertson about the barons' army and Cornwall," I said to Sergeant Cooper who was riding next to me.

"He is at Restormel and it is an important message, very important as I am sure you understand. So I am going to send two men to carry it in case one of them goes down. Which two of your men could be best depended on to ride hard and carry it as fast as possible at least as far as Okehampton? They can get remounts there, or even better, be replaced by fresh riders to carry it onward."

We rode off the road and into a stand of trees as soon as the *Three Bells* was out of sight. I dismounted quickly, called for the supply horse carrying my scribing materials, pulled out a quill and a piece of parchment, and hurriedly scribed a message including the Crediton tavern keeper's comments about the thin man "being ready." What took the longest was grinding the charcoal and mixing the ink with water from my water flask.

As soon as I finished my scribing I rolled up the parchment and placed it in one of the three leather courier pouches we were carrying on our supply horse. Then I spoke to the two archers Sergeant Cooper had selected to carry it.

"I am sending you both because this message must get through as soon as possible to Restormel. You are to carry it as far as Okehampton. It is unsealed so that Lieutenant Commander Courtney can read it. Hopefully, a relay of fresh riders can carry it onward from there. But if fresh riders are not immediately available to carry it onward you are to commandeer the best four horses in the Okehampton stable and carry it to Restormel yourselves. If one of you goes down or is slowed for some reason, the other must abandon him continue on without delay.

Sergeant Cooper stood next to me with a serious look on his face and nodded emphatically to indicate his total support for my order. The two men were wide-eyed with excitement. It was obvious that something significant was happening and they were part of it.

Chapter Eleven

Messages and messengers.

I did a lot of thinking on my ride back to Okehampton from the horse farm; and I had made a decision by the time my horse clattered over the outer moat's drawbridge and entered the outermost of the castle's three baileys—I was going to leave what was left of the Company's horse herd at the farm unless the Commander ordered me to do otherwise.

What I saw as I entered Okehampton and dismounted in the bailey to take a much needed piss was a much higher level of activity than usual. It was to be expected; suddenly having one hundred and forty-two additional horses and a couple of dozen additional men inside a castle's walls will do that for you every time no matter how big the castle's baileys and stables.

Anne, my wife, was waiting with a bowl of ale and a newly arrived messenger's parchment pouch. She had been alerted to my coming by someone who had seen me coming up the path behind the castle. Two dusty and tired-looking men were waiting with her. I recognized them immediately as a couple of the horse archers who had gone with Richard to escort him to London.

"A parchment for the Commander has just come in from Richard Adams," Anne said as she handed the pouch to me. "It must be important because Richard sent two men of his best men to carry it and they rode hard all the way. *She did not know they were the sergeant's best men, of course, but she said it and the men visibly puffed up when she did. Anne is good that way.*

"Captain Merton is at the horse farm and Lieutenant Johnson is still in his bed with the sweating pox so I was about to send the pouch on to Restormel with new riders when you were seen approaching. The Sergeant Major has two riders saddling up as we speak. The message was not sealed and the couriers said that Richard said you should read it, but that its onward carriage to Restormel should not be delayed for even a minute if you were not here to do so."

I removed the parchment from its courier pouch and read it quickly. "Damn," I said under my breath. And then I re-read it to make sure I had not missed something.

"Is it bad?" Anne asked. I thought quickly. She did not know because she did not know how to read and had no one to read it to her.

"Yes," I finally answered after I had given the matter some thought behind my eyes. "It almost certainly means the Commander will be here for his annual inspection much sooner than we expected." *It meant more than that, of course, but I would tell her later. And I wanted to*

think a bit more before I decided what I should say to the
men. Whatever they overheard or I told them later would
soon be known in the local taverns and beyond. Did we
really want the news to get out so barons would know they
were expected and we would be waiting for them?

"Sergeant Major," I bellowed. My shout was unnecessary. He was already coming through the gate in the middle wall and double-timing toward us. Two riders, each leading his horse and his remount were right behind him. One of them was Sergeant Sunday. It was a good choice for such a message; he was one of our best riders and likely to be the horse archers' next Sergeant Major.

"I need to add a message to the one that just arrived, Sergeant Major. Both messages are important and must get through to Commander Robertson as fast as possible. So I want you to quickly mount two additional riders to act as couriers. Both of them must be very dependable because the messages must get to Restormel as soon as possible. So make sure they are both riding the best available horses and leading the best available remounts.

"I will scribe my message whilst you are getting them ready. You have five minutes."

***** *Five minutes later.*

"Alright Lads, listen up, I said loudly to the two riders so the gathering crowd of on-lookers could hear me. "This pouch *must* get through to the Commander at Restormel as fast as possible. It is a test we have been ordered to make so the Commander will know how long it will take for him to get an important message to or from Okehampton if there ever is a serious need for speed. That is why I am sending both of you.

"I want you to ride as fast as possible to the tavern by the ford and change some or all of your horses there, but only if you think that replacing the horses you already have will help you get to Restormel faster. You are also to immediately leave behind any horse or man who cannot keep up. Do not slow down or waste a minute trying to lead a horse that has broken down or slow down for a rider who needs a rest or has taken a tumble. Just turn any horse loose that breaks down and keep going. We will recover it later.

Now Go!" I shouted as I handed the leather courier's pouch to Sergeant Sunday and slapped his horse on his arse to get him started.

Both of the men promptly kicked their horses in the ribs and galloped through the bailey and out on to the cart path. Sergeant Sunday was in the lead and slinging the strap of the cylindrical leather courier's pouch over his shoulder as they clattered across the drawbridge. Restormel was many hours away and Sunday was no fool; I knew that he would soon settle down to the rapid amble that their horses could maintain for hours.

"Is it truly just the usual annual inspection to see if we are ready for trouble or is it serious?" Anne asked somewhat anxiously as we stood in the bailey and watched them leave.

"There is nothing to fret about, my dear. It is just the Commander's annual inspection occurring a few weeks earlier than usual and nothing more. I will tell you all about it later."

I told my lie because the people standing nearest to us could hear me. Then I loudly shouted over to the Sergeant Major so everyone in the bailey could hear.

"Sergeant Major, we have brought in the horses in and sent off the messengers. Now we need to get ready for the rest of the Commander's inspection test by making sure our larders are such that we can withstand a long siege. He is coming in the next day or two and we do not want to be found to be short of supplies due to the additional horses and men, eh?" *Not that the horses and men will be eating here if the barons actually try to march on Cornwall.*

It was hard to know whether the men who heard what I said would believe what we were doing was for some kind of Commander's inspection. Hopefully they would and my lie would gull them into believing what we were doing with the horses was inconsequential. What was certain was that they would talk about it amongst themselves such that the local merchants and travelers would soon hear about it.

What was also certain was that news of our preparations would sooner or later reach the barons *if* they were interested enough in Cornwall or concerned enough to make inquiries. On the other hand, if the barons really were coming it might encourage them to mistakenly think we intended to hide behind our walls whilst their foragers ravaged the land. Fighting an unprepared enemy is always best.

Hopefully everyone would think of our hurried preparations as merely a response to a routine annual inspection and not reveal to the barons that we would *not* just hide behind our walls if they tried to enter Cornwall. I resolved to ask Anne what she thought of my efforts to mislead the barons when we had a chance to speak privately.

And I was certainly glad that it was the Earl, my Uncle Charles, and not me who was responsible for making sure that our villagers would have food and shelter when they moved west to get away from the fighting and foragers. The workers at the various stannaries, on the other hand, were employed by the king and were his problem—unless they had food reserves the barons' foragers might take; then they would be our problem and a big one. It probably meant we needed to "borrow" the food supplies of the stannaries before the barons' men could get to them. And, of course, we needed to do the same thing with the monasteries' food reserves even though their abbots would howl, Bodmin's in particular.

The stannary captains and the abbots could look to the barons and to the king and God for their food so far as I was concerned; and more power to them. But, now that I think of it, it was probably a good thing that I also asked the Commander for his permission to start gathering in the stannary and monastery food reserves in Devon when I dispatched Sergeant Sunday with news about the barons.

But do I have time to wait for an answer? Damn; probably not if the barons are already on their way. And then there are the grain merchants in Exeter and Plymouth. They almost certainly have grain we could buy for our horses and bread, and they would no doubt be willing to deliver here for enough coins. *If we do not buy it the barons will.*

"Sergeant Major, I need six horse-drawn wagons ready to roll out of here within the hour, each with a teamster, a reliable sergeant, and three archers. *No* remounts. They will need food for three days. I also need a party of ten archers with *no* remounts carrying saddle bags, two sergeants and bread makings and cheese for four days. They should each bring the bridles and lines so they can each lead three riding horses back."

Anne will be pissed if I am away for another couple of nights. But I need to gallop to Exeter and Plymouth myself to negotiate with the merchants for grain and riding horses and pay them. Hmm; what they cannot send to us immediately they can send by sea to Fowey Village. My mind was whirling as I went up the stairs two at a time to get the rather large amount of coins I hoped I would need. Hopefully there would be a lot of grain and horses available such that I will need a lot of coins. And I best send a message to the Commander telling him what I am doing. So many things.

Chapter Twelve

On the road.

Captain Adams and his six remaining men spent the rest of the day riding north on the old Roman road. They stopped well before dark to camp for the night on the west side of the road near a swiftly flowing little stream. After they burnt their meal of flat bread and meat strips and the sun finished passing overhead they quietly moved across to a new site on the eastern side of road. Two sentries were posted all night long and kept their horse saddled and their weapons close at hand. They left the fire burning on the other side of the road and carefully watched it for signs of activity until it flickered out.

This time both Captain Adams and Sergeant Cooper took their turns on sentry duty. They also set a rally point farther down the road toward London and required the men to keep their hobbled horses saddled and close at hand in the event a fast departure was necessary. As you might expect, nothing happened but both the captain and sergeant thought taking the precautions was a good thing because it kept the men on their toes and conveyed the seriousness of what they were doing.

The next morning Captain Adams shook the dust out of his tunic and rode out to visit Lord Randolph at his nearby Tiverton Castle stronghold and give him greetings from his cousin, Lord William. He, Captain Adams that is, had ridden a few miles out of his way to call upon Lord Randolph because of what he had been told at the *Three Bells*. He was accompanied by one of the archers, a grizzled two-striper from Wales by the name of David Owen. The captain had selected David to accompany him because the scar on his face from falling off his horse and onto a jagged rock years earlier made him look like a particularly ferocious mercenary instead of the mild-mannered fellow that he actually was.

The two archers easily found Tiverton Castle and were promptly admitted to see Lord Randolph, probably because his lordship was both bored out of his mind by watching his sheep graze and curious as to why a mercenary captain and one of his lieutenants would request an audience.

According to what Lord William had told Captain Adams at the *Three Bells*, his cousin Lord Randolph was one of the twenty-four members of the "Great Council" of English barons that met periodically to advise the king on matters of taxes and wars. Cousin Randolph, Lord William had said, was especially eager to participate in the baron's "Loyal Army" because he wanted the next king to do what King Henry had refused—give him permission to build his present pre-Norman stronghold into a much stronger castle by crenellating it. *Captain Adams immediately read between lines and decided that the king had probably*

refused the request because of Lord Randolph's rebellious
nature and lack of support.

"And who do you think is likely to be England's next king, your lordship?" Captain Adams had inquired of Lord Randolph as they sat with bowls of ale in their hands at the table in his lordship's low-ceilinged hall. Three of his lordship's knights sat with them and listened intently. They were obviously trusted retainers and present both to guard his lordship and to advise him.

"England must have a king. So it will likely be Edward if he returns in time from crusading in the east. But if Edward is not here when his father dies, it will probably be either the French crown prince or one of the de Montfort's. The Great Council will decide."

Then, after a pleasant belch from drinking his ale too quickly, Lord Randolph shouted for a refill and continued.

"Who becomes the next king does not matter to me so long as it is *not* one of the French princes. My cousin and I will both join in the effort to fight off the French because we will almost certainly be replaced and our people will lose the lands they have from us if the French are successful. And for the same reason we *will* go along with whatever the Great Council decides if the king dies and Prince Edward is not available to replace him.

"Whether getting a new king on the throne will involve fighting I do not know and neither does anyone else. Perhaps the French will not invade England once again and

Edward will return before the King Henry dies. It is in the hands of God."

His answer let me ask an important question.

"But what if Devon and Cornwall rise up to oppose your foraging whilst you and your fellow barons are waiting for the French or are waiting to put your own man on the throne if Edward has not returned?"

"We will be so far to the southwest that there will be no one to oppose us. It is well known that there are no lords with knight's fees on any of those lands. Poor franklins and monasteries hold all the usable land. But we will not want for food whilst we wait for even they must lay in food supplies for the winter, eh?

"In any event, I think whoever the Council chooses to be king will win and that if my men and I stand with them we will at least hold our own lands; and perhaps even add to them, particularly if I contribute a company of mercenaries in addition to my knights and levies. Accordingly, I am willing to contract to feed you and your men for a year and pay your company six silver coins for every fighting man who stays with me for the whole year. What say you?"

Captain Adams affected to think about the offer, and then opened negotiations by declining with a friendly smile. Both men understood that was what he would be expected to do. There was, after all, an established and well-known procedure for the hiring of mercenaries. Accordingly, he responded as his lordship expected.

"I know the value of my men well enough to know that we will have to be paid much more than that if we are to join your lordship's army and fight for you. And we are worth much more than a mere six silvers per year because we are all experienced fighting men and because we know that there *will be* fighting because of Cornwall even if you and the other members of the Great Council are not yet sure.

"It is not the French and possibility of fighting between the nobles as to who should become king that will concern my men; it is the archers of Cornwall. My men and I know the archers and their abilities. So we know *they* are the real danger, much more so than from the French and the English barons, and that there will be serious fighting if you and your men try to forage in Cornwall.

"We also know that there will be fighting even if the French do not come; because good English barons and their knights, such as yourselves, always want more land and are willing to fight for it such that God decides who ends up owning the land. Accordingly, there will be fighting such that six silver coins for each man is not nearly enough; and we would also have to be paid more for every man who is killed or loses an arm or a leg or an eye."

Less than an hour later a slightly tipsy Captain Adams and his false lieutenant rode away from Tiverton Castle after agreeing, subject to his men's approval as is always the case with free companies, to provide eighteen experienced mercenary soldiers for one year or until they were killed or wounded for two hundred and seventy silver coins plus twenty more for every mercenary who was killed and an additional ten silver coins for every eye or arm or leg or horse that was lost. The first eighty of the coins would be paid immediately upon the mercenaries arrival at Tiverton. It was a good contract.

"The terms are acceptable to me," the captain had said as he stood, made the sign of the cross in case any of the men present were truly religious, and shook Lord Randolph's hand in agreement. "If my men also agree to them, I will return with my men in ten days time to collect the first eighty silvers and we will each make our marks on a contract."

Lord Randolph did not have Captain Adams watched or followed when he rode off a few minutes later. Had he done so he would have been surprised to learn that the Captain continued riding east toward Oxford and Windsor with Sergeant Cooper and the five remaining horse archers instead of riding back to Plymouth to "consult with his men."

Captain Adams smiled when he thought how Lord Randolph would react to the scribed message he would receive instead of the mercenaries. It would politely say that his men had declined his lordship's offer as being much too low since Lord Randolph and his men were almost certainly going to die of starvation or being shot full of arrows in Cornwall and left to rot in ditches along its roads. It would also strongly suggest that his lordship and his men stay at home until they could fight the French somewhere else if they actually invaded.

"There are many ways to win a battle," he told Sergeant Cooper when he and archer Owen rejoined their men and he told the sergeant about his meeting with Lord Randolph. "And one of them is to discourage some of the enemy's soldiers from taking the field—which is exactly what Commander Robertson has ordered us to do." *What he did not tell the sergeant was that both he and the Commander had been learnt to do that at the Company school.*

******

Several days later Captain Adams and his six remaining men splashed their way across the River Thames at Oxford without paying a toll to use the bridge. They stopped in Oxford to spend the night because Commander Robertson and Lieutenant Commander Courtenay had explained to the captain why it might be a good place to gather information about the barons' intentions. One of the reasons was that Oxford had begun attracting some of the second and third sons of England's barons, knights, and celibate priests.

Their sons supposedly moved to Oxford to learn Latin at one of the little city's priories so they could begin their studies to become priests and clerics—although it was well known that many only pretended to do so in order to escape a dreary rural life without having to risk his life by becoming a knight and periodically having to fight for one cause or another. Oxford's halls and taverns and possibility of making new friends, it seems, were a splendid alternatives to staying down on the farm that you would never inherit or having someone periodically hacking at you with a sword—*and the lads, in turn, being naïve and illiterate young rustics who had a few coins and generally thought highly of themselves for some reason because of their fathers' lands and titles, made Oxford an interesting place by attracting the tutors, tavern girls, bed renters, and soothsayers who preyed upon them and systematically relieved them of their fathers' coins.*

The archers spent two comfortable nights in Oxford because Captain Adams was able to obtain three beds at the village's new tavern, *The Bear.* It turned out to be a fortuitous choice, and not only because it kept them dry during the several days of rain that occurred whilst they were there.

Captain Adams had heard about the possibility of finding beds at a new tavern in Oxford called *The Bear* from a traveler they had encountered on the road. And when they reached Oxford and learned beds were available, he promptly opened his purse to hire one room for himself and one for Sergeant Cooper and three of the men. The alternative would have been to camp outside the village in the rain or to hire beds in one or another of the little city's priories and monastic halls and risk being robbed or assaulted while they slept.

The rest of his men, the two most junior, slept in the stable of the nearby priory of Saint Frideswide to guard the horses and keep them saddled and ready for an instant departure should the need arise. The priory's stable was one of several where the visitors and residents of the city could pay to stable their horses if they had them.

The Bear turned out to be an inspired choice. The alewife was pleased to see them and effusively welcomed Captain Adams and his mercenaries as some of her very first customers for the new tavern's sleeping rooms and their beds. They were similarly pleased because the building and its rooms smelled like fresh cut wood instead of the usual smell of people and spilled ale that inevitably settled into a tavern's walls and dirt floor. What made the *Bear* so ideal for the archers was that the new tavern's public room was constantly crowded and friendly because the secular canons and students of the nearby priories and halls such as Saint Frideswide's were constantly coming in to inspect the new tavern and sample its ale.

The place was packed all day and most of the night. In addition to the sons of the gentry and would-be gentry who were supposed to be learning Latin and considering careers as priests, there were the usual local franklins and reeves from the lands nearby as well as the travelers that constantly came through the village because it was located next to the Thames bridge closest to London. Indeed, that is apparently how Oxford had long ago gotten its name—as the place closest to London where oxen-pulled wagons could cross the Thames where it was low enough to be forded and for a bridge to be built.

To the surprise of Captain Adam's and his less-informed archers who had never been there before or even heard of the place, there were a number of young men in Oxford learning to scribe and babble in Latin in order to advance themselves as priests and clerks—and many more who were merely pretending to do so in order to get away from home and avoid having to work.

Most of the young men lived in the priories and halls that rented inexpensive beds and stabled horses to supplement their donations and benefices. Others slept in the taverns or in rooms rented from Oxford's residents. What they had in common was that they all needed a place to drink and eat and meet their friends; in other words, a public house like *The Bear* where their fathers' lives and intentions could be discussed and disdained as "not for me" whilst they spent their fathers' coins.

What Captain Adams and Sergeant Cooper soon learned in *The Bear* was that much of the coins received by Oxford's priories' and taverns came not from the merchant and pilgrim travelers who passing through the village, but from the younger sons of the upper classes who had no land in their futures and preferred to listen to tutors from the local priories and talk with their fellows in the local taverns rather than become priests or, much worse, knights who might have to follow their lords when they went off to die in the crusades—or in the coming war for the throne of England which several of them had heard being discussed during visits to their baronial and knightly homes.

The Bear turned out to be a particularly fortuitous place for the archers to stop for the night because it was so new. That was because everyone drinking in *The Bear's* public room seemed to be mightily pleased by the arrival of the new tavern and that, in turn, somehow seemed to increase their willingness to talk to everyone else in the tavern; probably because the Bear's newness gave both the locals and the travelers an excuse to open a conversation to talk about how much they liked it and its ale.

And the talking yielded good information for the two archers from one particular drunken young man, a baron's willowy third son who had scurried back to Oxford to avoid having to accompany his fathers and two older brothers to Cornwall. After listening to the lad describe his father's plans, and buying him and his mates more than a few bowls of ale to keep them talking and friendly, Captain Adams promptly decided to stay over for another day to try to learn more. Indeed, the captain seriously considered staying even longer.

After giving it much consideration whilst lying in bed that night, however, Captain Adams decided to continue on to Windsor the next day *without* weakening his force by immediately sending another message to Cornwall. Instead, he decided to weaken it by leaving Sergeant Cooper and one of his men in Oxford for a few more days to attempt to gather more information. They were to continue on to London in two weeks if they had nothing important to report; and to ride hard for Cornwall with the news if they did. *By then, as you might imagine, the sergeant and his men were fully aware of the danger facing the Company and understood the importance of the information they were gathering.*

It was a good decision because Oxford was a fine place to gather information about the barons' plans and intentions. That was because of the priories and halls that attracted young men from keeps and manors all across England and also because it was the first crossing of the Thames above London with a bridge. As a result, the village of Oxford was a major way station on the road that many of the barons and their armies would take if they were coming out of London or the lands surrounding it and marching towards Devon and Cornwall.

Oxford was, as Captain Adams had been learnt years earlier when he was being schooled at Restormel, a "choke point" because its bridge was so narrow in addition to being a religious centre and a logical place for pilgrims and merchant travelers to stop for to spend the night or to refresh themselves. The latter, of course, was more important to most people.

Indeed, according *The Bear*'s beaming owner, a gregarious local resident whom the archers chatted up, he had built his tavern there for the same reason that there were always so many tutors and street woman in Oxford— because of the young lads with coins in their pouches who came from all over England to pretend to learn to read and scribe enough Latin to become priests and clerks, and also because almost every merchant, knight, and priest traveling west on the London road tended to stop in Oxford and spend a few coins for a drink or to find a dry bed for the night.

The monks and priests in Oxford's priories were important to the little city, of course, according to the tavern keeper, especially if a person believed in the power of prayer and the importance of chanting them out loud at all hours of the day and night, but the young people and the travelers and those who preyed upon them and serviced them even more so. Indeed, it remains so to this very day.

Chapter Thirteen

Windsor and the priestly spies.

Only once before had Captain Adams met Windsor's pudgy parish priest, Father John Clayton. That was two years earlier in London. The brief meeting had occurred when the priest had been paid by one of the Company's spies to carry a parchment message from Windsor to the Company's London shipping post so it could be forwarded on to Cornwall. Even so, Captain Adams immediately recognized the priest when he answered the door in response to the captain's knock.

The priest had obviously been surprised by Captain Adam's unexpected appearance on his doorstep, but he recognized Captain Adams as soon as the captain identified himself. The priest had promptly ushered him into the "living" of Windsor Village's Saint Peter and Saint Andrew Church whilst looking anxiously over the captain's shoulder to see if they were being observed.

Captain Adams, in turn, was somewhat surprised by the quality and size of the vicarage in which the supposedly celibate priest lived and the shapely young "housekeeper" who lived there with him and brought them bowls of ale and a plate of cheese and bread after they sat down and began talking. In the background, as she was placing the wooden bowls and plates on the table, he could hear children playing.

"I am impressed at the quality and size of your vicarage and its services, Father John," he said in an effort to be friendly. "I must admit that I did not know that parish priests lived so well" Captain Adams said to the amply proportioned priest with an amiable sound in his voice as he took a sip of ale and picked up a piece of the cheese to nibble on. It was a bit sour but he ate it anyway.

"My father bought the parish for me and a cottage on the outskirts of the village for my mother," the priest replied rather bitterly. "It was the only thing he ever did for us even though he is a rich man and could have easily done much more. That is why I am forced to do whatever I can to earn additional coins to feed myself."

"Actually, I did not come knocking on your door just to spend the night with you and enjoy a free meal; I am here at the request of the Bishop of Cornwall to ask you to help me arrange a couple of private meetings for him; one with Father Peter Cooper, the Angelovian priest who is one of the chamberlain's scribes, the other with Father Thomas White who is also an Angelovian. He is one of the priests in the Nuncio's household.

"They are both in residence somewhere here in Windsor; one in the Chamberlain household and the other in the Nuncio's. It was suggested to me that you might know them because they are fellow priests," he lied. "I need to pass a private message on to them from their bishop but I have no idea how to find them. Can you help me?"

Father John said not a word. But his eyes lit up and he leaned forward as if he needed an explanation before he could agree—and he got one even though it was untrue.

"I was asked by the bishop to privately tell each of them that he would like to pray with them and discuss their futures the next time he comes to London. I think it possible that the bishop wants them to think about taking new positions at parishes in the Holy Land where the Angelovians are attempting to bring Christianity to the local heathens. He asked me to talk to them privately so their current masters do not get upset by the possibility that they may lose their services. Can you help me meet with them without letting anyone else knowing?"

The priest did not say a word other than "it is a long walk from here to the castle and it looks like there may be rain. Besides, it is a risk for me to get involved in anything outside of my own church and order." He just looked across the table at the captain with a question on his face and rubbed his thumb on his pointing finger as if he were counting coins.

"I will pay you for your trouble, of course, if you will go immediately," Captain Adams hastily added. "And I will also need a place to sleep for myself and the six men traveling with me whilst we wait for the priests to respond to the message. And I also need a stable and food for our horses and two candle lanterns, one for me and one for my men."

The priest smiled a rather arrogant smile and leaned forward. Something was afoot and he intended to make the most of it. With a little luck it might provide additional coins that could be added to those he had been slowly accumulating to buy a bishopric. His mother would like that and so would his not-so-secret wife who was posing as his housekeeper.

"Three of the king's silver coins for each priest I take the risk of summoning for you and two for you and your men and horses for each night you are here and have to be fed. You can have a room here in the vicarage and your men can sleep in the stable. My housekeeper will provide your suppers and food and drink to break your fasts in the morning."

It was an outrageously high amount but I nodded my head in agreement and wondered how he would react when he discovered we each had two horses. It seemed to me that it was a very large amount of coins for a very small service. Perhaps contacting the priests and sheltering us was a riskier thing for Father Clayton to do than I thought. Even so, I could not imagine why it was risky for him or how the Company's coin-summing clerk would respond when I accounted for the coins I had been given for my trip to London.

I started to ask why summoning them to meet with me was risky but decided against it.

****** *Captain Adams*

It was later that evening on a moonless night when Father Thomas walked in the dark from the Nuncio's rooms at Windsor Castle to the vicarage. The portly priest and I were waiting and we both went to the door when Father Thomas knocked on it about two hours after the sun had finished passing overhead. Father Thomas, however, refused to come in out of the dark into the candle-lit vicarage. He whispered his insistence on meeting with me inside the church next to the vicarage. And that is what we did.

We were careful at Father Thomas's insistence; we spoke softly whilst kneeling side by side at the altar of the empty parish church. The parish priest, Father John, tried to accompany us to the church, but he walked away with a snort of disgust when I caught Father Thomas's desire for secrecy and motioned with a shake of my head that he should remain behind even though he was the church's vicar.

The only light in the church came from my placing the candle lantern I was carrying behind us on a pew. We were meeting in the church, the archer-priest softly explained, so that anyone who saw us or heard about us would think we were a priest and a believer with a problem that needed prayers instead of a spy passing on valuable information to someone who should not have it.

"I am much relieved to see you, Captain Adams," Father Thomas said in a whispered voice as he knelt beside me and crossed himself as he might if we had come to pray. "I have important information. It is so important that I was about to take a chance and rent a horse and ride to London tomorrow morning to deliver it. You need to get word to the Cornwall as quickly as possible that the barons of the Great Council, most of them at least, are forming a great army and will be marching to occupy Devon and Cornwall within the next few weeks. They call it the "Loyal Army" so the king will not get upset, but it really is not.

Father Thomas was absolutely astonished, and greatly relieved, when I nodded my head and murmured. "The Commander knows about their plans. But he needs to know more. That is why I am here. What else do you know? Do you know how soon and how many are coming and why? Can you find out?"

"The barons and the Nuncio are saying that they need to form an army and station it near Exeter and Plymouth in order that it be immediately available to fight off a French invasion which will come ashore at either or both of those ports. But it increasingly appears to be much more than that. From the conversations I have overheard and messages I have scribed for the Nuncio, I think the barons intend to have their army formed up so it can march on

Westminster Abbey and quickly install one of their own when the king dies.

"I also get the impression that once their army is formed some of the barons will not wait for the king to die. I am not sure of that; but what I am sure is that the barons intend to form an army and feed its men by foraging in western Devon and Cornwall."

Father Thomas had not known that his fellow priestly spy and cleric, Father Peter Johnson, was traveling with the Chamberlain and away from Windsor, but promised to deliver the bishop's request for a meeting to him as soon as Father Peter returned to Windsor. I told him that he need not bother if he was able to safely tell Peter what information the Commander needed.

"The request for a meeting with the bishop was only to get Father Peter to visit London so I could tell him about the information that the Company needs," I explained. "I will leave it to you to whisper it into his ear when he returns."

I also told Father Thomas I had decided to leave two horse archers at Windsor at the stable of the village priest's vicarage in case he or Father Peter obtained additional information of such importance that the Commander needed to know it as soon as possible.

"They will be waiting for you in their stall every night and follow whatever orders you or Father Peter give to them. Any significant *additional* information that needs to be sent to Cornwall should be brought to them in the dark of night, but only if you or Peter decides that it is so important that one or both of them should ride to Cornwall with it."

I also decided, but without mentioning it to Father Thomas, that I would immediately send two of our remaining riders to Cornwall with a message confirming the information I had already provided.

Father Thomas nodded his head in agreement and said he would tell Peter all about the situation and the archers in the stable. And then told me he was concerned for his safety and that of Father Peter.

"Be careful about what you and your men say to Father John; he is a two-faced liar and will sell us out in a heartbeat for a handful of coins. We are safe only so long as we pay more than anyone else."

******

The next morning I announced to Sergeant Cooper and the archers who were still with me that I had considered what I had seen and heard during our travels to be of such importance that I decided that two of them should act as messengers and carry a verbal message back to Cornwall. It was a simple message such that it would be easily understood by the Commander; and a total mystery to the two archers and, thus, to anyone else should they be captured and forced to talk. It was quite simple—"I have further verified what I told you earlier; it will happen soon."

Also, and because I did not want to take a chance on the messengers revealing that we had spies in the king's court, I deliberately waited until *after* the two horse archers ridden off to inform the last two of my men that they would be staying in Windsor to carry messages to Cornwall. Leaving both of the last two remaining horse archers and their four horses in Windsor was a difficult decision for me. It meant I would be riding alone to London and my shipping post would not be reinforced—and that could be disastrous because of what I had decided to do.

None of the four archers complained when they were told of their new assignments. To the contrary; they stood at attention, knuckled their heads, and repeated their orders so I could be sure they understood them. Even so, I think all four of them, and their mates I had already sent back to Cornwall or left behind, were to a man unhappy that they would not be seeing London after all. Little did I know at the time that none of them ever would.

As you might also imagine, I took great satisfaction the next morning before I rode off in *not* paying the priest the three silver coins for delivering a message to the unreachable Father Peter. But I took no chances; I settled my account with the priest by paying him only what he had earned *after* I finished arranging for the two archers to remain in Windsor. Specifically, they and their horses are to be fed each day and share three of the stalls in the vicarage's stable. For that, Father John, the village priest, was to receive one silver coin per week, in advance as he insisted, for so long as they and their horses were in the stable.

I paid Father John for three weeks in advance and said I would personally make any required payments if they stayed longer. And then I looked the priest in the eye and very sternly reminded him with a great deal of threat in my voice that he himself had said that helping me meant taking a risk—and that he was certainly right about that since both myself and others in the Company of Archers knew of his involvement such that he would be quickly and painfully find himself in purgatory if he ever mentioned a single word to anyone about my visit or anything else about the two priests.

"What that means is that your health and circumstances will quickly and permanently decline if anything bad happens to the archers in your stables or the two Angelovian priests. So it is up to you to keep them safe both now and in the future, eh Father John? Your life and your future depend on it. Do you understand what I am telling you?"

The portly priest turned red and nodded his head. "I understand," he said in a shaky voice.

Before I left to ride alone to London I ordered the two archers to never tell anyone that they are archers and to always keep the stripes on their tunics and their longbows and quivers hidden. I also ordered them to stay out of the taverns and in sight of each other at all times and to spend every hour of darkness at the Vicarage's stable until someone arrived in the night to send one or both of them off to Okehampton with a message. If either or both of the men were still at Windsor after the next three Sunday nights passed they were to ride for London and report in to me at the Company's stable. And of course I told them how to find the Company stable when they got to London.

What I did *not* tell the archers who were remaining in Windsor was *who* would be bringing the information to them, only that "he" knew where they were staying and would contact them at the Vicarage's stable after dark if he had anything that needed to be reported to Cornwall or any other order that he needed them to carry out.

Chapter Fourteen

Preparing for war.

It was not until four days later when I returned from Exeter and Plymouth with all the available horse and riders and Anne and I were alone in our bed that I quietly confirmed her fears about the coming war. She gasped, but said she understood, when I told her that I had lied earlier when I said the riders I sent galloping off to Restormel were part of the Commander's annual inspection.

"The truth is that an army is being raised by some of England's most powerful barons and it almost certainly will be based near here and foraging along the border and in Cornwall in the days ahead. There will be fighting and sieges."

And she gasped again and held me even more tightly when I told her that Okehampton would almost certainly be attacked and besieged whilst I was away fighting against the invaders. I apologized profusely for misleading her.

"I am sorry, my dear, but I lied to you when I said there was nothing to fret about. It was a gambit. I had to say it in order to gull everyone who was standing there listening to us. It had to be done because we do not want word to get back to the barons that we know their army is coming.

"And, for what it is worth, what I said was not actually tell a lie; Commander Robertson *is* coming for an inspection to make sure we are ready to fight. You must make a room ready for him and another for his aide, Captain James Franklin, as I expect we will see them here in the next few days. Indeed, I half expected to see him here when I returned from the coast."

Then I assured her that we would pass the inspection and reassured her by telling her what she already knew.

"We will pass the inspection because we *are* ready for a long siege. It will be inconvenient but you will be safe no matter whether you spend the war here or go to a refuge further to the west. I think we will be able to defeat the barons' army with just the archers who are already here in England. But if not, the men we have in the east will be recalled. They will come back in sufficient force to be able to defeat the barons and relieve the siege long before Okehampton and our other strongholds run out of food."

That was true. Or at least I hoped it was. What I did not tell Anne was that I was still not certain whether she and the other Company wives and their children would be safer staying behind Okehampton's besieged walls or fleeing to the west with the villagers. It would depend, I finally decided, on how much bread-making grain and firewood we had left in the castle's larder after we sent out the supply wagons for the additional horse archers.

******

Okehampton was the scene of much activity and overcrowding due to the arrival of so many additional horses and men the previous afternoon. And it got significantly worse on Thursday afternoon when an exhausted courier arrived on a blown horse after dropping his remount along the way. The parchment the courier was carrying was an important message from Commander Robertson.

The Commander had received Captain Adam's message from Tiverton and my message about going to Exeter and Plymouth to buy grain horses and the unexpectedly large number of horses that were available at Okehampton. As a result, he was making a forced march to Okehampton and bringing with him every potential rider, foot archer, and horse he could muster including all the archers who could ride or volunteered to learn from the Company's available galleys and transports including their lieutenants and captains!

I made some quick sums in my head and asked the courier a few questions. Damn, there was no doubt about it; hundreds of men were on their way to Okehampton and the Commander and the men riding with him could arrive as early as tomorrow. Our crowded conditions were about to substantially worsen. Moreover, from what I could gather from what the messenger told me, Commander Robertson may be intending to base himself at Okehampton for at least the next few days and perhaps for the duration of the war. An appropriate sleeping room needed to be prepared for him immediately, and many more beds would be needed depending the numbers and ranks of the men he was bringing with him.

According to the Commander's message, the handful of horse archers and outriders posted to Restormel and all boys from the school old enough to have horses assigned to them were riding with him. Also riding with the Commander on the rest of Restormel's horses and the remounts of the horse archers stationed there were some of the foot archers who already knew how to ride.

The rest of the potential riders for the horses we had just brought into Okehampton, including men who were not riders but said they were willing to learn, were coming along right behind them in commandeered horse-drawn wagons. Everyone else including all the archers off the galleys and transports that were stationed in Cornwall or newly arrived from the east were walking behind them and coming as fast as possible on foot along with a hundred or more of the new recruits who had been at the depot near Restormel being learnt to be archers.

"Commander Robertson ordered me to tell you that he is bringing every available man, horse, and boy and that he wants food, water and places for them to sleep waiting for them when they arrive. He also said to tell you that he was marching with more than five hundred men and about a hundred horses including those pulling the wagons that are loaded with the horseless riders and the heavy weapons and extra arrows of the foot archers.

"The Commander also said I was to tell you that about fifty of the foot archers and recruits would either be stopping at Launceston or continuing on to Plymouth without stopping. They are going to be used to reinforce Launceston and Plympton Castle in order to free up all the archers who know how to ride or are thought to be capable of being learnt."

About two hours later yet another courier came in on a staggering horse and literally fell off his horse with a message from Richard Adams. The courier was one of the two men Richard had dispatched after he had visited Windsor. The other courier and three horses had been dropped off along the way and would arrive later.

Richard's message was verbal, but it was important because it confirmed that his initial message was accurate. I debated whether or not to send the new message on to the Commander, but decided there was no use risking more good horses since I knew he was already on the road and coming as fast as possible.

We spent the day in frenzied effort to get ready for the new arrivals. Most of the day was spent re-organizing the archers' barracks, the castle's stables, and our horses and supply wagons so that we could accommodate the men who were about to unexpectedly descend on us with various states of riding expertise. We also set up four new kitchens, one in each of the Okehampton's three baileys and the fourth just outside its outermost wall.

You would have thought that the sudden arrival of so many additional men would have given us all the additional hands that would needed to get things ready. But that was not the case: Horses had to be trained and training enclosures built, arrows fletched, food supplies bought and brought in from the surrounding farms, grain milled into bread flour by our miller, firewood chopped, chickens slaughtered. The list went on and on and on. It was so long that I was afraid I had overlooked something.

It took some doing, had everyone running about like a chicken with his head cut off, and periodically resulted in a misunderstanding or outrage.

"Ignore what the sergeant just said, my dear. He is just doing his job." That was my response to a despairing look Anne gave me in response to a particularly foul threat from amongst the many that could be constantly heard in Okehampton's baileys as the sergeants desperately drove their men to finish one task and get on to another.

The sergeants were at times, I had to admit, incredibly crude. But their curses and threats seemed to work and everyone including the wives worked hard to help get things ready. I did my part by spending a good part of the day carrying firewood and helping to dig shite ditches. It set an example of the importance of the work that needed to be done and the need to hurry. If it was so important that I had to double time from place to place and work my arse off, then so did the sergeants and everyone else.

I had begun by moving about a hundred of my best and most experienced horse archers into the inner bailey along with their horses, remounts, and the supply wagons that would sustain them if they had to spend an extended period of time in the field. Their families were allowed to remain in their current stall-like hovels that were built up against the insides of the castle's middle and outer walls. These were the men that would almost certainly be going furthest out to intercept and prey upon the barons' army before it reached Okehampton. Hopefully Commander Robertson would allow me to lead them; I thought he would and I planned to insist on it rather strongly.

All the rest of the horse archers and the immediately useful riding horses, almost all amblers, were moved to the middle bailey along with the remaining supply wagons. The horses that still needed more training were moved to the outer bailey, the northern end of which would be the temporary camp of the absolute beginners amongst the archers and recruits who had volunteered to be learnt to ride. The stables and stalls in the outer bailey were where the arriving foot archers would camp whilst they were with us. Everyone else would camp in tents outside the outer wall. Tents were being hurriedly erected everywhere and additional shitting ditches dug both inside and outside the castle's three curtain walls.

I spent the day carrying firewood, supervising the location and erection of the tents that were available, putting out water barrels, and making sure that there were sufficiently numbers of shite and piss trenches in the outer bailey and outside the third wall for the five hundred or so additional men who were about to descend upon us.

Whilst all that was happening Anne and Harry Morgan, the Welshman who was the castle's chief cook and brewer, were organizing food and drink for the new arrivals with the help of the castle's small crew of servants and the wives of the horse archers who had been hurriedly mobilized to assist them. It was no small task to get everything ready, and in the middle of doing it Anne discovered that the castle's supply of salt and pepper, the spices needed to cover up the taste of food when it begins to smell foul, was running low. We would, she said, need to immediately send a wagon to Exeter for more in order to get back up to the required eighteen months supply.

I cursed at the news like one of my sergeants, and then apologized and told her I would arrange it immediately.

****** *George Courtenay*

Commander Robertson and the first of the men he was bringing with him were seen from the castle wall the next morning. I knew he was coming fast, but it was an even earlier arrival than I expected; he had obviously been riding hard at the head of a column that consisted of every available horse, rider, and wagon he could find at Restormel and gather up along the way.

Some of the horseless would-be riders were behind the Commander Robertson in commandeered wagons. The men in the wagons were mostly the foot archers and stripe-less recruits who would be mounted on the horses from the horse farm and on the remounts of the horse archers. They would find their horses and food and drink waiting for them in the middle bailey where they would camp and be learnt to ride. The foot archers and the recruits hurrying along behind them on a forced march would be temporarily barracked in the outer bailey and any non-archers with them, such as wagon drivers, would camp outside the outer wall.

How many of the newcomers would be mounted on the remounts that had until recently been assigned to the regular horse archers and outriders remained to be seen. I intended to recommend that one hundred of the most experienced horse archers keep their remounts. Indeed, I had already moved them into the inner bailey in an effort to strengthen my case. The remounts of the rest of the horse archers and the horses from the camp would be ridden by some of the new arrivals because we were going to need to get as many mounted archers into the field as possible.

Marching on foot behind Commander Robertson and the riders and the rider-carrying wagons were the last few of the archers coming for horses to ride. Also walking with them were the foot archers off the Company galleys and transports and the new recruits who would initially be posted to Okehampton. The men destined for Launceston and Plympton, I assumed, had already turned off the road and were marching toward them as fast as possible.

Captain Merton, a wan and still coughing Lieutenant Johnson, and the Sergeant Major were waiting at Okehampton's outer gate to direct the arriving men, horses, and boys who were coming here to their proper places where they would find food, drink and places to sleep waiting for them.

****** *Lieutenant Commander Courtenay*

Commander Robertson rode into Okehampton with all the available horse archers and every riding horse he could gather up on short notice—over sixty of them, horses that is. His senior aide, Captain Franklin, was riding with him and so was the apprentice sergeant who ran their errands. They ridden virtually non-stop and looked more than a little road-worn and tired as they and the men riding with them rather stiffly climbed off their horses in the inner bailey and accepted the traditional welcoming bowls of ale.

The Commander listened to the newly arrived message from Captain Adams whilst he was pissing and then got a fast summary of Okehampton's preparations from me as he alternated between taking gulps from his bowl and bites out of the flatbread he had been handed with melted cheese on it. He immediately convened a meeting in the castle's great hall with all of his available captains and began making decisions and issuing orders.

A detailed leather map of Devon and Cornwall covering an entire cow skin was spread out on the table in the great hall and everyone gathered around it. The Commander began by thanking me for getting everything ready for the men he had brought with him. Then he told everyone about the new message that had come in from Richard Adams in London confirming the information in his previous messages—that the barons' army was coming and intended to do its foraging in Devon on the approaches to Cornwall and in Cornwall itself. He also said how pleased he was with the information that Richard Adams had sent in and also that Richard had assigned archers to remain in Crediton and Windsor to act as messengers.

"Those were very smart decisions for Captain Adams to make because they will almost certainly give us more time to get ready. They also greatly increase the possibility that we will know when the invaders will arrive and the size and composition of their forces. Captain Adams is to be commended for his initiative." *Everyone grunted their assent and knew Richard's star was rising.*

Commander Robertson got right to the point as soon as he and his captains were seated around the table. In order that everyone would have the same background information, he began by having Captain Franklin read out the messages from Captain Adams. Then he had me report on the current and projected availability of horses, grain, and riders at Okehampton. When I finished he summarized for us what most of us already knew.

"I came with every available rider and horse when I heard the good news as to how many additional horses Lieutenant Commander Courtenay and his men could provide. I also brought some lads, both archers and new recruits, who said they were willing to board a horse and serve as horse archers. They will be posted here so they can be taught to ride and to push out arrows as they do so. I also brought all the available wagons to carry them even though some of the wagons will have to be sent back to Restormel immediately so the alchemists can use them to carry the ribalds they are preparing for use at the ford."

He had also, the Commander said, brought all the boys from the Company school who knew how to ride because they were old enough to be assigned their own horses.

"They can be horse holders along with the stable boys and any other non-archers we can recruit from the villages as riders. As things stand, it looks as though we can put just over four hundred horse archers into the field with about one hundred men and boys who can ride going with them as horse holders.

"It is a much bigger force of horse archers than I would have thought possible and it changes everything. It means we can hit the barons' armies harder and much further to the east before they reach us. It also means we will need more supply wagons and horses to pull them so the horse archer raiding companies can stay in the field as long as possible," he added.

"And that, in turn, may mean we will have to use the wagons and teams that we had planned to use to carry our families and the villagers deeper into Cornwall as supply wagons and to carry the ribalds."

"Our basic war fighting plan, however, remains unchanged: We will evacuate our women and children to the west and hold our four strongholds with the absolute minimum amount of men they will need to withstand prolonged sieges. The horse archers under Lieutenant Commander Courtenay will stay in constant contact with the enemy and whittle them down with constant attacks and ambushes, and the foot archers under my direct command with Captain Franklin as my number two will try to hold the Tamar ford and, if that fails, fight them in Cornwall."

Damn, George thought as he listened to the Commander. I like what I am hearing but Anne is not going to like it at all; she wants to stay here. Perhaps I can arrange it. But do I really want to do that?

"It is my intention to make a determined stand at the ford with all the foot archers who can be made available. Where and how we will fight if we cannot hold the ford will depend on the circumstances at the time. I would assume that means the foot archers would then fall back deeper into Cornwall and the horse archers under Lieutenant Commander Courtenay would continue to do whatever they can on both sides of the river to whittle down our enemies."

Actually, Commander Robertson had something very different in mind that he shared only with me and Captain Franklin after the meeting ended so that we would know what to do if he fell. It was bold and imaginative and I liked it.

We were assured that all the additional Company galleys and transports that come in from the east would continue to be stripped of most of their archers for use in England, even their captains and lieutenants if they were archers. Most, but not all, of the archers serving on the galleys would be replaced by hired rowers and volunteers from the villages so they could remain in service with the handful of archers remaining on each doing their best to make their galley appear fully manned and dangerous to approach. Their sailing sergeants would temporarily take command.

The galleys themselves would be held at the entrance to the Fowey and its estuary to carry messages and prevent the barons' army from using small boats to cross the Tamar River into Cornwall. Holding the galleys there with their sailors and a small force of archers on board each of them was significant; it meant our galleys would be available in the unlikely event we had to run for it. They could also function as hospitals where we barbered our wounded.

Even more importantly, holding the galleys at the mouth of the river would discourage the barons from trying to get their men into Cornwall by boat; they would be forced to march inland and cross at one of the fords upstream in order to forage in Cornwall—and the likely ford they would attempt to use, because it was both the closest to the sea and the only one with a road running to it, was just down the road from Okehampton.

Somewhat to everyone's surprise, but totally understandable once it was explained to us, we were also told that even though we needed every available man reinforcements would *not* be called in from the Company's shipping and posts in the east.

"There is no way we can get the lads at Cyprus to Cornwall in time to participate in this year's fighting and we would lose the services of the archers on the galleys we send to fetch them. We will send for them later if it looks as though the fighting will start up again in the spring."

By far the longest discussion of the meeting was the very last. It dealt with how soon we should evacuate various villages in order to deny the barons' foragers access to food supplies. After much discussion, it was finally decided that the villages and food stores under the Company's control on the Devon side of the Tamar should begin being evacuated when the main force of the barons' army was on the verge of reaching Tiverton. A decision about the people and stores in Cornwall's villages, monasteries, and stannaries would be made by Commander Robertson later when things were more certain as to whether or not we would be able hold the barons at the River Tamar ford "instead of just blooding them as much as possible when they cross."

What was not discussed, and should have been, were the stores of food in the cities and villages immediately beyond the lands under the Company's protection, particularly Exeter and Plymouth. How are we going to prevent the barons' army from buying them or taking them?

Similarly, to my great relief, at no time did the Commander mention the "lean man" at Crediton and what he was ready to do nor about the men who had been left behind at Oxford and Windsor to gather information. Our captains and lieutenants would learn about them if and when they needed to know.

As we looked at the map and talked about our alternatives and what should be done under various circumstances, it became increasingly clear that the Commander intended to hit the invaders hard and continually long before they reached Cornwall. At some point I made my case that one hundred of the horse archers should retain their remounts for the purpose of fighting the barons' armies as far to the east of Cornwall as possible—and was turned down when the Commander decided that only about fifty of the horse archers would be going to war with remounts. He did agree, however, that they should operate as far down the road toward London as possible.

All the other of the current horse archers' remounts including the fifty I would lose, the Commander announced, were to be ridden by the newly arrived foot archers and the horse holders recruited from the stable boys and school boys. That was the bad news so far as fifty of the horse archers in the inner bailey were concerned since it meant they would each lose one of their horses to new horse archer in training and be forced to fight without a remount.

The good news was that the Commander agreed that the men with remounts would be stationed as far forward towards London as possible to act as skirmishers and I would be in command of them and all our forces and strongholds east of the River Tamar. One of the galley captains, Harry Church, would be my number two and based at Okehampton. *Harry had attended the Company school and knew how to ride. He had smiled and nodded his head in agreement when I told him about my plans for defending Okehampton and the horse farm.*

"And how many horse-drawn supply wagons do we have to send out with our horse archers to support them whilst they are in the field?" the Commander asked looking at me. It was the same question I had been unable to answer when he had asked it of me days at the captains' annual meeting.

This time I knew exactly because counting them had been the first thing I did after returning from the meeting at Restormel.

"Nineteen are immediately available here at Okehampton with two-horse teams of plough horses to pull them and I expect the men I sent out yesterday will be able to buy at least five or six more in the villages. To that you can add whatever number of useful wagons and horses you have brought from Restormel and can additionally find in Exeter and Plymouth."

Not everything in Captain Adams' reports was repeated and discussed; only Commander Robertson and I knew what it meant that "the thin man is ready to do the necessary." We nodded grimly to each other when we heard that part of one of Richard's messages repeated by

Captain Franklin and it was never discussed. We were both hopeful that it never would be mentioned again. Unfortunately, or fortunately depending on how one looks at such things, some days later it became an important topic of conversation.

Later that afternoon the covered wagons carrying the untrained riders for the extra horses began arriving at Okehampton. There were eleven wagons full of them. They arrived separately and seemed to have been in somewhat of a race if the cheers of the men riding in the first wagon to come through the outermost gate meant anything. They were followed the next day by the main column of men marching on foot. As they had with the riders and wagons, Captain Merton, Lieutenant Johnson, and the Sergeant Major met them at the outer gate and directed them to where they would be camping.

Chapter Fifteen

Taking the initiative.

Captain Adams rode into London alone with orders to carry out and plans firmly behind his eyes as to how he might additionally help the Company get ready for the war that was almost certainly coming. But first things first; he needed to make sure the information he had received in Windsor got to Commander Robertson. He also needed to make sure his shipping post and its men and their families would be safe when the fighting started. His dilemma was that he had no idea how much, if any, danger he and his men and their families at the Company's post would face once the fighting started. Hopefully all of the barons and their supporters would be campaigning far to the west such that his shipping post would be ignored—but he could not be sure.

As a result, immediately after giving Elspeth, his wife, and his ten year old daughter great hugs and telling them he had things to do and would explain later, he began scribing an additional copy of his message reporting what he had learned in Windsor. It merely repeated the message the two archers were carrying overland. As soon as he finished scribing it he rushed off to get it on its way to Commander Robertson via one of the Company's galleys that had arrived the previous day from Lisbon and whose archers would be welcomed at Restormel as reinforcements. It had already unloaded its inbound passengers and cargo and loaded its outbound cargo including the forty or so recruits that had been waiting for transportation to Cornwall. It was scheduled to sail on the tide so he knew he had to hurry.

He got to the departing galley just in time to hand the message pouch to its captain and tell him that it was a war warning and that he should row hard all the way to Cornwall. Then he hurried back to the shipping post and once again told his increasingly anxious wife he would explain what was happening when he had more time.

Richard grabbed up a candle lantern started to climb up the ladder to his family's private room above the warehouse. It was his intention to inspect the post's escape tunnel which could only be accessed from a trap door in the darkened coin room that lay beyond the family's living room. It, the coin room that is, held the chests of the post's coins and flower paste and was totally dark because it had no wall openings.

He climbed the ladder with Elspeth right behind him asking questions. A few moments later he changed his mind when she followed him into the coin room and began shouting at him as he moved the empty chest at the back of the coin room that covered the trap door under it. It had been his intention to climb down the ladder under the trap door. He needed to do so in order to get to the little room that was deeper in the ground behind the back wall of the post's warehouse; the room with the entrance to the post's escape tunnel.

He and Elspeth had been married for many years so he knew her well enough to know that she would keep after him relentlessly until he told her what was happening. So he stopped after he opened the trap door, gave a great sigh, and explained to her what was happening whilst they stood there in the coin room amidst the lantern's flickering light.

Elspeth was only temporarily stunned into silence.

"Are you sure, absolutely sure?" she demanded when he finished. "Yes, I am sure," he told her. "Oh my God!" she said. "What can I do to help?"

******

After inspecting the tunnel with a now highly motivated Elspeth crawling determinedly along behind him, and finding it still usable, he brushed off the tunnel dust and hurried off to visit a reliable Mammonite merchant and moneylender, a man whose forebears had washed up on England's shores several generations earlier and whose family had somehow become merchants and established themselves as one of the Company's more reliable customers. Richard had selected him to help the Company do what must be done because Richard knew he had no love for England's nobility and was not likely to betray one of his best customers.

From the turbaned merchant, to whom Richard explained *some* of the situation, he rented a warehouse further down towards the mouth of the Thames. It was Captain Adam's intention that in the event of trouble the warehouse would become a "secret safe house" where his family and the families of the archers assigned to the London post could hide out until they could be evacuated to Cornwall by sea. The Mammonite knew where his bread was buttered and had no great illusions about England's nobles. He promised that within the day it would be stocked with water, food, and firewood.

Whilst he was walking with the merchant to see the warehouse that was to become his post's safe house, Captain Adams reached an additional agreement with his new landlord—the merchant and his two clerks would immediately begin hiring rowers to send to Cornwall to replace the archers on the Company's galleys that would be coming in to Cornwall from Lisbon on previously scheduled voyages. The two men then parted and Captain Adams hurried home to begin scribing a report.

******

Early the next morning Captain Adams carried out another order he had received from Commander Robertson—by getting a horse from the nearby Company stable and riding along the Thames until he found two transports, both three-masted ships, that would soon be outbound for the east with a stop in Lisbon.

Each of the transport's captains was handed a pouch containing one of the captain's hastily scribed parchments and a substantial payment with the promise of another even larger payment when he handed it to the captain of the Company's Lisbon shipping post. The message ordered the captain of the Lisbon shipping post to make the promised second payment and to send every available Company galley and archer on to Cornwall as soon as they arrived in Lisbon and could take on the necessary water and supplies. Captain Adams was fairly sure that one or both of the transports would make it to Lisbon. *It was after it sailed from Lisbon that a transport's fate would depend on either the Moors not spotting it or enough tribute having been paid in advance in Lisbon as a toll.*

No one had ordered Captain Adams to hire the rowers and have them transported to Cornwall, but he knew it was the right thing to do since it would free up some or all of the archers in their crews to fight in the coming war without taking their galleys out of service. Even more importantly, he knew from his recent meeting with Commander Robertson and the castle captains in Cornwall that riding horses would be in short supply. So he spent the next two days at London's livestock markets and visiting some the city's many stables to buy up all the useful riding horses he could buy on short notice. He also commissioned several merchants to help him buy more.

On the afternoon of the fifth day after Captain Adams' return to London two of the hostlers from the Company's stable and three of the five archers assigned to his shipping post set off under the command of the post's sergeant, Robert Shand, to deliver thirty-seven newly acquired riding horses to Okehampton. Three hostlers hired from one of the nearby stables rode with them. The Company men, if they got through to Okehampton, would remain in the west as reinforcements for the Company's horse archers for the duration of the coming war, and reasonably so since they would otherwise be hiding in London rather than fighting. The three hirelings would be free to ride back to London as soon as the horses were delivered.

Later on the same day Captain Adams watched as two chests of the post's coins, three chests of the priceless flower paste that kills the pain of a wound or a pox, more than a hundred newly recruited rowers, and five newly arrived archer recruits, were loaded on to a two-masted coastal transport he had chartered to carry them to Fowey Village. The post's two remaining archers went with them to command the new recruits and guard its cargo.

Captain Adams stood on the riverbank and watched until the transport cast off and began slowly moving down the Thames toward the sea. It galled him that he had had to pay out the coins needed to charter it but it had to be done since no Company transport or galley was immediately available to carry them. He also sent yet another copy of his message reporting the news from Windsor, in case the first two had failed to arrive. The new message also reported the actions he had taken since his return to London.

Adams returned to his shipping post after he had waved farewell to the rowers and the last of the post's five archers, one of whom, a steady chosen man who had been promoted to acting sergeant and sent to command the newly employed rowers and archer recruits during the voyage.

As Captain Richard Adams walked back to the post he once again tried to decide how soon he should relocate his family and the families of the post's archers to the "safe house." He had a covered wagon and two mules ready to carry them there on a moment's notice and there was already food, water, and firewood in it. Alternately, of course, in an emergency they could go out through the escape tunnel that was behind the false wall of the post's warehouse area, the one that was accessed from the upper floor where his family lived and emerged in a pig sty several blocks away behind a tanner's home and workshop.

Captain Adams had already decided to send his family and the post's other wives and children off to the safety of the safe house as soon as word of the fighting between the Company and the barons reached London. Then *he* and he alone would stay at the archer-less shipping post until the very end. When and if the barons' supporters came it was his intention to carry the remaining chests of coins and paste into the escape tunnel, pull enough of its dirt ceiling down behind him to block the tunnel, and then leave through the tunnel and walk to the safe house in the dark of night with his longbow and quivers slung over his shoulder and carrying a galley shield and short sword. He would recover the chests when the danger was past.

The captain had everything ready to move his people to safety on a moment's notice, or at least he thought he did. What he had *not* yet told his wife was that he had held back the two best horses and placed them in a neighbouring stable. He had done so because he intended to ride to Cornwall and join the fight as soon as he knew she and his daughter and the post's other wives were and children safe; she would be pissed when she heard about his intention to leave and join the fighting and there was no getting around it.

******

The virtually simultaneous departures of the horses and both Sergeant Shand and his men and the newly hired rowers turned the London post and its stable from being packed with horses and men to being empty and virtually unmanned. And that was certainly the case: Except for Captain Adams, the only people at the post other than the wives and children of its men were a couple of Company retirees living in London who had been hurriedly recalled to duty on a part-time basis and a young archer who was in great pain and totally useless because he had somehow broken his wrist whilst Adams' was away in Cornwall to meet with Commander Robertson. He immediately sent the two retirees back to their homes and the young archer off to live with a local bone-setter.

Captain Adams did not make his decision as to when *he* would evacuate his post and ride for Cornwall until he walked into his post after seeing off the rowers and his post's chests of coins and paste. But when he did he found a merchant waiting to arrange a cargo shipment and several pilgrims seeking to buy passages—at which point he decided to keep the post open and continue to sell passages, accept cargos, and sell and redeem money orders for as long as possible despite there being no able-bodied men to assist him. And to his great surprise when he mentioned his decision to them, his wife and the wives of the post's absent men were enthusiastic about pitching in to help him carry on.

Sergeant Shand never returned to London. His family joined him in Cornwall after the war was over. He subsequently attended the Company's scribing and summing school on Cyprus and rose to the rank of Lieutenant before the galley on which he was serving disappeared in a storm. He remains famous in the Company for his many descendents who subsequently served in the Company and for giving his name to a mixture of lemon juice and ale that he prepared for his family and his fellow students which they drank to obtain relief from the heat of Cyprus's extremely warm summer days.

****** *Restormel Castle*

Commander Robertson had stripped Restormel Castle and the Company's nearby training camp of every available archer and horse. All that remained of the castle's original inhabitants was the old earl and the families of the recently departed men, about twenty of the younger boys at the Company's school for likely boys who had been left behind because they were not yet strong enough to push arrows out of a longbow and had been too young to be assigned their own horses and taught to ride, and the Sergeant Major who was now the Company's alchemist and the two new apprentice sergeants who were his new and very unhappy assistants.

Even so, Restormel Castle's baileys were bustling as never before and only the Company's nearby training camp for archers was totally deserted. That was because a hundred or so of the newly arrived recruits from London had been moved into the castle along with three veteran sergeants who were charged with either making them into archers or discharging them with free transportation back to London. The recently arrived recruits had come from the Company's nearby training camp for archers and were now training and sleeping in the castle's baileys. The commander's plan was for them to complete their training inside Restormel's baileys and to then remain there to serve as the castle's defenders until they were needed elsewhere.

The newly promoted alchemist Sergeant Major, Arthur Tinker, and the two archers who had volunteered to be his assistants had been ordered to set aside their efforts to use man-made lightning to turn lead into gold and, instead, concentrate on building ribalds that could be mounted on Restormel's outer wall or on wagons so they could be carried elsewhere to be used.

The three men were working hard even though both of Sergeant Major Tinker's new assistants were unhappy because they now wanted to ride out with the Commander and serve in the field as either horse archers or foot archers. Temporarily working with the three men were two of the likely lads from the Company school whose arms were still not strong enough to push out arrows from a long bow even though they had been given a horse to care for and taught to ride.

****** *Okehampton*

George and Anne stood in the light rain and waved farewell to Commander Robertson as he led a handful of riders and a couple of horse-drawn wagons out of

Okehampton's outer bailey and on to the cart path that led down to main road between London and Exeter. They were outbound for Plymouth where the Commander would inspect Plympton Castle's defenses. He had already strengthened its defenses by adding a score or so of the foot archers and new recruits to its garrison.

As soon as the Commander arrived at Plympton the castle's captain, John Farmer, would be ordered to turn the command of the castle over to his Sergeant Major and lead the handful of outriders based there and all the available riding and wagon-pulling horses he could gather to join George's rapidly growing company of horse archers at Okehampton. John would be sent to Okehampton to command one of the horse archers' raiding companies because he had learned to ride when he was a student in the Company school. John's Sergeant Major was not a rider; he would take over command of the castle and be responsible for defending it.

As soon as Commander Robertson was out of sight Anne scurried inside to get out of the rain and George mounted his waiting horse and led Sergeant Morrison and six foot archers to the footpath leading up to the horse farm. The sergeant and his archers were riding in a covered wagon so they would not be too tired to walk the footpath to Hatherleigh when they arrived. The wagon was almost full because it also carried a couple of small leather tents that the men would use to camp along the footpath, some dry firewood and sacks of food, and an entire bale of extra arrows.

George's plan was for the sergeant and his men would stay at the horse camp and along the footpath to Hatherleigh until the barons' army arrived. Then it would be their task to hold the footpath for as long as possible by inflicting fearsome casualties on anyone who attempted to use it. A couple of stable boys too young to ride out with the horse archers as horse holders went with them in the wagon. They would be the archers' runners and carry their messages and supplies.

The sergeant and his men did not know it yet, but if worst came to worst and they could not hold the footpath they would be expected to retreat back to the horse farm and kill the horses in the hope they would rot before they could be used as food to help feed the barons' army—and then melt back into the surrounding forest to fight as skirmishers and raiders.

George intended to walk the footpath with the men and boys in the wagon all the way to the Hatherleigh tavern as soon as they got to the horse farm. He would do so in order that they could talk along the way as to the best places to set up ambushes and chokepoints.

And he had already decided that before they got to the tavern he would caution the archers to careful about what they said to Hatherleigh's villagers and not give them or any travelers they met even a hint as to why they were there or what they would be doing. That was because George was not at all sure of the loyalties and intentions of the local villagers. They were at best uncertain because the lands around Hatherleigh were further to the east of the lands that were under the Company's control; they belonged to a Kentish lord who lived in the midlands and were worked by serfs and tenants under the direction of a reeve who was one of the lord's nephews.

George also now knew from Richard Adam's messages about Richard's intention to leave a second messenger at *The Raven* when the horse archers returned from London. But what if the new man slept in the tavern because he was a tavern worker instead of in the stable with the horse archer who was there under the guise of being a hostler? George worried about the possibility because he was one of the few men who knew the real purpose of the tavern. It was a closely guarded Company secret known only to the Company commander and George because he was the commander's his number two. Neither Captain Franklin nor any of the other archer captains knew anything about it.

****** *Commander Robertson*

I did not stop for a second visit to Okehampton when I left Plymouth to return to Restormel two days later. I could not because my little entourage and I left our horses behind and sailed from Plymouth to Fowey Village in a fishing boat. Our horses did return to Okehampton, however, along with Plympton's Captain Farmer, the four outriders who had been stationed at Plympton, and all the riding horses and wagons that were still available in the Plymouth area. There were only a few because George Courtenay had made a quick visit a few days earlier and bought up everything he could find.

Captain Farmer and the four outriders and their remounts went no further than Okehampton. They remained there to reinforce the fifty-man company of horse archers and outriders with remounts that George himself would be personally leading against the barons. Similarly, most of the horses from Plymouth remained at Okehampton for the use of the Company's rapidly expanding company of horse archers. Only the personal riding horses of myself and Captain Franklin were sent on to Restormel; our remounts would be used to carry another two horse archers into battle far from Cornwall's border with England.

It is difficult for a man to ride on a galloping horse and at the same time push arrows out of a longbow with any degree of accuracy. It takes practice and requires a man who is both a good archer and a good rider. As a result, according to the messages I received almost daily from George, the number of horse archers continued to grow slowly despite the intensity of the volunteers' training and the gains that were made by the pairing of our most experienced horsemen with those who were still learning. Even so, and because most of the volunteers were already fully trained archers who knew how to use their longbows, within the week George was able to add forty men to his company of horse archers. As a result, he now had well over three hundred archers immediately available to lead against the barons and their men—with more and more of the archer volunteers becoming found fit to join them every day.

A controversial decision sped up the process—George ordered that all the new men be mounted on the much easier to ride amblers and that the non-ambling horses be assigned to the most experienced riders. Initially some of the experienced horse archers were unhappy about letting the newbie volunteers take over their horses, giving up their remounts was bad enough after all, but their sergeants put them right and riding on horses that were not amblers soon became known as a mark of excellence such that the experienced horse archers were much mollified by being recognized as such when they bounced along on their non-amblers. Even so, George made sure that all of the fifty men who would be going out with him had remounts and that at least one of them was ambler. *Of course he did; non-amblers were hard on a man's arse and he planned to lead them a long way towards London before the fighting started. George is a good man and I am lucky to have him as my number two.*

Chapter Sixteen

The archers in Oxford have to run.

It was Sergeant Cooper and Archer Bill Atkins who saw the initial elements of the barons' army first. The two archers were returning from visiting their horses and coming into *The Bear* through its rear entrance after pissing in the alley behind it. They came into the pubic room just as five men speaking English with strange accents came in through *The Bear's* open front door and headed towards a vacant table. The newcomers looked road weary and they brought their swords and shields into *The Bear* with them. This was the first time since the two archers arrived in Oxford that a party of men had come into the tavern carrying weapons.

The two archers saw them enter, and for a brief moment Sergeant Cooper was not sure what he should do. But then, with Bill following dutifully along behind him, the sergeant worked his way through the crowd of drinkers and deliberately sat down at the empty table next to the new arrivals. He did so in order that he and Bill could listen to them and, with a little luck, strike up a conversation.

Sergeant Cooper had no more than seated himself and waved to the alewife to let her know that she should bring bowls for Bill and himself than another even larger group of similarly armed men came through the door and walked over to join the first arrivals. They were obviously together and part of the same company.

"Would you like us to move over so you can sit together?" the Sergeant Cooper asked with a friendly smile and a welcoming gesture with his hand. The alewife delivered the two bowls to their table as he did as she beamed her appreciation at the sergeant for his offer after she gave a greeting and smile of welcome to the new arrivals. The new arrivals nodded their thanks and a moment later the sergeant and Bill did just that; they picked up the long linen wraps they had carried into the tavern and moved to the next table. Everyone seemed to be in good spirits including the new arrivals.

"Much obliged," one of the new arrivals said with a nod as the two men stood up to move and he took one of the stools at their old table. At least that is what they thought he said. They were not sure because the newcomer spoke in a dialect of English that Sergeant Cooper thought he recognized as East Sussex even though he could not understand it. The other recent arrivals joined the first man in sitting down at the table vacated by the archers and several of them nodded their appreciation as the sergeant and Bill reseated themselves.

"My pleasure; my pleasure indeed," said Sergeant Cooper with a smile. "Welcome to Oxford. What brings you here on this fine day?" he inquired most friendly. The man listened to him and then smiled and shrugged in such a way as to let the sergeant know that he was having trouble understanding him. It all happened whilst the new arrivals were settling down next their previously arrived friends.

The man who had sat himself down next to the smiler understood the question and leaned towards Sergeant Cooper so he could be heard over the noise of the now-crowded tavern. He explained that they were from East Sussex and on their way to Cornwall as part of an army to fight the French. A few minutes later Bill leaned over and whispered that he thought he heard one of the men joking that they had ridden right past Windsor without stopping to visit the king.

"How soon do you think you will get to Cornwall?" Sergeant Cooper asked the man with whom he had been talking and then took a big slurp of ale from his bowl. And then, when the man merely shrugged to indicate he did not know or care, the sergeant asked "and where will you be joining up with the rest of your army?" As soon as he said it Sergeant Cooper realized he had been much too direct.

"Why are you asking him such questions?" a man sitting on the other side of the little table leaned toward the two archers and demanded to know. He was a knight and had a cross on his tunic to indicate he had been a crusader. "Who are you?" he demanded to know rather threateningly and with a great deal of suspicion in his voice.

"Horse and mule buyers, good sir; horse and mule buyers." It was the cover story Captain Adams had ordered the two men to tell whenever they were asked what they were doing and why they were there.

"We have been staying here at *The Bear* and riding out to visit the villages around Oxford to buy them. We buy them in the villages and take them to London to sell. Buying in one place where they have them and selling in another where they are wanted and valued more is what we do. Might you be needing a good riding horse perhaps? We will have a splendid ambler gelding available in a couple of days. Fully trained and not more than four years old is what he is. I can give you a good price."

The suspicious knight snorted his disdain and turned back to his friends with a sneer on his face.

"Horse merchants, pah! They are Travelers most likely and they probably steal back the horses they sell so they can sell them over and over again," the man rather arrogantly announced to his friends as he shook his head dismissively and took another sip of ale from the wooden bowl he was waving about. At least that is what the two archers thought he said. His friends laughed, looked at the two archers, and then laughed again.

"Come on, lad, we need to leave before there is trouble," Sergeant Cooper said as he drained his bowl.

Then he stood up and headed to the door. Bill scrambled to get up and followed him out after him after taking one last big gulp from his bowl. The men sitting at the tables were too busy laughing and talking; they paid no attention to the two men as they hurriedly left.

"What should we do, Sergeant?" the archer asked anxiously.

"We will do what we told to do, Bill; what we were told to do." The sergeant was not aware of it but he tended to repeat himself when he was uncertain or worried.

The two archers hurried out the front door of the tavern and into the narrow street that ran in front of *The Bear* and separated it from the low wall that ran around the priory of Saint Frideswide. They could do so without delay because they had paid in advance for the bed they shared and, being rightfully wary of thieves, had left nothing behind in the room where their bed was one of several. The barons' soldiers in the tavern were still drinking and talking boisterously as the two archers stepped out into the lightly misting rain. It was cool for a summer's day and they could hear the faint chanting of the monks coming from the church of St. Frideswide's priory which was on the other side of the newly cobblestoned street.

"Where are we going?" Bill asked as he hurried to catch up with the fast walking sergeant.

"Back to Okehampton, lad, back to Okehampton. We have information about the barons' army that we need to report."

A few moments later they stopped in astonishment as they walked along the side street on which *The Bear* was located. They stopped because they could see the main road running through Oxford ahead of them—and it was now filled with soldiers and wagons slowly moving towards the river ford and the old stone bridge that crossed the Thames. Even worse, the crowded road was also Oxford's main street and stood between the two archers and their horses and equipment which were in one of the city's stables that was located three or four blocks away on the other side of the main road.

The two men waited for a moment for an opening in the densely packed and slow-moving column and then weaved their way through it to the other side of the cobblestoned street. As they did they could see that the column stretched into the distance as far as they could see in either direction—which was not very far because the road had bends in it. The road-worn armed men in *The Bear* must have come from it. The column was probably backed up in the city because the nearby bridge over the Thames was so narrow.

After they made it across the road the two archers stopped to look back at the column. What they saw appeared to be a totally disorganized mass of men and wagons that were slowly, very slowly inching their way through the village towards the bridge on the edge of Oxford, the bridge that crossed the Thames. The soldiers, for that was certainly what they were, looked to be mostly village levies with a sprinkling of knights and their squires and sergeants. They were mostly walking amidst a long line of horse-drawn carts and wagons that so totally filled the road that some of the wagons were two abreast. Almost all of the wagons were covered with sailcloth to protect the people, weapons, and supplies in them from the sun and rain. It looked, in other words, like exactly what it was—a column of disorganized soldiers on the march.

What was immediately obvious was that the soldiers in the column were not expecting to have to fight any time soon. That was obvious because only a few of them were actually carrying their weapons. On the other hand, the men walking all around the long line of slow-moving horse-drawn wagons almost certainly had their weapons close at hand in the covered wagons that were accompanying them to carry their equipment and supplies.

Also, and to the two archers' great astonishment, probably because neither of them had ever actually seen an army on the move before, there were women and even some children walking with the men and riding in the wagons. Even more to their surprise, some of the wagons obviously belonged to merchants called sutlers and at least one seemed to be carrying an assortment of street women and their protectors.

None of the men walking or riding in the column were wearing armour or helmets although some of the better-dressed and liveried men were walking with men and boys who were leading great huge horses on which armour and shields were tied along with the great long swords favoured at the time and great long lances suitable for jousting. They were almost certainly knights and their squires and servants. Many of the marchers were wearing sandals although quite a number of the more shabby of them were barefoot as were a good number of the women and almost all of the children.

"A hoy to you," Sergeant Cooper shouted out to a woman who was looking down at them from the one-horse wagon she was driving. She had curiosity in her eyes and was holding an infant to her breast. "Where be you from and where be you going?"

"My man and I be from a land called Sussex and be following his lordship to some war that be up yonder somewhere."

"Who be your man going to fight?"

"Some Frenchies I think," she said with a shrug as she slowly moved past them. "But not for a while. At least that is what Sir George told my man."

"Well good luck to you and your man, and Sir George too. You will certainly need it if you are going all the way to western Devon and Cornwall," Sergeant Cooper replied. "There is a great plague and no food there. It would be better to turn back than to go to Cornwall and die most horrible from the pox or starvation."

Sergeant Cooper loudly cautioned the wagon-driving wife about going to Cornwall because a few days earlier Captain Adams had told him in no uncertain terms that any man who was marching on Cornwall, and his horses, should either be killed or encouraged to turn back by suggesting that they were marching into lands beset by plague and famine. "It is your duty to do so whenever possible," the captain had told him and his men rather pointedly.

"What is that you just said?" a ragged man who had been walking a few steps behind the wagon stopped and asked. He had overhead the sergeant's exchange with the driver of the wagon and had stopped to talk. He looked like a farm worker who might be in some lord or knight's village levy. Several of the men walking around him also stopped. The wagon, however, kept moving.

"I told yon wife that there is a plague and a famine in Devon and Cornwall. That is God's truth. Whoever is leading you there, if that is where you are going, is taking you to a terrible and certain death. Moreover, it is well known that the archers of Cornwall are ferocious and will kill you with their arrows faster than the plague if you try to enter Cornwall with a weapon. It would appear that you and your mates are on a one-way trip to purgatory."

"It cannot be true," said one of the other men who had heard the exchange and also stopped. He had a very worried look on his face.

"It is true. And I should know; my mate and I are horse buyers and we just came from there. We fled for our lives. You are going to horrible deaths if Devon or Cornwall is your destination." The sergeant nodded to agree with himself as he said it. So did Bill.

The men who had stopped began to look worried and soon others began stopping and listening as well. In the background the column continued to slowly move through Oxford towards the nearby Thames ford and the old bridge that carries the road across the river. The two archers were surrounded by a constantly changing group of men and women from the very slowly moving column for at least ten minutes and perhaps longer.

The two archers learned a lot as they repeated their tale to their wide-eyed and clearly fearful listeners: The soldiers on the road were the knights and village levies of the Earl of Sussex who had seventy-two knight's fees. All of the earl's available knights were in the column and every one of them was required to bring at least a dozen men from his assigned lands and provide at least one covered wagon to carry their food and equipment. Even more men came from the lands the earl directly farmed under the direction of his reeves. All in all Sergeant Cooper reckoned that there were about a thousand men in the earl's army—and they and the women they had brought with them had been joined along the way by sutlers selling supplies off their wagons and various other merchants and hanger-ons.

What was interesting was something the Sussex men did not know, but one the sutlers who stopped to talk did, or so he claimed—that the army of the Sussex earl had started early and was trying to get to Cornwall first. The earl was trying to get there early, the man claimed, so he and his men would have the best place to camp and the easiest foraging.

The talkative sutler, a man with a great untrimmed bushy beard and incredibly snaggly teeth, seemed to know a lot about armies and immediately offered to sell us fire-starting rocks and strikers. The men gathered around us agreed somewhat angrily, when in response to a question from Sergeant Cooper, the sutler claimed the Earl of Sussex had started his march early, even before there was time for his people to harvest their first crops of hay and grain and finish their planting.

His lordship had marched early, the sutler said with a nod of his head to agree with himself, in order to arrive in Cornwall first and claim the best spot to camp and forage. The sutler also said the earl was angry at their slow progress because he was afraid that other lords would have the same idea, especially several from the midlands and the Earl of Westminster. The Sussex army was, the sutler claimed, in somewhat of a race to get to Cornwall and begin foraging. He said it over his shoulder as he ran to catch up with his wagon which had moved a few more feet down the crowded road before once again being forced to stop when the wagons ahead of it stopped. It might well have been Oxford's first traffic jam.

Sergeant Cooper yelled his response to the sutler—and in so doing greatly distressed the men and women gathered around him and those on the nearby wagons who heard it. It showed on their faces and caused them to begin whispering to one another.

"Well I can tell you that you are going to Cornwall and western Devon where God has laid a great famine and plague on the land. There is no food to forage there. That means these poor sods will have to spend their coins to buy food from you or they will starve to death." *Of course it distressed the people who were listening; they were clearly poor folk with little or no coins of their own.*

Suddenly the questions stopped and the men who had been standing around listening scattered to return to their places in the column—and everything changed.

"Uh oh. Here comes trouble," Bill said as he saw a man walking rapidly towards them from the front of the column carrying a bared sword and a knight's shield. Several similar sword-carrying men were following closely behind him. They all wore the same livery.

"Damn. Time to go. Hurry Will; run damn it, run," the sergeant shouted as he grabbed the linen wrap he had tucked under his arm and dashed away down the side street toward the nearby stable and their horses. Bill did not need any urging to follow him and soon caught up with Sergeant Cooper. At least three men began chasing after them—and now they were all three running after them with their swords drawn.

Sergeant Cooper surprised Bill by turning left at the first narrow alleyway he came to instead of turning right in order to run directly to the stable. And he unrolled the long linen wrap he had been carrying cradled in his arms as he ran. Carrying the wrap slowed him down until the linen came free after trailing along behind him and almost tripping him. The alleyway into which they had darted was foul and they ran right past a man who was in the process of squatting to relieve himself.

The two archers, with Bill Atkins in the lead, did not slow down even though once again the sergeant staggered and almost lost his balance and almost fell when his sandal came down on something slippery in a puddle of water he splashed through. But he was able to himself to keep himself upright and continue. Both of the fleeing men were running as fast as they could with the older sergeant slowly falling behind because of the unwieldy burden he was carrying. They could hear the pounding of feet and shouting behind them.

Sergeant Cooper did not hesitate when the alley came out into the next street. He turned right when he reached the street and kept running, actually getting past Bill for a moment because Bill had slowed down to wait for him in order to see which way the sergeant would go. People walking in the street stopped and looked up in surprise as the two archers came running past them. The two archers were desperate and looked it because they continued to hear running footsteps and shouts behind him.

"Go in the next alleyway on the left" … "and wait for me" … "just inside" …. "I will give yours to you there," the sergeant gasped as he pounded down the street and tried to catch up to the younger archer running ahead of him.

At least the shields they are carrying are slowing them down, the sergeant thought as he turned at the next corner. Then he realized he was much too tired to keep running at his current rate of speed. He slowed down and understood he would have to either rest or walk for a while when he reached the next alleyway. He could hear the shouting and footsteps behind him and was beginning to get desperate when an idea somehow popped into his head.

Chapter Seventeen

First Blood.

Archer Bill Atkins had slowed down enough by the time he reached the alley entrance such that Sergeant Cooper was finally able to catch up with him and hand him his unsheathed short sword. Sergeant Cooper did so, handed Bill's sword to him that is, just as the two archers reached the entrance to the alley. The piece of linen that had wrapped the two short galley swords to conceal them when they were in the tavern had come unraveled and was somewhere behind them in the street.

Sergeant Cooper stopped as soon as he entered the alley—and waited. He did not want to stop, but he had to stop. He could hear his heart was pounding in his ears and he was breathing so hard it was all he could do not to bend over and put his hands on his knees in an effort to recover. But he did not give into the urge; instead, he took a firm two-handed grip on his double-bladed short sword and gasped in deep breathes of air while he waited. He was just inside the entrance to the narrow alley with his back up against the alley wall. It was, he decided, all he could do. He was desperate and he knew it.

The still gasping sergeant did not have to wait long before the first of his pursuers dashed into the alley—and was going so fast that he almost got past Sergeant Cooper's heavy two-handed slicing swing. And to make things worse, the sergeant's intended victim somehow saw the sword coming and twisted away in a desperate effort to avoid it.

Sergeant Cooper had intended to swing his sword sideways and take the runner squarely in the stomach with a great slicing cut before he could raise his shield. It did not happen. Instead, because his pursuer was running so fast and trying to turn away at the same time, he ended up only giving the man a great bloody slice across the back of his tunic.

The pursuer screamed and dropped his sword and shield, bounced off the alley wall, and went stumbling deeper into the alley before he fell down. That is where he met Bill Atkins. Bill instinctively put the point of his blade on the back of the face-down and still-screaming man and pushed down on it so hard that the point of the sword went all the way through the screaming man and its tip broke off. The man abruptly stopped screaming in mid-scream and his legs began their death tremble almost immediately.

Sergeant Cooper quickly resumed his position against the alley wall at the side of the entrance whilst Bill was finishing off the first pursuer. He got himself in position not a moment too soon. Almost immediately another pursuer came running into the alley. He was not running nearly as fast as the first man such that this time the sergeant's great slicing two-handed swing succeeded in taking the second pursuer so squarely across the stomach that Cooper almost cut him in half. Bill did not try to finish him off. Instead he squared up holding his sword with both hands and joined the sergeant in waiting for the next pursuer to run into the alley.

The two archers quickly resumed their positions and waited. But the third pursuer never did enter the alley. Perhaps because the second man into the alley continued to scream loudly as he thrashed about in a great puddle of blood whilst unsuccessfully trying to hold his stomach together so his guts would not fall out.

Everything was quiet except for the sobbing and screaming as the two archers waited for the next pursuer; but no one else tried to enter the alley and they could hear no running footsteps.

"Time to go," Sergeant Cooper said a few moments later. He was still breathing hard and trying to catch his breath. With that the two archers hurried out into the little side street at the far end of the alley and began walking rapidly toward the stable where their horses and longbows were waiting. It was about five minutes away.

Bill had leaned down and picked up one of the pursuers' swords as they had hurried down the alley towards the street beyond it. He examined it as they walked briskly out of the alley and out into the narrow side street. It was double-bladed, at least two feet longer than the short swords the archers' were carrying, and it looked new and unused.

"We might get some good prize money for this one," he said somewhat shakily because he too was still somehow short of breath. "It is a good blade; it looks as if it has never been used and only dropped once."

Both men were still tremendously excited as they came out of the other end of the alley. Sergeant Cooper, in fact, was still trembling for some reason and felt weak in his knees. At first they barely noticed the people in the street who hurriedly moved to get out of their way and then stopped to watch them pass. But then they did. The villagers' curiosity was understandable; men carrying bloody swords on the streets of a quiet English village are likely to have that effect.

A few minutes later the two archers hurried into the stable where they had left their horses. They went straight to their horses and began hastily saddling them. A couple of the stable's hostlers saw them enter carrying their bare and bloody swords and one of them said something to them which the two archers probably never even heard. In any event, whatever was said was totally ignored as the two archers hurried to saddle all four of their horses and load their sparse possessions on to their remounts.

The hostlers watched in silence as the two men retrieved and strung their longbows and they each slung their bow and a quiver of arrows over his shoulder. Had the hostlers been asked, they would have said they did so with the speed and certainty of men who had done it many times before. Then, still without saying a word to each other or the hostlers, the archers each hung the sheaths of their swords on their tunic belts and sheathed their swords. Quickly getting themselves and their horses ready to ride was something every horse archer knew how to do without having to be told.

In a very short time the two archers were leading their horses out of their stalls and into open area between the front of the stable and the street that ran past it. As they passed through the stable entrance the sergeant scooped up a small sack of grain, horse food for sure, that was sitting on the stable's floor. They might need it, he decided. He quickly stuffed it into a larger sack tied to his remount's saddle without ever letting go of its reins or the reins of the horse he would initially be riding.

The stable's two hostlers had quietly stood to one side and watched as the archers saddled their horses without saying a word—they somehow knew without asking that something serious had happened and that they would not get an answer if they asked about it. The hostlers continued to watch in silence as the two archers led their horses out into open area in front of the stable, and then climbed aboard the horses they would be riding whilst all the while holding tight to the relatively long reins of the remount each of them was leading.

If the hostlers had been close enough to the archers, which they were not, they might have noticed the great involuntary sighs of relief and satisfaction each of them gave after he swung himself up onto his horse's saddle and nudged it in its ribs to get it and his remount moving—but they certainly heard the archers' spontaneous whooping cheers as their horses ambled out on to the cobblestones of the street in front of the stable.

****** *Hatherleigh tavern*

All six of the foot archers chosen to defend the footpath between the Company's horse farm and Hatherleigh accompanied George to the horse farm. They rode in a covered wagon and George rode his horse. The path defenders were commanded by a young sergeant who had been highly recommended by Commander Robertson—who had said "I know just the man" as soon as he had heard George's plan for the defense of Okehampton's and approved it.

The young sergeant's name was Phillip Morrison. He was the son of one of the Company's old sweats, a chosen man on the Company's roll as Morris the Cartwright. Sergeant Morrison had attended the Company school at Restormel and served for two years as an apprentice sergeant on Galley Fifty-one until a captain who could do his own scribing had been given the galley's command. Then he had served for a year as a cleric at the Company's fortress on Cyprus. George was never told what the sergeant had done that had called him to the attention of Commander Robertson. It did not matter; Sergeant Morrison was the man the Commander wanted on the footpath.

Sergeant Morrison, after having the situation and its requirements explained to him in some detail at Okehampton, was allowed to pick his own men. They were obviously all long-serving veterans and most of them appeared to be as old or older than the relatively young sergeant. George soon realized that they had been well picked.

George and the six foot archers started down the path to Hatherleigh as soon as they reached the horse farm. Their first walk down the path was intended to be an exploring trip both for them and for George; the foot archers to see for the first time the path that they were to defend for as long as possible, and George to visit Hatherleigh's tavern for the first time in order to evaluate it as a threat and also to begin spreading rumours to encourage the barons' men to turn back and desert.

Sergeant Morrison and his men did not take any axes, shelters, or food and water supplies with them for their first walk along the path. They would carry them down later after decisions were made as to where the sergeant's little band of archers would make its defensive stands if the barons' men tried to come up the path. They would also consider where they might block the path by cutting down trees to fall across it.

Walking on the narrow path through the very thick stand of trees through which the path passed was as damp and slippery as it had been the first time George walked it, and once again the little biting bugs soon became a serious distraction. There was no doubt about is; the men would need to cover their faces and exposed skin if they were to stay on the path for an extended period of time. George said as much to Sergeant Morrison who emphatically agreed and then surprised George by saying that on balance the bugs were favourable since he and his men would be prepared for them with linen covers over their heads and the barons' men would not.

The walk went slowly despite the bugs because they periodically stopped to consider the defensibility and weaknesses of various potential defensive and ambush positions along the path. By the time George reached the Hatherleigh tavern he had a very good idea as to why the Commander had suggested Sergeant Morrison and he was no longer concerned about the sergeant's ability to do whatever needed to be done. He also was wet and muddy and his face and hands were red and blotchy and itched most fiercely both from the bugs and some itching plants he had encountered without realizing what they were.

Hatherleigh's tavern was located in a key position—it was on the south side of the main road running between London and Exeter in the southwest of England *after* the road had been joined by all the roads and most of the cart paths feeding in to it from the north. In other words, most and perhaps even all of the armies of the barons coming to invade Cornwall and its approaches would pass in front of it.

The seven men came out of the trees and trudged across a recently ploughed field to reach the tavern and the little village in which it stood. Before they came out of the trees, however, George gathered the men around him and joined them in turning their tunics inside out so the stripes of their ranks would not show and mark them as Company men.

Turning their tunics inside out and wearing them that way, George explained as he began removing his, was necessary so that they could go into the tavern claiming to be deserters fleeing from Cornwall. They would be doing that, pretending to be deserters that is, so they could claim that they were running away from a plague and famine in Cornwall.

"Hopefully, the men of the barons' army, or at least some of them, will believe us and be encouraged to desert themselves," George explained to the men. And they nodded their appreciative agreement and mumbled "ayes" when he added "It is better that they run away than us having to fight them and run the risk of getting ourselves hurt.

"Anyone from amongst the local people who is in the tavern will almost certainly mark us as archers even with our tunics turned and they know about the footpath and the horse farm," he said to the six men. "So when they ask why you are deserting, which I am sure they will in one way or another, you are always to say that you went up to the horse camp to see if there was any food or horses left that could be eaten, and that when you saw there were none you and your mates decided to use the footpath and come to Hatherleigh because it was the fastest way to get out of Cornwall.

"And when whoever you are talking to expresses their great surprise at hearing your story, which they also will almost certainly do, every man is to say that he left the Company because everyone in Cornwall is starving and there is a plague on the land—and that you did not want to wait until after the last of the horses were eaten to leave because by then it would be too late. That is our story and you must stick to it if we are to gull any of the barons and their men into turning back.

"Almost without a doubt the next questions will be where are you going and what do you intend to do now? When those questions are asked you are to tell your questioners that you and your mates heard about a noble who was loyal to the king and looking for men to serve as mercenaries in a war between the king and some barons who were pretending to form an army to fight the French.

So you are off to try to find him or someone like him to employ you as mercenaries.

"Then you are to say that you are happy that you will be out of Cornwall and on the winning side since you have been assured that this time all the rebel soldiers will lose their heads to the king's axe-man instead of just their captains. As you might imagine, that will also help encourage the barons who are loyal to the king, or fearful of him, to desert and take their men with them."

Sergeant Morrison and several of his men understood immediately what they were to say and why. Both he and his chosen man, a foot archer by the name of Roger Boggs, assured George that they would see to it that every one of their men would always say what they were supposed to say. Right then and there, because they had both understood the purpose of his plan and their part in it so quickly, George decided that both the sergeant and his chosen man would each be sewing on another stripe if they succeeded in holding the footpath for a reasonable amount of time.

******

Hatherleigh's *Red Ox* tavern had the familiar smell and appearance of a roadside public house. It was also larger than many despite its isolated location, probably as a result of having all the travellers passing in front of it who were coming to and from Exeter, Plymouth, and Cornwall.

The tavern's location was significant; it meant that most and perhaps all of the barons' army were likely to pass in front of it on their way to Devon and Cornwall. There was after all, no other way to get to them except by sea.

George walked into the *Red Ox* with himself and Sergeant Morrison and his men firmly determined that more of the barons' men would pass in front of the *Red Ox* whilst marching towards Cornwall than would ever pass it whilst travelling in the other direction after the fighting ended—and that many of the barons' men who were on the road would never live long enough to ever see the *Red Ox* in the first place. The not-so-minor problem, of course, was that destroying the barons' army or gulling some or all of the men in it to turn back was easier said than done. Their visit to the *Red Ox,* as George saw it and had explained it to Sergeant Morrison and his men in some detail, was just one of the many things that had to be accomplished to make that happen.

"God bless all here," George said brightly as he ducked his head to get through the door and led Sergeant Morrison and his men into the public room of the *Red Ox.* He had known that he and his men would find travellers in the public room because there were two horse-drawn wagons and four saddle horses and a mule tied to the hitching posts in front of the tavern in addition to any local drinkers who might be present at such an early hour. In addition, the shutters over the *Red Ox's* wall openings were open because of the warm weather and he had seen some of the men who were inside as he and his footpath defenders had walked up to the tavern's open front door.

Walking up to the *Red Ox* brought back old memories to George; its appearance on the outside had not changed a bit since his last visit some years earlier when he was a recently promoted sergeant and riding back from London with a string of newly acquired brood mares for the Company's horse farm. That was before he had gone east as a Sergeant Major and met the daughter of one of the Company's captains who would become his second wife.

George smiled and raised his hand in a friendly greeting to the people standing and sitting in the *Red Ox's* public room as every one of them turned to see who might be coming in to join them. There were eleven or twelve people in the room, all men including a couple of priests, and most of them nodded or waved their hands to acknowledge his friendly greeting, and then continued looking in his direction with a more than a little interest as George's men filed in behind him.

The alewife was the first to greet them out loud.

"A hoy to you good sirs and welcome to the *Red Ox*. This is the place to wet your throats if you are walking this hot day." ... "Archers down from the horse farm are you?" she added a moment later in response to the bows and quivers each man had slung over his back. Almost every man in the room leaned forward to hear his answer.

"Oh aye, mistress," George said. "That we are. We were just up there at the horse farm and what we saw was horrible, just horrible. We went up to the horse farm to see if we could find some food. We knew the horses had been taken off to be eaten because of the famine. But we went up there anyway because we thought there might be some grain for the horses that we could find and grind for bread. Unfortunately what we found was no horses and everyone either dead or dying. We did not wait to find out if it was starvation or from the plague because all the dead ones lying about was smelling most horrible. So we came down the path because it was the fastest way to get out of there.

The alewife's eyes widened, her mouth gaped open, and her face turned white.

"Dead you say; plague? Everyone at the horse farm is dead or dying?"

"Oh aye. And the horses have all been taken away to be eaten. The crops in Cornwall failed again this year, you know. Dead and dying people are everywhere. Me and the lads were lucky because we were stationed at Launceston Castle and could eat its siege supplies. But now even those are gone which is why we left. All we have are some coins and our weapons; do you have any food we can buy?"

The men who had been drinking and eating in the tavern when the archers entered were now on their feet and aghast. Several of them including one of the priests made the sign of the cross. Famine! Plague! It cannot be!

"Best to head toward the east and escape," suggested Sergeant Morrison helpfully as the archers settled themselves around a table next to a wall opening with its shutters thrown open. "That is where we are going."

Seeing the priests gave George an idea; and a few moments later Sergeant Morrison gave him another.

Chapter Eighteen

Sergeant Cooper's ride.

Sergeant Cooper and Archer Bill Atkins began riding at an easy pace down the narrow Oxford street and tried their best to look as though they were just passing through. They felt better about things now that they were finally on their horses and had their longbows strung and safely slung over their shoulders.

As you might imagine, both men had an urge to put their heels to their horses' ribs and gallop away to safety as fast as possible. But they did not because of all the people and wagons on the street in front of the stable; they could not ride faster than everybody else without attracting attention to themselves—and the last thing in the world they wanted to do was call attention to themselves and the direction they were heading. They had no idea who they had killed or if there were any searchers out looking for them. It might be early days for searchers to be out but they could not be sure.

At first they had had no plan other than to get away to the relative safety of the nearest open fields and pastures as quickly as possible. As soon as they were clear of Oxford's narrow streets they were confident they would be able to outrun any pursuers. But then, without a word being spoken between them, they both remembered that what they needed to do most of all was get back to Okehampton and warn the Company that the first of the barons' army was on the march.

Soon thereafter, and still without a word passing between them, they each realized that they had an immediate problem—Cornwall and Devon were to the west on the other side of the Thames and the Thames bridge was packed with the barons' army which might well leave guards posted there even after the army finished crossing the river.

They had only ridden to the eastern outskirts of Oxford when Sergeant Cooper said out loud what Bill had already been thinking—that they dare not risk using the Thames bridge for fear of being recognized by the barons' men and getting taken whilst they were on it.

"We cannot use the bridge, Bill. We might be recognized and trapped on it with no way to escape. So we will have to continue to ride east towards London on this side of the London road until we can safely cross over to the other side of the road and come back towards the river. It is the only way we can get back to warn the Company that some of the barons' army is already on the march. Do you agree?"

"There is no question about it, Sergeant. You are right about the bridge being too dangerous; we will have to go upstream from the bridge and swim our horses across if we are to get back in time to alert the Company."

What Bill really was thinking behind his eyes, but did not say to Sergeant Cooper and never would, was entirely different—"risking my arse to alert the Company be damned; getting safely back to my wife is what I want to do no matter how long it takes."

* * * * * *

The two archers rode out of Oxford toward London in the fields and pastures on the south side of the crowded London road. It did not take long because Oxford was so small. As they rode east through the fields and pastures, they tried to keep the road in sight off to their left. It was not hard to do, keep the road in sight that is. It was easy because the road as it entered the village was still packed with the wagons and men of the barons' army slowly moving westward towards the bridge over the Thames. But after a few minutes of riding through the countryside east of Oxford the two archers suddenly realized that the traffic on the road was back to normal. It was almost as if the barons' army had been a bad dream.

"Come on lad, it is time to ride for home and sound the alarm," said Sergeant Cooper as he turned his horse and began slowly riding toward the distant road. They were continuing to move slowly because Sergeant Cooper was determined to keep their horses as fresh as possible in case they had to make a run for it.

As they approached the road they saw a horse-drawn covered wagon on it without a left front wheel. The wheel had apparently been removed from the wagon in order to be replaced or repaired. The sides of the wagons linen cover were rolled up so as they got closer they were able to see that the bed of the wagon was filled with, among other things, a suit of armour, a jousting lance, and another broken wheel along with various sacks and some bedding.

A well-dressed man with an angry look on his face was standing next to the wagon watching the efforts of a couple of men to reinstall its wheel. They were farm workers from the looks them, almost certainly serfs or slaves. The well-dressed man was obviously not happy with the progress they were making, or so it looked from the way he was waving his hands about as they rode up to him. The idled wagon horse, a brown mare, was in the wagon's traces and worrying the ground in front of it for something to eat. There were two other horses tied to the rear of the wagon; a riding horse with a saddle on it and a great huge beast of a horse that would be ridden into battle by a knight who was wearing heavy armour.

"They look like stragglers who got left behind when their wagon broke," suggested Bill helpfully as they came nearer. An empty ox cart heading in the direction of London had just finished passing the broken wagon and people were working in the fields on either side of the road.

"Aye lad, so they be; so they be. They are our enemies, eh?"

A moment later, Sergeant Cooper, when he saw the armour and lance in the wagon, whispered a quiet order to Bill out of the corner of his mouth as he un-slung his bow from his shoulder and plucked an arrow from his quiver.

"Well lad, we might as well start here; we will do for the baron's man whoever his is and set his serfs and slaves free. We will take his lordship first; but not the horses. I have an idea that a couple of the horses and the armour might make good prizes. The wagon too for that matter."

The sergeant started to kick his horse into an amble to close on the wagon, but then he changed his mind and held out the reins of his remount to Bill who was riding next to him.

"Here. Hold my remount. This one is mine." He leaned over and handed the reins of his remount to Bill as he pulled his horse to a stop near the broken wagon. He could see into the wagon bed because the wagon was leaning over on to its wheel-less left front axle. The two men working on the wheel were obviously the angry man's serfs or slaves from the looks of their clothes and his attitude towards them.

"Hoy there. Broken down I see. Be you on your way to Cornwall?" The sergeant asked most friendly to the man who was once again angrily shouting at the two men who were beginning to try to put a new wheel on the left front of the wagon. It was obviously intended to replace the broken wheel that was on the ground next to the wagon.

"And who be you to be asking?" the angry man said with an arrogant snarl. He was clearly not in a good mood.

"We be the men who may help you fix your wheel and help your men put the new wheel on your wagon if you tell us why you are on the road and where you are bound. Who be you and where are you headed?"

The man drew himself up and looked down his nose at the two riders as arrogantly as could since he had to look up to where they were sitting on their horses.

"I am Sir William of Falmer, the nephew of John Fitzalan, the Earl of Sussex. My uncle is up ahead with the rest of our men. We are bound for Devon and Cornwall as part of an army to fight the French. Is that good enough for you?"

"Yes it is. But you gave the wrong answer," said Sergeant Cooper who promptly nocked the arrow he was holding in his hand and grunted as he leaned forward in his saddle and pushed it as hard as he could straight into Sir William's chest. The sergeant was a veteran horse archer and it took him barely a heartbeat to do it.

Sir William staggered backward a couple of steps and would have fallen if he had not been pushed up against the wagon and been able to steady himself. There was a look of absolute disbelief and astonishment on his face as he regarded the feather fletching of the arrow sticking out of his chest. Then he looked up at Sergeant Cooper, said "no" ... "no" ... "but" ... several times. He was obviously trying to say more but nothing else came out.

For a few moments the knight stood there leaning up against the wagon and looking incredulously at the two men on horseback. Then his panicked eyes tipped up as he went to sleep and he slid down to the ground on to his knees. When he went down on his knees they could see the bloody arrow sticking a foot or more out of his back. A moment later Sir William toppled over on to his side and his mouth moved as if he was chewing on something and trying to speak, but he was out of air and nothing came out. And then his legs trembled for a few moments and his dying was over.

"Get his purse and retrieve the arrow, Bill; retrieve the arrow. He may have some coins and we may need the arrow again."

Sergeant Cooper gave the order as he swung off his horse and wiped his brow. The two serfs were wide-eyed were still holding the wheel. It was newly repaired from the looks of it and men were absolutely terrified. Sergeant Cooper was surprised to find that he was out of breath and his hands shook as he began talking to the terrified and shaking men.

"Your lord is dead of trying to go foraging Cornwall and rising up against the king," the sergeant bellowed at the now-trembling men. You two and the horses and wagon and everything in it are prizes of war and now belong to me and my mate. As your new owner I am ordering you to take the horses and the wagon to London to the stable owned by the Company of Archers. It is near the road that runs along the river about a twenty minute walk beyond the city walls and the great fortress next to the city that is called The Tower.

"You will be able to find the stable if you stay on this road until you are on the other side of the Thames. Then turn off the road that runs along the river and stay on it until you get all the way past the city wall and the great fortress next to it called the Tower. When you get that far start asking the local folk where you can find the horse stable of the Company of Archers. You are to tell the stable's captain what happened here and that I said he is to find places for you if you wish to be free men instead of returning to Falmer."

Then he gave the two terrified men, who had dropped the wheel and were now down on their knees in front of him, a stern warning as he climbed back aboard his horse.

"I know you can be found at Falmer. So I will send men there to find you and kill you if you do not take the horses and the wagon and everything in it directly to the stable of the Company of Archers in London. I will also find you and kill you if you tell anyone except the captain of the stable about what happened here. Do you understand?"

Then he turned and looked over at Bill who was in the process of dismounting from his horse and put what he had done into perspective.

"One down and a lot more to go; a lot more to go."

******

The ease by which Sir William had been killed and his horses, wagon, and armour taken as prizes was not lost on either of the archers. They also had the coins from Sir William's purse and would split the prize money if Sir William's horses, weapons, and armour actually reached the Company's stable and were sold as prizes.

The coins they found in Sir William's purse and the very real possibility of prize money greatly excited the two men. That was because they knew that they alone would share the prize money because they were the only Company men in sight when the prizes were taken. Moreover, the horses and the armour and weapons in the wagon looked to be in good shape so that there would be a lot of prize coins for each of them *if* the wagon and the horses reached the Company's stable and were sold.

Bill quickly realized he would have more coins than he had ever had before in his life even though the prize coins would not be divided equally. According to the Company's rules on the distribution of prize money, which every man in the Company knew because it was so important, Sergeant Cooper would get four prize coins to each one of Bill's because of his higher rank. It would be the first prize money either of the two archers had ever received.

"Well, what do you think, Bill? We need to ride hard to get word to Okehampton as soon as possible about the Sussex column and the barons' early arrival, eh? The fastest way would be to ride on the road or along side of it. We could cross the river up from the bridge and ride back to the road. We would be alright if we go back on the road toward the front of the column where they do not know us. None of them has seen us on horses; they would think we were part of the army or, perhaps, travellers who are passing by. What do *you* think?"

Sergeant Cooper did not need to ask Bill his opinion, of course, but he did. They had somehow become mates and their relationship had changed because they had shared the danger of their narrow escape, earned prize money that they alone would share, and had fought together as a team, albeit a very small one, without letting each other down. It was something that would bind them together for the rest of their lives.

"Whatever you say, sergeant; whatever you say."

Bill said it with a big smile and deliberately repeated himself exactly as Sergeant Cooper often did. He did so without thinking because he was excited about the prospect of finally earning some prize money and because he somehow understood behind his eyes that their escape and fighting together had created a bond between him and Sergeant Cooper that would last for as long as they lived.

The sergeant recognized Bill's jest and smiled his appreciation at it. Yesterday he would have been outraged by the archer's familiarity; today they were mates who had fought together side by side and he was pleased because Bill agreed with him. It is often that way; differences in rank seem to dissolve and become less important when men fight together and share dangers.

A moment later Sergeant Cooper pulled his horse's head about and the two archers began riding into the farmland on the other side of the road. Both men were smiling as they rode and little wonder—they had more coins to spend, their horses were fresh, the sun was out, and their memories of their narrow escape had been pushed aside by their easy victory over Sir William and the prospect of prize money. It was a very fine day and they were happy to be alive.

Chapter Nineteen

On the road again.

Things were going well at the *Red Ox* until Sergeant Morrison tactfully brought up a problem I should have foreseen before I started talking about the plague and the horses being eaten because of a famine.

"Uh, Commander, do you think our story about what we found at the horse farm will hold up? What if we are seen leaving here and walking across the hay field to the entrance to the cart path so we can go back to it before it gets dark?"

"Damn. I did not think about that, Sergeant. You are right, of course. We will have to walk down the road a ways until the tavern is out of sight and then walk out to the tree line and back to the footpath. And we better start soon if we are going to spend enough time on the path." *Which is what you very gently just reminded me we need to do.*

What I did not know until a few days later was that almost at the same moment Sergeant Cooper and Archer Atkins were further down the road towards London and facing a somewhat similar need to circle back to avoid being seen.

******

We reached the footpath more than an hour or so after Sergeant Morrison's tactful suggestion that it was time to leave if we were to get back to the horse camp before the sun finished passing overhead. It took us that long because we did not walk directly from the *Red Ox* to the entrance to the path. We could not do that because the people in the tavern would have seen us and it would have raised questions as to the truth of our stories and warnings—we had, after all, claimed we had deserted and were fleeing *from* the horse camp.

What we did, instead, was walk down the road towards London until we were out of sight of the *Red Ox*. Once we could not be seen from the tavern we continued walking until we saw *both* that there were no workers in the fields who might inadvertently report us and the road was clear towards London so no travelers could see us who might stop at the tavern. Only then did we walk through a pasture full of sheep to the distant tree line and start walking back until we came to the entrance to the foot path.

Finding the entrance to the path was easy; walking back *up* the slippery narrow path to the horse farm was even more difficult than coming down it. The problem was that we all had to walk with our hoods up and our hands stuck through the openings on either the side of our tunics that allowed their wearers to put their hands inside their tunics to get warm.

It was not the need for warmth that caused us to walk in such a way, it was the bugs. We also wore our distinctive archers' knitted caps with their eye holes pulled down all the way over our faces so that the only openings were for our eyes. It kept us mostly safe from the bugs— and very much overly warm and constantly in danger of losing our balance and falling hard because we could not get our hands out from under our tunics in time to break our falls.

On the other hand, our efforts were not in vain despite our discomfort. We found and used our personal knives to mark not less than four possible ambush sites, two excellent locations for cutting down trees that would fall across the path to discourage its use, and a relatively un-buggy site for Sergeant Morrison and his men to use as a sleeping, cooking, and resting camp. They would, the sergeant promptly assured me, only use the camp site when there were a couple of sentries on duty further down the path toward Hatherleigh. *I was liking Morrison more and more.*

We finally reached the horse camp in the early minutes of darkness—and in a state of total exhaustion. It had been a long, hard day. Fortunately, Lieutenant Smith knew we would be returning and had a meal and a skin of ale waiting for us. After we finished eating and drinking I led my intrepid band of bug-bitten and muddy men to the camp's little "tavern" for some additional well-earned refreshments.

Sergeant Morrison and his men were still in the camp's little tavern and still drinking when I returned in the moonlight to a bed Lieutenant Smith had set up for me in an abandoned horse stall. But before I did I stood up in the little tavern and loudly announced a new policy—starting immediately anyone, Company or not, who used the path for any reason without Sergeant Morrison's permission would be hung from a tree at the beginning of the path. In other words, no one would be allowed to encourage an attack on the sergeant and his men by going down to Hatherleigh and letting the rabbit out of the bag about the Camp still having horses in it.

The next morning I awoke at dawn and was pleasantly surprised a few minutes later to find that Sergeant Morrison had already implemented the new policy of preventing the path from being used. He had done so by camping with his men at the entrance to the footpath such that anyone attempting to use the path would have to literally walk on them to get on to it. He intended, Sergeant Morrison told me a few minutes later when I walked over to talk with him, to immediately begin cutting the trees needed to block the path at its far end and to keep a couple of his men stationed to watch its entrance at all times. His men, he said, would serve in pairs with each pair of men having one of the stable boys assigned to them to carry their messages and bring them food and drink. I told him I approved. *And I certainly did.*

After my early morning talk with Sergeant Morrison I mounted my horse and rode back to Okehampton. As I rode I decided to put a file of archers and a dependable sergeant on the road between Okehampton and Hatherleigh so that no one would be able to reach Hatherleigh and report that there was no famine and plague in Cornwall. I also decided to implement another of Sergeant Morrison's suggestions.

****** *The London shipping post*

Captain Adams had ridden into London from Windsor and immediately dispatched a parchment to Commander Robertson via a Company galley with the news from the Company's priestly spy in the Nuncio's household. And then a few days later he had sent Sergeant Shand off to Okehampton with three of his post's archers and all the available horses he could acquire. He had also sent another follow-up message with Sergeant Shand in the off chance that his initial warning messages had not arrived. It was a verbal message; he had not scribed it in case Sergeant Shand was captured during his attempt to deliver the horses.

The Company's shipping post was quiet as a result of most of its men going off to assist in the horse delivery. The women and children were still there, of course, but

Captain Adams was the only man. That was because the archer with the broken wrist was still at the bonesetter's hovel and everyone else was at the Company's stable—a couple of elderly stable workers, and three boys who were allowed to live in one of the stalls in return for helping muck out the stalls and carry messages. The stable men and the boys did not have much to do since all of the useful horses were gone and the recruits who had been sheltering in its stalls with the horses had just been shipped off to Cornwall to begin their training.

Captain Adams, on the other hand, was busy all the time and, in fact, busier than he had ever been before. He rose before dawn every day to go to the markets to talk to the city's merchants and moneylenders and gather up whatever new information they might provide.

The merchants and moneylenders already knew about the barons' "Loyal Army" and soon realized what Captain Adams was doing and became quite helpful by passing on the latest information and rumours. Of course they were helpful; not only was the Company an important customer, but if there was one thing London's merchants and moneylenders did not like it was illiterate courtiers and land barons looking down their noses at them and arrogantly dismissing them. And, of course, the ever-increasing number of merchants and moneylenders who knew the captain was gathering information and sending it on to Cornwall meant that sooner or later one or more of the rebel barons would learn about what he was doing and take steps to stop him.

What did not change for Captain Adams was the periodic arrival at his shipping post of merchants with cargos to ship or receive and the buyers and redeemers of money orders. There was also the usual constant stream of people attempting to buy passages or inquire about their availability and cost. London's everyday life, in other words, was unchanged by the king's health, the barons' unrest, the missing prince, and the absence of a Pope. To the contrary, life in general did not change in any way for and people continued to appear at the shipping post in their usual numbers.

What did change was that Elspeth, the captain's wife, and the wives of the archers volunteered to try to take their men's place—which was sometimes not possible because none of the women knew how to scribe and sum. Fortunately, it was soon worked out that the women would do what they could when a customer arrived and then, when they were unable to fully meet a visitor's needs, they would ask him to return later in the day to talk to the captain.

Captain Adams, in turn, soon learned that he needed to return from making his inquiries and be available to sort things out at least two hours before the sun went down. Afterwards, when it got dark and things quieted down, he would light a candle and scribe a parchment with the latest news.

Early the next morning as soon as the sun rose, the most reliable of the hostlers would carry several copies of Captain Adam's latest report and some coins down the road along the Thames until he found a couple of captains who were about to sail southerly along the coast. They would be offered some of the Company's coins to deliver the parchments to Plymouth's Plympton Castle even if it meant calling in at Plymouth when they had no other reason to do so. It was a common practice and did not raise any eyebrows or cause any questions to be asked. If the past was any guide, there was a good chance that at least one of the parchments would be delivered.

Sometimes, of course, the hostler could not find anyone willing to carry the captain's messages and returned with the parchments to try again the next day. All in all, however, a constant stream of reports came in to Commander Robertson from London and many of them were important enough for the Commander to send on to George Courtenay in order to keep him informed.

It all came to an end on a Tuesday morning early in July when there was a great pounding on the door of the shipping post. Elspeth looked through the little peephole that had been drilled in it and saw a wagon and a band of sword-carrying men wearing livery. She quickly motioned to send the post's women and children hurrying up the ladder to the safety of the floor above the post's reception room and warehouse. The eyes of the women were wide with fear and uncertainty as they climbed the ladder and carried their smaller children up with them. The two would-be pilgrims who had come to buy passages to the Holy Land and money orders so they would for sure have coins to spend both when they got there and later when they returned to London just stood in the little entry room and looked confused.

"The post is closed. All the post's men are away. What do you want?" Elspeth shouted at whoever was banging on the double-barred door and trying to open it.

******

Sergeant Cooper and Archer Atkins rode north on the road that ran along the eastern side of the Thames until they came to an isolated stretch of the river. It was isolated only in the sense that they could see nothing on the other side of the river except periodic fishermen, the inevitable camps of homeless people and travelers, the normal traffic of barges and small boats going up and down on the river and people and wagons on the road that ran along the other side of it. They could not see the Oxford Bridge but believed they were a good four or five miles upstream from it.

There was, or so it seemed to them, no need to ride further up the river. This was, they told each other with a false sense of certainty, as good a place as any to swim across to the other side. So they dismounted and un-slung their longbows and quivers from their shoulders, lashed them alongside the other weapons being carried by their remounts, and prepared to swim their horses across the river. Before they walked their horses slowly into the river, however, they each checked to make sure his saddle was tied tight to his horse and that his extra quivers and his sword and shield were securely lashed to his remount.

Of course they dismounted and checked to make sure everything was properly stowed and their saddles cinched tight to their horses before they re-boarded them and walked them into the water; swimming across a river with two horses would not be the easiest thing in the world for them to do since neither of them knew how to swim. It meant they would have to tie themselves to their horses and then hold on for dear life and let the horses do the swimming. As veteran horse archers they had both swum horses across rivers a number of times before, especially Sergeant Cooper. The Thames, on the other hand, was by far the widest river either of them had ever attempted.

Sergeant Cooper was particularly anxious that his fear not show such that he talked too much and gave unnecessary orders.

"One more turn around the saddle should do it to keep your wrist tight up against your saddle, one more turn, Bill. Now wrap your reins around your wrist many times and hold them tightly so your reins cannot come loose or slip off your arm when you slide off, as you will, over the back of your saddle."

Sergeant Cooper said it loudly to Bill, but he was actually talking to himself. And no wonder as he admitted to Bill a few hours later—he had once almost drowned when he was a boy and fell into a pond. As a result, he was terribly afraid every time he had to swim a horse across a stream or river.

When they were ready they looked at each other and nodded. Then they each took a deep breath, shook his head in resignation, and slowly rode their horses into the water with the sergeant leading the way.

It seemed to take them forever to get across the river because horses do not swim very fast, or very well for that matter, especially when they have riders hanging off to one side because one of their wrists is tightly tied to the horse's saddle. Indeed, it was all the two men could do to keep their heads from only periodically going under the water like a hungry duck, particularly when the horses they were leading swam far enough apart so their riders were stretched out between the two horses.

Fortunately, and sometimes spitting our water after their heads went under, they both finally made it across even though the arse ends of their horses almost immediately sank so deep into the water that they floated free of their saddles and ended up being pulled along by their horses as they instinctively swam for the distant shore.

Worse, although they did not understand it until they reached the other side, Bill slipped off his saddle on his horse's downstream side and Sergeant Cooper on the upstream side of his. Bill's weight and the periodic pulling of the remount swimming behind them seemed to turn Bill's horse's head slightly downstream and the sergeant's upstream such that the two men and their horses began drifting further and further apart as the river's current carried them downstream and ever closer to the Oxford bridge.

In the end, both of the archers made it across the Thames because their horses made it across and, therefore, so did their riders because each of the men had a wrist that had been tightly lashed to his horse's saddle. Being properly lashed to the saddle meant that not only would he not sink into the river and drown unless the saddle came loose and slid under the horse, it also meant he could hold himself high enough out of the water to breath whilst holding tightly to the reins of the remount horse he was leading with his other hand.

That the two horse archers and the horses they were leading had all gotten across the Thames safely was the good news. The bad news was that they came ashore more than half a mile apart and that they reached other side much further down the river from where they had hoped to come ashore. And when they did finally struggle up on to the riverbank every inch of their bodies and everything else including their bowstrings and saddles were hopelessly wet and they were totally exhausted. Even so, and still dripping water, both men were greatly relieved and smiling with satisfaction as they unwrapped their wrists and untangled themselves, and hurriedly checked to see if their weapons and everything else their horses had been carrying had come untied and been lost in the river.

The river's current had caused the men to drift down the river far further than they expected. They realized that it was happening almost immediately. For a while Bill actually began worrying that he might come ashore near the Oxford Bridge and be recognized by some of Sussex men. Additionally, instead of coming ashore in the isolated area across from where they entered the river, they had come ashore downstream on either side a small village that was more than a mile closer to Oxford from where they had entered the river.

Sergeant Cooper's horse had swum more directly for the other side of the Thames such that he came ashore first. As a result he had already re-mounted and was riding down the river road when Bill staggered out of the river with his horses even further downstream. The two men were more than a little pleased at seeing each other safe and briefly thought about celebrating the fact that they had not drowned at the village's nearby riverfront tavern. Indeed, the sergeant had ridden right past the tavern's open front door as he rode down the river road to rejoin Bill.

"But what if some of the barons' men ride up while we are inside?" Bill asked and, in so doing, killed the idea.

"Aye, you are right, Bill, you are right. They are on both sides of the river, eh? We would be trapped. Besides we need to get going if we are to ever get back to Okehampton. Are any of your bowstrings usable?"

******

The two horse archers' tunics and bowstrings were quickly dried by the summer's warmth. It was a comfortable ride and their ordeal at the river and their chase through Oxford's streets and their killing of the Sussex lord all too soon became distant memories. It was the taking of the armour and horses and how they might spend the prize coins that they would receive that they thought about and talked about as they rode west across the fields and pastures along the Thames.

The two men kept riding toward the west until the sun started to go down. It was slow going because of their many detours around the periodic stone and wooden fences and hedgerows they encountered. But they were moving faster than the column even so and most of the time they were able to keep the slowly moving army of the Sussex earl in sight on the road to their left.

"Look Bill," the sergeant said as he squinted into the setting sun and pointed. "That looks like the front of the column up there ahead of us. Am I right?"

"Oh aye, that you are sergeant, that you are; it is the front of them for sure."

An hour or so later the two archers stopped for the night. They were tired but somehow could not sleep. So they spent the first couple of hours sitting around their little cooking fire talking about the difficulty they had had riding overland as opposed to riding on the road. It had taken them more time than usual to get their fire going, perhaps because the river water in the leather pouches that held each man's metal striker and fire stone had kept them wet. It was when the sergeant was finally blowing on the spark that would get their fire going that Bill asked a question that led to a change in their plans and almost caused the Company to lose its first battle with the barons' men.

"I wager we could ride over there and join the column in the morning and no one would even know who we be, eh Sergeant? They have never seen us on our horses or wearing our tunics or carrying our bows, have they? They would not be expecting us, would they? Just think of the damage we could do with our longbows as we rode past them and kept on going."

Sergeant Cooper thought for a bit, and then he smiled.

"Aye lad, you are right about that. It would learn them tossers a big lesson so it would; learn them a big lesson for sure." *And it would likely please Red now that the fighting has started. I might even get another stripe.* Besides, this is not the barons' main force so the need for us to hurry in with a report about it is not so great. *I hope.*

The two men just looked at each other until Bill finally spoke.

"I like the idea, sergeant; but how can we do it? We have no horse holders and we cannot abandon our remounts."

"Well, you could be the horse holder and wait for me in front of the column until I come up to you," the sergeant suggested.

The sergeant thought about it some more, and then added, "I would be fine if I started in the middle of the column and rode toward the front. They would not be expecting me if I came from behind them and gave them some arrows as I came past. You could wait for me up ahead of them with my remount. It would work, by God, it would work!"

"No, that is not even close to being good enough," Archer Bill Atkins told Sergeant Cooper most emphatically. "What if your horse stumbles or someone gets lucky with an arrow or sword? There would be no one around to pick you up and ride off with you. How would I explain what happened to Red if I left you behind and you were taken, eh?"

Sergeant Cooper just grunted. After a minute or so of riding silently, Bill made a suggestion.

"We could take our remounts up the road past the front of the column and hobble them out of sight somewhere where no one was likely to stumble upon them. Then we could ride back together and wait until some of the column gets past us. When enough of them buggers got past us we could ride back up the road toward our remounts and push out arrows as we rode past them—and keep going until we reach our remounts. If one of our horses goes down the other of us could pick him up just like we do in practice. Why we might even be able to get away with a horse or two to take with us as prizes, eh?"

The sergeant was clearly skeptical. He had suggested it but he was increasing sorry that he had done so. *What was I thinking?* So he brought up the best argument he could think of for the two men sticking to their original plan.

"We are supposed to ride hard to Okehampton to sound the alarm so Red has as much time as possible to get our lads out into their positions and ready to fight."

But the archer was not to be denied.

"All true, Sergeant, all true. But that lot over there on the road is only the beginning, not the barons' main force at all, is it? Besides, if we push arrows into a few of their wagon horses it would likely slow the whole column down much more than any time we would lose in sounding the alarm, eh? That would give Red even *more* time to get ready the lads ready than if we ride to Okehampton straightaway. He would want us to do that and we can do it."

It was a good argument and Sergeant Cooper thought about it for some time. Then he slowly nodded his agreement.

"Aye, it would do that. It would do that."

It could be argued that the two archers' greed for recognition and more prize coins caused them to temporarily forget that they were supposed to carry word to Okehampton as fast as possible. Their defenders would say that they were trying to delay the Sussex men so the Company would have even more time to get ready to fight them. But the real reason for their decision, as every veteran knows, was that they had become mates and depended on each other—and each of them was secretly afraid that the other would think poorly of him if he did not step forward. Soldiers are like that.

Chapter Twenty

Before the storm

Sergeant Cooper and Archer Atkins held their horses to a slow but steady ground-eating amble for almost an hour after they regained the road ahead of the Sussex Column. They kept it up until they decided it would take the front of the slow-moving enemy column a good four hours or more to reach them. Sergeant Cooper then led them off the road and into a small stand of trees. It was out of sight of the nearest roadside village and too far off the road to be a place where a traveler might go to camp for the night. The sun was a couple of hours past high noon.

The horses were immediately hobbled and given grain and water. Then all of the men's arrow quivers were draped across the necks of the two horses they would be riding during their attack and lashed into place and the cinches of the saddles on their remounts were checked to make sure they could be instantly tightened and the remount horses quickly boarded if the two archers were being hotly pursued. Then in the final minutes while their horses were still resting to get them back to their peak strength Sergeant Cooper began to have second thoughts.

"Do you really think that our attacking the Earl of Sussex's men will slow them down so much that it will give the Company more time to prepare for them than if we just ride on from here and report that they are coming?" The sergeant was clearly uncertain; it was the same question he had asked several times previously.

"Oh aye, I do sergeant, I do. At least an additional day or two I would think." As he said it Bill realized he was beginning to repeat himself more and more like the sergeant. "If we kill a few of their men and wagon horses they will have to spend time burying and barbering the men and reloading their wagons and deciding what to leave behind."

Sergeant Cooper just grunted. And then he began pacing about. He was clearly worried about making the wrong decision. Finally he decided. Glory and the possibility of a promotion had won.

"Well lad, it is time to mount up if we are going to go slowly at first in order to reach them with horses that are fresh. Time to mount up."

Bill smiled at him and nodded. The sergeant thought Bill was smiling because the sergeant had been slow to make up his mind to do the right thing by attacking the column. He was wrong. Bill was smiling and nodding to encourage the sergeant because the sergeant had become a good mate who had become so nervous that he was repeating himself.

The loud knocking on the post's now-always-barred door to the street stopped when Elspeth, the Captain's wife, asked "who is it and what do you want?" It had been a hard and demanding knock; not the "friendly" knock of a merchant or potential passenger or someone with a money order to redeem. She looked through the tiny little hole that had been carefully drilled in the door and she could see half a dozen armed men and a horse-drawn wagon that was halted on the street behind them. They did not look friendly.

"We want to talk to whoever lives here. Let us in," someone shouted from the other side of the closed door.

"Just a minute," Elspeth said without moving to open the heavy triple-barred door. "I will go get my husband. He is out in the alley relieving himself. The shipping post of the Company of Archers has moved to the other side of the market if that is who you are looking for. Are you sure you have the right place? This is the home of Alan, the king's coach maker."

Richard had explained that there might be danger and what to do and say if any dangerous-looking men appeared at the door. King Henry did not have a coach maker, of course, at least not one that she knew about, but Richard had explained to her that claiming that whoever was trying to get in had come to the door of a king's man might cause them to go away.

With her attempt to gull them still hanging in the air, she fled into the meeting room beyond the little entrance room into which the street door opened. Once inside she began lifting its two sturdy wooden bars into place to seal the meeting room off from the entrance hall. As she did she yelled at one of the post's wives coming into the meeting room with a child in her arms to "get to the back and tell everyone to climb the ladder and wait in the captain's room up above. Make sure my girl goes up too; tell her I will be there shortly." ... "Hurry Marie, run. We need to get everyone to safety."

As soon as the meeting room door's two bars were in place she hurried across the room and entered the much larger room that served as the shipping post's warehouse and the living quarters of all of its archers and their families except the family of the post captain; he and Elspeth and their daughter lived in one of the two rooms that were *above* the warehouse.

The women and children of the archers assigned to help Elspeth's husband man the post had heard the noise and commotion and listened to the conversation. They had responded to it by getting on their feet and gaping at her in confused surprise. Despite her order not one of the women had started up the ladder to the room above the warehouse. They were confused and uncertain.

"Up the ladder, all of you; hurry damn you!" ... "Do as you are told and take the children!" she screamed at them over her shoulder as she began putting the bars in place to double seal the heavy door between the warehouse and the meeting room. The wives finally began moving towards the ladder with Marie, the new wife of the post's youngest archer, going first and faster than the others.

"Light the candle lantern when you get up there, Marie. Hurry girl. We are going to need it. The fire-starters are in the pouch next to it. Hurry lass."

Elspeth began grabbing the women and children and pushing them towards to the ladder. Finally they understood what she wanted and began climbing it as fast as they could, which was not very fast because of the children several of them were carrying or trying to drag up the ladder with them.

The captain's wife continued to push the women and their children towards the ladder until the only one left was the young cow-like wife of one of the archers. She had an infant in her arms and seemed to be totally confused. She was standing in the room and looking about with wild eyes.

Elspeth did not hesitate. She gave the young woman a hard slap on the side of her face and then grabbed her and pushed her to the foot of the ladder. "Climb the ladder damn you, Molly; climb if you want to save your baby." The wild-eyed young woman suddenly turned docile and began climbing with Elspeth right behind her and periodically pushing on her arse and shouting at her to hurry.

It was slow going because of Molly's infant, but the ceiling was not high and someone reached down through the opening in the floor and helped by taking the infant from the woman's arms, and then helped the young woman climb off the ladder after she got through the opening. Elspeth came up the ladder right behind her. She could hear pounding and shouts from the street in front of the post, and then there was a great crashing noise and, moments later, the sound of voices in the post's little entry hall.

"Pull it up," she shouted to the wide-eyed women who were standing about in the room at the top of the ladder. As she did her daughter rushed to her and tried to hold on to her skirts. She pushed her away and grabbed the end of the ladder sticking up into the room.

"Help me pull it up," she shouted to the women were standing around her with confused looks on their faces. "Hurry." … "Good." … "Good." … "Yes, all the way up" … "Now put the trapdoor down."

Elspeth put the trapdoor down and barred it herself as the increasingly confused and hesitant women and their children watched. Light was flooding into room because the wooden shutters on the narrow wall openings on three sides of the room were all open. She could see the women and children in the room clearly including her daughter. And what she saw was Marie tending to one of the other women's children and that the candle lantern had not been lit. *The damn fool.* She angrily pushed the once-again grabbing hands of her own daughter aside and ran to the lantern.

Below them the increasingly terrified women and children could hear more shouts and banging. A moment later they heard the faint sound of great blows beginning to fall on the door between the little entry hall and the larger meeting room behind it. The women had never heard such a sound before but somehow they all knew exactly what was happening. Several of the shaken women and confused children started crying and one of the babies began screaming hysterically.

Moments later the captain's wife was desperately trying to light the candle lantern by making sparks by hitting the metal striker she had pulled from the fire starter pouch against the fire rock.

"Marie, put down the child and light this lantern," the captain's wife ordered with a shout. "And this time do as I tell you. We must light this lantern. Hurry damn you."

"Quickly," Elspeth shouted to the other women in the room as she jumped to her feet and thrust the fire-starting stone and the striking iron into Marie's hands. "The rest of you are to go into the coin room."

She did not wait for the wives to respond. She grabbed one by the arm and pushed her toward the door that opened into the dark coin room. The others began to follow.

Visibility in the coin room was very low because the only light in it came through the open door into her family's living room. That was because the room had no wall openings to let in light. There were none because it was where the post's chests of coins and flower paste were kept. So the only way robbers could get to into the room was to come up the ladder and move through the room of the post's captain family and enter it through its only door.

What the Elspeth knew, and the other women did not, was that the coin room also had a trap door in its floor. It was next to the room's far wall and opened down into the secret little room that was beyond and below the false far wall of the warehouse. It was down there where the entrance to the post's escape tunnel began. Elspeth knew all about the escape tunnel. It was where, a few days earlier, she had helped her husband take the post's chests of coins and flower paste. It had been a long and exhausting task and she knew the chests would have to be crawled over if anyone was to use the tunnel to escape— but they would certainly do it if that is what it took to save themselves.

The captain's wife did not wait for the other women to come to their senses and start moving. She rushed into the coin room ahead of them. In the dim light provided by the open door she pushed aside the empty crate, reached three of the fingers of her right hand into what appeared to be a crack in the wooden floor, and lifted the trap door.

"In here," she shouted as she rushed back to the women and children who were still not coming through the door into the darkness. "Everyone get in here. Hurry damn you," the captain's wife shouted. They were surprised and taken aback; she had never cursed at them before.

This time they got the message. Some of the women began moving even though the howling children that were trying to hold on to their skirts at the same time tended to slow things down.   They could all hear the muffled shouting and banging that was going on somewhere below them. The raiders were had broken into the post's entry room and were now trying to break through the door to get into the meeting room that lay beyond it.

A moment later Elspeth rushed back into the room where she lived with her family and began pushing everyone who was still there into the dimly lit coin room. The fine wood shavings the much-chastened Marie had been desperately blowing on were beginning to give off smoke. A minute or so later one of the shavings burst into flame and Marie was able to use the end of it to light the candle lantern. As soon as she did she hurried into the coin room and handed the lantern to Elspeth. "I am sorry," she whispered.

****** *Sergeant Cooper and Archer Atkins*

The two men rode their horses back to the road at a leisurely walk in order to keep them as rested and ready as possible. When they reached the road they began walking their horses towards London and the on-coming army of the Earl of Sussex. All of their arrows were in the quivers that were slung over their horses' backs in front of them. Their unstrung longbows were also slung over their shoulders and they were still wearing their workmen's clothes.

They had considered changing out of their working man's clothes and into their distinctive Company tunics, but after talking about it for some time they had decided to continue leaving their archer tunics rolled up and in one of the sacks carried by their remounts along with their shields, fire-starter pouches, and food sacks. They still might, after all, want to continue to pretend *not* to be archers. Besides, the rolled up tunics made good pillows for their heads at night and could be used to cover their hands and faces at night to keep the bugs away.

The two archers' swords were in their sheaths and hanging from their leather belts as they rode. Their shields and supplies and everything else were carefully packed on their hidden and still-hobbled remounts such that all they needed to do before they boarded their remounts was snatch off their hobbles and quickly tighten their saddle cinches. It would take them about five or six heartbeats to do so and then begin galloping away to safety. They had each made fast horse changes so many times previously in practice, and Sergeant Cooper several times for real, that neither man would even have to think about what he was doing whilst he was doing it.

They rode their horses at a leisurely walk in order to keep them as fresh as possible. About an hour after they started walking their horses back down the road toward London they finally saw the front of the Sussex army coming toward them on the road. They knew the Sussex column was getting close even before they saw it because they had met fewer and fewer travellers coming towards them, only those who had recently gotten on the road ahead of the on-coming army of the Earl of Sussex.

On the other hand, and despite the fact that their horses were only walking, they had constantly overtaken a number of even-slower moving pilgrims, farm-workers, and miscellaneous other people on foot along with a couple of oxen-pulled hay wains and a mule-pulled merchant wagon. They were all on the road and travelling in the same direction as the archers. The usual greetings and nods of travellers were exchanged and everyone kept going. It was clear from the greetings that were exchanged that none of the people they met or overtook were aware that the Earl of Sussex's army was on the road and marching westward towards them.

The relatively normal behaviour of the people on the road lasted until the two archers saw the first signs of the on-coming army in the distance. As they did they could see the travellers ahead of them on the road begin to move off the road to let the soldiers pass. And more than a few of the travellers moved well off the road, apparently because of their fear that the soldiers might be hostile or hungry or, and much more likely, would rob them if they had a chance.

A few minutes later the two archers themselves moved off the road and out into a pasture to the north. It was full of sheep with a young boy and a dog watching over them. The boy was standing and staring at the on-coming column.

Everyone else on the road was doing the exactly the same thing as the archers so that their moving off the road attracted absolutely no attention. The lack of attention paid to them was not surprising; all eyes were on the approaching army and wondering who it might be and what it meant. Where the two archers differed from the other people on the road was that they knew it was the Earl of Sussex's army coming toward them. They also differed in that they did not stop and wait for the earl's soldiers to pass; instead they kept moving slowly eastward through the fields and pastures next to the road whilst the Sussex army at the same time was on the road moving slowly westward away from London.

About thirty minutes later, when it was about two hours before sun went down, what appeared to be the end of the Sussex column finally came into sight in the distance. At that point Sergeant Cooper decided to stop so they could dismount and make any last minute adjustments in their equipment and plans.

The two archers dismounted and pissed as they stood by their horses without a word being spoken. After they shook their dingles each man strung his longbow and fussed with his quivers to make sure they were slung correctly in front of his saddle and properly lashed to it so they would not slide off if the horse suddenly stopped or turned. When they finished getting ready they each of them took several swigs from his water flask and once again checked the tightness of his saddle cinches and made a few last minute adjustments to the placement of his quivers. Finally they stood next to their horses and looked at each other. The sergeant spoke first.

"It is time to get on with it, Bill; time to get on with it," he said as he gave his horse a friendly pat on its shoulder and climbed aboard. Bill did almost exactly the same thing a few seconds later.

"Our horses are in good shape," Sergeant Cooper said as he looked over at Bill. He said it more to reassure himself than anyone else. And when Bill nodded and said "Aye," the sergeant pulled his horse's head around to point him at the road, and then very gently nudged his ribs to get him moving. They began by walking their horses side by side across the pasture toward the distant column.

"Men on horseback are the best for us to take out so they cannot chase after us," the sergeant said for at least the third or fourth time. Bill just nodded and said "Aye sergeant you are right about that." He had a great feeling a sense of relief now that the action was about to begin.

"We will ride on the same side of the column so we can pick each other up and ride off if one of our horses goes down," Sergeant Cooper said as they got closer, also for the third or fourth time. He was obviously getting more and more anxious about what they were going to do. Bill was just the opposite and it surprised him; he was anxious to get started.

Both of the archers had been looking for men on horseback as they rode towards the column. They would be the most dangerous of all the men in the column, particularly if they were carrying their weapons.   As they got closer they could see that there were a few individual riders strung out all along the column, but none of them appeared to be carrying weapons. Most of the men in the column were either walking or riding on a wagon. The walkers were almost certainly not carrying their weapons.

"That lot over there to the left looks like a good place to start," said Sergeant Cooper as he increased his horse to a trot and led them on a course that would intercept a group of four men riding together in the rear half of the column. At least one of them appeared to be carrying a sheathed sword. "Best to take them four toffs out first, aye lad? No sense leaving them aboard their horses to chase us, eh?"

The four men pulled their horses to a stop when they saw the archers coming across the pasture and it became evident that the two archers were riding directly toward them. The arrival of two riders who were obviously coming to speak with them was something new so far as they were concerned. It broke up a hot and boring day on the march and perhaps the approaching riders knew something interesting.

As the two archers rode up to the now-waiting riders they could see that they were well-dressed and at least two of them were wearing sheathed swords. Their horses looked quite useful but, of course, they could not be sure. In any event, if everything went as the archers planned these men in particular would not be able to chase after them and it was much too early in their attack to be trying to make off with their horses as prizes.

It did not seem to at all bother the four waiting men that stopping where they had been riding in the middle of the road also halted the forward progress of everyone who was marching behind them. They were apparently important enough not to worry about it; knights or nobles for sure. They just sat on their horses and watched with a great deal of curiosity as the two archers rode peacefully up to them. Also watching them approach with great interest was almost everyone walking and riding nearby in the now-stopped column. The archers' arrival was apparently one of the more interesting events of the warm and boring day.

Chapter Twenty-one

August second, 1271.

The four riders who were waiting for the archers to ride up to them were all wearing livery on their tunics. Fortunately, it not appear to be the same livery as the livery of the men who had chased the two men out of Oxford and died for their troubles. None of the four was wearing armour or a tunic with the cross of a crusader. But two of them were wearing sheathed swords on their belts. It was a warm summer day and they were obviously not expecting trouble. One of them began busily fanning his face with a straw hat as he waited.

"Hoy lads," said Sergeant Cooper cheerfully as he raised his hand in greeting as they trotted up holding their longbows to the side of their horses. "We are couriers bringing a message from the Earl of Surrey to the Earl of Sussex. Who might you be and do you know where we might find him?"

The inquiry did not have the effect it might; it made the four men suspicious.

"How can that be?" one of them asked as his horse pawed the ground only a few feet away from the horses of the archers. "The old earl died last year and his heir is but a boy."

"I do not know, Sir Knight. That is what we were told to say. We are just couriers with a message for the Earl of Sussex."

"Well, what is the message and who gave it to you? You can tell us. We are some of his lordship's knights and will be sure to deliver it to him."

The man who claimed to one of the earl's knights spoke to the archers rather arrogantly as knights usually did when they spoke to men whom they considered to be their inferiors.

Sergeant Cooper's response was to lift his bow from where he had been holding it along the far side of his horse—and in one smooth motion nock the arrow he was holding and push it deep into the chest of a man who was sitting on his horse a few feet away from the man who had demanded the message. The sergeant's first target, by a last minute arrangement with Bill spoken out of the side of their mouths as they rode up to the waiting men, was the left-most of the four men. He lifted his bow and pushed out the arrow so quickly and so unexpectedly that none of the four had a chance to react.

Less than half a heartbeat later Bill did the same for the man who was farthest to the right. The archers initial positioning of their horses and their targeting was according to a previous arrangement to avoid both of them taking the same man when the fighting began: Sergeant Cooper would establish his position and start with rider most to the left and work to his right; Archer Atkins would position his horse on the sergeant's and start with the man on his right and work to his left. Assigning targets in advance whenever possible was part of the Company's basic training to reduce the chance that multiple archers would target the same man charging at them and let the others get through to hurt someone.

Instant confusion and chaos was caused by the totally unexpected and virtually simultaneous attack by the two archers. The people in the column who had been watching the meeting shouted in surprise and began pointing, and the two surviving riders instinctively kicked their horses in the ribs, jerked on their reins, and twisted their bodies away before either of the archers could get his next arrow nocked and on its way.

The horses of the two survivors began moving almost instantly, but that was not enough to save their riders. Sergeant Coopers was able to hit one of the remaining riders in the back of his shoulder and Archer Atkins got the fourth rider out of the fight by putting his second arrow deep into his horse's hindquarters—which was a bit embarrassing because he had been aiming at the middle of the man's back.

Neither of the two archers waited to see the results of their surprise attack. They kicked their horses in the ribs, shouted "Hiya," and briefly used their reins to pull their horse's heads around such that their horses immediately began ambling along on the north side of the road in the direction the column had been marching. Once their horses were properly underway each of the archers dropped his reins and nocked another arrow.

Archer Atkins initially rode in the lead and held his horse to a steady amble, with Sergeant Cooper following close behind. They did not look back but behind them they could hear angry shouts. The next arrow came from Atkins a few seconds later as his horse ambled past a horse-drawn wagon that had been on the other side of the meeting. It had continued moving when the tail-end of the column was stopped. He put an arrow deep into the side of the wagon's horse which responded with a scream and a desperate lunge to the left which pulled the wagon off the road and overturned it. Sergeant Cooper put his third arrow into the leg of rider on a black horse a few moments later. It went part of the way through his leg and into the side of his horse which promptly bolted and threw him to the ground most painfully as it did.

Picking targets and continuing to ride as their horses ambled along the side of the column turned out to be a very good decision by Sergeant Cooper. The walkers and the people in the wagons they reached were almost always looking forward as they walked and rode. They inevitably turned around when they heard the shouts and screams coming from behind them, but then did not have time to do much more than watch as the two archers came riding past them and continued on towards the front of the column. They did so whilst pushing out their arrows as fast as they could.

Unfortunately, at least for some of the men in the column, they did not understand what was happening and the danger they and their horses were in until it was too late to take cover or try to fight back. Others were more fortunate in that the archers rode past them and left them unharmed because they were in the process of nocking another arrow or were focussed on what they considered to be a better target.

Sergeant Cooper and Archer Atkins were too busy riding and pushing out arrows to keep any kind of count on the damage they were doing. Everything was a great exciting and noisy blur with everyone watching them with a dumbfounded look on their faces as the archers rode past them—and then after the archers passed they inevitably began running around in every direction like chickens did after they lost their heads. At some point Sergeant Cooper pulled ahead of Bill and took the lead.

Periodically during their arrow-pushing ride up the road the two archers had to seize their reins to guide their horses out into a field adjacent to the road or around a wagon or a group of people who had come off the road for one reason or another. Other times they had to thread their way through the people of the convoy who were innocently going to or from the field next to the road for a moment's relief or to get a drink of water from a pond or stream near the road.

The two archer's horses were constantly moving along the column at a fast amble and any pursuers they may have attracted were still behind them. That it would take time for a pursuit to begin was understandable and the two archers were counting on it; by the time a potential pursuer realized what was happening and was able to get his hands on his weapons and mount his horse the two archers would already be far ahead on their constantly-moving horses. That, at least, was the plan.

On the other hand, there came to be more and more of them, pursuers that is, and their horses were inevitably galloping whereas the archers' horses were merely ambling to provide the smoothest possible arrow-pushing platform for the two archers, and also to save the horses' strength for the serious pursuit that was soon or later sure to occur. Indeed, it was only a matter of time before the first of the pursuers would catch up to them and the archers would either have to turn around in their saddles and shoot him down or break off their attack, kick their horses into a gallop, and make a run for safety. What they would do would depend on the situation.

Everything had gone well until each of the archers was well into his third quiver of arrows. Then it happened. A quick-thinking and totally non-descript man from a village levy caused a disaster. He had been walking with his spear for some reason and had spun around when heard the cries and sounds of confusion behind him. As a result, he had time to step out from behind a wagon and push his spear into Sergeant Cooper's horse as he came riding past. Sergeant Cooper had just pushed out an arrow was just reaching for another when he saw the man come out from behind a wagon and lunge at his horse with his spear. It happened so fast that Sergeant Cooper did not have time to even try to swerve out of the away.

The force of the sergeant's moving horse drove the tip of the spear deep into his fast-moving horse. At the same time the butt of the spear slammed into the man holding it so hard that he went over backwards, bounced off the side of a wagon, and went down on his back. Sergeant Cooper did somewhat the same. He went flying out of his saddle and landed on his back as the force of the spear pushed his horse over into the ditch next to the road—and then the horse landed on top of the fallen sergeant and began thrashing about and screaming in pain as it desperately tried to get to its feet.

Sergeant Cooper felt the heavy weight of the struggling and screaming horse as it rolled over him and distinctly heard the sharp cracking sound of bones breaking. He could hear faraway shouts and felt nothing. Then everything faded away.

Archer Atkins had been riding eight or nine horse lengths behind Sergeant Cooper. He had just pushed an arrow into the side of a horse in a wagon's traces and was reaching for another arrow when he saw the sergeant's horse go down and turn a somersault. Then he watched in growing horror as the tumbling horse landed on top of the sergeant and rolled over him in the ditch that ran alongside that section of the road.

Atkins instantly grabbed his reins and jerked them hard in order to stop his horse so he could turn back and begin a rescue. He actually rode about twenty feet past the fallen sergeant before he was able to pull his horse to a stop and get it turned around. Even as he began turning back he could see that the terribly wounded horse was still on top of the sergeant. It was on its back screaming and struggling desperately to get back on its feet despite a long spear sticking out of its side and a leg that was obviously broken. One look at the twisted and broken body of his mate once the horse struggled clear of him and he immediately knew that Sergeant Cooper was gone.

Bill was starting to dismount to do what he could to help when he saw the first of the pursuers coming up at a fast gallop from the rear of the column with a sword in his hand and at least half a dozen other riders trailing out behind him. The wide-eyed and shouting people nearby on the road were also moving toward the scene of the catastrophe. It was, as the sergeant had always been fond of saying, time to go. He had no choice if he was to have any chance of living long enough to report what he and Sergeant Cooper had seen and done.

Archer Atkins' main problem was that the first of the pursuers were galloping hard and closing rapidly. It was going to be very close Atkins suddenly realized as he pulled his horse's head around, yelled "Heya," and began kicking his horse in the ribs and lashing it with the reins so it would know to begin running at a fast gallop instead of its usual smooth and steady amble. His horse was a sturdy long distance ambler and still somewhat fresh, but making a run for his remount was still his best hope for an escape. That much Atkins knew for sure. Now if only his horse did not fall or get caught by a faster horse.

****** *The London shipping post*

The post's terror-stricken women and children were standing and sitting in the dim light of the coin room as Elspeth took the lantern from Marie. The only light in the coin room was from the lantern and the open door to the family room next to it which was lit by the sun coming in through its open wall openings. Everyone was listening to the rampaging invaders who were somewhere below them and anxiously and instinctively waiting for Elspeth to tell them what to do.

The women assumed she would tell them to climb down the ladder into the unknown darkness and it terrified them because those who looked could not see the bottom of the ladder or what might be down there in the darkness. Indeed the lantern's flickering light did less than the open door to light the darkness of the room in which they huddled at the top end of the ladder sticking out of the dark hole. But at least if one of the women climbed down the ladder with the lantern those who followed her down would be able to see what was at the bottom and where to put their feet if they had to climb down.

Everyone was waiting for Elspeth to tell them what to do.

"Quiet. Everyone quiet!" she hissed once again in a semi-whisper. "And give that child a teat to suck for God's sake, Mary; and everyone stop talking!" she hissed in the direction of a howling child whose mother was trying to console her.

Silence finally; at least somewhat. There were still sniffles from some of the children and whispered words from the women as they attempt to consol them. Then the sounds of banging and crashing started once again below the terrified women. This time the noise was closer. Their attackers were obviously trying to break down the double-barred door between the post's meeting room and the warehouse immediately behind it where most of the women and children lived.

What the invaders did *after* they got into the warehouse would determine what Elspeth would do next. Hopefully the invaders would just loot the warehouse and leave. But they had heard Elspeth speak and knew there had been people in the post. Richard had explained to her about the Company unexpectedly having terrible new enemies from amongst the English barons including a local landowner known as the Earl of Westminster who was thought to be second only to the king as the richest man in England.

But were the invaders after loot or were they after the post's people such that they would keep searching for them after they finished looting the warehouse? She knew that if they fetched a ladder and tried to climb through the trapdoor they would find it barred. But then what would they do? And where was Richard?

****** *The road home*

Bill Atkins looked over his shoulder as he leaned forward in his saddle and shouted and used his reins to try to whip his horse into running even faster. He and his pursuers were thundering up the side of the road past gawking men and women. He himself was in a desperate race to get away from a rider who had closed to less than twenty lengths and was holding a sword out in front of him as if he knew how to use it. Even worse, someone else had pulled ahead of the pack of pursuers who were galloping along further behind him and was also coming up fast. Any idea about continuing to raid the column was long gone the young archer's mind; getting to his remount and staying alive had become the only thing he could think about as he desperately galloped along the still-moving column.

Up ahead he could see the road was thick with wagons and walkers. They might block or trip his horse. Without even thinking about why he was doing it he turned his horse toward the field next to the road. His horse jumped the ditch next to the road and they galloped into a field of hay being cut by a line of men and women wielding scythes. The road packed with marchers and wagons flashed by on his left and the men and women cutting hay flashed by on his right.

The hay cutters stopped and watched as Bill galloped through their field and then jumped his horse over a low wall and into the pasture full of sheep that was beyond it. The pasture ran along the gentle slope of a hill and then levelled out into grassy open area that continued for as far as he could see. There were sheep scattered about everywhere and they scrambled to get out of his way as he galloped among them. He was shouting as he leaned over his horse's neck; both to encourage his horse and in the useless hope that it would somehow encourage the sheep to move out of the way.

As he galloped and shouted he was leaning low over his horse's neck and periodically looking back over his shoulder. Behind him Bill could see his two closest pursuers make the jump and follow him into the sheep pasture. They had fallen back during his horse's initial burst of speed but were now once again slowly closing the gap. The nearest of his two most serious pursuers was once again only forty or fifty lengths behind him and had started lashing his horse to encourage it to keep up the pace and close the gap. On the other hand, he could see that the other pursuers were finally beginning to fall back and some of them were beginning to abandon the chase altogether and walk their horses back to the road.

The young archer's horse was bred for endurance and distance. It continued to run well as the archer led his pursuers deeper and deeper into the seemingly endless pasture full of sheep. Even so, Atkins could feel his five-year old gelding beginning to weaken under him and knew that one or more of the men behind him would catch up to him in a few more minutes if he did not do something. So he did the only thing he knew to do; he dropped his reins and reached into his quiver for an arrow and nocked it.

Atkins twisted in the saddle and began to rapidly look back and forth between where he was headed and his pursuers. The road was now half a mile or more off to his left as he continued to gallop through the sheep with his head going back and forth between what was ahead of him and the two riders riding hard behind him. They were definitely starting to close the gap, especially the nearest man.

It was when he saw the pasture was clear ahead that he twisted around in his saddle and launched an arrow at his closest pursuer—and it missed by a mile even though the horse his closest pursuer was riding was now only ten or fifteen lengths behind and he was supposed to be able to make such shots. Instantly plucking a new arrow out of one of the quivers hanging in front of his saddle was second nature to him and he did so without thinking. That was when he knew that God was smiling on him.

Although Bill did not know it and never would, the hard riding pursuer was the young and ambitious son of a knight with a knight's fee from the Earl of Sussex. He had been more than a little surprised when Bill turned in his saddle and loosed an arrow at him, and greatly relieved when it missed. He knew he had had a close call and had already been having second thoughts about continuing—particularly since he was increasingly alone and it had finally dawned on him that he chasing after someone who knew how to fight. Besides, he was now quite some distance away from the column such that no one would see his bravery and victory when he won. To make a long story short; he decided to abandon the chase and turn back. He did not know it at the time, of course, but it would be the last decision he would ever make.

Unfortunately for the young man, he did not just pull up his horse and abruptly stop. Instead he turned his horse away from the chase with the idea of letting his horse begin to gradually slow down so it would gradually cool off. It was what he had been taught to do after a horse had had a very hard run. It was also a fatal mistake because in the process of veering away he turned his horse broadside to Bill just as Bill was getting ready to twist around in his saddle and push out another arrow.

Turning his horse to the left to ride away and end his chase turned the ambitious young man and the right side of his horse into a target that was too big and too close for an experienced horse archer to miss, especially now that he was much closer to Bill and Bill did not have to twist all the way around in his saddle to push out his arrow. This time the arrow did not miss. The heavy blow as the arrow slammed into the glory-seeking young man's side and knocked him all the way out of his saddle after a moment or two of hanging off it to one side; he went down hard and tumbled end over end in the pasture's grass and sheep shite. He never moved again except for the trembling in his legs. His uninjured horse kept running.

Bill immediately pulled his horse around to face his distant but still on-coming second pursuer and nocked another arrow—and then brought his horse up into a smooth amble and set his course *toward* the second pursuer. "Best to get this over with one way or another," was Bill's thought as he dropped his reins and focussed on the on-coming pursuer.

The sword-carrying pursuer was a middle-aged knight who held one of the Earl of Sussex's lesser knight's fees. He was chasing Bill because he was trying to distinguish himself in order to be able to ask for a better piece of land. He had been surprised when saw the young son of one of his fellow knights go down, and then again when the man they had been pursuing suddenly turned and began riding towards him instead of continuing to flee. It suddenly dawned on him as he continued galloping towards the on-coming archer that his sword did not have the same reach as the archer's bow; he was bringing a blade to a bow and arrow fight.

"Time to quit this shite before someone else gets hurt," was the knight's thought as he began pulling his horse to a stop and turning its head so he could ride away to safety. It was not to be; he had waited too long—the knight's effort to stop his horse and turn it away let Bill's rapidly moving horse quickly close the gap until he rode right past the now-fleeing man whose horse was still in the process of turning. Bill's arrow took the man high on his back up by his right shoulder and caused him to drop his sword.

It was then that the knight instinctively made a very smart decision. He began pulling his horse to a stop and, while the horse was still moving and he was still holding on to the reins, he deliberately fell off his horse even before it stopped just as Bill was ready to push another arrow into him. The reins were jerked out of his hand and the horse kept going.

"Take it," the knight shouted with a wave of his good hand towards his fleeing horse as he sat on the ground propped up by his good elbow and looked up at the archer.

Bill looked down at the man for a moment whilst his Company horse danced about the fallen knight; and then nodded.

Chapter Twenty-two
The archers begin to deploy.

All three of Okehampton castle's bailies were the scene of intense activity as George Courtenay hugged his wife tightly for a long moment and then turned to climb aboard his waiting horse. All around him horse archers were climbing into their saddles. The supply wagons assigned to his fifty-man main battle group and the various twenty-man raiding companies had already begun moving out through the castle gates and clattering over the cart path's ruts and stones towards the nearby old Roman road that was still the main road between London and the Exeter.

It was noisy and chaotic departure with several hundred or more of emotional women and children saying farewell to their husbands, fathers, and sons. To his great surprise, George felt a sense of relief as he boarded his horse. It meant he would finally be getting away from the constant need to make decisions and for things to be changed and problems solved.

Truth be told George was glad to get on his horse and leave Okehampton. Captain Merton, his deputy, would now be in command of the castle and have to make whatever new decisions had to be made on the Devon side of the River Tamar until George returned. *Commander Robertson, the Company's commander would make the decisions for the Cornwall side of the river. He would use all of the Company's remaining archers, the foot archers who were not tasked with staying in the Company's four strongholds, to hold the ford over the River Tamar and then fall back into Cornwall if they were unable to do so.*

Almost five hundred horse archers and eighty horse holders were riding out with George including his personal battle group of more than fifty experienced horse archers and outriders with remounts. These were the men that were to go the farthest down the road towards London and he would personally lead into battle. The rest of the five hundred included more than two hundred and fifty new horse archers with varying abilities to ride who had been hastily recruited from the foot archers serving in the Company's four Cornwall-related strongholds and from the galleys and transports that had arrived in Cornwall during the previous weeks. They even included some of the new recruits who had been at Restormel Castle being learnt to be archers and the veterans who were training them. Among the five hundred was George's new personal aide and errand runner, the newly promoted Sergeant Atkins.

The Company's horse archers had been based at its Okehampton Castle stronghold for exactly the purpose they were riding off to try to do—preventing invaders and other undesirables from reaching Cornwall and helping to expel them if they got into Cornwall despite the horse archers' best efforts to keep them out. Okehampton was the ideal place for the Company's two hundred or so regular horse archers and outriders to wait and train because it was strategically located close to where the Company-maintained road branched off from the London to Exeter main road. It was the only road into Cornwall.

George was leading his men out to meet the enemy because it was now virtually certain that a "grand army of loyal barons" composed of the individual armies of many of England's biggest land barons was on the march towards eastern Devon and Cornwall. As a result both the Company's regular horse archers and outriders, and the foot archers and new recruits who had been hastily invited to join them, were going out under George's command to whittle the enemy down. Hopefully George and his men would be able to kill or wound enough of the would-be invaders such that some or all of the barons' men would either fall or decide to turn back before they tried to force their way across the Tamar and enter Cornwall.

The day George and his horse archers out of Okehampton had been a day of great turmoil with gallopers having already been dispatched to Restormel three different times with updated news and information. There was now absolutely no doubt about it; the first of the barons' armies, those of Sussex, Chester, Westminster, and Derby, were on the march towards Cornwall and there was going to be a war.

The intense activity at Okehampton was understandable. Several hours earlier an exhausted Archer Atkins had arrived with three horses he and Sergeant Cooper had take as prizes and an exciting tale to tell. He had arrived only an hour or so after two archer messengers had ridden in from Windsor carrying the war warnings from the Company's priestly spies.

George had moved quickly. The horse archers, both the new lads and the veterans, had already been organized into raiding companies and their captains assigned to rally points and camps on the leather map draped over the wooden table in the great hall. As a result of George's careful planning everyone knew where they were to go and what to do when the horns began tooting for the archers to assembly with their horses so the final announcements could be made and orders given to the assembled men. Their supply wagons had already been loaded with supplies and had been waiting for their horses and drivers for several days.

The horses newly arrived from London and those still being trained would stay behind with an experienced outrider sergeant newly promoted to the rank of Sergeant Major who had been placed in charge of getting them ready to join the fight. More specifically, the Sergeant Major was tasked to getting what was left of the archer volunteers ready so that they could simultaneously ride on the horses assigned to them and push out arrows at the Company's enemies. His was an important job as there were still more than sixty foot archers and "almost ready" recruits still being learnt to ride. They and their horses would be sent out to the raiding companies as reinforcements when the Sergeant Major decided they were ready to both push out arrows *and* ride at the same time.

George himself would be leading just over fifty experienced horse archers and their remounts and three supply wagons out of Okehampton along with eighteen or nineteen stable boys and hostlers to be their horse holders. The horse archers riding out with George were the only ones going out with remounts. They had them because they would be going out the greatest distance and staying out the longest. The archers of the more than twenty raiding companies under the command of the Company's captains, lieutenants, and Sergeant Majors who knew how to ride would be riding out right behind them. They would then disperse so that the Company's raiding companies were scattered all along the London road and on the major roads that joined it.

"You must," George had repeatedly told the captains and lieutenants of the twenty-man raiding companies who would be following him out of Okehampton, "stay in the field and keep the armies of the various barons under pressure with constant attacks until we either destroy them or their army breaks up and turns back." It was understood that the conduct of every single man would be evaluated after the war and that there would be immediate promotions, demotions, and retirements. Doing so after a fight was a Company tradition.

George rode out of Okehampton at the head of his men on a nice sunny day. His number two, Captain Merton, remained behind to command the castle. One of the galley captains, an archer who had risen from the rowing deck and did not know how to ride, stayed with him to serve as his number two. The leaders of the additional raiding companies resulting from the hasty recruitment and training of additional horses and riders included a dozen horse archer and outrider sergeants, three galley captains who knew how to ride because they had attended the Company school as boys, the two Sergeant Majors from Plympton and Launceston, and two galley lieutenants. They all knew how to ride because they too had attended the Company school. The experienced horse archers and outriders were scattered amongst the raiding companies to be their backbone.

In his heart George knew that the confusion and last-minute changes of assignments and tactics during the past few weeks had been inevitable once the war had become certain. Years of careful preparation are inevitably cast aside when a war suddenly arrives and the enemy is not exactly who you anticipated. It is always that way when soldiers are suddenly and unexpectedly forced to go off to war; you prepare for one kind of war and then you usually have to fight another. It is a soldier's lot.

In George's case, some of the problems that were unexpected were actually quite encouraging—for instance the need to suddenly find and outfit several hundred foot archers and new recruits with horses, saddles, arrows, and the supplies and supply wagons they would need to operate independently until the war was over.

Also changing was the way the horse archers were to launch their attacks; by doing what the late Sergeant Cooper and the newly promoted Sergeant Atkins had proved successful—starting at the rear of the enemy columns and rapidly working their way forward. It had been a last minute addition to their battle orders.

The captains and lieutenants of the raiding companies had been assembled in Okehampton's great hall a few hours earlier to hear the latest news, get their final orders, and ask any last minute questions. While they were there they heard Sergeant Atkins' report, and received a very strong suggestion from George that the idea rolling up enemy columns from the rear whilst they were marching was how their attacks should be conducted whenever possible.

That there might be more effective ways to attack their enemies and that additional horses, wagons, and men had been found to strengthen the Company's efforts to whittle down the barons before they reached Cornwall was the good news.

The bad news was that the last minute addition of the additional men meant that most of the horse archers would not be riding out with remounts to help carry them off to safety if the horse they were riding went down or they needed to run. It also meant that each of the raiding companies would be riding out with significantly fewer arrows in its supply wagons than its captain had anticipated. That was because the existing supply of arrows had ended up being apportioned between many more riders.

Moreover, and almost unbelievably, the arrow shortage had been made even worse by a mountain weasel that had just taken some sort of prey in the swampy area next to the Plymouth road. The wagon's driver was not sure what the weasel had in its mouth, only that it was a newt or a snake, when the weasel stepped out on to the road in front of a wagon that was carrying arrow bales from Plympton Castle to Okehampton. The nasty little beast had its still-writhing victim in its mouth when it darted in front of the wagon horse and so startled the horse that it bolted and the wagon ended on its side up with one end of it under water in the River Plym. As a result, some of the bales of arrows it had been carrying to Okehampton were last seen floating down the Plym despite the wagon driver's desperate efforts to retrieve them.

All that George and Commander Robertson could do was make the best of the unexpected changes and shortages and carry on. They had no choice so they did everything they could think of to do: The Company's strongholds were stripped of their horses, riders, saddles, and arrows and their gates closed for the duration—with almost every man and woman remaining in them now working throughout every day and into the night to produce the replacement arrows they would almost certainly need for their own defense if the barons' men reached their walls.

Other important last minute preparations included the sending out of several of the retired "old boys" from the Company school as soothsayer priests to Hatherleigh and to a village further down the road *beyond* Crediton. They were to base themselves in the villages' taverns and sell very inexpensive prophecies and indulgences to the men of the barons' armies as they passed by on the road.

The two retired Angelovians, both lieutenants who had retired in Cornwall and still periodically worked at the Company school to help the boys learn to scribe, would pretend to the fortunes of the barons' men by examining the lines and creases of their hands in return for a small coin or piece of bread. They would then sorrowfully return the coin or bread and offer to give last rites to those of the men who were sadly told by a whisper into their ear that they had no hope *unless* as they left quietly in the dark of the night and returned to their homes or ran away to somewhere else—and as their payment was being returned to them the inevitably horrified men were warned that the prophecy would come true, even if they quietly deserted, if they ever told anyone what the priest had said to them.

As you might imagine, every enemy soldier who was worried enough to pay to have his future foretold by a priest would receive the same message. It was the Angelovian priest's return of the coin or bread and his offer to give the man his "last rites" if he chose not to desert that convinced the gullible amongst them that what the priests told them was true.

Using priests to gull enemy soldiers into deserting had been successfully used several times in the Company's early years and was a battle practice taught in both of the Company schools. It was quite effective because it was always understood by the man whose palm was being read that something significant and terrible must have been revealed; priests, after all, rarely passed on accepting a coin or something to eat.

Another last minute preparation was the assignment of a handful of horse archers to set up three-man observation posts along the main roads to bring in early word of any approaching enemy forces and intercept the barons' couriers and small scouting parties. The archers at the observation posts would, on the other hand, smile warmly on all those who were going in the other direction, even if they were some of the barons' men and armed, and congratulate them on escaping the plague and famine. The latter, of course, was done so that word would spread both that western Devon and Cornwall should be avoided as unsafe places to visit and that those of the barons' men who deserted would not be harmed.

****** s

Things were not going as smoothly as the de Montfort brothers and their priestly cleric had hoped they would. Queen Eleanor had begun to make promises in her son's name to get support from the uncommitted barons and some of the less committed barons to change sides. Even worse, a number of the barons had started to move toward Cornwall before the agreed starting date. And to top it off, the rumours that the French were seriously considering another invasion of England were getting stronger.

The cleric explained the immediate problem.

"The Earl of Sussex and some of the others do not want to spend their coins to buy food for their men so they have started early in order to get their foraging done and find the best places to camp before the other barons can get there with their men and take them. The Earl also wants to be the king or at least a king-maker such that he can negotiate for more of the lands that are to be taken from the lords who support the crown. He also wants a separate title of nobility for his son and heir.

"And he is not the only important lord who has done so; according to the messages I received earlier today the earls of Chester, Westminster, and Derby and only God knows how many of the others have decided to start marching early so they too can stake out the best places to pitch their camps and forage. Even worse, I am told on good authority that the queen has already sent word to Prince Edward asking him to hurry back from the Holy Land."

"I knew we should have chosen someplace other than the southwest to muster the army," suggested the older de Montfort bitterly. "It is too far away." And after a short pause he asked "Is it too late to recall Sussex and the others and get them to muster their men someplace in the midlands?"

The priest shook his head and disagreed. *The older de Montfort is certainly a useless worrywart, the priest thought to himself. But, of course, he could not say that out loud or mention it to anyone even though that was what he really thought of the man.*

"Selecting western Devon for the army's muster and Cornwall for the foraging was the right decision for you to make, your lordship. It was the only place for the Loyal Army's mobilization that would attract the other barons to join you. The earls of Sussex and Chester and the other barons would never have agreed to bring in their men if the Loyal Army was mustered anywhere else. For one thing, it would have eliminated a French invasion in the southwest as an excuse for them to bring their men and join you.

"More importantly, nothing would have ever have happened because each of them would have been afraid to march for fear he would be accused of treason for taking his men to join an army that was being formed for the purpose of going against the king. Marching to Cornwall is acceptable because it requires marching *away* from the king; marching to the midlands, or anyplace else for that matter, would have been too risky for most of them because it would have been seen as marching *toward* the king.

The younger de Montfort agreed with the priest.

"Father Pierre is right, brother; the only thing we can do now is send word to everyone that they should start their men marching for Devon and Cornwall. You can tell them that they need to do so immediately because the latest word from the French court is that the French army is gathering and is about to sail for England. That is not true, of course, but it is a good excuse to get the laggards started."

Actually, it was true and Father Pierre knew it; the "special friend" of his fellow French Franciscan, the Nuncio, had told him about it several days earlier.

"But why confuse the de Montforts and the others with facts that might distress them?" he had decided behind his eyes. "There is nothing they can do about it and, besides, a

French victory might encourage the appointment of a French Pope."

****** *Captain Richard Adams*

Captain Richard Adams was returning from the market with the latest news and information he had gleaned from its merchants and moneylenders. It looked bad. The armies of some of the barons were already on the march. He was composing his next message to the Commander in his head as he walked back to the post.

As Richard turned the corner to enter the street on which his post stood he saw a wagon in front of post being loaded. He instantly knew something was wrong because some of the neighborhood people were standing around on the street and watching the wagon. They never did that; something was up. He stopped walking and watched.

A moment later Richard recognized the livery worn by one of the two men who had come out of the post's door carrying a wooden crate and began loading it on the wagon. It was the livery of the Earl of Westminster who the merchants were sure was one of the leaders of the Loyal Army—and there had been no cargo in the post's warehouse waiting for the earl to retrieve. It was some kind or a raid or robbery for sure.

What should he do and where were Elspeth and his children? His mind was racing as he hurried back around the corner of the street to get out of sight. He peeked his head around the corner and watched until he was sure as to what was happening. A moment later he turned around and began trotting to the Company stable which was several blocks away to the south. He did not think anyone had seen him. He also did not know how many men were inside his shipping post and home.

Captain Adam's sheathed sword banged against his leg as he ran for the Company's stable. He only carried his sheathed sword when he visited the market, not his longbow or his shield. As a result, he was running to the stable to replace it with his longbow and a couple of the quivers of the arrows that were kept there. They had been taken to the stable a few days earlier so he would not have to sneak them out of the shipping post when he left to join the fight for Cornwall.

The mouth of the elderly hostler on duty at the stable gaped open and he started to say something when Captain Adams, breathing hard, trotted past him and went directly to the inner-most stall where a few extra quivers of the post's arrows were stored in one chest and his private gear and the stable's records and scribing materials were kept in another. He grabbed up his longbow and quickly strung it, quickly removed his sheathed short sword from his belt and retied the belt, and then picked up a couple of quivers full of arrows and slung them over his shoulder. He already had a replacement string for his bow because he always carried one in his coin pouch along with some coins and his fire stone and its iron sparker.

"Saddle both of my horses and put a sack of grain for the horses, a full skin of water, and my sword and shield on the remount. Also get one of the covered wagons ready to go with the brown mare and put a couple of sacks of grain and some water in it as well. And tie my horses to the wagon so it can lead them."

Richard shouted his orders over his shoulder to the hostler as he left at a run. "I will be back for them shortly and will want to leave immediately."

He did not really think he would immediately need either the wagon or the horses. But he did not know what was happening and wanted to be prepared if he and his people needed to run.

****** *The London post.*

Elspeth carried the candle lantern to the hole in the floor of the coin room. As she did she realized that if she carried the lantern all the way down the ladder to the entrance of the escape tunnel it might then become so dark in the coin room that no one would be able to find the ladder to climb down it and escape. Even worse, even with enough light it would be nigh on to impossible for the some of the women and children to get on the ladder because it did not stick up out of the hole.

All she could do, Elspeth finally decided, was to wait with the dimly lit coin room's door open and the candle lantern by her side so she could carry it to where it was needed most. Only if the raiders began a serious effort to climb up to get into the room used by her family would she bar the door to the coin room and try to send the women and children down the ladder to the tunnel. She was hesitant to close the door and send everyone down the ladder in the darkness until it was absolutely necessary because she had only one lantern and it was quite a ways down. All of the post's other lanterns were in the shipping post.

Having only one lantern, she had suddenly realized, was a serious problem because it could not be in two places at the same time—if it was at the bottom of the ladder in order to light the ladder's steps and the entrance to the escape tunnel the women still in the coin room would be left in total darkness and might have trouble finding the ladder in order to climb down it to escape. On the other hand, if the lantern stayed in the coin room it would be dark at the bottom of the ladder and the people who climbed down it in the dark would have trouble finding the tunnel entrance. She was frustrated by the realization and felt a sudden moment of panic.

The muffled noise of men talking and shouting in the warehouse continued for some time. Then there was the sound of something thumping against the ceiling trapdoor. Someone was testing it; probably pushing on it with a spear or a piece of wood to see if it would open. It held because it she had barred it but the constant banging of something against it worried her. Elspeth decided to quietly walk back into her family's room to listen and to make sure the bar was firmly in place to prevent the trapdoor from being opened. She was concerned that repeated pushings and hittings against the trapdoor might cause the wooden bar holding it closed to slowly work itself out of position so that it could be pushed open.

She left the lantern by the trapdoor in the coin room floor that led down to the escape tunnel and went into her family's better lit and much larger sleeping room to check on the trapdoor. When she reached it she got down on her knees and put her ear against the trapdoor and listened. A chill suddenly ran down her back a moment later when she realized what she was hearing—the men in the warehouse were stacking up cargo crates so they could climb up to the ceiling; and they were talking about getting axes to chop their way through the trapdoor.

Elspeth ran back into the coin room and began whispering orders. Moments later the women and children slowly, very slowly it seemed, began hesitantly climbing down the ladder into the darkness of the little escape room far below. Elspeth did her best to help them. She stood above the opening with the lantern and dangled it down into the darkness so that it would provide a bit of light both for the coin room and for the little tunnel entrance room at the bottom of the ladder.

There was much confusion and crying out by the younger children. As a result, it took a very long time before everyone finished climbing down into the pitch black little room at the bottom of the ladder—and throughout the ordeal many of the children picked up on their mother's fear; they started to get hysterical and most of them had to be carried down into the total darkness.

It seemed to take forever but in the end everyone was able to climb down. That was because one of the more reliable of the women had gone down first and was holding the ladder steady with one hand whilst holding an infant to her breast with her other arm. What Elspeth did not realize was that the men in the warehouse could hear the noise on the other side of the brick wall that separated the back of the warehouse from ladder which continued on down past the warehouse wall to the little escape room where the tunnel entrance was located.

When the women and children were finally all down the ladder Elspeth closed the door between the coin room and her family's living room. Then, feeling her way in the darkness in order to do so, she doubled-barred the door in the total darkness. As soon as the bar was in place she felt her way back across to the other side of the room to where she thought the ladder was located. She finally found it, helped by the noise and lantern light coming out of the escape room below, and started down. After she got a few steps down the ladder she attempted to pull the woven carpet back over the trapdoor to conceal it as she closed it.

What she then *forgot* to do was put the bar in place that would keep the escape room's trap door in the floor above it from being pulled open from above. She only remembered that she should have done it almost an hour later when she heard the pounding of an axe as someone standing on the cargo crates tried to break into the room above them from the warehouse. Then her heart sank because she realized she had left the bar in the coin room.

The noise and the talking that accompanied the chopping were quite loud and could be clearly heard because it was only eight or nine feet above them on the other side of the warehouse wall. By then all the women and children were sitting jammed together in front of the tunnel entrance. The children, fortunately, were somewhat settled down except for periodic sobs and childish talking.

Then everything changed and she stopping thinking about whether she should go back up the ladder and get the bar: The banging on the warehouse trapdoor suddenly stopped and there was a lot of excited shouting.

Chapter Twenty-three

The fighting begins.

The commander of the horse archers and his lieutenants and sergeant majors were sitting on their horses watching the long, wide, and totally disorganized column of men and wagons moving slowly toward Cornwall on the road below them. There were five of them and they were watching the road from just inside the tree line at the top of a grassy hill that stretched upwards from it. Each of the men had a longbow and several very full quivers of arrows slung over his shoulder and at least four additional fully loaded quivers hanging over his horse's back in front of his saddle. Every one of the five men was an experienced horse archer and a long-serving veteran of the company of archers based in Cornwall—and they had almost fifty similarly trained and equipped men who were waiting further back in the trees.

There was no doubt about it so far as the veteran archers watching the road were concerned; the sight of their disorganized and unprepared enemies moving slowly past them was very encouraging to men who were highly trained, superbly armed with the most modern of weapons, and willing to fight for their free company and its holdings in western Devon and Cornwall—men like them and the archers they commanded.

****** *In the city of London*

George Courtenay and his senior men were not the only archers watching the Company's enemies. Captain Richard Adams was peering around the corner of a building in the city of London and watching men in the livery of the Earl of Westminster. They were periodically coming out of the entrance to the shipping post he commanded with a crate or sack and loading it on a horse-drawn wagon that was standing in front of post's now-damaged entrance door. There was no sign of his wife and daughter or any of the other residents of the post

Several of the captain's neighbours had obviously been attracted by sight and sound of the post's door being battered in and were still standing in little groups across the street from the front of the post's front door. They were watching and whispering to each other. So were a half dozen or so young boys who lived in the neighbourhood. Other men and women were walking up and down the street and going about their normal lives. Some of the people on the street looked at the wagon and the post's battered door as they walked past them; others looked the other way and tried to pretend that they had not seen anything.

Captain Adams was fairly sure he knew why the post was being attacked. Westminster, after all, was a leader of the "northern folk" who used to be called Vikings and well known to be one of the most rebellious of England's barons and almost certainly amongst the barons marching on Cornwall. And that Westminster's men did so whilst wearing his livery probably meant something; he just did not know what it was. It could be that he thought the Company would be defeated or tied up fighting in Cornwall for so long that he could get away with it. *Or could it possibly be someone else who was trying to shift the blame to Westminster as the Company always tried to do?*

What Captain Adams did not know was how many of Westminster's men were inside his post or what had happened to his wife and daughter; but he did know three things that were important—one was that there was only one door that could be used to get in or out of the shipping post and he was looking at it. Another was that the city's night watch would not be on the streets for three or four hours at the earliest, if at all, and probably would not do anything to help even if they knew there was a robbery in progress. The third was that whoever was doing it had made a great and almost certainly fatal mistake.

After watching Westminster's men for a few minutes and thinking about what he should do and how he should do it, Captain Adams decided that the best way to get close enough to the men who were periodically carrying crates and sacks out of the post was to act normal and walk up to them as if he had nothing particular on his mind. If he did so, he hoped, they would not be alarmed until it was too late for them to do anything to stop him from doing what he felt he had to do.

So that is what Richard Adams did; he put on a cheerful face, walked casually around the corner of the building, and proceeded down the street towards the wagon in front of his post. He did so whilst carrying his longbow in his left hand in an unthreatening way as if he was relaxed and carrying a pole or stick for some reason. Had anyone looked closely, however, they would have seen that his left hand was also holding an arrow against the wooden shaft of his bow. The captain's right hand was swinging casually as he walked down the street and he was moving his head about as if he might by humming a jaunty tune as he walked.

The Captain's ruse worked. The two men coming out the door carrying another chest paid him no attention at all as he came around the corner and began cheerfully walking down the other side of the street. A number of his curious neighbours were standing around watching the removal of the post's property take place. They were standing across the street on the captain's side of the wagon; Westminster's men and the crates and sacks they were carrying were on the other side of the wagon and much closer to the post's door.

Several of his neighbours looked up as Captain Adams walked past them. One of them started to say something but the captain cut him off with a wave of his and a terse comment.

"I know Sam, I know. Well, there is bound to be a bit of a dustup I would think. It would be best if you and Charlie and the others would go on home now, eh? It would not do to get yourselves caught up in someone else's troubles would it?"

He said it loud enough so that the men and women standing about nearby could hear him. But he did not wait to see how they would respond. Instead, he continued walking steadily forward until he reached the side of the wagon and had a clear view of the inside of his post though its one and only door. Then he raised his already strung bow, nocked the arrow he had been holding, and pushed it straight into the chest of one of the two crate carriers who was less than ten feet away.

And then with one practiced motion he immediately plucked another arrow out of his quiver and pushed it into the side of the second man almost before the crate the first man had been helping him carry hit the ground. Richard's second arrow took the second man while he was still looking in disbelief at the man who had been at the other end of the crate they had been carrying—who was now leaning against the wagon with a look of surprise and confusion on his face, bulging eyes, and about a foot of the front end of a very bloody arrow sticking out of his back.

"Go home, lads," the captain ordered loudly to his neighbors as he nocked a third arrow without taking his eyes off the door. As he did the man his first arrow had taken slid down on to his knees and then toppled over on to his side. He was trying to talk between his gasps and groans. The second man had been leaning forward over the fallen crate when the arrow hit him; now he was sitting on his arse with his back against the fallen crate. A trickle of blood was starting to run out of his mouth and he was staring at the captain with rapidly blinking eyes that were having trouble focusing. They were definitely out of the fight.

Captain Adams backed up about ten paces almost immediately after he told his neighbours to leave. The extra distance would give him time to nock another arrow and get both the first man out of the door and the second man if two of Westminster's men came charging out of the post's doorway at the same time. If three or more came charging out together at the same time, however, he would take out the closest man the moment he appeared in the doorway and then run off down the street as if the devil himself was after him—and keep running until his chasers were strung out far enough behind him. Then he would turn back and begin taking them out one man at a time before the next man could reach him. It was the old "wounded bird" ploy that every boy in the Company school was repeatedly told to use when he was outnumbered.

It did not happen that way but that was his plan.

****** *Somewhere in Somerset or Wiltshire*

"Remember lads, tell your men that no one is to show himself or move forward for any reason. We are going to stay here and wait here for the end of the column to go past us. Then we are going to do what we practiced yesterday and roll them up from the rear."

It had certainly worked for his new sergeant, and as he watched the slow moving column he thought he understood why: It was always better to fall on an enemy from behind before he could get ready to fight you off.

George had said the words loudly without taking his eyes off the people and wagons passing on the road that ran through the fields of hay and grain that stretched out below the hill. A few moments later, he and his lieutenants moved back deeper into the trees and rejoined their men.

There was one exception. One of the outriders, the outriders being the best of the Company's best riders, was sent out leading his remount into the open pasture land to ride along the tree line toward London to see what he could see and come back with a report. He was only sent eastward because George already knew that another column was not marching immediately in front of this one; for if there had been an enemy column marching in front of this one he and his men and his scouts would have already seen it as they came down the road in the other direction.

The outrider was sent out because George wanted to know if a column or columns of other barons' men, perhaps those of the Earls of Sussex or Westminster, were coming along close *behind* the column passing below them. The scouts who had come back earlier had reported there was no else coming towards Cornwall from the east except for the usual travelers who made the road one of England's busiest. But that was several hours earlier and George wanted to be sure. If there was another column nearby that was also marching on Cornwall, he would have to decide whether or not to have his men attack it in addition to the column passing on the road in front of him—or leave them both to pass unmolested.

Lieutenant Commander Courtenay was being especially careful because he wanted his first big fight to be both successful and significant. If it was, it might convince some of the barons and their men to turn back instead of continuing to march westward to invade western Devon and Cornwall. He also wanted to show the barons that they would not be safe anywhere in England if they continued to think in terms of basing their "Loyal Army" on the lands that the Company had for many years considered to be under its protection. Accordingly, he and his fifty-plus horse archers and their eighteen horse holders and three supply wagons had deliberately traveled quite a distance along the road toward London before they found a suitably large enemy column to engage.

George had kept his little army moving towards London until his outriders brought back word that a large column of armed men was up ahead on the London road. The outriders had chatted up some of the column's stragglers and learned that the column was composed of the knights and levies of half a dozen barons from Kent and Essex. They had started early, one of the stragglers had told the scouts, because they had further to go and wanted to get to Cornwall before the other barons' armies arrived in order to find the best place to camp and forage.

Many of the barons, or so it seemed, had the same idea and did not trust the others to share the best places to camp—which gave the lieutenant commander another idea.

******

The archers on the hill had stayed off the London road and avoided villages after they crossed the River Exe. In doing so they avoided contact with the smaller enemy columns that were on the road ahead of the big one they were planning to attack. As a result, George and his men were not exactly certain where he and his men were located. He thought they were probably in Wiltshire but perhaps they had travelled far enough to reach Berkshire. It really did not matter; the relatively large and disorganized column of men and wagons moving slowly and peacefully towards Cornwall on the London road was exactly what he had been looking for.

As soon as he had been informed of the on-coming column's existence and its size George had stashed his supply wagons in an isolated wooded area a good hour's ride to the north of where he intended to attack the column in the rear and roll it up. Now he was waiting for the last of his scouts to return and tell him if another of the barons' armies was coming along behind this one; and, if so, how fast it was moving. If there was another column and it was close behind he would have to decide whether or not to go after both of them in one great and continuous sweeping charge from their rear or just this one.

George and his men had seen and ridden around several much smaller enemy columns in the past several days. This was by far the largest column they had yet come across. He had passed up three earlier columns they had seen because they were too small; he wanted to make his first attack an example of the Company's strength that would encourage some or all of the other barons and their men to return to their homes before it was too late. Besides, he was sure that the captains of his twenty-two raiding companies would be giving the smaller columns he and his men had bypassed a warm welcome in the near future if they had not already done so.

In any event, George knew it was time for the fighting to start if only because it is always best to fall upon an enemy when he is unprepared to fight. Besides, his men were as ready as he could get them and he already had an idea behind his eyes as to what orders he should give *after* the coming fight on the road—if he and his men were able to decisively win it.

****** *The fight on the road is about to begin*

The time had come. The scout's report was that there were no other enemy armies within an hour's ride of the one that had just finished passing below us on the road that ran along the bottom of the hill.

George faced the fifty horsemen and gave them their final orders. It was expected of him even though most of the men already knew what he was going to tell them.

"An enemy column of about a thousand men is on the road that runs along the other side of this hill. We are going to start in the rear of the enemy column and work our way to the front whilst staying together in one great battle group just as we have been practicing for the past few days. Some of you are to ride on the left side of the column with Captain Evans; some of you are going to ride on the right side with me. You know who you are.

"What is important is that no man is to stop moving towards the front of the column for any reason and that you only ride past your mates on the outside so you do not get in the way of the arrows they are pushing into the column. Rely on the men behind you to put an arrow into any horse or man you ride past whilst you are nocking another arrow. Do not stop to get someone you missed. Sergeant Smith and his men will pick up anyone who is wounded or loses his horse. They will also be leading spare horses to replace any man's horse that goes down. So you do *not* need to stop to help a mate; that is the responsibility of Sergeant Smith and his men.

"The important thing to remember is that you are to keep riding towards the front of the enemy column and *only* push out an arrow when you see an unwounded man or horse. There are a lot of enemy men and horses down there on the road so it is important that you *not* waste a single arrow, and certainly not on a man or horse that has already been wounded or on women and children.

"Not wasting arrows is so important that any man who wastes one will lose a stripe for every arrow he wastes on a wounded man or horse. The same is true if you waste an arrow on the women and children or break off from the main attack to go chasing off after an enemy soldier who runs away from the column. Let them go and keep riding towards the front if you cannot reach them with an arrow when they first start to run.

"And remember that when we finally reach the front of the enemy column we are going to stop and turn around and then ride back to gather up our arrows so we can reuse them and gather up any enemy weapons or armour that might be available. That is when you can finish off the wounded horses and the enemy skulkers who played dead and were not smart enough to run away after we rode past them the first time.

"Finally, also remember that you are *not* to bother the enemy wounded unless it is necessary to put them to sleep with a blow to their heads because they are jumping around too much when you pull out your arrows to retrieve them. That is because we want some of them to live long enough to tell the others who come along about what will happen to them if they keep marching towards Cornwall."

Chapter Twenty-four

Whittling them down.

Captain Adams did not have to wait long before someone came to the post's door to see what the sudden outburst of shouting and the commotion on the street was all about. Whoever it was that appeared made a bad mistake—he stepped into the doorway to look instead of quickly and carefully darting a look from around the corner of the doorway. It was also his last mistake in that Richard's arrow took him squarely in the stomach and had been delivered with all the force that the totally prepared and extremely outraged archer captain could put into it.

Richard could not see the final result of his shot because it pushed the man back into the entry hall and he fell off to one side. But Richard and everyone in the street behind him could definitely hear his squealing and screams before they became fewer and fewer and faded away.

What Richard *did* see a moment later as he was nocking another arrow was someone briefly stepping into view inside the room as he rushed to the fallen man's assistance. Richard snapped off an arrow at the would-be helper and, if the resulting thud and the screams that followed meant anything, either he or someone else in the room had been hit.

Richard was not sure, but it was probably not a fatal hit since the room was dimly lit and he had only seen the man for an instant and he had been moving. On the other hand, whoever was hit had immediately started screaming and shouting. Richard heard it and grimly nodded his acceptance of the fact that he had almost certainly taken another of his post's attackers out of the fight.

"Well, they know I am out here. Now what will they do?" Richard thought to himself as he nocked another arrow and once again darted a very quick look behind him to make sure that no one was coming up behind him.

He saw no one close or even coming toward him and certainly no one who looked like a threat. To the contrary, there were still people on the street talking and shouting but they had moved even further back. And when he directed his attention back to his shipping post he could see for the first time that the door from his post's entry room to the reception room immediately behind it had also been forced open. It was hanging crookedly off to one side.

As you might well imagine there continued to be a lot of noise both on the street in front of the post and from inside the shipping post itself. Part of the noise on the street was related to the horse that had been pulling the wagon; it had responded to all the noise and shouting around it by somehow pulling its reins loose from where they had been loosely tied to a hitching post and bolting. It had apparently galloping away down the narrow street with the wagon bouncing along behind it and the people ahead of it on the street running to get out of the way. All Richard knew was that it was gone.

"Who are you; what do you want?" a voice shouted loudly from inside the shipping post in the midst of the screams coming from it.

"What did you say?" Richard replied. "I cannot hear you. We are the men of the city's night watch and we are here to keep the peace. Who are you? Come out peacefully so we can talk and get things settled down."

The answer came quickly.

"We are the men of the Earl of Westminster and we are here because this shipping post is owned by his enemies. I am Sir Eric, Lord Giffard's son."

"What was that? Did you say you are the son of the esteemed and respected Lord Giffard?" Richard shouted back. *Actually, he was trying to gull the shouter into showing himself; he had never even known there was such a thing as a Lord Giffard.*

"Yes, and I am his son, Sir Eric. My men and I are here at the request of the Earl of Westminster himself," the man shouted back. His voice suggested that whoever he was he had become much more sure of himself and arrogant now that he knew whoever was attacking him and his men knew and respected the name of his father and his father's cousin, the earl.

"At the request of the Earl of Westminster you say? That is good news because we are all king's men out here and we certainly know our very own Earl of Westminster. Well then, Sir Eric, everything will soon be put right if you really are Lord Giffard's son and here at the request of the Earl himself. You can come out now and we will work this out. I will make things right between your men and mine, I swear it. Then he quickly reached over his shoulder and pulled a new arrow from his second quiver.

A moment later a young man angrily strode into the doorway with a petulant look on his face. It instantly changed into one of distress and great anger when he saw the bodies of the two crate carriers lying in great pools of blood.

"My God you have killed them. You will pay for …..," the young man's voice trailed off as he took in the scene and realized that Captain Richard Adams of the Company of Archers was the only man in front of him.

"Who are you? What is happening here? What is the meaning of this? Where are the men of the night watch?" the angry young man's questions flooded out of him. Richard could see that Sir Eric was wearing a chain shirt under his tunic. *Of course he was wearing a chain shirt; a young nobleman who thought he and his men might face armed resistance when they raided a building where valuable cargos and coins were stored would almost certainly wear one. It was to be expected and the reason*

Richard had nocked a new arrow, a heavy with a needle-nosed iron point.

"How strange," said Richard with more than a little cynical wonder in a voice that was not particularly loud. "Those are the very same questions I was going to ask you. Are you really the son of the famous Lord Giffard who is a vassal of the Earl of Westminster?"

As Richard was speaking he deliberately took the arrow from his bow as a sign of his peaceful intentions and Sir Eric moved a couple of steps out into the street to survey the scene. As Sir Eric stepped into the street, several of his men moved into view in the post's reception room and stood behind him in entry room. Sir Eric may have been emboldened to come out for a look because he could see that Richard was not carrying a sword, only an empty bow. Besides, everyone knew that an arrow could not pierce chain.

"Of course I am Lord Giffard's son, you damn fool. The Earl of Westminster is my uncle."

"In that case I have a message for your father and the Earl from his king's loyal subjects, although someone else will have to deliver it to him."

And before anyone could move Richard nocked the arrow he had removed from his bow and pushed it straight at Sir Eric with all his strength. The arrow was what the men of the Company called "a heavy" and was well-known to the Moorish knights because its heavy weight could drive its slender iron point through most armour.

It happened in an instant. All Sir Eric had time to do was open his mouth and start to protest. But before he could get the words out the force of the arrow striking him in the chest drove him back into the arms of the two men standing behind him. For a brief instant they held him up and he just stood there and stared in amazement at the feathered fletching of the arrow that had gone through his chain and was sticking out of his chest.

"You said everything would be alright. You promised," the young man finally gasped in surprised protest as Richard nocked another arrow and in one smooth gesture pushed it straight at one of the men who was holding Sir Eric up. Sir Eric, it seemed, still did not understand that he had just been killed.

"Aye, so I did," Richard snarled in reply. "And even though everything is not yet totally alright, it is certainly getting there fast—for I have just killed you and a couple of the other rotten bastards who attacked my wife and my shipping post."

By the time Richard had started explaining things to Sir Eric he had already pushed out a second arrow—at a wide-eyed man with a gaping mouth who was standing to the left of Sir Eric and helping to hold him up—and was nocking a third.

The second arrow was also a heavy and it certainly did what it was supposed to do—it must not have hit any bones because it went almost all the way through Sir Eric's un-armoured helper and pushed him backwards against the wall behind him.

As Sir Eric's first helper was hit and went backwards. The other man who had been helping him let go of Sir Eric's arm, desperately pushed himself away from the knight, and jumped backwards through the post's door before another arrow could be launched.

It all happened in the blink of an eye. Sir Eric's other helper moved so fast that all Captain Adams could do after nocking his third arrow was watch as the man who he had just hit with an arrow bounced off the wall behind him and fell forward so that he was partially on top of one of Sir Eric's trembling legs. That was when he began screaming and shouting for help whilst at the same time staring and grabbing frantically at the few inches of arrow feathers sticking out of his tunic whilst simultaneously desperately trying to untangle himself from Sir Eric and get to his feet.

It was about then that Richard realized he was standing outside in the sun and getting more than a little warm; and he still did not know how many more men were inside.

****** *Closing the Giffard account*

Richard stood in the street and waited in the sun for a while. Then he moved closer so that he stood in the shade of the building. He thought it unlikely that any of the Earl's men still inside the post had bows or else they probably would have tried to use them by now. His best move since he did not know how many men were still inside, he decided, was to wait until they started coming out. But then he remembered that his wife and his children were in there and needed him and so did the families of his men. So he changed his mind and decided not to wait.

He had already nocked another heavy by the time he realized he had no time to lose and could not wait. So he took a deep breath and with his bow raised and aimed toward where he most expected someone to appear, he began slowly and carefully inching his way forward toward the battered door that hung off the entrance to his post. Suddenly he darted to his right and gained the front wall of the post to the right of its entrance door. The shouting and talking behind him in the street increased as he made his run and then quickly began to subside as he pressed his back against the wall. Everyone was waiting to see what he was going to do next.

Captain Adams took a deep breath and kept his arrow nocked when he reached the wall and put his back up against it. He was keeping his nocked arrow pointed towards the door but he could more easily check the street that was in front of him now that he had his back against the wall. He saw no danger, only a large and growing crowd of noisy gawkers. The crowd grew quieter and quieter and watched in fascination as he began slowly moving toward the post's entrance door with his back still against the wall and his head and bow pointed at the door. It was probably the closest any of them had ever come to real fighting in their entire lives.

When Richard was about ten paces from the entrance door he began slowly moving out away from the wall and into the street whilst always facing the post with his nocked arrow pointing at the empty doorway. When he was far enough out into the street he began slowly inching his way sideways to the left so as to move more and more toward being in front of the door. He continued moving until he was about ten feet out from the wall and could see a very small sliver of the inside of the post's entry room. No one was in sight.

Slowly, very slowly, and always ignoring the noise and shouted questions coming from the street behind him, and always facing the doorway and ready to instantly push out an arrow, he once again began inching his way very slowly to his left. Each inch he moved let him see a little more of the inside of the entry room.

He stopped moving for a second when he saw a foot with a leather sandal on it. It was lying in a puddle of blood and its toes were pointing slightly upward so he knew it was not a standing man. He continued slowly inching his way leftward. As he did, more and more of a leg came into view and then a body with the feathered fletching of an arrow sticking out of its chest. It did not appear to be moving; it was probably the first man who came into the doorway or the one he caught with his snap shot when he ran to the first man's aid.

After Richard had moved a few more inches to the left he could see the head of the man on the floor and the edge of the doorway into reception room behind him. It was definitely not the man who had been helping hold up Sir Eric. The dead man was lying in a spreading pool of blood.

There were men's voices shouting to each other inside the post but nothing to be seen as Captain Adams continued slowly inching his way to his left so that he could see more and more of the entry room. A few more inches later and he could also see the beginning of the door into reception room behind it. And a few inches after that and he could see into part of the reception room and another body which he did not recognize. It too was lying in a great puddle of blood.

Now he could see more of the entry room and all the way through the doorway into the reception room behind the second body. He had also, without planning to do so, moved closer to the entrance. *Where are they? He could not sure but he thought the voices he had heard had come from both the entry room and the reception room.*

"Come out," he shouted. "This is your last chance."

Suddenly a man's head popped out from behind the entrance door and was instantly withdrawn. He was so close, perhaps just five or six feet, that Richard was startled and jumped. Even worse, the head had appeared and then disappeared so quickly that he had no chance to push an arrow into it. He froze and aimed his nocked arrow at that very spot and waited.

"I am leaving to go for help," Richard shouted.

His announcement was followed by a long period of silence except for a couple of questions that were shouted from somewhere deep inside the post, he could not tell for sure but they might have come from inside the warehouse. He did not respond to them. Instead he stayed silent and ready. Suddenly the same head was poked out from behind the door entrance in the same place for another look. It did not even finish coming around the corner for the look when the Captain Adam's iron-tipped arrow hit it with a great splatting sound.

Chapter Twenty-five

Fighting on the road.

Fifty-two horse archers followed George down the hill to the London road. As soon as they were on the road they divided as he had ordered and began riding down the road toward the rear of the westward bound column. They did so in two very long single-file lines of about twenty-five men each. One line led by George was riding along the right side of the road towards the rear of the enemy column; the other line was riding towards it on the left side under the command of Captain Fisher, the battle group's number two.

Their plan was quite simple as all good plans are—to "push out arrows and ride along both sides of the column without stopping until they reached the front of the column." At that point they would turn around and ride back along the column to finish off the wounded horses, empty the purses of the dead and wounded and pick up whatever captured weapons and armour they could carry away on their horses, and retrieve their arrows. They would turn back earlier if they ran out of arrows or met serious resistance.

George was leading the single-file line of archers on the right with Sergeant Atkins proudly riding immediately behind him. George did not know it, and perhaps never would, but Sergeant Atkins and the chosen man riding in the third position behind him had been taken aside by Captain Fisher and told in no uncertain terms that they were to stop if George's horse went down and protect him until the designated rescue men bringing up the rear arrived with the spare horses. Everyone else was to be waved on past them to continue the attack without stopping.

They began overtaking the usual travelers and local people walking and riding on the road and the column's stragglers almost immediately. The first inkling that the column was somewhere ahead of them was a wagon with a half dozen men standing around looking at the wagon horse whilst one of them examined its right rear hoof. The horse had obviously gone lame.

The men the archers were riding toward appeared to be a knight or his sergeant and some of the men from his village levy. They just stood there and watched as the two long lines of archers trotted toward them. George nocked an arrow and brought his horse up to a slow amble as he approached them. An amble was always preferred by a horse archer pushing out arrows because it was a smoother gait.

"These men are like sheep in a pasture and we are their wolves" was George's thought as he grunted as he pushed his arrow into the side of one of the men's legs up by his arse. The man yelped and George shouted "For the king and Sussex" as he did. The other men standing around the wagon stared with looks of astonishment on their faces for a brief moment and then several of them began running in a forlorn effort to get away. It did them little good; they all were hit by the arrows of one or another of the men riding behind George and so was the horse.

There was a gap requiring several minutes of riding past more of the regular travelers who had gotten back on the road after the column passed before George once again reached another little group of stragglers. They were all on foot and not a one of them was armed. Their horse drawn wagon had stopped and was waiting for them.

Once again George brought his horse up from a trot to an amble and nocked an arrow. This lot appeared to have stopped for a man who had gone off to the side of the road to relieve himself. Perhaps he was their sergeant or just a good friend with whom they had been walking. Whatever the reason, it was bad luck for them. George pushed an arrow into the middle of one of them and kept on riding. Behind him he could hear screams and shouts including those of his men who were also bellowing "for the king and the lords of Sussex and Kent" as they rode past the killed and wounded men.

"Well that battle cry ought to confuse the barons when they hear about it," George thought to himself as he slowed his horse back down in order to conserve its strength. "And they will from both the wounded who survive and the regular travelers on the road."

Pretending to be acting in the service of King Henry and a couple of the two earls was a deliberate part of the Commander's war plan. Gulling your enemies into falling out so they begin fighting each other is always better than risking your own life and the lives of your men to fight them directly. And George knew the barons would hear about his men's battle cry because there always seemed to be a few survivors from the losing side of every battle. Indeed, he had taken steps to insure that some of the barons' wounded would not all be killed so there would be survivors to tell the tale. Whether or not it would gull the barons into fighting amongst themselves or deserting the "Loyal Army" remained to be seen.

******

Less than two minutes after taking out the two parties of stragglers George and his men came up over a rise in the road and saw the column stretched out before them. A minute or so later they reached the tail end of the enemy column.

What they saw in front of them looked to be a mixture of walking men and the wagons of the army's sutlers, knights, and village levies. There were a surprising number of women among them and even a few children. From aboard his horse George could see that some of the people who were walking or riding in wagons at the very rear of the column were looking back at George and his on-coming horse archers. That was to be expected. People are always curious and hoping for something new to talk about. On the other hand the people who were walking and riding beyond the men and wagons at the very rear were mostly looking in the other direction and seemed to be unaware that the two long single-file lines of archers were rapidly approaching in their rear; most of them were looking to the front. That too was to be expected.

George and his archers reached the rear of the enemy column as it was moving through an open area of pastures and croplands. George had deliberately chosen the general area to be the place for his attack and had waited for the column to reach it. He did so in order that his hard-riding horse archers would be able to safely swerve out and around the column and keep going without getting delayed or prevented from continuing by some kind of bottleneck such as might occur if the road it was passing though a thick stand of trees or a bolting horse pulled a wagon in front of them. Catching the enemy column out in the open, of course, had the additional merit of there not being any place where the enemy soldiers might run and hide.

Captain Fisher riding on the left hand side of the road reached the enemy column a few hoof beats before George. As a result, he had the honour of pushing out the first arrow of the Company's attack on the column itself—at a very confused man who was standing on the driver's seat of the wagon bringing up the very rear of the column. He was looking back and forth between the two lines of approaching horsemen in an unsuccessful attempt to understand who they were and what was happening.

George distinctly heard the man scream and saw him fall back into the bed of his wagon when Captain Fisher's arrow hit him. So he contented himself with pushing an arrow deep into the side of the horse pulling the wagon. The wounded horse promptly bolted off the road with the wagon bouncing along behind it such that the archers riding behind George and Sergeant Atkins had to ride around it. Such sudden and unexpected impediments of one type or another began to occur constantly and caused the two lines of archers to get longer or longer instead of each archer riding immediately behind the next. Unexpected obstacles had not been part of the practice attacks George had organized. They were unexpected and, every so often, allowed some of the men in the enemy column time to get to their weapons.

Despite the unexpected problems, the two lines of archers continually flowed westward along on both sides of the column and pushed out arrows whenever they had an arrow nocked and saw a man or horse who had not yet been hit. As you might imagine, very few of the barons' men and horses escaped unscathed by the time the last archers in the two single-file lines had ridden past them.

As a general rule the priority targets for the archers riding up front with George were the men who were carrying weapons and those who were trying to escape by running out into the empty fields and pastures. They were targeted by the archers riding at the front of the attack because they knew archers coming behind them would take the men and horses who remained on the road. Even so, every so often a runner was able to get far enough off the road to survive the archers' arrows and a few were even able to escape by running between the passing archers' horses without being hit. There were screaming, shouting, and bolting horses and men everywhere. Chaos rippled up the column along with arrival of the first archers.

George himself led the archers of the line moving up the right side of the column until he had used all the arrows in two of his quivers, about twenty-five in all. Then he and Bill Atkins and the three riders behind Bill pulled out of the single file line and began waving their hands to signal the others to move forward to take their places at the front of the line. This much, at least, they had practiced. George gave up the lead both because his arms were getting tired and because he wanted to see how the rest of the archers were performing. He also wanted to know if his men had suffered any casualties. Truth be told, he was getting tired of shooting down unarmed men and horses even though he knew it was necessary.

It was wonderful battle in the sense of it always being best to fight an unarmed enemy; most of the soldiers in the enemy column were walking and riding without their weapons and had no chance to defend themselves before they were hit with an arrow. That was because they did not have time to get to their wagons and retrieve their weapons before they were shot down by the archers riding past them toward the front of the column.

* * * * * *

Sergeant Atkins and the three men who had been riding behind him waited next to road while George ordered the archers riding in the rear to move towards the front to take the place of those whose arrows were being rapidly depleted and whose arms were getting tired. It did not take long as the archers' horses were all ambling as they came past and there were only about twenty-five of them in each single file line.

All around them as George and Sergeant Atkins sat on their blowing and snorting horses were the ear-piercing screams of wounded horses and the shouts and cries of agony from the wounded men and the women attempting to assist them. It was everywhere an absolute and noisy chaos by the time the last archers in the two single-file lines finished riding past. Behind them they had left dead and wounded men and horses everywhere on the road and along both sides of it. George's horse and those of the men who had stopped with him were very skittish, probably because of the screams of the wounded horses and the general excitement that was all around them.

By the time the last man in each line of archers finished riding past many of the column's wagons were in the ditches next to the road with dead and wounded horses or mules in their traces and many of those were turned over on their sides and backs. Dead and wounded men, supplies, bedding, and weapons were strewn about everywhere. It was like that as far as the eye could see towards the rear of the enemy column.

The attack had proceeded very much as George had envisioned, at least it did at first. That was because George and his men had ridden very rapidly along both sides of the enemy column without stopping or slowing down. It undoubtedly helped that he had also laid down very firm orders as to how the archers were to use the hundred or so of arrows that each man was carrying. And as you might imagine, it also helped that George's sergeants and their archers agreed with his orders and followed them because they made good sense.

First and foremost the horse archers were to take out any man on horseback or standing next to a saddled horse so that an enemy rider could neither gallop along the column ahead of them and sound the alarm nor draw his sword and fall upon the archers as they rode past him. Secondly, they were to take out any man with a weapon or riding in a wagon where they might have weapons close at hand. The priority after that were the wagon drivers and their horses, and then, finally, the men walking in the column without their weapons. Arrows were not to be wasted under any circumstance on women or children or on wounded men and wounded horses.

In any event, most of the weapons the barons' men had brought with them were spears and swords and knightly lances, weapons that would not have been useful against the archers' longbows even if the barons' men had been able to get to them. The barons' men, in essence, were bringing blades and spears with an effective range of a few feet to a war with archers equipped with longbows whose arrows could reach out for hundreds of feet.

At first it was one long rapidly moving slaughter with very few of the barons' men and horses able to escape by the time the last of the archers rode past them. Everything changed after the first six or seven minutes, however, when the fast-moving leaders of the two lines of horse archers were about half of the way up the enemy column. Word had somehow reached the men walking and riding at the front of the column that their mates were under attack behind them. At that point, the men the archers had not yet reached went for their weapons and those with horses began climbing aboard them to fight or run.

It did not take long before the horse archers riding in the front went from being unopposed to coming upon men who were armed and as ready as they could be to defend themselves with their swords and spears. But even that was not enough to stop the attack because the archers immediately began doing what they had been ordered to do—for a minute or two longer they rode further out from the column and continued riding forward and pushing arrows at the men who were futilely waving swords and spears at them.

Everything changed once again when the horse archers at the front of George's two long lines of riders learned the hard way that some of the barons' men were using bows, albeit short bows, and also that some of the enemy horsemen had been able to get mounted and appeared to be gathering for a counter-attack. At that point, following George's orders, the archers at the front broke off contact with the column and began riding back down the devastated rear two-thirds of the column. They carried their dead, wounded, and unhorsed men with them, in some cases slung over the backs of the horses of the archers who were still able-bodied.

As they began to retreat the horse archers began looking back over their shoulders as they rode and got ready to push arrows at anyone who might be pursuing them. They had lost one man killed by a crossbow quarrel, six men wounded with varying degrees of severity, and a number of horses had been lost for one reason or another.

At first the enemy did not make a determined effort to follow the now-withdrawing and turned around archers with a counter attack. As a result, the archers were able to stop along the way to pick up some of their arrows and the coin pouches of some of the enemy dead and wounded.

By the time the returning horse archers reached George and Sergeant Atkins enemy riders waving swords had begun slowly riding through several miles of devastation toward them. Others of the barons' men and women had begun walking cautiously through the devastation seeking family members and friends. It appeared they were doing so more for the purpose of looting and making rescues than as a counter-attack.

Indeed, the initial arrivals of men and women from the front of the column were so tentative and cautious and loot-seeking that George briefly thought about having the archers ride out around them and continuing to attack the front of the column that the counter-attacking walkers and riders had gone off and left unguarded. But he soon abandoned the idea and began motioning with his arm to withdraw his men as more and more of the barons' men from the head of the column began to arrive carrying their weapons.

In any event, the slowly developing return of armed men to the devastated portion of the column forced George and his archers to move further away from the road. But they did not leave the field. Instead, as they had been previously ordered, they split off into little groups of six or seven men under their sergeants and continually ranged along both sides of the destroyed portion of the column and continually pushed arrows at all of the baron's horsemen and anyone on foot who appeared to be carrying a weapon, especially when they saw someone who did not appear to be a threat.

More specifically, the archers began harassing the would-be rescuers and looters in order to encourage them to turn back. Unfortunately, that also periodically brought them within range of the handful of the barons' men who were armed with crossbows and another horse archer was badly wounded.

An hour or so after the attack began the barons' surviving riders, mostly knights and squires from the front of the column equipped with their traditional swords and lances, finally got themselves into their armour and tried to launch a counter-attack. They rode down the column toward the archers with their lances and swords outstretched whilst aboard their lumbering large horses. It was how they had been learnt to fight similar equipped enemies.

The charge of the barons' sword and lance carrying horsemen was impressive but did not succeed; the archers galloped away whilst turning their saddles and peppering the pursuers and their horse with arrows in the Saracen style. This inevitably continued until the pursuers stopped their futile chases and turned their large and lumbering horses back to rejoin what was left of their column.

And when the barons' knights did turn back, the archers turned back with them and followed them and all the way back whilst constantly showering them with arrows. A good number of the counterattacking knights and squires went down, mostly when their horses were hit and then either fell or threw their riders off. The archers would then stand off and push arrows at the knight until he was killed or wounded. Surrenders were not accepted from horsemen.

It was quite a sight. Everywhere on both sides of the devastated column there were little groups of horse archers riding together and periodically retreating and attacking. It was a way of fighting that most of the barons' men had ever seen before unless they had been crusaders and experienced Saracen attacks.

The archers' horse holders watched and waited idly in the distance except when an unhorsed but otherwise able-bodied archer was carried to them to get another horse or a wounded man was brought there so that one or two of the horse holders could try to get him back to the camp where the archers' supply wagons were hidden.

It did not take long before the barons' knights and other riders to learn, often fatally or painfully, about what the archers called "the wounded bird." That was where the archers pretended to flee until their pursuers, inevitably waving swords or lances, were strung out behind them on tired horses. At which point the archers being pursued would turn back to pick off their now tired pursuers one at a time—it is, after all, as everyone knows, always easier and safer to shoot someone in the back whilst he is riding or when he is standing helpless and with no way to defend himself.

******

Several hours were spent in such endeavours and additional dozens of barons' men fell, especially among the surviving knights who became increasingly aggrieved, and finally retired, because the archers were not willing to "fight properly." It was not until an hour or so after the fighting began when there were no more foolish knights and other riders coming out to be killed that George and his men began shouting an offer to the people who were still alive and in the column's devastated middle and rear.

"We will not shoot arrows at you whilst you are moving your wounded and the women and children to safety at the front of the column," the archers shouted. "Have at least one person who is helping to carry each wounded man walk with his or her hand raised so we know that is what you are doing."

And then later when the barons' wounded were being successfully moved and the truthfulness of the archers' offer had been established, the archers were ordered to begin shouting something new—"turn around and return to your homes; we will not attack anyone who ends his rebellion against King Henry and begins walking eastward on the road to return to his home."

They also began shouting "every unarmed man who walks eastward on the road will be unharmed, neither today *nor* in the days that follow; those who do not return to their homes will be killed or die of starvation."

The shouted offers of George and his men were surprisingly successful. The barons' men in devastated portion of the column, tentatively at first and then in a great surge, began frantically raising their hands and moving their wounded and the women and children to temporary safety at the front of the column. And more than a few threw down their arms and began walking in the other direction back toward Oxford and London. Whether they would keep on walking or turn around when it got dark and try to rejoin their mates remained to be seen.

The archers remained quietly on their horses and rested and watched as the barons' men abandoned their dead and dying. In doing so the barons' men did exactly what George wanted them to do most of all—the wounded would help eat up the barons' food supplies and the dead men and horses behind to rot in the sun would serve as warning to the men of the barons' armies who would be on the road in the days to come.

George and his archers moved back to the road once the barons' wounded and women began being moved to safety. When they reached the road they counted over three hundred dead and dying men and over two hundred dead and dying horses and mules, most of them still in the traces of the wagons they had been pulling or still moored to the wagons behind which they had been walking. The severely wounded horses and mules were mercied whenever possible.

The archers also found a number of seriously wounded barons' men who had been left behind even though some of them might have been able to survive with proper barbering. They were left untouched where they had fallen unless, of course, they had an arrow in them that could be retrieved. Then they were mercifully hit on the head so they would go to sleep for a while whilst the arrow was being pushed on through so that it could be cleaned up and re-used. And, of course, it was not that the archers were being merciful in temporarily putting the enemy wounded to sleep; it is, after all, much easier to get an arrow out of a wounded man when he is not jumping around and screaming as it is pushed out or cut loose. *Pulling them out rarely is successful as the valuable heads tend to come loose such that only the shafts are recovered.*

The archers who returned to the road were there primarily to retrieve their arrows and pick up any loot they might find. Accordingly, except when they were attempting to recover their arrows, they ignored the enemy wounded who had been abandoned by their mates and promptly began burning the wagons and scattering their contents. Unfortunately, the wounded men who were "walking wounded" and the women who retreated to the head of the column carrying those of their badly wounded friends and husbands they wished to rescue had also carried off the coin pouches of the dead and seriously wounded and most of their swords, armour, and other valuables.

Scribe's note: Pilgrims and other travelers in the decades that followed the war sometimes wondered in their letters why several of England's main roads suddenly and for no apparent reason veered off in a great half circle in several places along them. It was certainly no secret to the travelers at the time—the bodies and bones of hundreds of dead men and horses smell most foul for years if they are never buried. It seems that they were in such a terrible state by the time the fighting ended that either no one cared enough to bury them or there were not enough barons' men left alive to do it. The reports vary.

Chapter Twenty-six

The aftermath and more.

George began thinking about what had gone wrong as soon as he and the main body of his men had broken off contact with the enemy column and begun riding back to their isolated temporary camp. In one sense it was a great victory. On the other hand, the column had *not* been totally destroyed as he had hoped to do. But why had it not? Was it because the enemy column was longer than he thought because there were more men and horses in it than he had expected. Or perhaps one of the barons' men who was already mounted had somehow been able to do what George had most feared would happen—he had galloped from where the column was being attacked and warned his mates at the front of the column that there was fighting behind them. Or perhaps the road at the front of the barons' column was going up a hill so that the men on horseback or riding in wagons could see the rear and realized it was under attack.

By the time George and the first thirty or so of his men reached the wagons and supplies at their secluded camp carrying their two dead and seven seriously wounded men George realized that how the barons' men at the front became aware of the attack did not matter. Nor did it matter that the enemy riders had begun riding back to see what was happening and join the fight had been not been a problem since it allowed his men to kill and wound some of them and their horses—what had stopped him and his archers from totally destroying the column was that the barons had a few archers with short bows and crossbows in their column. And also, of course, they had begun to run out of arrows.

As a result of the barons' archers and the shortage of arrows, George and his men had not totally destroyed the column and he had ended up losing two men killed and seven badly enough wounded and hurt from various causes that they would not be able to ride and fight again for weeks, including two poor sods who were so seriously wounded that they might require a mercy along with anyone else whose wounds turned black and began to smell. They had also permanently lost at least eleven horses and another five or six that were temporarily unavailable whilst they were being barbered.

A dozen or so of the archers under Captain Fisher had remained behind with their remounts and five horse holders to make sure the barons' men did not return to bury their dead or butcher the horses for food. They were under strict orders not to hinder people that returned to try to barber the wounded that had been abandoned or people that were trying to leave the column and move eastward towards Oxford and London—so long as they did not stop and try to bury the dead or cut meat off the horses.

The barons' men, for their part, the survivors that is, responded to the attack and their disastrous losses by moving their wagons off the road and into a great defensive circle in a nearby field. They ended up staying there for several weeks until the lack of food and unrest and numerous desertions from amongst the survivors resulted in all but three of the surviving barons to lead what was left of their disheartened men back to their homes. Captain Fisher's archers helped them reach their decision by letting the deserters leave and by constantly prowling around the barons' encampment and picking off anyone who tried to go out to forage.

Only the men who left the barons' camp without their weapons and began walking eastward toward London were not shot down. Two of the three barons who pressed on had been marching with their knights and levies near the head of the column and suffered relatively minor casualties. The third did so because he apparently did not want to go home to his wife and had nothing better to do.

The baron who did not want to go home to his wife got what he wanted; one of the archers' raiding companies wiped out what remained of his little army three days later and left no survivors. The names and fate of the other two big land owners and their men is unknown.

****** *Ilchester*

The kindly old priest put the man's broken piece of a small copper coin on the wooden tavern table and nodded his thanks. And then, with the man watching with fear in his eyes, the priest put his left elbow on the table and used his left hand to hold the man's outstretched calloused and grimy hand in place above the table. The old priest immediately began mumbling a prayer in Latin and running the pointing finger of his right hand slowly and carefully over the hand's many lines and creases. The man had said his name was Julian and the he was a serf without a family name in the village levy of a knight called Sir Randolf.

"Oh," the priest said after almost a minute of searching and touching the man's hand. "Oh my." Then, still holding on to the man's hand with his left hand, he crossed himself with the hand of his pointing finger. Then he returned to slowly running his pointing finger over the lines and creases he was intently examining.

A few seconds later the priest dropped the man's hand, picked up the piece of broken coin, and handed it back to the man with a sorrowful look on his face.

"I cannot take this if you are going to continue on to Cornwall with Sir Randolf," the priest said very quietly in almost a whisper. "It would poison my soul and send me to purgatory. You should give it to your wife if she is with you or have a friend carry it home to her as a memory of what she has lost."

The man's face turned white beneath his beard and his rough and calloused hand began shaking as he held it out to accept the return of the broken little piece of copper.

"Am I really doomed?" he asked in a shaky voice.

"Yes, I am afraid so *if* you continue marching toward the west where the sun goes down. It will be a long and painful death *unless* you do what is necessary to avoid it by returning home immediately."

The man's face brightened for a moment, and then faded.

"But what can I do? Sir Randolf will be hard on me if I run. He will flog me and kill me when he returns after the war." The man's hands were shaking as he explained his problem.

"There is no need to worry, Julian. Your Sir Randolf will not be returning home to bother you unless he too leaves immediately. Nor are any of your mates from the village likely to return to their hovels unless they also return home as quickly as possible. I cannot be sure until I see their hands, of course, but it is likely that every man who even tries to set foot in Devon and Cornwall will die most horrible and spend eternity in purgatory for trying to rise up against King Henry and his heirs, the kings that God himself has chosen for them."

Then the priest whispered another warning to the white-faced and trembling Julian.

"You will be safe only if you go home as soon as possible and *only* if you never tell anyone that I warned you to do so. I am a priest and protected by God as I am sure you know; so you need to remember that God will make sure that you die in horrible pain and stay in purgatory forever if you ever tell anyone that I warned you what would happen if you continued to march toward Cornwall. In other words, my dear Julian, I told you a priestly secret and you must always remember that anyone who reveals a priestly secret is doomed to die in great agony and stay in purgatory forever."

The priest crossed himself as he spoke, mumbled a few words in Latin, and then spoke again to Julian.

"Now smile as you leave since God has told you how to save yourself and send in the next man."

Was it true about what would happen if someone revealed a priestly secret? The old priest was not sure it was the word of God since he had neither heard of it whilst he was at the Company school being learnt to be an archer and an Angelovian nor in the years that followed. But it certainly sounded like something a Pope might have announced as the word of God if he was found with coins that belonged to someone else in his possession or a woman or boy in his bed—and that was close enough since the priest knew it was quite likely to have already happened or might in the future when a new Pope was chosen.

****** *Fish Street, London*

Captain Adams was on high alert as he moved cautiously down the narrow cobblestoned street toward the doorway of his post's little entrance room. As he did he could see the man who had just taken an arrow into the side of his head—he was lying on the floor in a rapidly spreading pool of blood that was flowing in little spurts out his mouth and from both sides of his head both where the arrow had gone in and where its bloody point had come out. The still-flowing blood did not surprise Captain Adams; he knew from his experiences fighting in the east against Moorish pirates that the blood would keep coming for several minutes as it always does when a man is killed by an arrow or sword that hits him in his head.

The captain was moving cautiously because he thought that there might be another of Giffard's men alive in the post's entry room and also because he knew for sure that there were several more of them in the reception and warehouse rooms behind it. His problem was that he did not know how many there were or where they were located.

Captain Adams had his longbow up and its nocked arrow pointed toward the doorway of the entry room as he moved very slowly around the corner and saw more and more of the room. He did so from the right hand side of the entrance door that opened on to Fish Street, the street that ran in front of the post.

He had already been able to look in through the door and several of the narrow wall openings and seen that there was no one in the middle and left side of the room. But he had not been able to see the entire room when he quickly looked in and then pulled his head back. There was at least a possibility that was still another man or even two crouched with their weapons ready below the wall openings so they could not be seen by anyone looking in. He thought there might be at least one but he was not at all certain.

As he started to enter the room through the doorway he suddenly realized he had made a truly major mistake. He gotten overbalanced with fear about his wife and family and had moved against his post's attackers without doing enough thinking. It suddenly came into the space behind his eyes that what he should have done was go down the narrow alley next to the post's building that was used for shitting and pissing and look through the wall openings that lit the post's rooms to see what he could see.

It could be done, looking in that is, because the shutters for each of the post's wall opening were only closed in the summertime when it was dark in order to prevent the entry of the city's night vapours which were well known to be quite dangerous. It was a summer day and he knew the wooden shutters would still be open to let in light.

The post's wall openings were only good for letting in light. That was because they were deliberately much too narrow for even the skinniest child to squeeze through and unbar the door so thieves and robbers could enter. But they certainly were wide enough for him to be able to look in to see where Giffard's men were located and how many were left.

Hmm. Was the alley also wide enough for him to face the post's wall openings and use his longbow to push arrows at the men inside? He was not sure even though he had been in it many times to relieve himself or to empty his family's chamber pot. Hopefully, the alley was wide enough for him to do more than just look inside and relieve himself; but even if it was not he would be able to look in and see what he could see.

******

Richard slowly backed away from the post's entrance. Then, bending low so he would not be seen by anyone inside who was peering out into Fish Street through the narrow wall openings of the entry room, he hurried around the front of the building and ran into the extremely narrow alley. As he did he noticed the crowd of onlookers had continued to grow on the other side of the street.

There were a lot of "oohs" and "ahhs" and people pointing at him as he ran towards the alley and turned to enter it.

The alley smelled most foul, probably because it had not rained since the previous morning and was frequently used by the people living in the buildings on either side of it. It was also used by people passing on the street in front of the alley. Richard was so used to the smell coming into his post through its narrow wall openings that he barely noticed it as he entered the alley, although he was well aware of the need to be careful where he put his feet down and did so without thinking.

What he immediately realized when he entered the alley was encouraging: The alley was wide enough for him to stand facing the openings in his post's wall and fully draw his bow with the point of a nocked arrow protruding from it plus the extra foot or so he would need to push his arrow forward with sufficient force without banging his hand into the daub and wattle wall.

Richard immediately crept up to the first of the wall openings and cautiously peered in. What he saw surprised him: There was no one in the entry room! They must have either run out the front door into the street after he began moving toward the alley *or* they had moved back deeper into the post's reception room or the warehouse that was immediately beyond it.

As Richard moved cautiously down the alley to the first of the wall openings into the next room, the reception room where the post's affairs were conducted with its customers, he decided that whoever had been in the entry room must have moved back deeper into the building. It was almost certainly what had happened because the noise from the gathering crowd would have changed if the watchers in the street had seen someone suddenly try to make a run for safety.

He very slowly and cautiously approached wall opening. Yes! There were three of them crouched against the wall less than ten feet away—and they were all intently looking toward the door! Two of them were holding bared swords and one, the man closest to the wall opening, looked to be ragged and unarmed, probably one of Giffard's serfs or slaves from the look of the rags he was wearing and the fact he was barefooted and the other two were wearing sandals.

The better dressed of the two swordsmen was cautiously leaning his head into the doorway so he could see both the entry room and the street beyond it. There was a body lying in a pool of blood just beyond the doorway. One of the men he had hit in the entry room must have tried to crawl to safety; or perhaps he had been pulled there by one of his mates before he was abandoned.

Richard did not hesitate. He pushed an arrow at the man who was trying to peer through the door to see what was happening. But as he did he must have made a noise because everyone turned to look at him just as he pushed out the arrow. And as he did, he simultaneously heard the familiar sounds of the splatting "thud" of an arrow hitting flesh and the slapping sound as his bowstring bounced off his leather wrist protector.

The arrow aimed at the man's back hit him in the side of his shoulder as he turned. His yelp and the look on his face were those of stunned surprise, but not yet those of pain and fear. They would come soon enough.

Everything happened at once. Richard began pulling another arrow out of one of his quivers, the raggedly dressed man screamed and cowered against the wall, and the other swordsman made a serious mistake—he ran for the door into the warehouse and got safely through it before Richard could push an arrow at him. It was a mistake because there would have been no way for Richard to stop him if he had run in the other direction and out into the street; now he was even deeper into the shipping post and still had to get past Richard. Perhaps he did not know there was only one way in and out of the post.

Richard did not hesitate. He grunted as he pushed another arrow at the wounded man who was still staring at him with a look of total disbelief on his face. This one took him full in his chest and drove him backwards such that he tripped over the dead body and went over backwards.

"Who is your master?" Richard shouted at the ragged man who was down on his knees with hands clasped together and staring at him with big and frightened eyes. He shouted out his question as he nocked another arrow and pointed it at the man. "Tell me who your master is and I will let you live."

"My master is James, the stable captain," came the quavering answer. "I clean the stalls and carry water and hay to the horses. Sometimes James lets me drive a wagon and sometimes I work in the kitchen. Please Master, do not kill me."

"Who is the stable captain's lord?"

"James is the captain of his lordship's horses. Please Master, I mean no harm. Do not hurt me, please." The man obviously did not understand the question.

"Who is his lordship?"

"The earl is his Lordship, Master." He said it beseechingly whilst on his knees and wringing his hands in a manner most abject and pleading. "The Earl of Westminster."

"Does the Earl of Westminster know the men who brought you here? Did he send them here?"

"Yes Master, I am sure he knows them. I saw him talking with Sir Robert and Sir Eric before we set off. It is the Earl's wagon that is in the street out front. I be driving it. Please do not hurt poor me."

"Alright. Alright. I will let you live and not hurt you. But only on one condition: You are to run to the stable that is two streets further down the river from here and wait for me there. It is the stable of the Company of Archers. If you are waiting there when I return I will give you two copper pennies; if you are not waiting there for me I will have the Earl flog you until you die. Do you understand?"

"Yes Master, I understand; thank you, thank you. God will bless you. God will bless you," he said while nodding his agreement and continuing to wring his hands most abjectly. He was still on his knees.

"Then get up and be off with you. And you must run all the way and not stop until you reach the stable. If you stop and talk to anyone I will see flogged to death."

And with that, Richard turned away and began to make his way further down the alley. He did not wait to see the slave leave. If he had, he would have seen the ragged man's trembling fingers as he took the coin pouches off the two dead men before he hurried out on to Fish Street and began running.

Chapter Twenty-seven

The fighting continues.

Richard moved slowly down the alley and approached the first wall opening of his post's warehouse with a great deal of caution. His bow was at the ready with an arrow already nocked. Of course he was cautious; there were men in there and they knew he was in the alley—and then he nearly jumped out of his skin when he started to raise his head to look in the narrow opening and its wooden shutters were literally slammed shut in his face. A moment later he could hear someone grunt and then there was the familiar sound of a wooden shutter bar being dropped into place.

The archer captain did not waste a moment. He moved as quickly as he could down the alley to the next wall opening. It was still open and he could hear men talking back and forth to one another in excited voices. There were at least two of them, he decided, and possibly even three. He crouched slightly so that he was just below the wall opening and drew his bow with the arrow pointed at the wall opening which was only inches away—and waited.

A moment or two later he heard someone talking loudly who was walking towards the wall opening, apparently to close its shutters. Suddenly a head and arm popped into view as a man reached across the opening to close the shutter. He was less than three feet away.

The shutter was never closed. Richard's arrow was pushed out with all his strength. It went through the man's neck all the up to the arrow's fletching feathers and he staggered away backwards into the room, and then began to make a great commotion as he stumbled about banging into things and making strange gagging noises. There was a lot of shouting from others in the room.

Richard instantly nocked another arrow, drew his bowstring, and held the arrow's fletching up to his eye as looked into the room along its length. He was as ready as he could be—and he could see nothing, not even the man who had staggered away from the wall opening with an arrow in his neck.

"Are you the Earl of Westminster's men?" Richard finally shouted in through the wall opening without showing himself. "Who sent you and where are the women and children?"

"Who are you," someone shouted from where he was hiding behind a stack of crates. There was more than a little touch of fear and hysteria in his voice.

"I am the man who is going to order your hands and feet to be cut off one at a time if you do not answer my questions." ... "Does the Earl of Westminster know you are here?"

"I think so. Yes, of course he does. He sent us,"was the somewhat quavering reply.

Suddenly a man came out from behind the crates carrying a bared sword and ran for the door. Richard instantly pushed an arrow at him—and missed.

Cursing and nocking another arrow as he ran, Richard hurried down the little alley until he reached Fish Street. He got there just in time to see a man with his sword in his hand run through the crowd of watchers and moments later get safely around the corner of the building on the Thames Road. It was the very same corner where Richard had paused to watch the raiders before he had moved forward and begun attacking them.

For a very brief moment Richard considered running after the fleeing man. But he quickly decided against it; he was gone and would likely bring back reinforcements. Instead, he very cautiously entered the shipping post through it front door with his nocked arrow pointing the way and his longbow at the ready. Was the man who had answered him still in there or was he the runner? He had heard voices calling back and forth so he knew there was at least one more man inside.

******   *Inside the shipping post*

It would not be long before the runner returned with reinforcements. Even so Richard moved very slowly and carefully through the entry room into the reception room beyond it and then into the post's warehouse. The first thing he saw even before he moved through the door to the warehouse was a man in the doorway with an arrow in his neck. He was lying in a rapidly spreading pool of blood.

Everything was totally silent once the archer captain stepped over the body and entered the post's warehouse. As he did he left some of the noise of the street behind. He saw the crates piled up under the closed trapdoor to his family's room as soon as he came through the door into the warehouse. A moment later he realized that the overly long ladder used to climb up to the room was missing. A great relief swept over him as he realized what the empty room and the missing ladder and closed trapdoor meant—that his family and the post's other women and children had climbed the ladder to his family's room and pulled it up behind them.

About then there was a rustling noise in the far corner of the warehouse and any thoughts he might have had about calling out to his wife disappeared.

"We have you greatly outnumbered," He shouted rather loudly but not unpleasantly. "If you come out now and surrender we will let you live if you answer our questions; if we have to come in there to get you, then for sure you will die. You must surrender immediately. It is your only hope of staying alive."

It was all a lie, of course; Richard wanted whoever was there alive.

"Will you really let me surrender and not kill me?" A very tentative and quavering voice asked after a pause. It came from behind a large pile of wooden cargo crates. There was great fear in the voice and rightly so.

"Come out now with your hands in the air where we can see them," Richard said with authority in his voice. It was about then that it really dawned on him that he was about to have a problem, a very serious problem, if the escaper returned with reinforcements before he could get his family away. "Hurry. Come out now or we will come in after you and kill you. Is anyone else with you?"

A moment later a voice shouted "I am coming out. I am coming out. A moment later it added "I am alone." There was the sound of someone moving and a few seconds later a well-dressed man wearing leather sandals poked his head around a pile of crates. Then he slowly and very tentatively came out from behind the crates with his hands in the air. He had a very frightened look on his face—and he was wearing the well-known livery of the Earl of Westminster. It was prominent in London and Captain Adams recognized it immediately.

"Face down on the floor and spread out your arms and legs. Do it now or die most painful," Richard shouted at the man. Then, as the man complied, he shouted as loud as he possibly could.

"ELSPETH, CAN YOU HEAR ME, ELSPETH?"

There was a reply but it seemed to be coming from somewhere far away. WHERE ARE YOU? He shouted again. The response again seemed far away. And then he knew—she was in the escape room on the other side of the warehouse wall and six or seven feet further down at the entrance to the tunnel.

"COME OUT IMMEDIATELY. BRING ALICIA WITH YOU. YOU TWO COME FIRST; I NEED YOU HERE AS SOON AS POSSIBLE. HURRY. EVERYONE OUT."

There was a muffled reply. "We are coming. We are coming."

******

Elspeth's arrival seemed to take forever. Richard spent the time questioning the man who surrendered. He learned more and more and got increasingly anxious as he did. Finally he heard footsteps hurrying across the floor above him. A few seconds later he heard a familiar sound above him as the wooden bar that prevented the trap door from being opened was pulled loose and thrown aside. A moment later the trap door was pulled open.

"Hurry, you must hurry," he shouted as Elspeth pushed the ladder through the opening and began climbing down it with his daughter and the other women and children coming down right behind her.

"Run to the stable with Alicia as fast as you can," he shouted at her as she came down the ladder.

"Do not wait for the others. I will send them to you. There is a wagon waiting in the Company stable with two saddled horses tied behind it. Lead the wagon horse to the Acorn Tavern on the next street and wait there with it. You know where it is.

"Take any hostlers in the stables with you and be ready to gallop off to the safe house if you see anyone carrying weapons who looks dangerous. As soon as all the women and children arrive and can be loaded into the wagon you must drive it to the safe house. Stay there until I come to you. Now run. Hurry."

His hurried orders, the strained and anxious sound of his voice, and the look on his face were enough to convince her. Elspeth took Alicia's hand and ran for the door. She had seen the ashen-faced prisoner and the bodies lying about in pools of blood and understood that this was not the time to stop and ask questions.

* * * * * *

Richard sent the post's women and children hurrying after Elspeth as fast as they came down the ladder. They had been scared out of their wits by all the unexpected events and were more than happy to run past the dead men and leave. Then Richard turned his full attention to the prisoner. He had already found a line and tied the man's hands behind his back whilst the last of the women and children were coming down the ladder and being told to run for the Company's stable. Another line was tied around his neck for Richard to hold so the man could not run away.

"I hope you understand that I will not hesitate to knife you or put an arrow through you if you try to run away," Richard said very emphatically. He was very convincing because he truly meant it.

When the ashen-faced and trembling prisoner nodded and in a tremulous voice said he understood, Richard told him to get up and walk to door. "And you better move as fast as you can—because I will leave you behind with your guts cut open or an arrow in your belly if I have to run for it and you do not keep up."

The prisoner took Richard's words seriously, as well he should in view of the bodies he saw and the sticky pools of blood he stepped in as he hurried to the door. His sandals made strange sounds and tried to stick to the floor as he did.

"Turn left on the street and keep going without saying a word to anyone. Now start running," Richard ordered as they came out of the post's entranceway. The prisoner obeyed and they both ran with Richard right behind him with his bow in one hand and holding the neck rope with the other. Turning left as they came out of the post meant they were headed away from the river road instead of toward it.

The crowd of watchers on the street had grown even larger and there was much shouting and pointing as they emerged and began hurrying down the street. The fact that the prisoner's arms were tied behind his back and he was being kept from running away by a rope around his neck was clear to everyone.

They had gotten out of the shipping post just in time. Richard and his prisoner had just gone past the first cross street when a band of twenty or more men led by a man on horseback came running around the corner from the road that ran along the Thames and entered Ship Street. They paid no attention to the two men running down the street away from them and headed straight for the door to the Company's shipping post.

"Turn right at the next corner and then slow down to a fast walk," Richard ordered to the man who had already gone past the cross street and was jogging about ten paces in front of him. He had not liked the way the people in the street looked at them and called out as they had hurried out of the post. The last thing he needed was some busybody or a reward-seeker in the crowd pointing out which way they were running to the new arrivals.

Accordingly, as he turned the corner he un-nocked his arrow and began holding his bow by his side in order to attract less attention. He also linked his left arm with his prisoner's right arm so they could walk together and appear to be friends—and talk. But he still held tight to the neck rope and was instantly ready to stick his knife in him.

"We will have to walk the long way round to get to the safe house," he muttered to himself as they made the turn.

******

Richard's prisoner's name was John and Richard resumed questioning him as soon as they began briskly walking to the Company's new safe house. John was a reeve in the household of the Earl of Westminster and desperately willing to do anything to avoid the fate of his fellow robbers. The reeve had seen first-hand what Richard had done to his fellow robbers so, as you might expect, he anxiously did his best to answer all the questions that were put to him. As you might also expect, the archer captain learned quite a lot about the Earl of Westminster and the raid on his shipping post by the time he saw the warehouse that was his post's new safe house up ahead of them about an hour later. Richard believed that the terrified man's answers were true.

One thing Richard learned was that John reeve had been sent on the raid because he was in charge of collecting the Earl's rents and guarding his coins. Another was that the Earl had begun marching west six days earlier with a huge army of more than two thousand of his vassals and more than five hundred mercenaries from France and the lowlands—and they would be joined along the way by hundreds more men from the Earl's traditional lands in the north.

In fact, Richard had already heard that the Earl's army had begun marching from the merchants at several of the markets which operated on land owned by the earl. Indeed, he had already sent word about the Earl's army to Cornwall—but he was glad to hear about it again because it helped confirm that the reeve was telling the truth about what else he said.

"His lordship told Sir Eric to wait for six days until after he and his army were well past Windsor so he would not be blamed for the raid if it went foul. We were to see the coins safe in his London castle and then Sir Eric and his men were to ride hard to catch up with him on the road to Devon and Cornwall. But not me because I am not a fighting man; I was to stay in London and continuing collecting the Earl's rents."

John said he did not know how or when the Earl had learnt about the Company's wealth and that there were coin chests in the Company's London shipping post. But he said he was not at all surprised that the Earl knew about them. According to the reeve, the Earl of Westminster was one of England's richest men and consumed with the idea that he needed to get even richer. He was also, according to the reeve, extremely jealousy of anyone, including the king, who might have more coins in his chests than he did.

"His lordship is always trying to find out who might have more coins than he does. The merchants and moneylenders probably told him about the Company of Archers and its London shipping post. It is well known, after all, that your Company promptly pays the money orders that are constantly being submitted to it and also accepts coins for safe-keeping. So it stands to reason that you must always have a big reserve of coins available in your chests, eh?"

The reeve also told Richard that the Earl of Westminster had been so inspired by the way the Church selected its Popes that he had recently had one of his clerics draw up lists of the barons whose support he would need to be proclaimed king when Henry died—and how much he estimated it would cost to buy each man's support. But it was not King Henry's crown the Earl really wanted, according to the reeve, it was the rents that the king collected from his lands and the king's ability to collect taxes and tithes.

"If a rich cardinal can buy the support of enough of the Church's cardinals to become the Pope and make himself even richer," the reeve claimed to have heard the Earl say on more than one occasion whilst he was tipsy from drinking too much, "then so can an English noble such as myself buy the support of England's barons and become England's king and make myself even richer, and without having to waste my time mumbling prayers."

According to John Reeve, the Earl of Westminster had a burning desire to possess even more coins and to collect more rents than anyone else in England including the king. He also thought there would be no knights or nobles to oppose the barons in Devon and Cornwall and had become convinced of the barons' inevitable victory. As a result, he had decided that he might as well go ahead and take whatever coins the Cornwall-based Company had in London since if he did not take them one of the other nobles would.

What truly galled and greatly infuriated Richard was that the Earl actually would, in fact, end up with the coins that were kept in Company's shipping post for safekeeping and to pay the money orders that the Company sold in London and its other posts. And not only that, the Earl would also end up with the Company's chests of the priceless pain-killing flower paste.

What galled Richard the most, however, was that *he* was partially responsible for the loss of the coins and the flower paste. That was because *he* had ordered Elspeth to come out ahead of the others because he needed her to run to the stable and get the wagon and his riding horses moved before the Earl's men got to the stable as he was sure they inevitably would.

Elspeth had done what he told her to do and come out first, and in so-doing the trapdoor in the coin room floor had almost certainly *not* been closed and re-hidden as the last of the wives came up the ladder from the tunnel entrance and ran to safety. As a result, now that the Earl's men had re-taken control of the post, the chests of coins and flower paste would be found where he and Elspeth had left them in the escape tunnel.

By the time he began loudly and insistently knocking on the warehouse gate with the hilt of his personal knife Richard was absolutely furious both at the Earl of Westminster and himself.

"I will cut that murdering son of a bitch's heart out if it is the last thing I ever do," was one of the more mild promises Richard made to himself as he heard steps approaching and an eye appeared in the little peephole in the little door that was cut into the warehouse's entry gate. But then he totally forgot about it a moment later as he pushed his prisoner in through the door and had a joyous reunion with his wife and daughter.

Chapter Twenty-eight

Okehampton three weeks later.

Captain Merton and Anne Courtenay talked quietly as they descended the circling stone steps to inspect Okehampton's water well. Each of them was holding a candle lantern and going slowly and carefully because the narrow stone steps were wet and slippery. The captain walked ahead of her even though it was only his second trip down the stone stairs to see the water well that was so important to the castle he commanded. Without it the castle would not be able to withstand a siege. The captain understood that the well was vital to the castle's defense, but it was something he had taken for granted until the Commander's had specifically inquired about its condition and, in so doing, implied that he would be closely inspecting it.

They were making the inspection because Commander Robertson had mentioned the well in his most recent message wherein, in addition to many other matters, he had inquired about the current state of Okehampton's readiness to withstand a siege. The Commander's message had arrived a week earlier just before the arrival of the barons' army cut the castle off from news of the outside world. There had been no word from him since then.

Captain Merton had just gotten around to doing the inspection because he had been so distracted by other events, namely the arrival of part of the barons' "Loyal Army" that was now encamped all along the Okehampton cart path from the castle to the Exeter Road. The barons would have spread their personal armies out into more of western Devon except that the constant raids by the horse archers' raiding companies had inexorably forced more and more of them to gather their men together for safety—and Okehampton had been by far the best place for them to gather such that the barons one by one had begun gravitating towards it with more of their personal armies arriving every day.

Climbing down to the water was always dangerous because the steps were narrow and sometimes slippery. Truth be told, Anne was afraid to use them. Whenever possible she let the younger and more sure-footed women fetch up the water that apparently seeped into the well from the stream that ran next to Okehampton on its north side. Some said the water was coming from the nearby stream that provided water for the horse farm and the castle's three moats. Anne thought that doubtful because the well water did not have the same horsy taste to it as the water and morning ale she drank when she visited the horse farm.

Anne was accompanying Captain Merton on his inspection because the castle's women were responsible for bringing up the water from the well and she was supposed to know something about it. In fact, she was the only woman left in the castle; all the others had been evacuated to western Cornwall several weeks earlier. Now the water was being carried up by the stable boys and archer recruits who were helping the remaining archers garrison the castle. Already one of the recruits had slipped and was being barbered for a broken ankle.

Anne had jumped at the chance to accompany Captain Merton to inspect the well because she wanted to know more about what was happening outside Okehampton's walls. It seemed that George's horse archers had failed to stop the barons' Loyal Army from reaching the approaches to Cornwall and now, to Anne's horror, they were mustering right in front of the castle on the cart path that ran from the castle to the London road.

From the ramparts atop the citadel it was obvious that many thousands of the barons' men were already here and more could be seen coming in almost every day. Anne was so worried about the castle falling to them that the previous day, without telling anyone, she had carried a candle lantern and walked the entire length of the castle's long escape tunnel despite the periodic deep puddles of water. What she had not done, however, was try to open it at the other end to see where it came out.

The armies of the various barons coming together in front of Okehampton "was inevitable and had been expected," Captain Merton explained, when they first began to appear and Anne had expressed her shock at their arrival. "They are camping here for the same reason Okehampton Castle was originally built here and the Company has constantly strengthened it—because the ford over the Tamar is nearby and they are going to have to cross the ford in order to get into Cornwall and forage. It is not even fall and the Loyal Army's men are already starting to go hungry as a result of your husband's horse archers cutting off and destroying so many of their foraging parties. We know that from talking to deserters and prisoners."

Captain Merton was exceedingly deferential as might be expected from someone who was speaking with the wife of someone in his chain of command with a much higher rank. Besides, he knew she had a good head on her shoulders and might have useful ideas behind her eyes that she had gleaned from her absent husband.

In fact, things were not going as well as the Company's captains and commanders had hoped they would both generally and for Okehampton specifically. This was despite the fact that the Loyal Army had taken significant losses from the constant raids of the horse archers who had been sent forward to engage it. In addition, several of the barons had lost their lives and most of their knights and important retainers at Crediton when the local tavern burned to the ground in the middle of a rainy night. The barons and their knights and sergeants sleeping and drinking in the tavern had been lost because all of the shuttered window openings turned out to be too narrow for a man to squeeze through and all the doors had somehow been barred from the outside before the fire started.

Unfortunately for the Company of Archers and Cornwall, the "Loyal Army" was really just a collection of sixty or seventy smaller independent armies each commanded by the individual baron who had raised it. Each baron, in effect, commanded his own army of knights and their village levies. Some of the barons such as the Earls of Essex and Westminster had large armies with thousands of men whilst the smallest of the others had only a few dozen. There was as yet no unified command or single commander who could be defeated or encouraged to withdraw.

In essence the Company's problem was that each baron's army was marching independently of the others. As a result, the losses the barons had suffered at the hands of George's horse archers and at Crediton had fallen heavily on the individual armies of some of the barons whilst the armies of the others had remained virtually intact and reached the approaches to Cornwall full of enthusiasm for what their barons hoped to accomplish. Indeed, if anything, the destruction and losses and departures of some of the barons' armies had encouraged the others when they heard about them; because they would not have to share the food they expected their men to find when they foraged in Cornwall and the lands of those who did not support the new king that would be apportioned out after their victory.

As a result, a large number of the baronial armies had reached the approaches to Cornwall intact. And even worse, the foragers they sent out had already seized the Company's horse farm that was a three hours ride to the north. Fortunately, as a result of desperate last minute rescue operation, the stallions and most of the breeding mares and colts had been brought into castle's baileys whilst the first of the barons' men were still arriving and setting up their camp. The new arrivals were presently occupying the empty stalls and eating the hay and grain that had been left behind when the horse archers had ridden out with most of Okehampton's horses some weeks earlier. If the castle was not relieved before the horses' food ran out they would be eaten by the handful of archers still at Okehampton.

Lieutenant Smith the horse farm's captain and Sergeants Morrison and Greene whose men had been guarding the access routes to the farm had been had come in with the horses and all their surviving men—and then had slipped away through the trees along with many of the castle's defenders to join Commander Robertson's effort to hold the ford over the Tamar. At least that was what they had been told they would be doing. All that were left were about a hundred defenders under the command of Captain Merton.

Also joining the Commander in Cornwall were George and the men directly under his command and about half of the raiding companies that had been hanging like wolves along the London Road and around the barons' encampments. It had been pre-arranged that if the barons reached the Tamar in force George and certain of his men, about half of them, would leave their wagons and temporary camps behind and swim their horses across the Tamar to join up with the foot archers at Launceston on the Cornwall side of the river.

Richard Adams was also with the Commander on the other side of the Tamar. He had sailed for Cornwall in coastal cargo transport with his prisoner even though the London post had been abandoned by the Earl's men after they had stripped it of its coins and flower paste. Richard had given serious thought to staying and attempting to rebuild the post but decided against it for fear that the Earl's men would return seeking vengeance for their dead; the next time, he decided, he might not be so lucky.

Another of the reasons Richard sailed for Cornwall was that no more Company galleys would be coming in to London during the foreseeable future; the Lisbon shipping post was sending them directly to Cornwall as soon as they arrived from the east. Yet another was that he was anxious to bring his prisoner to Cornwall and get into the fight. And a fourth, and truth be told the main reason he did not stay, even though he would never admit it, was that he was too embarrassed to face the Company's creditors and customers who were clamoring for their coins and to be compensated for their missing cargos. Besides, he did not want to be forgotten when the next promotions to the rank of Major Captain were announced.

Word had reached Richard before he left London that depositors and the holders of money orders were besieging his shipping post in an effort to get the coins to which they were entitled. He did what he could to placate and reassure them: he commissioned a craftsman to repair the doors to show everyone that the Company was back in business and arranged for two of the Company' elderly retirees living in London to spend their days in front of the post's entrance to assure its customers that every penny of theirs was safe because the Company had more than enough coins elsewhere in its many other posts.

The retirees were there to assure the unhappy creditors that the Company's other posts had already been asked to send coins to replace those stolen by the Earl of Westminster and to fully pay for the lost cargos. What the two retirees told the Company's creditors was all true and the creditors believed them, but they were still unhappy because everyone knew that it would take many weeks for the replacement coins to arrive. They also knew that there would have to be some sort of peace between the Earl and the Company before the coins to pay them could be safely brought to the shipping post and distributed.

The retirees reported that the bodies scattered about in post had been removed by the Earl's men and that it had been totally looted including the crates and sacks of cargos awaiting shipment or delivery. There were also reports that some of the Company's depositors and money order holders had gathered outside the Earl's stronghold at Westminster and were demanding that he return the money he had stolen.

News of the creditors' protests heartened Richard but did not accomplish much since the earl and most of his men had already "gone off to Cornwall to fight the French." It did, however, give him an idea.

****** *The betrayal begins*

An elegantly dressed Captain Merton wearing a fine sword and a young lieutenant, James Sawyer, wearing a ratty leather helmet and a patched and battered old tunic stepped out of the castle's little door in the outermost of the castle's three gates and waited in front of the raised drawbridge as the door in the great wooden gate closed behind them. Behind them on the castle's walls a horn began loudly braying and tooting. Lieutenant Sawyer began enthusiastically waving a long tree limb with a piece of dirty linen attached to it as the drawbridge was lowered in front of them. It was obvious that the two men had come out to talk; what the barons' men would never know is that they had spent several hours carefully rehearsing what they would do and say.

The two archers walked out on to the drawbridge and stopped half way across it. Nothing happened at first except the horn on the castle's ramparts kept tooting and some of the barons' men walked to the edge of the barons' encampment and stared at them. The horn finally stopped when a young man came running up from the barons' encampment and breathlessly shouted out a question asking who they were and what they wanted.

"I am the commander of the castle's garrison. I am here to parley with whoever is your commander or his representative."

The young man ran off and a crowd of curious barons' men began to form at a distance. A few of them started forward, but Captain Merton waved them back and he and Lieutenant Sawyer began slowly retreating back toward the castle gate to emphasize that the barons' men should not come any closer. The overly curious thrusters got the message and withdrew to the fringes of the gathering crowd.

About ten minutes passed before half a dozen well-dressed men, several wearing armour with crusaders crosses on their tunics and a couple of men wearing priestly cassocks, pushed their way through the gathering crowd and began walking toward the drawbridge. One of the priests was wearing a bishop's mitre.

Captain Merton immediately held up the open palm of his left hand and pushed it at them; the age-old signal to stop. They stopped. He pointed at himself and then at the sergeant. As he did he loudly counted "one" and "two." Then he pointed at the approaching men and again counted and pointed and said "one" and "two." His meaning was instantly clear to everyone who was watching and it was not at all surprising.

There was a hurried consultation amongst the approaching men. A few moments later the two priests came forward and the rest of the men retired to stand at the front of the gathering crowd. One of the men who came forward was wearing a bishop's mitre and carrying a crosier.

"I am the Bishop Cuomo of London and this is Father Alan who is a cleric in the service of the Earl of Westminster," the older of the two men announced rather arrogantly as he walked up to the two archers. "And who be you and what do you want? Do you wish to discuss the terms of your surrender?"

"Surrender? You must be joking, Your Holiness. I be the Constable of Okehamption and this be Sergeant Black, the captain of the castle's gate. Tradition requires that I bring the sergeant of the gate with me even though I have a very private matter to discuss only with you," the captain replied to the bishop. *There was no such tradition but the bishop would not know that and it explained why Lieutenant Sawyer, posing as the sergeant in command of the gate, was with the captain.*

Captain Merton immediately took the bishop by the elbow and led him out of the hearing of the other two men. He obviously wanted to talk privately with the bishop without being overheard by the sergeant. *What he really wanted was to give "Sergeant Black" a chance to talk privately to the priest. It had all been planned long ago.*

Sergeant Black and Father Alan watched the captain and the bishop move away and put their heads together. As soon as they were out of hearing "Sergeant Black" leaned forward, dropped his voice, and whispered conspiratorially to Father Alan.

"I am the sergeant of the men who guard the castle's gate at night. If you can come up with enough coins for me and my men I will drop the drawbridge and open the gate for you in the middle of the night. Do you think your captains would be interested?"

"Of course they would be interested," the priest said. He was clearly more than a little surprised at what he had heard and responded with a level of interest in his voice that the sergeant found encouraging. "What do you have in mind?"

"I need forty silver coins for me and ten each for my four men; eighty in all—and your sworn word in the name of God that we five can hide in the castle's little church and go in peace after the barons and their men take the castle. And you best tell them to bring as many knights and men at arms as possible. The archers in the castle will fight hard even though they will surely lose because there are only four hundred of them." *Actually, of course, there were only a little more than one hundred of them.*

"Yes. Yes. That might be possible. When would this happen?"

"I will leave that up to you. Each morning when the sun arrives I always come out of the door in the gate to inspect the gate and drawbridge. If I find a pouch you have thrown over the moat with the coins in it I will open the gate and put down the drawbridge that night. I will do it about two hours before dawn's early light so that you will have time to assemble enough men. Then my lads and I will run off and hide in the castle's church with the door barred until the fighting is over. It will not last long if you bring enough men."

After a moment or so "Sergeant Black" added more.

"A night when the moon is small and there are clouds to hide its light would be best. I will give you most of the night to assemble your men and then lower the drawbridge and open the gate about two hours before dawn. And for God's sake bring as many real fighting men as possible and tell them to be quiet when they form up to rush across the drawbridge and into the castle. There are archers in the castle and they are fighters. If you bring too few men they might defeat you and then my men and I will surely be hanged."

"Oh aye, Sergeant, the Loyal Army will do that *if* its captains agree to what you propose, of that you can be assured. But how do we know we can trust you to let us in after we have given you the coins?" the priest asked suspiciously.

"Of course you can trust me, Father. I want to live to spend the coins and I know full well that if the coins are paid and I do not lower the drawbridge and open the gate the barons' men will kill me and take the coins back when they finally capture the castle. And I will do the same with for your entry into the citadel; I will disable the door to the cookhouse on the far side of the citadel so that your lords and their men can enter the citadel there and get the chests of coins in the castle's treasury."

"And if there is a portcullis? Will it be up as well?"

"Absolutely, Father. There are two on the gate behind us and I will make sure they are both up. Your barons and their lads will get into the bailey unmolested and the citadel's door to the cookhouse will be open; I swear it in the name of God. But only if *you* swear in the name of God that *my* lads and I will get our coins and be left in peace in the castle church and free to leave afterwards. Will you so swear?"

"Aye. As Jesus is my witness; if the pouch is thrown it means we swear it. I will personally see to your coins and freedom and I guarantee it in the name of God." Both men promptly made the sign of the cross to seal the deal.

"Oh by the way," the sergeant said as Captain Merton and the bishop began to walk back to join them. The rear of the castle's church is the first thing your men will come to when they come through the gate. It will be dark and when they come to the church they will have to turn to the right or left and feel their way around it to get to the open area of the bailey on the other side. So be sure to tell them to keep on going forward in the dark until they come to the wall and then to follow it around."

Both of them, of course, were lying even though they had crossed themselves and sworn in the name of God to the truth of their words. The sergeant was lying because there was no church inside Okehampton and the priest because he knew the bishop was so greedy that he would never let eighty silver coins get away without trying to take them back.

In fact, the first stone wall the invaders would feel in the dark, in the unlikely event they got across its moat and reached it, would be the castle's middle curtain wall, the one that could not be seen by anyone outside of Okehampton because both it and the inner curtain wall were ever so slightly lower than the outer wall—and Sergeant Black had *not* promised to raise the drawbridge over the middle wall's moat and open its gate. What was more likely was that the invaders would fall into the middle moat in the darkness before they reached the wall. That, of course, would not be a problem if they knew how to swim whilst wearing their armour and helmets.

Both Captain Merton and the bishop returned from their private conversation with a disappointed looks on their faces. The captain and the "sergeant" then retreated over the drawbridge, which was immediately raised behind them. They talked as they listened to the screeching sound as the drawbridge rose and they waited for the little door in the gate to be opened so they could re-enter the castle. They could see the priest and the bishop walking briskly towards the distant crowd of watchers and talking as they did.

What Captain Merton had proposed to the bishop had obviously *not* been enthusiastically accepted. The bishop had not been pleased when the captain refused the bishop's offer to peacefully surrender the castle and instead offered to buy pepper and salt from the barons' sutlers. It did not matter: In the discussion that had led up to the captain's request he had been able to clearly convey to the bishop that the castle had more than enough food in its larders for a long siege *and* that there were important chests of coins in Okehampton such that he could not surrender.

"Did he bite?" Captain Merton asked the "sergeant" under his breath when they reached the door in the gate.

"Aye. At least I think so. And yours?"

"Apparently not," he said with a laugh that sounded like a giggle. "I told the bishop that it looked as if we would continue to be in a Saracen standoff for some months since I could never justify surrendering the castle. I could not do it, I explained to him, because that would mean surrendering the chests with the coins the Company had been accumulating at Okehampton so it could continue to feed its men during the coming time of peace that would start when Jesus returned.

"Then I told him that the Company would hang me or chop me for sure if I surrendered the castle and the coins the Company was going to need to feed and pay its men when Jesus returned, but that I might survive if the castle could hold out long enough for Jesus to return, which it probably could because it had enough food and men to last for at least a year and perhaps two.

"But you should have seen his eyes light up when I mentioned the chests of coins. He promptly started telling me that Jesus might not be returning as soon as everyone thought and that Jesus would want the fighting to stop even if it meant losing the chests of coins—and that he was absolutely sure that he could convince the barons to spare me and the rest of the garrison if we surrendered.

"Men's lives are more precious than coins, the bishop said to me most earnestly.

"But I was having none of it. I told him that *all* the priests were saying Jesus's return and peace in the world was imminent. As a result, the Company was taking no chances on not being able to feed and pay its men until Jesus leaves again and the fighting and piracy in the Holy

Land and elsewhere resume. That is why I could not
surrender the castle and let the barons have the chests.

"Only when Jesus leaves again," I told him, "would the
Company be able to once again earn the coins we needed
to feed and pay our men by carrying refugees to safety
and cargos and money orders past the pirates. Whilst he
is here and there is peace we will have to spend the coins
we have been accumulating in our chests to pay and feed
them. I can survive surrendering the castle to an
overwhelming force such as yours; but if I surrender the
Company's coin chests, I told the bishop, I would almost
certainly be hung or have my head chopped off.

"I finally told him that all I could do was try to defend
the castle and its coins until Jesus returned and there was
peace, but that I could take a few of the coins from among
those that had not yet gotten into the chests to buy a
pound of pepper and a pound of salt from the barons'
sutlers every few weeks to improve our food. That, I told
him, was reason why I had wanted the meeting—to see if
the barons would let their sutlers sell us some pepper and
salt."

*It was all the two men could do not to giggle like the
schoolboys they once had been as they waited for the little
door in the gate to open. They were quite pleased with
themselves and rightly so.*

"Do you think they will fall for it?" Lieutenant Sawyer
asked.

Chapter Twenty-nine

The Barons' Attack.

The barons immediately gathered to listen to the priests' report and discuss the sergeant's offer to lower the drawbridge and open the gate. There were fifty-three of them present including seventeen members of the Great Council whose members advised the king—and to a man the nobles liked the sergeant's offer. That was probably because they could see the high and crenellated stone curtain wall around the castle and the roof of the citadel that poked up toward the sky from a motte in the middle of the castle's particularly large bailey. They looked formidable; it was entirely believable that the Company of Archers would store some of its coins at Okehampton so as to be prepared for Jesus's return.

Of course the barons liked the idea of bribing the guards; even the youngest and most inexperienced among them understood that it would, at best, take many weeks before a siege would starve out the defenders and that there would be very heavy losses if they attempted to take Okehampton by storm. Moreover, it was obvious to everyone that their foraging would go better in the days ahead if they did not leave the castle's defenders free to sally out into their armies' rear after they crossed into

Cornwall. There was also the matter of the chests of coins that were in the castle and who should get them.

* * * * * *

There were more than a few disputes later that day when all the barons who were available assembled on short notice met at the Earl of Westminster's camp upon receiving his urgent request that they attend. The barons and their advisors had all come; probably both because they were curious as to why the meeting was so "urgent" and because the messengers carrying the verbal invitations "confidentially" mentioned there would be a free meal with horse and chicken meat, all the cheese you can eat, and French wine immediately following it.

Everyone listened carefully and was impressed. Most of the arguments that ensued were related to who should put up the coins needed to pay the required bribe and whose men should lead the attack. They all wanted their men to be involved and lead the way because they understood that whoever got to the coins first would probably end up walking away with the lion's share of them. They also, of course, wanted someone other than themselves to pay the bribe. The problem was that the Loyal Army still did not have a single commander to make the necessary decisions.

Both the older de Montfort brother and the Earl of Essex had tried to claim the leadership of the Loyal Army and they each had their supporters but, much like the Church whose cardinals could not agree on who should be the Pope, none of the aspirants had enough barons supporting him. The Earl of Westminster also wanted the position and claimed it was his due because his army was by far the largest now that the army of the Earl of Sussex had turned back because of its severe losses on the road.

The archer sergeant's offer to open the gate and the door to the citadel brought the question of the Loyal Army's leadership to a head. In less than an hour of shouting, accusations, whispered negotiations, and the enthusiastic waving about of bowls of wine and table pounding, it was sensibly agreed that the Loyal Army would have the three main claimants as co-commanders and the agreement of all three would be required before any major decision was made.

As soon as the leadership issue was resolved the EaFrl of Westminster immediately moved to make himself first amongst the three equals. He did so by proposing that *he* advance the eighty silver coins to get the gate opened and that the coins in the castle be divided, after he was repaid his eighty coins, according to how many men each baron sent into Okehampton as part of the initial wave of attackers.

Westminster announced his plan loudly by standing on a stool and shouting—and then the other two aspirants to the throne had no choice but to agree when they saw the enthusiasm with which it was received. Actually, even the other two co-commanders liked the earl's proposal since it would cost them nothing. And then, as was inevitable, each of the three immediately began thinking about how he could get rid of the other two so that he would be able to keep all the coins and be the sole commander of the army.

What the Earl of Westminster did *not* tell his fellow barons was that he was going to hold almost all of his knights and mercenaries as well as most of his better commoners out of the attack. He had recently received several eyewitness reports about the losses of Sussex and certain other barons had suffered on the road at the hands of the archers, and he also knew of his own losses in London during the taking the archers' shipping post. As a result, he now had a very different view of their fighting abilities than most of his fellow barons.

Moreover, as he and his priestly advisors saw it, the losses suffered by the other barons in their attack on Okehampton would further *increase* his army's already greater strength relative to the other barons, especially those whose men who led the way to the coins since he was sure they would have to fight their way past the archers to get them. Then, as a result of his increased strength of his army relative to those of the other claimants to the throne who had lost casualties pursuing the coins, he was even more likely to be able to successfully claim the throne.

Besides, when he had the throne safely in his hands he would be able to use his army to take the coins away from those who initially seized them and maybe even their lands as well on the grounds that they had not shared them properly. In other words, he would take the long view and concentrate on seizing England's throne and revenues whilst letting the others fight to get the archers' coins he intended to end up owning when the dust settled.

* * * * * *

Dawn was just breaking three days later when "Sergeant Black" walked out of the little door in the castle's entrance gate and saw the leather pouch that had been thrown over the moat with the coins in it. He picked it up with a smile and made a surreptitious little wave of acknowledgement towards the barons' camp with his back to the castle. He did so in case anyone was watching from the barons' camp—which they most certainly were. Then he hurried back to the door in the gate and was inside the castle before the sun was fully arrived on its daily trip around the world.

It was noisy that night as the nobles and their knights attempted to quietly bring their men to the open area opposite the drawbridge. Fortune seemed to favour the barons in that the sound of their men's many whispers and muttered curses did not carry over the high stone wall immediately beyond the drawbridge in front of them. At least no one in the castle appeared to have heard the men of the various armies jockeying for position and whispering threats against possible usurpers to the favourable positions nearest to the drawbridge. That was to be expected since the only ones who would be on the wall in the middle of the night and be able to hear it would be the sergeant and his men.

By agreement, and at their insistence, some of the barons and the knights of most of them would lead the way into the castle's bailey. They would do so, the barons told each other, for the glory of being first to get inside— and then each of the barons quietly directed his knights to ignore the expected fighting and, instead, hurry straight to the citadel and find the windowless treasury room next the Constable's sleeping room where they thought the coins were most likely to be found.

* * * * * *

Captain Merton and Lieutenant Sawyer spent the night on the castle wall overlooking the gate. They chuckled and shook their heads in disbelief at all the noise being made as the barons' men assembled. They had both a candle lantern and an hour glass with them in order to be sure it was still too dark to see anything when they lowered the drawbridge, raised the two portcullises, and opened the gate. The lantern was lit in an effort to help the barons' men find the gate and encourage them to believe the guards were there to admit them.

"Well, Jim, you did tell them the truth," the captain chuckled once again. "Well mostly; except for suggesting that they continue moving forward in the darkness until they found the wall of a church."

"Yes, and I bet we will fish at least twenty of them out of the middle moat as a result," the lieutenant replied.

"Twenty? Not a chance. Four or five maybe; but never twenty. Mind you, I would be happy for even one or two," the captain said with a little shake of his head that said no.

"I have a silver coin that says there will be at least a dozen?" the lieutenant replied.

"You have a bet even though I hope I lose it," the captain said.

The two men were about to spit on their hands and shake on the bet when a sergeant walked in on them to report. He was slightly out of breath and more than a little excited.

"I walked all the way around on the top the outer wall, Captain. The men are in place and every man has his extra bowstrings and all the extra arrows he was given. And I hailed the middle wall when I was in the back. The Sergeant Major said to tell you that he just finished walking the middle wall himself and his lads are ready too."

****** *Twenty minutes later*

"Well, Jim, what do you think?" the captain said to the lieutenant. "Might as well let the lambs in for their slaughter, eh?" Their bet had been totally forgotten.

The captain did not wait for an answer. He picked up the candle lantern and carried it over to the inner side of the portcullis with the others following close behind. A couple of chosen men who had been standing silently nearby followed after him. The lieutenant followed him for no other reason than he was starting to get nervous and it gave him something to do.

A moment later the chosen men were turning the great crank that noisily raised one of the two portcullises in the entry way just beyond the gate. As soon as they got the first portcullis up and secured they began raising the other portcullis and lowering the drawbridge. Whilst they were doing that the captain and lieutenant themselves climbed down a long and sturdy wooden ladder to remove the three great wooden bars that held the castle's gate shut, and then hurriedly climbed back up the ladder. It was promptly pulled up behind them.

It had been a long and mostly sleepless night for the barons' men who would be entering the castle if and when its gate was opened. They had mostly settled down and were sitting and whispering to each other in the moon-less dark when they heard the noise of the portcullises being raised and then the sound of the drawbridge as it suddenly began being lowered. The waiting men quickly leaped to their feet and began grasping their weapons tightly even before the great rattling noise of the drawbridge being lowered was finished and there was the familiar crashing sound as the end of drawbridge came over the moat and hit the ground.

The drawbridge coming down could not be seen by the waiting men because of the darkness caused by the clouds that had totally blotted out the moon's feeble light but they had all heard drawbridges come down many times and everyone knew exactly what was happening when they heard the familiar sound of Okehampton's drawbridge being lowered. Those at the very front of the leaderless mob also heard the loud creaking sound as the great gate in the castle's curtain wall was swung open.

There was no doubt about it behind the eyes of the small handful of barons and several hundred armour-wearing knights who were at the front of the waiting attackers; the gate "sergeant" and his men had been true to their prayerfully sworn oaths and earned their eighty coins.

The crash of the drawbridge hitting the ground resulted in a great and continuing cheer and shouting in the black darkness as the waiting knights ran on to the bridge and through the gate into Okehampton's great bailey with their men hurrying along right behind them.

Unfortunately it was so dark and crowded at the front of the waiting and totally disorganized mob of attackers, and the pushing and jostling amongst them to get to the waiting coins so intense, that there were a number of splashes as some of the men trying to get across on the narrow drawbridge were either pushed into the moat or fell into it because the darkness caused them to misjudge where the drawbridge was located. It was total chaos. Some of the attackers even fell down and were trampled in the rush.

The screams and cries of the attackers who did not make it across the drawbridge went largely unnoticed in the darkness and noise and, in any event, did not last long since most of them did not know how to swim and the moat was eight feet deep. It did not matter; no one would have stopped to help them even if they could have seen them fall—because everyone was too anxious to get into the castle and those who might have done so were pushed along in the surging crowd and could not have stopped even if they wanted to do so. Besides, the sad fate of those who went into the water or were trampled was clearly the will of God since he had obviously caused the night to be too dark for them to be found in time to save them.

******

Captain Merton and Lieutenant Sawyer stood on the wall above the gate and listened to the shouting and battle-cry screaming mob of men as it surged over the drawbridge and began to pass under them in the darkness. They were amazed and impressed.

"My God," Merton heard his lieutenant say to someone above the din coming up through the kill holes below them. "I never expected so many of them. How many do you think there are?" He did not hear the reply if there was one.

The barons' men kept coming and coming for what seemed like a very long time, but actually was not. Even so, in a few short minutes many more than a thousand men had followed a couple of barons and several hundred knights into Okehampton's pitch-black outer bailey.

It did not take long, less than a minute after the first attackers started passing under the archers standing on the wall above the gate, than there began to be heard the screams and splashes coming out of the darkness. They began as the men at the forefront of the attackers reached the castle's second moat, the one that circled all the way around Okehampton's middle wall and had its own drawbridge—which had not been lowered.

Okehampton's middle moat was not quite as deep as the castle's outer moat, but deep enough when a man blundered into it in the darkness and his feet sank down to its muddy and shite-filled bottom, especially if he was wearing armour.

It seemed like a long time but it was only a few minutes after the attack started that the sound of men running and shouting into the bailey began to tail off. A few minutes later there were the shouts and other sounds that suggested that some of the attackers might be starting to come back the other way. That is when Captain Merton ordered both of the portcullises to be dropped and the drawbridge over the outer moat to be raised.

The noise from the attackers inside the bailey rose and fell throughout the rest of the night. Splashes and screams could be heard intermittently throughout the night along with many loudly shouted questions that were increasingly fearful and rarely answered.

****** *The slaughter begins*

The noise of the attackers' shouting and calling increased as dawn's earliest light began to appear. It then increased again and got louder and louder as more and more of the attackers began to see the moat and the castle's middle wall in front of them. And the shouting and wailing got even louder and desperate when the attackers realized that the portcullises had been closed behind them and that there were archers on the walls above them on both the middle wall in front of them and the outer wall behind them.

As you might imagine, the noise then got even louder and dramatically changed in tone when the archers began plying their trade and the increasingly panic-stricken attackers realized they were doomed because they had nowhere to hide.

Those of the attackers who could run, and initially that was almost all of them who had not fallen into the moat, desperately tried to run away from wherever they were standing in order to find a place of safety where the archers on the walls could not see them. That caused a good number of them to end up running in a great circle all the way around the middle wall. Others sought refuge behind the dead and wounded or in the stalls against the outer wall that were the homes of the castle's horses and men.

Both efforts failed; nowhere was there any useful cover, not even in the stalls that housed the horses and the archers' families that ran all along the inside of the outer wall. That was because coverings in front of their entrances had been removed so their interiors could be seen by archers standing behind the arrow slits atop the opposite wall. Their occupants had long ago been removed; the families to safety in villages and camps deep inside Cornwall and the horses to the middle bailey.

It was only when the arrows began arriving and no place could be found to hide that the barons' men still on their feet finally realized that Okehampton had more than one crenellated curtain wall surrounding it. In essence, they had not known Okehampton's citadel was surrounded by no less than *three* curtain walls. They had not known there were two additional crenellated curtain walls inside the outer wall because all three walls were all about the same height such that the inner two could not be seen by anyone standing on the ground outside the castle.

The inner walls could not be seen because the castle was built on a slight hill so there was no place higher where someone could stand and look down at it. As a result, anyone standing on the ground outside the castle could only see the outer wall and would think there were no other walls behind it. That was deliberate: Okehampton had been carefully designed to make each of its baileys a murder ground for anyone foolish enough to enter it without permission; and now the attackers were in the outermost of the three baileys with no way out and no place to hide.

At first the attackers did not at fully understand their fates so they began running about like chickens with their heads cut off as they desperately tried to find a way to escape or a place to shelter. They found neither. Those who lived long enough discovered that they had been sealed inside the bailey when the portcullises at either end of the tunnel through the outer wall were dropped. Once that happened there was neither a way out for any of them nor anywhere to safely hide.

As you might well imagine, hysteria and panic set in amongst the attackers when they saw the archers on the walls above them and realized they were in a death trap because every inch of Okehampton's outer bailey could reached by the arrows of one or more archers. And they were right to be panicked and hysterical—being able to use a longbow to accurately push out arrows was the one thing that every single one of the one hundred or so archers on Okehampton's walls had to prove he could do before he was allowed to make his mark on the Company's roll.

Chapter Thirty

The slaughter.

The archers on the ramparts followed the order they had been given by Captain Merton to make it a priority to shoot down the men in the bailey who appeared to be nobles and knights. Unfortunately for the barons' knights and nobles, they tended to be identifiable because of the quality of their tunics and the armour they were wearing. But the archers certainly did not wait to push out their arrows until they spotted a knight or noble who was still alive. To the contrary, their grunts as they pushed out arrows and the sound of their bowstrings slapping against their leather wrist protectors were as constant and on-going as the screams and pleas for mercy of the leaderless men running about and cowering in the bailey below them.

It took longer than you might expect for the archers to finish off the invaders. That was because there were only a little more than a hundred archers in the castle and they were spread out all along two long walls such that there were, at least at first, dozens of targets for each of the archers. It was as one of the archers remarked to Lieutenant Sawyer when he finally walked along the ramparts to tell them to stop pushing "almost like shooting fish in a barrel."

Most of the archers shot the invaders down willingly and cheered each other on with a great deal of enthusiasm as they did so. They also jeered each other most friendly when one of their nearby mates on the ramparts missed a shot—which was fairly frequent because it is harder than one would think to hit a running man who is also on the ground below you and trying to dodge and twist to avoid your arrow when he watches you push it out and sees it coming. There was no surprise at the archers' enthusiasm and lack of mercy; they were, after all, trying to kill armed invaders who in some cases were attempting to hide in the family home of the archer who was pushing arrows at them.

And, of course, compounding the difficulty of the archers on the walls was that many of their shots were long shots pushed at runners coming past them and even longer shots from the archers standing atop the middle wall because only they could see the barons' men trying to hide behind the tables and beds and feeding troughs in the homes and horse stalls lining the outer wall.

****** The aftermath*

The slaughter finally stopped when Captain Merton, Lieutenant Sawyer, and Sergeant Major Cook began walking along the top of the two walls and ordering the men to stop pushing. As they did they loudly called out a generous offer to the surviving invaders on the ground below them.

"If you wish to surrender you must throw down your arms and take off *all* of your clothes and lie face down in the middle of the bailey with your arms outstretched. Anyone who does this will be taken prisoner; anyone who does not will be killed."

It did not take long before naked and trembling men were everywhere stretched out on the ground amongst the dead, including some of the wounded with arrows sticking out of them. More than half of the archers on the walls initially stood watch with their bows at the ready as some of their mates and the twenty or so stable boys lowered ladders from the top of the wall and began to go down into the bailey to gather up the invaders' armour and weapons and, most important of all, the many hundreds of arrows that were sticking into the ground. The boys had served on the walls carrying arrows and water to the archers and, although they did not know it yet, would be entitled to wear a battle dot on their tunics if they lived long enough to subsequently go for an archer.

Captain Merton and some of the archers went down into the bailey with the boys to help them collect the attackers' weapons and to look for skulkers who were trying to hide instead of surrender. Within an hour the naked prisoners on the ground had stopped shaking in fear that they would be painfully killed and begun turning red from the sun which had suddenly popped out from behind the clouds. The exceptions, of course, were the enemy wounded who were still shaking as they waited to have arrows pulled or cut out of them so the arrows could be re-used; they were inevitably terrified and began pleading and trying to crawl away when they realized what was about to happen to them.

"Nobles, knights, and priests are to stand up with their hands in the air. Any man of rank who does not do so will be immediately killed."

The new order was passed from mouth to mouth along the top of the walls. It turned out that there were only three or four dozen of the invaders' gentry still alive including five or six with arrows sticking in them who were able to struggle to their feet. They were embarrassed at being seen without clothes but, even so, many of them looked about expectantly as they stood.

Several of those who climbed to the feet were actually smiling in the belief that they were about to start receiving better treatment than their men and that they would be offered for ransom and treated well until it arrived. It was a reasonable expectation as treating captured gentry better than their men was the custom of the day when armies led by kings and nobles faced each other. Unfortunately for them their optimism was misplaced.

The surviving nobles and knights did not know it yet but they would *not* receive better treatment than their men. If anything it would be worse because of the vengeance required by the Company's articles on which every archer had made his mark. If any of the gentry were thought to be in any way responsible for the attack they would be almost certainly hung or have their necks chopped; if not and they were able to survive on whatever rations were sent to them from the barons' camp. It was more likely they would be placed in chains and forced to help to row a Company galley to the Holy Land rather than be ransomed to rejoin their families. Moreover, when they reached the Holy Land they would almost certainly be delivered to the Templars as "volunteers."

The alternative to the nobles and knights "volunteering" to go crusading with the Templars for a while would be to go for a long ocean swim in waters where there was no land in sight; it was a Company tradition for miscreant nobles, knights, and priests to be cut no slack. *The Templars, always short of knights and volunteers due to their money lending resulting in ever more lands for them to defend in France and elsewhere, were always grateful for the new recruits who inevitably stayed with them for some years or permanently because they had no coins to buy passages home.*

Before all that, however, there was work to be done at Okehampton and the nobles, knights, and priests were set to doing it whilst they remained unclothed—having lines tied around their waists so they could be lowered into the castle's moats to pull the bodies out and strip them of their armour and weapons. The captain explained his decision to the lieutenant and the Sergeant Major.

"Our moats smell bad enough as it is and the fish already taste a bit off. Adding dead men to further foul them would be too much. Besides, some of the men in the water are wearing armour and carrying weapons that we can sell for prize money."

The similarly-naked commoners from the knights' village levies, at least some of them, were set to gathering up their wounded mates and burying the dead in a meadow in the nearby forest. They did not know it yet, but they would be used to help row a Company galley for a while and then set free in either Cornwall or London to make their own way back to their homes. The only thing certain about the futures of the prisoners was that no one would be sold to the Moors or anyone else as a slave or serf—because it was a Company tradition and specified in its articles that the Company would neither buy nor sell slave and serfs; probably because so many of the archers were former slaves and serfs or their sons.

It took all the rest of the day for the prisoners to collect and bury the bodies of the dead and to assemble and begin barbering their wounded mates. And it did not always go smoothly, at least at first. At least one of the nobles and several of the knights arrogantly refused to tie a line around their naked bodies and jump into the moats to help pull the bodies and weapons out of the moats. Their refusal was cheerfully accepted by the no-nonsense archer sergeant who was directing the recovery of the bodies from the middle moat—he and his men promptly and very rapidly ran the refusers into the moat at the point of their personal knives such that their fellow nobles and knights had to pull their bodies out as well. It greatly encouraged the others and, as a result, the prisoners began working with an even greater will.

****** *The barons' camp*

The magnitude of their defeat and the large number of missing men, especially knights, weighed heavily on the barons' great encampment. There was much wailing and lamenting by the women and anguished looks on the faces of most of the more than fifty barons who assembled late that afternoon for prayers and drinks at the invitation of the Earl of Westminster. A number of them had missing relatives and many of them, including the de Monforts and the Earl of Kent, were missing a considerable number of their knights and men. To a man, they dreaded the ransom demands they expected to be coming.

Once again it was the secretly-pleased Earl of Westminster who rose to the occasion. Following a brief prayer for the souls of those who fell and the safety of those who had been captured he announced that he would take into his service as his vassals, if they so requested, all those who had lost their lords as well as the families of the men who had fallen. He also offered to loan the necessary ransom coins to any of the captured nobles and knights who might need them.

"It is a very Christian and kingly thing he is doing," his clerics and retainers made a point of telling everyone who would listen. They inevitably nodded somberly even though more than a few, knowing the Earl's history, muttered something to the effect that they would believe it when they saw it. "More likely he will sell them for slaves and keep their lands," one man was heard to say.

******

Commander Robertson was at Launceston on the Cornwall side of the Tamar with George Courtenay and all of the Company's available foot archers when he and his men received news of the great victory at Okehampton. At almost the same time Captain Adams arrived from London with an important prisoner and the distressing news that the Earl of Westminster's men had raided and looted the Company's London shipping post. That was no small loss in that there had been a number of chests of coins and flower paste in the post.

The Commander and his captains knew the Earl was almost certainly the second richest man in England after the king, and also that he was one of the leaders of the "Loyal Army" that had reached Cornwall's border and were about to invade it in order to forage for food. Now he was even richer. As might be expected, Commander

Robertson and his captains responded to the news about the attack on the Company's London shipping post with seething anger and many swearings of a terrible revenge.

The Commander and his captains were also concerned about how things were going in general, and rightly so. Adding Westminster's men and mercenaries to the men of the other barons who had gotten through to Devon meant the barons' Loyal Army might well have as many as seven or eight thousand men in it. The archers had less than a thousand and that included several hundred recruits who were still being trained and several hundred horse archers and outriders that had previously been skirmishing with the barons' foraging parties and had recently swam their horses across the river and entered Cornwall to join them.

Worse, there were still other barons on the road whose armies might be able to get past the horse archers who remained outside of Cornwall and join the barons' main force—and when they did it would make the odds against the archers even worse. Indeed, even now the barons might have enough men to force the ford over the Tamar despite the seven hundred or so foot archers that Commander Robertson had available to oppose them.

There was no question about it, the situation was dire. It was time for the Company to do whatever it could to strengthen Cornwall's defenses against the almost certain attempt by the barons to cross the Tamar and begin foraging in Cornwall.

On the other hand, and fortunately, how best to defend Cornwall against invaders coming out of England was something that had been constantly considered by the Company's captains and commanders. Indeed, how to defend Cornwall from an invading army was a major topic that was discussed and examined every year by the students in the Company school at Restormel Castle, the school for likely lads that the Commander and most of his captains had attended.

Indeed, defending Cornwall from invaders was the basis of the "pretend wars" that were conducted each year wherein the older boys at the Company school were given their first experiences at actually commanding real archers in "mock battles" even though most of the "real archers" in the war games were archer recruits who were being trained at the Company's depot near Restormel and had not yet been allowed to make their marks on the Company's roll.

Commander Robertson and his captains, in other words, had a fairly good idea as to what needed to be done. They had already begun giving the necessary orders and making the necessary inspections to insure that they were being carried out.

Chapter Thirty-one

The Tamar ford and the need for decisions.

Launceston Castle's garrison and the army of archers assembled at the Tamar ford continued to grow as more and more archers arrived from Lisbon. In addition to the new arrivals some of the raiding companies began coming in from Devon and more and more of the archer recruits completed their training. There were soon just over a thousand foot and horse archers at the Tamar ford. Importantly, most of them were long-serving veterans armed with the most modern of weapons and serving under battle-hardened sergeants and captains.

Commander Robertson and his captains had not known about the possibility of reinforcements actually arriving from the east until the first galley from Cyprus had arrived two days earlier. They had been pleasantly surprised to learn that word of the fighting in England had somehow reached Cyprus from Lisbon and that the senior lieutenant commander commanding the Company's great Cyprus stronghold had taken it upon himself to send as many archer-crewed galleys as possible directly to Lisbon without the usual port calls along the way to take on food and water.

Cyprus's commander had given the galley captains their orders with the understanding that the galleys would be hurriedly resupplied in Lisbon and continue on to Cornwall if the archers rowing them were still needed—and would merely turn around when they reached Lisbon and return more slowly to Cyprus if they were not.

Most of the cargo each galley was carrying, in addition to extra archers, consisted of extraordinary amounts of food and water that totally filled its cargo holds and covered its deck. That was important because the apparent need for speed required the galleys to minimize the port calls they needed to make. The only other cargo each galley was carrying were bales of arrows from the defensive stores of the Company's Cyprus stronghold and all of the long-handled bladed pikes that could be found. The bladed pikes, of course, were the vicious modern weapon manufactured by the Company's smiths on Cyprus that were so effective against charging knights.

The relief galleys coming out of Cyprus, in other words, were both over-crewed with veteran archers and dangerously overloaded.

Word that a second Company galley had been seen entering the Fowey estuary with reinforcements on board had reached the Commander at the Tamar ford by a galloper from Fowey Village only that morning. As you might expect, news of the galley's arrival spread rapidly among the men at the ford and further encouraged their morale and confidence. Both the men and the

Commander were eagerly awaiting a follow-on galloper from Restormel carrying information as to the number of the archers the new arrival was carrying and who was among them.

There was much speculation and talking amongst the men at the ford as to how many additional archers the new arrival was carrying and who they might be; but they would not know for sure until it came up the Fowey to Restormel and the archers on it disembarked to begin a forced march to the Tamar ford to join their fellow archers who were already gathered there. The new arrivals would carry their personal weapons and start a forced march to the ford as soon as their feet touched the ground; the arrow bales and additional weapons the galley was carrying would follow as soon as they could be off-loaded onto carts and wagons. A galloper would ride ahead to report their numbers as soon as they were known.

What the Commander and his men *did* know was that the first galley had arrived with a total of almost one hundred and fifty archers on its oars after record-breaking voyages from Cyprus. It had been dangerously overloaded with supplies of food and water at Cyprus and rowed straight through to Lisbon without making port calls and then, after hurriedly taking on more water and food, sailed straight to Cornwall. Even better, according to its captain, more galleys carrying additional archers were already being loaded when his galley set its sails and he began his record-breaking run to Cornwall. This new arrival was almost certainly one of them.

All of this was immediately made known to the men at the Tamar ford. As a result the rank and file archers and their sergeants continued to remain highly optimistic about their prospects. And they were already quite high, probably because the men had confidence in themselves and their weapons as a result of their training and past experiences and also because the Commander and his captains followed the Company's tradition of living and eating with their men and sharing their hardships in the field—and keeping their men as fully informed and well fed as possible.

It undoubtedly helped that the Commander and his captains deliberately let themselves be seen so their men would know that their hardships and dangers were being shared and that they had not been abandoned. The archers' good cheer was probably also helped because the men at the ford had not actually seen the huge size of the barons' forces on the other side of the river and because Commander Robertson was greatly respected because he was very good with a longbow.

The newly arrived galley was almost certainly one of those that had been hurriedly sent from Cyprus. If it was, the men rowing it would be significant and timely reinforcements for the archers Commander Robertson had assembled at the Tamar ford. *Even more important, as things turned out, the arrival of the additional archers subsequently encouraged the Commander to make a fateful decision that would greatly affect both the Company and England—when in the days that followed he decided to go ahead with what he would come to think of as his London gambit.*

If the past was any guide, many of the archers newly arrived on the galley from Cyprus would have weak legs from being at sea and would drop out on the forced march to the Tamar ford. But they were all men strong enough to be archers so it was also reasonable to expect that they would march all night without stopping and most of them would join the force assembled at the ford by sometime in the morning of the next day, and also that the rest of them would hobble in and reach the ford sooner or later thereafter.

Whilst the new arrivals were marching to the ford their galley's sailors and every other available man and woman would be loading the bales of extra arrows and pikes the galley was carrying on horse-drawn wagons and carts. Each of the wagons would set out for the ford as fast as it could be loaded. Everything was being greatly hurried because a major effort by the barons' armies to storm across the ford was overdue and expected to begin at any minute. There was no such thing as having too many men or weapons.

Even so, there was a feeling in the archers' camp that was a combination of confidence, excitement, and uncertainty. That was because it was widely believed that the barons would make at least one major effort to take the ford. They would do so because it was the only way they could get their foragers into Cornwall. Accordingly, Commander Robertson had ordered almost all of the archers in England to the ford as soon as fast as they became available. The only exceptions were the horse archers who remained east of the Tamar to harass and weaken the invaders and those in the very small garrisons that were needed to defend the Company's four major strongholds in the event they were besieged.

The only question on every man's mind was "how soon" the barons' Loyal Army would try to come across the ford.

Also at the ford, at Commander Robertson's order even though no one understood why and he was not saying, were many of the horse-drawn cart and wagons the Company had come in carrying men and supplies from Restormel. They had been kept at the ford with their horses in their traces and were presently parked far enough inland to be out of sight of anyone on the Devon side of the river.

At the moment the wagons were being guarded by a fast-reaction force consisting of an entire galley company of archers with an additional dozen or so of horse archers to act as "early warning" scouts further to the rear. The foot archers of the galley company were there in case the barons' men were somehow able to get across the Tamar somewhere else and tried to attack the ford defenders in the rear. They would also, of course, rush to reinforce the archers at the ford when the main attack coming out of Devon was imminent.

The only thing that had surprised the Commander and his captains was that a major effort to take the ford had *not* yet occurred. They were certain that there would be such an effort because they understood, or at least they thought they did, why the barons needed to fight their way across the Tamar at the ford above Launceston, and then hold the ford in force. More specifically, they knew that if the barons' men could *not* take the ford and hold it they would have to abandon their plans to forage in Cornwall and be forced to live off of whatever food they could find or buy elsewhere and bring back to their camps—or go home.

Indeed, although the archers did not know it yet, the barons and their knights were finding it increasingly difficult to send their men out to forage unless they personally led them. The men's increasing unwillingness to go out foraging existed because it was becoming more and more dangerous to leave the camp. That was because there were still no less than a dozen raiding companies of horse archers operating east of the Tamar. They were like packs of wolves hanging around of the edges of a great encampment of sheep—and that is how they saw themselves and acted.

The barons' problem existed because as soon as a foraging party left the relative safety of the barons' encampment the horse archers were likely to begin stalking it and periodically skewering its men with well-aimed arrows. As a result, and sometimes even when the barons ordered one of their knights to lead them, the men who were ordered to go out to forage increasingly only pretended to go. Instead, they either marched out a short distance and then hid for a while, or they skulked off to visit friends elsewhere in the great encampment. Then, after enough time had passed, they would return and claimed to have been out foraging with no success.

Either way, they then came back and reported they could not find any food. Besides, it had become well known in the barons' camp that there was little food left to find in western Devon because the villagers had taken much of what they had with them when they fled into Cornwall and the archers had burned their fields as soon as they left.

In essence, most of the barons' armies were already running low on food and they had no choice but to help take the ford across the Tamar *if* they wanted to enter Cornwall to forage. They had to cross at the ford because there were no bridges over the river and the handful of small boats on river had long ago been dragged ashore on the Cornwall side.

The scouts and foraging parties of the individual barons' armies had made a number of half-hearted efforts to cross the river, but these had been easily turned away by a few well-placed arrows. A major assault by the entire

Loyal Army, on the other hand, would almost certainly succeed if the barons pressed their attack. At least that was what the barons and their men assured each other with a great deal of confidence in their voices. They believed it because they did not know how many archers were waiting for them at the ford or how well they were armed. To the contrary, the barons and their knights continued to think the archers were poorly led because they had no nobles and knights to lead them and were poorly armed because they had rarely been seen with swords and shields.

There was a similarly degree of certainty behind the eyes of Commander Robertson—the Tamar ford had to be held until the barons suffered enough losses such that they would give up trying to enter Cornwall and go home. And that, the Commander and his captains believed, would require that the barons' men suffer a great enough of a defeat at the ford such that their knights and levies would not be willing to try again.

Only if the barons were soundly defeated in their efforts to enter Cornwall, or so the Commander and his captains believed, would the barons lead their men back to their homes to avoid starving to death. Moreover, the barons leaving to go home was something they would be able to safely do because men and riders moving eastward on the road were *not* being attacked.

In any event, there was no doubt about it in the minds of the archers; in the very near future the combined armies of barons' men who considered themselves unstoppable because of their numbers would begin coming to blows with a much smaller army of archers who considered themselves to be unmovable because of their superior weapons and training.

****** *The barons' co-commanders meet.*

The three co-commanders of the barons' "Loyal Army" met on the same day the Company's second galley carrying reinforcements began unloading its archers at Restormel. Two of them were more than a little concerned; things were not going well and they were increasingly worried because some of their fellow barons were obviously preparing to leave camp and return home whilst they still had a chance of making peace with King Henry and the queen. The third was pleased and quite satisfied—because, at least so far as he was concerned, things were going exactly as he had hoped they would.

The surviving barons and knights had counted on their men being able to forage in Cornwall whilst they waited for the king to die or, in the case of the more gullible, the French to arrive. So far neither had happened. Moreover, the fighting has been vicious and the foraging parties had not been all that successful. That was because the foraging parties were constantly being attacked and harassed by roving bands of mounted archers and also because most of the farmers in western Devon had been evacuated into Cornwall before the Loyal Army arrived—and had taken their food supplies and livestock with them.

Desertions in general had increased, but not noticeably, once the men reached the increasingly foul-smelling camp sprawled out along the cart path in front of Okehampton Castle. That was because there was safety in numbers and there was still some food in the camp. Even so, the three co-commanders and just about everyone else in their camp knew it the time was rapidly approaching when they would have to either force their way into Cornwall and begin foraging or disband and go home with their tails between their legs.

When the three co-commanders met that afternoon two of them knew they must quickly get their army into Cornwall to begin foraging and the third had another idea that he did not share with them. What they all three agreed, or so it seemed, was that they must either force their way over the ford or abandon their efforts to wait for King Henry to die due to their inability to get food for their men. Actually, the Earl of Westminster had a very different third alternative in mind but he kept it to himself.

Their discussions were heated and revolved around which of them should lead the fight at the ford. All three of the co-commanders understood they would have to take the ford and destroy the pesky archers who were demoralizing their men. They were also encouraged because they knew that most of the barons and their knights were optimistic because they were not yet suffering the same privations as the hungry men of their levies. That was because some of the barons had resorted to *buying* food in eastern Devon and Exeter as well in Dorset and Somerset; and some of the food was getting through, albeit less and less.

The problem, and it was more demoralizing to many of the barons than their losses of knights and men, was that they had to pay for the food they bought and most of them had very few coins. And, of course, a good number of the barons had no coins at all, at least none that they were prepared to spend to buy food for their men.

The continuing optimism of the barons and their knights was somewhat surprisingly in view of the growing shortage of food. It was based on the size of the Loyal Army which was now really just an aggregation of more than fifty small baronial armies—it was still quite large, six or seven thousand men, no one knew for sure, despite the losses that had occurred at the hands of George's horse archers and the catastrophes at Crediton and Okehampton.

Individual baron's armies had been decimated on the road and some of the barons had lost their lives, and a few had taken what was left of their men and gone home, but the forces of most of the barons had remained relatively unscathed except for the loss of many of their knights inside Okehampton and the desertions from their levies.

In other words, the main concern of those who remained was not the defenders of Cornwall, they could be handled; it was the expected shortage of food in the months ahead unless they bought it and could get it delivered *or* they foraged for it in Cornwall. Fortunately, or so the barons and their clerical advisors thought, the shortage of food would be resolved when they moved into Cornwall and began foraging where they thought there would be no opposition.

The meeting in the Earl of Westminster's tent did not last long. Less than an hour later the word went out that the Loyal Army would gather in front of the Tamar ford in the morning and then move into Cornwall to begin foraging. The Earl of Essex and the older de Montfort would have the honour of leading it across the ford due to a minor affliction the Earl of Westminster had suffered the previous night when he had apparently tripped on a rock and fallen whilst going out to piss.

Westminster manfully struggled to his feet and smiled and nodded at his departing co-commanders until they walked around the corner of his tent and were out of sight. Then he sighed, walked over to a skin of wine without limping, and sent for his three most ambitious knights.

Chapter Thirty-two

Preparing for battle.

The barons' encampment was a beehive of excitement and activity even before the sun arrived the next morning. One after another each of the barons and his knights led their men out of the huge encampment and began moving toward the ford that was several hours away on foot. The nobles and knights were riding and their men were walking behind them. Some of the barons had broken camp and were taking their tents and families with them in their wagons. Others left their families and tents behind and were marching with only their weapons. Today was the day.

Both sides thought they were as ready to fight as they could be even though there had been a great difference between the barons' preparations for assaulting the ford and the Company preparations to defend it. The Earl of Essex and the older de Montfort had prepared to lead the attack by riding down to the ford a week or so earlier and spending a few minutes sitting on their horses whilst they looked at the handful of archers sitting about on the other side of the river and the water running over the shallow river bottom in front of them. Everything looked deceptively peaceful and the two co-commanders were quite satisfied.

Most of the nobles and knights in the Loyal Army, on the other hand, had never even seen the Tamar ford and neither had most of their men. That was no surprise because it was a several hours walk from their camp that was stretched out all along the cart path that ran from the main road all the way to Okehampton Castle. Besides, there was no need to look at the ford so far as they were concerned; if you have seen one ford and splashed across it you have seen and experienced them all. The only difference was how deep the water might be and how fast it would be flowing, and even that differed from day to day. A ford, in other words, was just a ford and they could reasonably expect that if enough of their men splashed their way across it they would overwhelm and defeat the defenders on the other side.

In contrast, and because holding the ford was so important to the defense of Cornwall, for as long as anyone could remember the Company's men had been talking about how best to defend the ford, studying how to do so in the Company school, and practicing its defense every year as part of the Company's annual make-believe battles.

******

The Company had a number of outriders posted as watchers on the Devon side of the river. The first of them came galloping back as soon as they saw the size of the disorganized mob of weapons-carrying men that were coming down the narrow road that ran through the forest towards the ford. A large number of men were coming, they reported, and they consisted of mostly riders who appeared to be armoured knights. That was to be expected because the knights being riders could, if they so desired, move faster than the men of the village levies who would be walking behind them. What was not yet at all certain was who the barons would send forward to try force their way across the ford first. Would it be the horsemen or the foot?

Except for some men on some wagons on the Devon side of the ford and about a hundred men who were casually standing around in plain sight by the side of the river and on the embankment above it on the Cornwall side, almost all of the Company's available foot archers, now almost a thousand of them including the hastily recalled men of the galley company that had been guarding the wagons, were hiding, crouched or laying down out of sight, atop the river embankment in front of the ford. About half of the hidden men were on one side of the road that ran up from the river and continued on into Cornwall and about half were on the other side.

In addition to the men at the ford, the Company's available horse archers under the command of George Courtenay were constantly patrolling up and down for miles along the path that ran along the river. They were there to sound the alarm if the invaders had somehow managed to cross the river above or below the ford or were about to try to do so. And, of course, all those who were available at the time would fight alongside the foot archers if the ford was attacked. Gallopers were immediately sent out to bring in as many of the horse archers as possible. The barons were coming and every man was needed.

The ford itself was where the river widened appreciably so that the water spread out and was not so deep that a man could not wade across. That was why the road into Cornwall crossed it at that location. Only when the river was extremely low during a severe drought, which fortunately was not the case at the moment, could the Tamar be waded across elsewhere downriver from the ford. Even so, the Commander was taking no chances; there were ways by which an army could cross a river where it was too deep to cross even though it might mean losing some of the men who could not swim.

The only other defenders at the ford were in six horse-drawn covered wagons that were side by side on the Devon side of the ford and pointed at Cornwall. It was not certain why they were waiting there with one man holding each wagon's horse and three or four men sitting idly in the bed of each wagon. Perhaps to carry any last minute refugees across the ford without getting their feet wet. There were also six covered wagons parked atop the river bank overlooking the ford with what looked to be tree trunks sitting in them and that were pointed over the water at the narrow road that ran up to it through the forest.

All in all there were just under a thousand archers in place to defend the ford against the seven or eight thousand men of the barons. It was a warm and partially cloudy day and ford across the Tamar was definitely usable by men on foot if they did not mind getting their feet and the bottoms of their tunics wet.

In the distance on the Cornwall side of the river, as the knights approached the ford, the distant beat of a marching drum could be heard. A few minutes later almost a hundred footsore and exhausted archers from the newly arrived galley Number Sixty-eight could be seen marching in to strengthen the defenders with even additional men limping in behind them.

The new arrivals were met by one of the Commander's aides, Captain Adams from London. He rode out to greet them and lead them directly to their place in the Company's defensive line on the embankment overlooking the ford. As he did Captain Adams gave the new arrivals' captain his orders and explained what was happening and why the Commander himself had not come out to welcome them in person—because the barons' attack was about to begin.

Commander Robertson was one of the men who appeared to be standing around idly at the top of the embankment. After Captain Adams had hurried off to welcome the newcomers he thought of something he had forgotten and gave an order to another of his aides.

"Harry, run back to the reinforcements coming in. They have already been seen by the men on the other side of the river. So I want you to tell whoever is their captain to keep his men standing in a fighting formation. They can sit down and rest but they are *not* to lie down and try to hide with the rest of the men who are hiding behind the embankment. And tell their captain not to let his men give away the men who are hiding by walking over and talking to them."

Then he turned to another of his aides and gave yet another order related to the new arrivals.

"Charlie, get your arse back to the wagons and bring up the wagon that we saw yesterday that still has some extra arrow bales on it. I want you to stay with it and make sure the arrow bales get distributed to the new lads. Also the lads who are coming in are sure to be hungry and thirsty after marching all night, so I would appreciate it if you would try to organize some water skins and some bread and cheese for them. The boys from the school are back there with the wagons. They can bring them up."

"It is time to get things started," Commander Robertson remarked to no one in particular. "Come on over, lads" he shouted loudly across the ford to the men in the wagons parked next to the water on the Devon side of the ford. At the same time he repeatedly waved his arm toward them and then brought it back in the age-old reaching out and pulling back hand signal that meant "come."

The men in the wagons had seen the outrider galloping in and splashing across the ford to sound the alarm. They knew what his arrival meant and had been waiting for the Commander's order. The wagon drivers immediately began snapping their whips and the wagons began slowly moving side by side across the ford. The water was only up to their axles or a bit more. There was no doubt that both the barons' riders and their foot would be able to get across if they were not turned back by the waiting archers.

Strangely enough, it looked as though the men in the slowly moving wagons were scattering things into the water as they moved across the ford. When they reached the Cornwall side of the river the wagon drivers whipped up their horses and went up over the embankment and kept on going.

A few minutes later the last of the mounted watchers swam his horse across the river downstream from the ford and the knights riding at the front of the barons' column could be seen by the Commander and the other men on the Cornwall side of the river. The knights pulled up their horses out of arrow range and watched as the six wagons continued to slowly move side by side across the ford. If they had any sense they would have asked themselves why the rider swam his horse across instead of following the wagons and riding his horse across the ford.

The knights also watched and listened as the hundred or so new arrivals on foot marched up to the embankment overlooking the ford with their feet coming down to the beat of the drum, and then assumed a position on the north side of the road that came up out of the ford. The way they moved interested the knights but did not alarm them; they had never seen men moving together with all of them putting their feet down at the same time to the beat of a drum. They were not alarmed because new arrivals were neither mounted nor wearing armour.

The knights approaching the ford did not know it, probably because they had never before fought against English archers, but what they were watching as the wagons came out of the river and disappeared from sight was the new arrivals forming up into the seven-man deep lines of defenders the Company used when its men were facing the possibility of a charge by mounted knights. As you might imagine, the knights saw nothing to worry about because there were so few of the new arrivals and they were all on foot. There still was not a knight to be seen on the Cornwall side of the river.

The only other defenders the barons' men could see were a couple of men standing around the line of wagons that had moved so slowly across the ford, the back ends of a line of wagons each with a tree trunk in them that were parked on the river embankment above the ford, and the no more than a hundred or so men wearing Company tunics who were milling about down by the river or standing about on the river embankment overlooking the ford and watching their arrival.

What the knights did *not* see were the almost a thousand archers who were lying hidden with their bows and other weapons on either side of the road after it came up the thirty or forty feet from the river to the grassy embankment overlooking the ford.

In other words, the knights and their two commanders did not see anything to suggest there would be much opposition to their crossing. The two nobles could safely lead the way and claim the victory.

Chapter Thirty-three

The battle at the ford.

It took the better part of the morning before the Loyal Army finished assembling on the river bank opposite the ford and on the narrow road that ran up to it through a very thick stand of trees and brush that effectively prevented people from straying off the road. The men at the front of the Loyal Army were almost all of the Loyal Army's remaining knights. They had been ordered forward by their lords and had pushed their way forward through the mob of men on foot. The foot soldiers were packed into the narrow road behind the knights for as far as the eye could see. They could not get off the road because they were hemmed in by the thick stands of trees and brush on either side of the road that made the forest virtually impassable.

The Earl of Essex and the two Lords de Montfort had arrived several hours after sunrise and, like the knights who had arrived before them, rode up to the very front of the assembling assault force to see what they could see. What they saw on the other side of the river was no more than a hundred or so potential defenders standing about down by the water and up on the grassy river embankment above it. They had also watched and pointed as a hundred or so new arrivals marched up to the sound of a beating drum and assumed some kind of defensive position on the north side of the road that ran into Cornwall.

"We will roll over them without even slowing down," the younger de Montfort crowed gleefully when he saw how few defenders were on the Cornwall side of the ford and that none of them appeared to be knights in armour.

The older de Montfort and the Earl of Essex were also greatly encouraged. The two co-commanders immediately agreed that they and their knights should be the first to come to grips with the defenders of the ford. It was necessary, so they told each other, that they should go in with the knights in order to provide them with the necessary leadership and, although they did not mention to each other, so they would be present on the battlefield at the time of the victory so they could claim credit for it.

In fact, each of the men, without saying anything about it to the other, saw his participation in the forthcoming victory as being both low in risk and another step towards becoming accepted by the Great Council of Barons as being sufficiently brave and warlike to be England's next king; and they were both pleased that the Earl of Westminster was confined to his tent by his injuries and that his knights would not be riding with them except as volunteers attached to one or the other of their armies.

Westminster had insisted on some of his men accompanying his co-commanders at the ford "so I can be with you in spirit if not in body." They had agreed because they could think of no reason to deny such a reasonable request.

******

It took some time for the two co-commanders to bring all their knights forward and begin to get them ready to charge across the ford and begin skewering the defenders on their lances. But they were finally beginning to get it accomplished with the two de Montfort brothers and their knights mostly on the left and Essex and his knights mostly on the right. The knights of the other barons were behind them on the very narrow road that led up to the ford with the mercenaries and the foot soldiers of the levies following in a great disorganized mob immediately behind the knights.

By the time the co-commanders had begun to get their men into some semblance of order their knights had moved forward almost all the way up to the edge of the river. There was not much room on the riverbank so some of the knights and all of the men on foot were still packed together on the narrow road that led up to the ford. The road itself was bordered by a heavy growth of trees and bush on both sides such that the men on it were increasingly jammed together as they tried to move toward the river. Crucially as it turned out, most of the knights were looking at river in front of them and that was the way their horses were pointed.

The co-commanders were just beginning to shout and wave their arms in an effort to move their men into position when their troubles began.

An order must have been given to the men standing on the Cornwall side of the river because all at once they took their longbows off their shoulders and began pushing arrows across the river into the densely packed mass of knights and the foot soldiers immediately behind them.

The co-commanders and their knights obviously thought they were out of arrow range, if they had even thought at all. Accordingly, they were more than a little surprised and totally unprepared for the torrent of arrows that suddenly began raining down on them.

Fortunately for the assembled nobles and knights, they were prepared for a fight and wearing armour despite it being a warm and sunny summer day. As a result, only a few of the riders at the very front of the barons' column were wounded despite all the arrows that bounced off their armour. Their horses, however, were at best only partially armoured. And, as everyone knows, horses do not react well when an arrow suddenly wounds them, even the great and ponderous destriers that many of the knights were riding.

The result was similar to what you would expect if someone dropped a nest full of wasps into a room crowded with people—much shouting, confusion, and milling about as the closely packed wounded and screaming horses of the knights and nobles desperately tried to get away from whatever it was that was biting them.

Huw, the older de Montfort brother, was trying to get control of his suddenly panicked horse when he felt a sharp blow hit the unprotected area of his back just below where his armour was tied together. He screamed from the pain even though no one in the shouting and screaming pandemonium around him paid any attention or even heard him. The pain was excruciating and it felt as though something moving about inside him. There certainly was; it was a long double-bladed knife in the hand of the unknown knight without livery who had been riding immediately behind him.

A moment later most of the great mob of several hundreds of closely packed horses, including Huw de Montfort's destrier, began surging towards the river. The panicked horses were desperate to move and there was no place else for them to go. De Montfort was still on his horse and screaming from the terrible pain when the horse in front of him fell as it went over the riverbank and Huw's horse stumbled over it. That was when he fell off his horse and got kicked and trampled by numerous hooves. It happened just before he reached the water.

Mercifully, de Montfort did not last long enough to know what had happened and, in any event, it was the horses' hooves, not the knife, that killed him.

******

Commander Robertson was standing out in the open on the river embankment when he gave the order for the archers who could be seen by the barons' men to begin pushing arrows at them. The closely packed barons' men had obviously not realized the range of the archers' longbows and were too good a target to be ignored. So he gave the order for the archers who could be seen to start pushing out their arrows. As a result, a great and continuing storm of arrows began falling on the knights whilst they were still trying to form up on the opposite bank of the river for a charge.

The hundred or so experienced archers who were loitering along the riverbank in view of the knights were each armed with longbows and were each capable of pushing out an arrow every few seconds. And they certainly did. The result was a great and continuing storm of well-aimed arrows falling on the mounted knights and horses who were packed together at the front of the barons' forces. A few moments later another order was give and the galley company of new arrivals began adding their arrows to the storm. And a moment after that George Courtenay and the forty of so horse archers rode forward from where they had been waiting in a little stand of trees and added their arrows to the deluge.

The great majority of the archers, however, remained hidden and unseen in their ranks behind the top of the riverbank overlooking the ford—except for a few who got so overly excited by what was happening in front of them that they stood up to add their arrows to the storm that had suddenly begun descending on the men gathered on the other side of the river. Fortunately, the miscreants were quickly hauled back out of sight by their sergeants such that their sudden appearance had no effect on the knights at the very front of the barons' forces who, in any event, did not notice their sudden appearance because they were too distracted by the continuous arrival of more arrows and the chaos and confusion the arrows were causing in their ranks by causing the horses to bolt.

Commander Robertson watched calmly as the constantly arriving stream of arrows caused confusion in the ranks of the mounted knights on the other side of the river, and then as the confusion led to somewhat of a charge by some of the knights. They rode towards the ford and into the water, probably because that was the direction most of the horses were facing when they began their panic-stricken efforts to escape.

The Commander and the archers were somewhat surprised by what happened next—the barons' knights and men packed in the narrow roadway leading up to the ford began surging forward. It seems as though the riders behind the leaders thought the movement and the cries and shouts of the arrow-stricken knights in front of them meant the attack had begun. So they had urged their horses forward to join the charge.

Within seconds a great mob of horsemen and men on foot came surging out of the narrow roadway and on to river embankment and into the shallow ford that lay in front of them. The attack of the Loyal Army on Cornwall had begun without any order being given.

Commander Robertson waited to give his next order until the first of the charging horsemen actually came out of the ford and set foot on dry land on the Cornwall side of the river. It took a while because many of the knights' horses suddenly went berserk and began throwing off their riders as they splashed their way over the ford. The literally thousands and thousands of rusty old caltrops that had been scattered out of the beds of the six wagons as they came across the ford from the Devon side were doing their job. Their time had come after waiting in Launceston's dungeon for as long as fifty years for some of them

"Stand up and start pushing," the Commander roared in his loudest voice as the first of the charging horsemen successfully made it all the way across the ford and the first of the enemy foot began coming out of the narrow tree-lined road that led up to the ford. The bugler standing by his side instantly began tooting the signal for everyone to commence pushing arrows. At the same time the chosen man with the signal flags who had been sitting next to the bugler jumped to his feet and began frantically waving the flag that ordered all who saw it to commence pushing out arrows.

******

The hidden archers had been waiting for the signal and instantly jumped to their feet. The sudden appearance of almost a thousand additional archers and the great increase in the cloud of arrows being pushed into the attackers' ranks did *not* deter the knights' attack and the charge of the foot soldiers running behind them, at least not at first. More and more men kept coming out of the roadway and spilling down the riverbank on to the ford, probably because they did not know what was happening in front of them and the knights and foot soldiers jammed together behind them on the road were pushing them forward.

It was total chaos and confusion in the ford with many of the knights' horses falling as they came over the edge of the riverbank or bolting in great distress as a result of subsequently stepping on a caltrop or being hit by arrow. There was shouting and distress and horses screaming and running everywhere. Many riders were thrown off their horses and floundering about in the river including some wearing armour who were under water because they could not get back on their feet or had been stepped on.

The bodies of horses and men were soon floating down the river, but not all of them because armour does not float.

Despite the chaos a fortunate few of the knights were able to splash their way across the ford because their horses were not hit by an arrow and did not step on one or more of the thousands of caltrops that the archers had scattered behind them as they drove their wagons from the Devon side of the river to the Cornwall side.

Those who made it across were initially encouraged both because they were looking ahead and did not see the disaster unfolding behind them and also because the archers they could see, those who were immediately in front of them down by the river, were in full flight. They were desperately trying to climb the embankment in order to get away from the on-coming knights—at least that is how it appeared to the knights riding across the ford.

The archers fleeing from where they had been standing and sitting along the riverbank had no more than reached the wagons parked on road above the ford on the Cornwall side of the ford when suddenly there was great and terribly loud roar of thunder. A great cloud of smoke and flames came out of the end of one of the logs in the back of one of the wagons, and then there was another crack of thunder and then another and another and another with barely a pause in between. There were six loud thunders and lightning flashes in all and they each produced a great cloud of black and yellow smoke that hung over the river and smelled like rotten eggs.

All six of the ribalds had been pointed towards the jam-packed road in Devon that led up to the ford. But they certainly lived up to their name as the stones they threw went everywhere else in addition to some of them going where they had been aimed: those of the stones that went low devastated the knights and horses struggling to cross the ford and one of the ribalds must have been totally mis-pointed as it cut down a swath of trees far off to the left of the road.

Unfortunately for the barons and their men, however, a good number of the stones the ribalds threw went more or less to where they were aimed and acted like balls being rolled on the village green—they flew down the road and treated the men and horses on it as if they were wooden pins being knocked over by the a ball being rolled at them. Except in this case there were many stones in the air at the same time and they knocked over many men and horses.

Everyone was struck speechless by the noise and the result, including the archers. There was a moment of stunned silence after the thunder ended and the arrows stopped flying. Then the screaming and shouting started again, the arrows resumed flying, and the handful of knights who had somehow made it across the ford and were still on their horses pulled them around and tried to run for their lives. Some of them made it back across the ford; some did not.

Chapter Thirty-four

The Company's victory comes to naught.

The two remaining co-commanders of the Loyal Army met late in the morning on the day after the fighting at the ford. The purpose of the meeting was to decide whether the army should try again to force its way over the river and whether or not to send more of their dwindling supplies of food to feed the prisoners who had been taken at Okehampton. The meeting was friendly and went well because the Earl of Westminster was very solicitous of the injured and distraught Earl of Essex.

It seems that the Earl of Essex had injured his leg because his horse had been hit by an arrow, or so he thought, and thrown him on to a jagged rock when it bolted and fell over the river embankment. Even more significant, he was distraught because more than half of his knights were either missing or known to be dead including his brother and one of his sons. Some of the commoners in his levies had also been lost but that did not seem to concern him all that much.

Westminster's concern for the earl's injury was more than a little insincere since it was he who was responsible for it—in the dust and confusion caused by the arrows coming down on the riders who were all jammed together one of Westminster's knights, unable to get close enough to Essex himself, did the best he could by using his knife to deeply slash the earl's horse high up on its right leg. As a result the earl's screaming and hurting horse had bolted and subsequently stumbled and fell when its leg went out such that it tumbled over the river embankment and went down. The earl had been thrown clear and, so far as he knew, his horse was still there amongst all the other horses and men who would not be coming back.

The only thing certain about the fate of the missing men and horses was that they were almost certainly dead. The ground around the ford were scattered with horses and dead and dying men who had been stripped of their weapons and armor. Already the bodies of many those who had died or been wounded whilst crossing the ford had floated away down the river and the rest were already beginning to puff up as the summer sun heated them.

It was not yet known for sure who was dead and who was only missing and probably dead. That was because arrows were immediately pushed at anyone who tried to approach the bodies. The archers, it seemed, wanted the enemy dead and dying left where they fell as a warning to the barons' men not to try again.

After a while Westminster gently led the conversation around to the question of who should be the next king.

"I know you want the throne, Jack, and you would make a fine king. But after so many grievous personal losses would it not be better to forego the many great expenses that would be needed to get the throne and settle for the certainty of being a duke and having more land?"

Essex sat up in surprise and took the question for what it was meant to be—an offer to begin negotiations.

"Aye, you are right about that, Edmund, and who is the next king hardly matters to me now that my son and brother are gone. We can try to force the ford again, of course, but I fear the worst. It is all over for us, I suppose. If we cannot get into Cornwall to forage for food we will have to go home and try to make peace with the king. I fear he will go hard with us."

"Not necessarily, Jack, not necessarily at all—if you will support *me* and be content to be a duke with more land."

And then the Earl of Westminster told him what he was willing to do to hold the Loyal Army together until King Henry died.

****** *The Earl of Essex speaks to the barons*

Almost all the nobles who survived the attack came to the meeting that the two earls jointly called later the next day including two who had to be carried to the meeting due to their injuries. As usual, some of them brought their senior knights and clerical advisors with them; some did not. To a man they arrived with dejected looks on their faces and without the usual bantering and friendly nods and greetings that had accompanied such gatherings in the past. Their despair was quite understandable; almost every one of them had lost a number of men and friends at the ford and many of them had lost close relatives.

Even worse, they had arrived at the meeting thinking that they either would have to have another go at forcing their way into Cornwall, something they were no longer at all keen to do, or they would be forced to go home for lack of food. The only other alternative would be to buy food with their own coins in the villages and cities beyond western Devon where there were no horse archers and try to bring it back to their men.

None of the alternatives held much appeal and they were all concerned that if they went home they would have to face the wrath of the king who was believed to have become increasingly furious as a result of the result of the reports coming in from his spies. Apparently King Henry's spies and informants had been telling him that the so-called Loyal Army was anything but loyal. According to them, the Loyal Army was waiting for King Henry to die and that many of the barons wanted to march on Windsor immediately and install one of their own as king. It was basically true even though some of them did not want to admit it.

The Earl of Essex waited until everyone arrived. It took a while because many of the nobles brought their senior knights and clerical advisors with them and others had been injured in the fighting and moved slowly or had to be carried. The earl began with a lie and told them what they wanted to hear about their resounding defeat.

"Our men all fought bravely, there were no slackers, but we have all suffered great and unexpected losses because it was God's Will that some of our brave knights were so enthusiastic that they began their charge before everyone else was ready. All we can do now is pray for the souls of the men who were lost and carry on as they would wish us to do."

But then he truly surprised and pleased them with what he so enthusiastically said next.

"My dear friends, there is *no need to despair* if we are unable to forage for food in Cornwall. As it turns out, we do *not* need to do so. That means we will *not* be forced by a lack of food to go home such that the king and his supporters can pick us off one at a time. I am happy to tell you that the man who will be our next king, Edmund, the Earl of Westminster, has a very fine solution that I like and I think you will like. I will let him tell you about it himself so that each of you can hear it directly from him."

"Essex is now supporting Westminster for king?" …. "Did I hear that right?"

His words caused a sensation among the assembled men. There were gasps and many expressions of surprise from everyone who heard them, especially from the younger de Montfort and his supporters. It was a great surprise since it was well known that Essex wanted the throne for himself.

Everyone leaned forward and listened closely when Edmund got up off the three-legged camp stool on which had been sitting and then climbed up to stand on it so that everyone could see and hear him as he addressed them.

"England is too dear to us, my friends, for us to let it descend into leaderless and lawless chaos when our good king dies and passes to his just reward in the kingdom of God. The French will invade for sure. And if we fight again to get into Cornwall to get the food we will need over the winter we might lose so many men that there would be not be enough of us left to fight off the French.

"It is a great problem. They, the French that is, are already preparing to invade because they know our dear King Henry is in ill health and spending his time, quite rightly, at his prayers. The French are coming for sure and might well succeed if we are too few in number or too weak from hunger such that we cannot turn them away."

There was no doubt about it behind the eyes of everyone who heard him speak; Westminster was carefully choosing his words because he knew they would get back to the king at Windsor—and he was right to be careful since Henry might recover his health or Edward return from his crusade or the Queen could begin issuing orders in the King's name that the loyal barons would accept. There were many things that could go wrong. He was not about to publicly proclaim himself a traitor until he had the barons firmly behind him.

The assembled men knew all that, of course. And the fact that he was choosing his words carefully caught their attention and appealed to them. But what they heard next truly surprised them.

"Accordingly, I am going to use *my* own coins to buy all the food we will need to feed ourselves and our men in the days ahead whilst we wait for the French. I know that a few of you have been using your own coins to buy food for your men in Somerset and Wiltshire and have been somewhat successful in bringing it back past the bandits on the roads. Moreover, it is well known that many of the men assembled here are rich in lands but do not have enough coins to buy enough food because they have paid such great and unnecessary taxes to the king so he can buy prayers for himself in Rome.

"As many of you know, God has blessed me with lands near London that produce rents for me from London's merchants and money lenders. Moreover, I am so sure that God will protect me that I have no need to spend them to buy prayers in Rome for my safety and salvation. Accordingly, I am going to spend *my* coins to feed the entire army for as long as it is necessary and no one will have to repay me.

"We will send strong knight-led companies out beyond where the archers patrol to buy the food we need from our friends in western Devon, Somerset, and Dorset—and bring it back past the archers on the road with every man in the Loyal Army receiving a share as a gift from me."

There was a moment of stunned silence. Then the cheering erupted and there were many cries of "Westminster for king."

Of course there were cries of "Westminster for king." He and Essex had scattered the most trustworthy of their men amongst the crowd to make them—and to watch and see who joined in the cheering and who did not.

******

It took the Company almost two weeks to find out what had happened. The archers continued to wait on high alert at the ford for the next attack, but the barons and their armies did not return. Instead the horse archers who had remained on the Devon side of the river watched as several strong companies of barons' men moved east with their wagons. The archers followed Commander Robertson's order not to attack or bother the eastward movers in any way in order to encourage desertions and withdrawals. The Commander and his captains were increasingly ecstatic; they thought the barons were turning back.

But even the horse archers still in Devon who saw the barons' heavily guarded wagons return a few days later with food did not understand what was happening. They followed their orders to not unnecessarily risk their men's lives and did not launch serious attacks on the strong force of men guarding the returning wagons. Instead the horse archers contented themselves with picking off the stragglers and prevent the barons' men from foraging for food, which the returning barons' men did not try to do because their wagons were full of food and they had no need. Moreover, the barons had learned from their previous experiences and brought all their available archers with them to help keep the Company's horsemen at a distance.

Commander Robertson and his captains did not learn any of this or why it was occurring for several weeks. And when they did learn about it the news came from an unexpected source—Sergeant Thomas White, the graduate of the Company school at Restormel who had been serving as a priestly cleric and Company spy in the household of the Nuncio. He had been present when one of the Nuncio's spies made his report to the Nuncio and explained why the Loyal Army would be remaining in the west until the king died or until its new leader, the Earl of Westminster, decided to march against the king.

According to the Nuncio's spy, the Earl of Essex and the younger de Montfort had seen their hopes of becoming king evaporate like the drops of water on the hay when the sun comes out. But the Earl of Essex was a practical man and had seen the light; he would accept Westminster as England's next king and settle for a dukedom and enough additional land for six knight's fees. Young de Montfort, so the spy said, would see his family's lands and earldom restored and be relegated to Leicester to spend the rest of his days futilely wandering around in its fields and poorly attended tournaments.

There was no question about it according to the Nuncio's spy; Edmund of Westminster had become the frontrunner to be the barons' choice to be England's next king, especially now that he had strong support amongst those barons whose lands were close enough to earn the coins he was spending to buy food for the Loyal Army. Indeed, the Earl was paying so much that some of them had apparently sold him their entire harvest and reserves such that their own people were likely to starve during the coming winter.

Sergeant White was a very bright young man. He instantly realized the implications of the spy's report and knew he had to get the news to Cornwall as soon as possible. Accordingly, he hired two horses at the Windsor Village's stable and immediately left for Cornwall riding the less reliable of the two so that the better horse would be as fresh a remount as possible in case he was chased and had to make a run for safety. He did so after leaving a hastily scribed note for the Nuncio informing him that his mother in Manchester was on her deathbed and he was rushing to her side.

* * * * * *

The sergeant, still dressed as a priest but now carrying a sword he had hastily acquired by paying too much to a traveler on the road, rode hard and only stopped to rest his horses and to feed and water them. Once he had to swing off the road to get around a heavily guarded column of wagons. And the next day he was chased by a handful of riders who were definitely not archers. Even so he made good time until he was intercepted in eastern Devon by a patrol from one of the archers' raiding companies.

They greeted him cheerfully when he revealed himself as a fellow archer and asked for their help in reaching Cornwall with a very important message for Commander Robertson. And to a man they became very determined to do so when he took their sergeant aside and told him that he and his men must carry the message to the Commander if he went down.

"Tell him that Sergeant Thomas White from Windsor said that the Earl of Essex ~~Westminster~~ has committed to providing the coins necessary to feed the entire Loyal Army and is now its choice to be England's next king."

Two days later Sergeant White and four horse archers swam their horses across the Tamar and reached Launceston where Commander Robertson had made his headquarters. The exhausted sergeant was soon telling the appreciative Commander all about what he had overheard in the Nuncio's rooms.

What it all meant, Commander Robertson instantly realized, was that the defeat of the barons at the ford had come to naught in terms of driving the Loyal Army away from Cornwall—because the Earl of Westminster had countered the defeat by sending out heavily armed columns to *buy* food from the nobles further to the east and also in Exeter. His willingness to do so had succeeded, just as Westminster had hoped, in solidifying him as the barons' choice for the next king. His retainers and the others, according to the Nuncio's spy, were increasingly referring to him as Edmund the Generous.

Chapter Thirty-five

The gambit begins.

Commander Robertson sat with his maps spread out on the long table in Launceston's great hall and studied them carefully. He now had six useable galleys anchored in the Fowey estuary that were available to carry his men away to safety if the barons somehow overwhelmed the outnumbered archers and they had to run for it. The six included the galley whose crew had arrived in time to reach the ford just before the attack started and three more that had arrived in the days that followed. But was it the time to do something different now that he had the extra men and galleys or should he wait? And what should he do if he decided to act?

After he sat and thought about it for a while the Commander sent for his new aide, Captain Adams from the London post, and asked him many questions. Then he made a decision—and promptly began telling the captain what he intended for the Company to do and giving him the orders that would get things underway. Captain Adams could see a role for himself in the plan and was more than a little pleased as he began to understand more and more of the Commander had in mind.

"We can do that, Commander, I am sure we can," Captain Adams had exclaimed just before he rushed off with a list of orders for Lieutenant Commander Courtenay and the various galley captains who were with their men at the nearby ford. Another of the Commander's new aides rode with him, the recently promoted Lieutenant and priestly spy, Thomas White. Lieutenant White was now somewhat rested and recovered after a good night's sleep and a couple of big meals. His new and significantly higher rank had been hurriedly sewn on to a hastily acquired archer's tunic.

Both men were very excited about the Commander's plan and they talked incessantly about it and the various roles they might play. Their horses ambled all the way to the ford as they did. Even better, they came up with many fine ideas as to how the plan might be best carried out and were well on their way to becoming good friends by the time the wagons of the archers' encampment came into sight.

In fact, the two men talked incessantly as they rode including the sharing of many personal things. It was as if they each had suddenly realized that he desperately needed a friend in the Company with whom he could talk about his life and his hopes and fears.

What the captain and the lieutenant now understood, and most of their fellow archers did not, at least not yet, was that the barons had successfully countered the archers' efforts to drive them away from Cornwall with the unexpected arrival of coins from the Earl of Westminster for food purchases. There was no doubt behind the two men's eyes that the Commander Robertson was right that the food the Earl's coins were buying would enable the Loyal Army to *remain* on the approaches to Cornwall. They agreed with the Commander that something had to be done to make the barons *go away*—and they particularly liked what he had in mind.

******

The meeting of the Commander's envoys with George Courtenay and the captains of the men guarding the ford did not go particularly well, at least not at first.

"Our galleys are being brought up the river and we are to abandon our efforts to defend the ford? And we are to march our men back to Restormel and board our galleys and sail for Lisbon? Are you sure that is what Commander Robertson ordered?" one of the galley captains asked incredulously as he and his fellow captains gathered around Captain Adams. They all had shocked and skeptical looks on their faces.

"Aye, I am sure; that is what you are to do. As I understand it, the Moors have learned about the Company sending many of its best fighting men back to England. They see you and your men being here as a chance to dislodge the Company from Cyprus and the Holy Land ports and are gathering to do it. As a result you and your men are needed back in Cyprus even more than you are needed here." *It was a lie, of course. The Commander told me to tell it so his plan would not be leaked to the barons by a deserter or spy until it was too late; the captains and their men would be told the truth after they got out to sea. They would understand.*

"In any event the Commander is the Commander and he has given his orders. He is already on his way to Restormel and will meet you there. He will be sailing with you and no doubt will be sharing what he knows and his plans when next you see him. In fact, I know he will; you and your men have an important role to play in the defense of Cyprus."

"Are we really going to sail back to Cyprus? I find that hard to believe." another asked. He had just rowed in from Cyprus a few days earlier and was astonished that he and his crew were already being ordered to return.

"Of course you are going to Cyprus. We must defend it even more than Cornwall because that is where we earn most of our coins, eh? Adams responded.

"But there is no need to worry about Cornwall because not everyone is going. Captain Smithson's company is to remain to hold the ford along with Lieutenant Commander Courtenay and his horse archers. Indeed, the Commander has ordered that there always be enough horse archers at the ford so that every foot archer will be able to ride double if the barons launch a major attack and Captain

Smithson and his men have to run for it because they cannot hold them despite the caltrops in the water."

"And my ribalds," Sergeant Major Tinker asked, "what about them?"

"You are to return to Restormel with them immediately. But you are to park six covered wagons where the ribalds are now placed so the barons will not know that they are gone. Close the ends so no one can see in."

* * * * * *

Orders are orders and must be obeyed. Even so, George Courtenay immediately rode to Launceston to "confer" with Commander Robertson whilst most of the foot archers at the ford hastily began breaking camp. They intended to start out before dark and march all night—and keep on going until they got to Restormel and were on board their galleys.

Of course the captains would break camp and start their men moving immediately; the need to obey orders even if they did not fully understand them or agree with them was ingrained in every archer. Besides, they could turn around and march back if the Commander's orders had been wrongly conveyed to them. But it did not seem as though they were wrong; according to Captain Adams messengers had already been sent by the Commander to order the galleys to come up the river to meet them.

George galloped to Launceston and then smiled in relief and nodded his head in agreement when he heard the details of the Commander's plan.

"I like it, Commander. I really do. It is a good idea and will certainly surprise those bastards."

That was George's comment when the plan was explained to him. Then he respectfully declined an invitation to stay for supper in order to ride back to the ford before the sun finished passing overhead. He was fully onboard with the Commander's plan and anxious to begin doing his part.

"Thank you for the invitation, Commander. It is most generous and I would love to stay to sup with you, but I best be getting back to the ford and begin bringing in more of my horse archers so there will be enough of us if Captain Smithson and his men need help with the fighting and running."

George did not know it and never would. But his putting the interests of the Company ahead of a chance to sup with the Commander and have an opportunity to further ingratiate himself finalized the Commander's decision—George would be the Company's next commander if he was still around when the Commander stepped down.

Chapter Thirty-six

The surprise destination.

Commander Robertson rode to Restormel to meet with the six galley captains and arrange for them to put to sea as soon as possible. It went well when he met the footsore and thirsty captains in the middle of the afternoon in Restormel's great hall. Commander Robertson explained his plan *after* he swore them to secrecy just as he had done with Captain Adams and Lieutenant White. The captains, of course, promptly swore that they would tell no one where they were going and what they were going to do when they got there, not even their lieutenants, until they were at sea.

A few moments later the six galley captains were all smiling and nodding their total agreement and understanding when the Commander told them about his plan and began pointing to various places on the map on the table and explaining where they were going and what each of them was to do when they got there. He would himself, he told them, be in command and sail with them in Captain Jeffrey Smith's Galley Seventy-three.

The announcement both pleased and pained Captain Smith. It pleased him since it meant his galley would be the command galley and he would know what was happening; and it pained him because he would have to give up sleeping in the forward deck castle and sleep with his lieutenant and senior sergeants in the larger castle aft.

Immediately after the meeting the captains joined their men on their now-loaded galleys and one after another they began slowly and carefully making their way down the Fowey to the river's estuary off Fowey Village. When they got to the estuary they would anchor and rest their exhausted and foot-sore men for the night. In the morning at first light, if the weather was not too unfavourable, they would raise their anchors and follow the command galley east in a six-galley fleet.

Commander Robertson said he would follow them down the Fowey a few hours later in a large dinghy and meet them in the village's tavern for more talks as soon as he arrived. The tavern was *not* to be emptied so they could talk about their voyage back to Cyprus "to fight the Moors who have taken advantage of our absence and begun threatening the Company's Cyprus stronghold."

They were meeting in a public place, the Commander explained, because he wanted the reason for their sudden departure to be known in the barons' camp. Of course he did—because it was not true.

In fact, all six galleys would be sailing east down the Channel towards London and then up the Thames instead of to Lisbon and then on to Cyprus. And they would be fully crewed with archers, and then some, when they lifted their anchors and rowed out of the Fowey's estuary. More specifically, the galleys the Commander would be leading out of the estuary would be sailing with almost nine hundred archers on board because *all* of the captains' men had made it back to their galleys. That was because the supply and ribald wagons at the ford had followed along immediately behind the marching men and picked up those who dropped out for one reason or another, mostly leg cramps and sore feet.

Early that evening, after they had successfully come down the river and anchored their galleys in the estuary, the captains came ashore in their dinghies and gathered at the village tavern to talk whilst they waited for the Commander to join them. Commander Robertson arrived about half an hour later to sit with them in a corner of the public room of Fowey's only tavern.

Fowey Village's *Black Hart* tavern was a good place to spread rumours to gull whomever the Company wished to gull. That was because it was usually packed with villagers, fishermen, and passengers assembling to travel to the Holy Land on the next outbound Company galley or ship. The fishermen, in particular, were useful because they sometimes sold their catches in Exeter which was reported to be crawling with barons' men trying to buy food with the Earl of Westminster's coins. That evening some of the would-be drinkers came in, took one look at the rank assembled around the corner table, and hurried away.

Others, however, sat as close to them as they could get and tried to listen.

Before the Commander arrived several of the captains lowered their voices so no one else could hear them and expressed the opinion that having the wagons ready at ford to make sure that all of their archers made it back to their galleys meant that what they were going to do in the days ahead had been the Commander's plan all along. *They were wrong: The Commander had held the wagons at the ford so they would be available to quickly carry the Company's wounded away to safety if the barons' men were able to force their way across the ford. But it did not matter; the wagons had been there and, as a result, every man had made it back to Restormel and their galleys would be sailing with two experienced archers on every oar.*

The Commander arrived at the *Black Hart* a few minutes later with his aides, Captains Franklin and Adams and Lieutenant White. They sat together with the galley captains and joined them in alternately drinking bowls of ale the alewife dipped out of her barrel and cursing the perfidious Moors who were threatening Cyprus such that they had to return to the Holy Land immediately even if it meant leaving Cornwall vulnerable to the barons who were trying to overthrow England's dear King Henry.

"Better that the barons try again to move into Cornwall and risk getting another bloody nose than they march against our dear king," the Commander was heard to say.

****** *Captain Charles Weaver, Galley Eighty-eight*

As soon as the sun came up in the next morning we set our sails and began rowing out of the estuary and moving eastward. It was a cloudy day and there was periodic rain but we were helped by a quartering wind and having so many extra rowers. Despite the rain and the resulting reduced visibility the fleet was able to stay together and keep England in sight as a grey mass on the horizon off to our port.

The sea was calm on our first night at sea so the fleet's six galleys were lashed together into one great floating raft and the six of us captains once again met with Commander Robertson in Galley Seventy-three's forward deck castle where he would spend the voyage. As you might imagine, we all had more questions and there were quite a few helpful suggestions, including one from me about how we should moor our galleys when we reach London.

Captain Adams brought in the prisoner, one of the Earl of Westminster's reeves, so we could ask him questions. He, the Reeve that is, answered many questions and gave us a lot of information about Westminster's castle on the outskirts of London. We had heard all about Richard's prisoner but this was the first time we had actually seen him and been able to question him.

He, the prisoner that is, seemed to be speaking honestly and trying to be helpful by providing information and agreeing to do what we required of him, probably because he was so scared for his future and trying to save himself. He was right to be concerned; I certainly would be scared if Adams caught me breaking into his home and threatening his wife and children.

Westminster's reeve was lucky to still be alive and that was a fact. But what he told us seemed truthful and what he promised to do would be quite helpful—if he really did it. After he was taken away the Commander told us that the man had been promised his life and freedom if he was in all ways truthful and helpful; and that he would lose both if he was not.

******

Four days of hard rowing later the lookouts reported that we were slowly overhauling a fleet of four sails that were ahead of us and off to starboard. The Channel is always busy and every day the sails of numerous individual boats of all kinds from small fishing boats to big three-masted ships had been sighted. These sails were different; they were sailing together as if they were a fleet. They were also heading in somewhat the same easterly direction as we were sailing.

A few minutes later the lookout on my forward mast reported that the four sails ahead of us were changing course. "A hoy to the deck. Them buggers have seen us coming up behind them and are turning back towards us," the lookout shouted.

I immediately climbed back up the mast to look again. Sure enough, they had come around and begun sailing toward us. It was instantly obvious that they were coming around to check us out.

Galley Seventy-three with Commander Robertson on board was ahead of me and in the lead. I could see that its captain, my friend Jeffrey Smith, had not brought his archers on deck so I did not. The Commander was obviously ignoring the on-coming sails just as he had told us he would do no matter who we met, even if it was a French invasion fleet. So the rest of us did likewise and continued sailing together easterly as the unknown sails bore down on us. As they got closer we could see that they were cargo transports out of Dover.

We ignored them. First things first as the saying goes; and everyone understood that getting to London as fast as possible was first.

The Commander's reason for ignoring the sails coming towards us was understood and appreciated by everyone including the crews to whom a very detailed explanation had subsequently been given as to why they had been misled about their destination—so that the barons' men would not be alerted by any loose lips or spies in time to get there first and be waiting for us.

What was certain to everyone was that time was of essence; we needed to get up the Thames to our destination, the city of London, before word of our departure from Cornwall reached the barons' army in time for its commander, the Earl of Westminster, to gallop to London with his men before we arrived. Time was a very real concern because sooner or later the Earl would learn of our departure of most of the foot archers from the ford and start asking himself where we might be going and what we might intend to do when we got there.

About ten minutes passed before the four sails got close enough for us to identify them for sure: They were bulky two-masted cargo transports and probably out of the Cinq Ports according to the ancient sailor who was the galley's sailing master.

"They be Portsmen out of Dover and looking for the Frenchies," was how the sailing sergeant put it to me after we had climbed up to the lookouts' nest to see what we could see about the sails that were bearing down on us.

We never did find out for sure who they were for the Portsmen's lead transport suddenly turned away as its sailors began frantically resetting its sails. The others immediately began turning away as well. Their change of heart occurred when the wind whipped the pennant on the Commander's galley's mast so that it could be seen. The Company's flag was a white cross on a piece of black linen and just seeing it was often enough to intimidate a possible prize into surrendering without a fight.

The frantic change of course by the Portsmen's fleet was understandable. The Portsmen were familiar with Company's galleys and archers due to past "misunderstandings" and wanted nothing to do with anything that might make us angry enough to chase after them. Their concern was well-placed since we had had periodic confrontations with the Portsmen ever since the beginning of the Company's time in Cornwall—and, so the Company story goes, the Portsmen had always come out of them rather badly. In this case it was as if a herd of four curious sheep had come investigate something on the horizon and suddenly discovered it was a pack of six wolves.

There was no question in my mind why the Portsmen suddenly turned away and would have done so even if we were only one Company galley instead of six—*we* were highly trained fighting men and equipped with the most modern weapons and galleys whilst *they* were a bunch of untrained cargo-carrying tossers from Dover who were only good for carrying sea-poxed knights and foot on their decks out to fight the similarly sea-poxed knights and foot being carried on the decks of their French counterparts.

I myself had never had to fight the Portsmen. But what we had been learnt in the Company school was that in the past whenever the Portsmen had intercepted their French troop-carrying counterparts, both the Portsmen and the French would be carrying sea-poxed landsmen who could barely fight such that more men on both sides were usually lost from falling over the side whilst barfing than were able to kill each other with their weapons.

But why were the Portsmen out with weapons-carrying landsmen on their decks? Was it because someone had reported the French were coming or was it to intercept us or someone else? It was a mystery.

After doing some quick sums in my head I realized so little time had passed since we left Cornwall that it was highly unlikely the Portsmen were out because couriers had ridden from Cornwall to Dover to inform their king-appointed Warden that we were en route to London and that the king wanted us stopped. We never did learn why the Portsmen were out that day; at least I never did.

Chapter Thirty-seven

We reach London.

Our galleys did not stay together as we rowed up the Thames. To the contrary, they deliberately arrived separately at the mouth of the river and began rowing up the Thames about thirty minutes apart in order not to attract attention. As was the usual practice on the Thames one of each galley's dinghies led the way with a tow line attached to the galley's bow. It was there mainly to help pilot the galley through the crowded river's heavy traffic by helping it make quick turns to avoid collisions.

The day was a warm and partly cloudy day in late August and the river was its usual busy self with boats and barges of all kinds and sizes going and coming in every direction. Fishermen with both fishing poles and barbed spears lined the riverbank because a run of salmon was on its way upstream. Their families would be eating well for the next week or so if the size of the fish several of them proudly held up for our sailors to admire meant anything.

We attracted a bit of attention despite our efforts to look peaceful and stay out towards the middle of the river. That was to be expected; a war galley rowing up the river towards London was unique enough to catch everyone's eye despite the fact that our pennant was not flying and the deck was deliberately kept almost empty of men to avoid causing alarm or drawing attention. It was empty because all of our archers were on the rowing benches and only allowed to come up and use the shite nest in the stern of their galley if they turned their tunics inside out to hide the fact that they were archers. Our fellow galleys coming up behind us would be similarly doing their best to look peaceful.

Indeed, in a further effort to make our galley appear peaceful we had several of our older and more benign looking sailors sitting on the railing of the stern castle's roof whittling on wood and cheerfully answering any hoys they received with a cock and bull story about coming in from the lowlands with this year's linen fleet from Anvers. A handful of similarly employed sailors with the same story would be standing about on the decks of the five galleys coming up behind us. It was part of an all-out effort to gull the hailers and lookers into enough complacency such that no alarm would be sounded until it was too late to prevent us from carrying out our raid. It was all part of the Commander's plan.

****** *Captain Adams*

I was standing on roof of Gallery Seventy-three's forward castle with Commander Robertson, Captain Franklin, and my friend who was Seventy-three's captain, Jeffrey Smith. Jeffrey's sailing sergeant was on the roof with us and the two of them were giving a constant stream of orders to the galley's rowers and to the four sailors and their sergeant who were in the dinghy that had a tow line attached to our bow. They were rowing ahead of us to keep our bow pointed such that we would not hit anything on the river as we came up against the current. The usual apprentice sergeants were on the roof with us to listen, learn, and run any errands that might need to be run.

Jeffrey's galley was leading the fleet up the middle of the Thames in a "one galley every half hour or so" single file with its decks clear and only a portion of the bottom tier of its oars rowing in response to Jeffrey's orders. The other galleys were strung out behind us to avoid attracting undue intention.

We had timed our entrance into the river so the last galley in our fleet to follow us up the Thames would arrive an hour or so before dark at the quay where we hoped to tie up for the night. And we were careful to appear peaceful and attract no attention: Our galley's Company pennant was struck, all the rowing ports not in use had their heavy weather shutters closed so no one could see that our galley was carrying so many archers, and the tunics of everyone on the deck were turned inside out in order that our galley could not be easily identified as belonging to the Company of Archers. The galleys coming up behind us were doing the same.

My mind almost became overbalanced behind my eyes when we rowed past the street leading to the warehouse where I hoped my wife and daughter were safely sheltering, and then again as we came past Ship Street where my now-abandoned shipping post was located. I strained my eyes to see what I could see each time but I saw nothing. Hopefully no one saw the tears in my eyes that I wiped away as we slowly rowed past the sites of my hopes and fears.

It was the middle of the afternoon by the time we finally reached the quay on the city side of the river where I told the Commander I thought we would be able to find enough quay space to tie up all six galleys using only two side by side berths. I had recommended it because I was fairly sure we would be able to find mooring space available because the berthing fees were uniquely high in an effort to attract only the best custom. The road that ran along the city side of the river was immediately next to the quay

Fortunately for my career in the Company I was right about there being space at the quay; there were three or four berthing spaces available and we only needed two for what the Commander wanted to do. We did not have to continue up the river to find another place to tie up. *I was greatly relieved; I would not be embarrassed by having made a bad suggestion to Commander Robertson—thank you Jesus and all the saints.*

Jeffrey's sailing sergeant was an experienced old salt who had sailed in and out of London many times in his long career. He had our galley row up the river beyond the quay in front of the city wall where we wanted to tie up. When he got far enough up the river past the quay he swung our galley around so its bow was pointed downstream and came slowly and carefully back down the river to the quay of wood and stone that ran next to the road. It was smoothly done and the sailing sergeant smiled when I told him so. We ended up mooring in front of some warehouses that stretched along the river immediately in front of the city wall.

The half dozen or so fishermen who had been fishing off the quay began packing up to move away as soon as they saw us approaching and realized that we were coming in to tie up where they had been sitting and fishing. One of them, a man wearing a rough straw hat he probably wove himself whilst he waited for a fish to bite, must have been the king of London's fishermen; he hurriedly pulled a stringer line with a three or four large fish on it out of the water. He was clearly unhappy that our arrival was making him move from where he had been doing so well.

A couple of wharfies lounging about in the sun sprang to life as we approached the quay and they saw our bumper baskets, fishing nets full of old linen and tree branches, being thrown over the side to protect our galley's hull. Without them there was very good chance the hull would be damaged by being periodically banged up against the quay. The wharfies quickly threw some of the quay's own similar bumper baskets over the side of the quay in order to add them to ours. Then they caught our galley's mooring lines when Jeffrey's sailors threw them and expertly tied us up to their quay. The first galley coming in behind us would take the vacant berth just behind ours and the others would tie up against the hulls of first two such that they would protrude out into the river.

We had rowed past the Tower and were about three miles upstream from the quay on the city side of the river that was usually used by the Company. We had come further up the river so that we would be well past the Tower and close to the city wall when we berthed. We had done so in order to be able to come ashore where we were not well known. It would cost a few more coins to tie up immediately opposite the city wall, but it was well worth the extra coins since it would also reduce how far we would have to walk to get to our destinations—or run carrying our dead and wounded if everything turned to shite and we had to retreat back to the galleys and leave in a hurry.

As soon as we were securely tied to the quay Jeffrey ordered a couple of sailors to put down a boarding plank so he could go into the nearby warehouse and pay for five days of moorage. He would also pay for the moorings of the other five galleys of "the Anvers linen fleet." We were taking two of the mooring berths; the other four galleys would lash themselves to the two moored along the quay so that our galleys would be protruding three-deep out into the river.

Mooring in such a way did more than save a few berthing coins; it also reduced the quay frontage that would have to be defended if our fleet was attacked. Its downside was that our galleys extended out into the river so far that several sailors had to be permanently stationed in their bows with long poles to push off any errant boats or barges that were traveling downstream too close to the shore.

****** *Commander Robertson*

The sun was just starting to go down as the sixth and last of our galleys and its dinghy came rowing slowly past us and then, as the others had done before it, spun around to point its bow downstream. Then, amongst loudly shouted rowing orders and an impressive stream of great cursing from its sailing sergeant, it was gently floated and rowed downstream until it slid smoothly into place and its sailors quickly lashed it to Number Ninety-two in the last available space.

I was smiling as I listened to the sailing sergeant's curses and threats. As you might imagine, it was a great relief to me when the last of our galleys finally arrived and began the process of safely tying up; I had begun worrying that I had not started the fleet up the river early enough for the final galley to arrive when there was still enough daylight left for it to find us. But now it was finally here and I felt much better about what we were going to start doing in a few hours; we were likely to need every man.

Absolutely nothing happened after our galleys began arriving and tying up except that the usual large number of merchants and the protectors of London' street women, brothels, and taverns arrived to solicit our galleys' custom and that of their crews. There was a steady stream of them and they were all sent away with the suggestion that they come back in two or three days "when our crews who went ashore downstream return from their shore leaves and the owners of our galleys decide what to do after the bolts of wool and linen we are carrying from Anvers are delivered to the merchants to whom they have been consigned."

Chapter Thirty-eight

We prepare to fight.

Commander Robertson waited until the middle of the night before he gave the order for the galley captains to begin quietly unloading our army of heavily armed archers. No talking was allowed as the tense and excited archers carefully and silently shuffled their way over the bobbing galley decks and boarding planks in the darkness and assembled in their galley company ranks on the quay.

Each of the archers had his unstrung bow and a couple of quivers slung over his shoulder and each was wearing a sheathed short sword on his belt and carrying a galley shield. He would need the sword and shield for fighting at close quarters inside castle keeps or if rain fouled his bowstring and made it difficult for him to use his bow. About half of the men were also carrying the Company's fearsome long-handled hooked and bladed pikes on their shoulders, the new ones that caused such havoc and destruction amongst armour-wearing knights both when they were aboard their horses or on foot. Every man was also, as was the custom, carrying extra bow strings under his cap and in his leather coin pouch and slices of cheese and salted meat in his coin pouch, and every seventh man was carrying a water skin. They were, in other words, fully ready for a fight.

After much discussion it had been decided by the Commander that our men would *not* turn their tunics inside out to conceal the fact that they were archers. To the contrary; it was decided that we wanted the barons to know we were archers from the Company of Archers—so the barons would know it was really us who were coming for their castles and fortified farms and would continue to do so until they left the lands under the Company's protection Devon and Cornwall.

In an effort to encourage the barons' return we were starting our gambit to lure them back with an attack on the castle near London that belong to one of the baron's commanders, the Earl of Westminster. He had been selected for the first raid of our gambit both because of the relative ease we would have of reaching his lands using our galleys and also because he was reputed to have a lot of coins in his chests—which we knew to be at least somewhat true because he had sent some of his men to raid our London shipping post and they had taken some of ours and some we were holding for others.

What we were hoping, of course, was that the Earl of Westminster the other nobles whose holding we intended to attack would respond to our gambit by hurrying back to London with their men to save what they could of their possessions. If that happened their departures would cause the barons' army to begin to fall apart. In the case of the Earl of Westminster, we were also hoping that he would not reach London until we had recovered the coins he had taken from our shipping post and had them safely back in our coin chests along with all of his coins to help fill our chests even fuller. That was our second objective and the reason his castle on the outskirts of London was at the very top of our list.

In essence, since Westminster and his baronial friends had decided to go to war with us we were going to oblige them by giving them a war such as they never before seen and never would forget—and it would continue and be fought on *their* lands and in *their* keeps until they marched out of western Devon and stopped trying to take our strongholds and forage in Cornwall. We did not give a whit what the barons did after they left, and that included who they decided to support to be England's next king.

We knew, of course, that we would have to have a simpler and more easily understood explanation for the king and queen and their relatives. It had to be simple for the Royals to be able to understand it. Accordingly, we would tell *them* we were attacking Westminster and the other barons because Cornwall's archers loved the king and queen dearly and the barons were trying to take their heads. It was not true about the archers loving such useless fops enough to fight for them, of course, but it was an explanation the royals were likely to accept because it was what they heard from their courtiers and supporters.

That we were acting to save the king and his heir was something the royals were likely to believe because their courtiers and supporters always lied to them and said everyone loved and respected them. Trying to explain that our only motive was the saving of Cornwall and some of our Company's prosperity would clearly be a step too far because it would be hard for the royals to understand. That was because they were well known for not having much space for thinking and understanding behind their eyes, a physical condition that was widely believed to be God's punishment on the royals for marrying each other's sisters and daughters instead of taking their dingles further afield as is done with horses and pigs.

****** *Captain Adams on the Thames*

Our men divided into two battle groups as they came ashore in the dark: One battle group was the led by Captain Franklin. The other was led by Commander Robertson himself with me as his number two and principal guide. That was because I was familiar with London and the area immediately around it. And also, I must admit, because I was the only four-striper available who was not busy commanding a galley. As you might imagine, I saw it as a great opportunity to distinguish myself and was determined to do so if at all possible.

Commander Robertson's plan was simple and easy for everyone to understand as all good battle plans must be: He and I would march our battle group upstream for a couple of miles on the river road and then use the road that ran along the outside of the city wall to go around to the other side London until we reached the relatively large and prosperous village of Westminster. It was here that many of the servants of the king lived when he was in his nearby residence, which he had not been for some years whilst it was once again being rebuilt. Also living in the village were some the servants who worked in the stronghold of one of the barons' commanders—the nearby and much smaller castle of the Earl of Westminster.

Major Captain Franklin and his men were to march downstream to seal off London's great fortress, the Tower. We were not sure of the loyalty or intentions of the Tower's constable and garrison so Captain Franklin's battle group was going to prevent them, peacefully if possible, from coming to the assistance of the Earl of Westminster's castle whilst we were trying to take it and the keeps of the other rebel barons that were in the vicinity of London. We were taking no chances on the Constable being one of the rebel barons and coming to his assistance.

As you might well imagine, I was looking forward to guiding the battle group marching on the Earl's castle and leading the attack to take it. That was because the Earl was a man I had sworn to kill even if I had to hire an assassin to do it after the war. The idea that he might know it was the captain of the Company's London shipping post who had led the men who destroyed his stronghold and taken his coins appealed to me greatly. I was determined to take a full measure of the vengeance to which I was entitled. It was something I thought about constantly.

It was relatively easy to get the men of each of the two battle groups assembled on the road next to the quay despite the darkness. That was because all the men in each of the battle groups were on the same string of three galleys protruding out into the river such that they came ashore over the same boarding plank. They walked across the decks and planks in the darkness with only a lantern at the beginning of each boarding plank. They did so with each man holding on to the tunic of the man in front of him in order not to lose his way or his place in line. Additional lantern holders walked at the very front of each line of men to lead the way.

Our men's disembarkation and the forming up of our two battle groups was made even easier because the men in each battle group were going in different directions when they came off their boarding planks such that their paths never crossed: The men from the three galleys of Captain Franklin's battle group were turning to the right as they came off their single boarding plank in order to go *downstream* to the Tower on the river road; the men of the other three galleys were turning to the left as they came off their single boarding plank in order to march *upstream* on the river road until they reached the turn-off onto the road that would ultimately take us to Westminster's castle.

Commander Robertson and Captain Franklin were the first men to come ashore. They stood together in the darkness on the quay and watched as the archers from the two strings of galleys came ashore two abreast and then moved down the road following the man who was carrying the lantern to lead them. Each archer was holding tight to the tunic of the man in front of him with his left hand and would continue to do so throughout the night until daylight arrived.

As the two men watched the first of the archers begin to come off their galleys and began to move two abreast down the road in opposite directions, the Commander whispered a few last minute instructions and words of encouragement into Captain Franklin's ear and they shook hands. Then Franklin stood to attention, saluted, and hurried off towards the lantern at the front of his column that was leading his five hundred or so men on a silent march back down the river road toward the Tower.

Captain Franklin was totally on board with the plan and determined to do his best just as I was. He had received a promotion to acting major captain so there would be no question of his authority over the other two galley captains in his battle group; and he was determined to do well so that it would be made permanent.

The new major captain and the Commander would each lead his men from the very front of his two-abreast column of walking men. They would each do so with the help of an archer walking at the very front carrying a candle lantern so the lantern carriers could see where to walk. The long lines of men following them would thus be able to stay on the road and continue walking whenever the constantly moving clouds covered the faint moonlight such that the road could not be seen.

When Franklin and his men got to the Tower they would divide up into six small companies and each would block one of the Tower's four entrance gates and two small postern doors so that no one could leave the Tower. Penning in the Tower's garrison was to be done to reduce the chance that Commander Robertson's men would be attacked in the rear whilst they were busy attacking and sacking Westminster's castle and the castles and fortified houses of the other London-area rebel lords. The Tower itself was immediately next to the road along the river so Captain Franklin did not need a guide to help him find it. He did, however, have several men who had spent time in London before they went for archers to act as messengers and couriers.

The Commander's three galley companies with approximately the same amount of archers began to march *up* the river road in the other direction at the same time Captain Franklin's men began marching *down* it to the Tower. Commander Robertson himself marched at the front of his column. With him were myself, my prisoner John the reeve, an archer carrying a candle lantern, and some archers who had grown up in London and knew the city. Also marching at the front of the column was the

Commander's junior aide, my new friend Lieutenant Thomas White, and several apprentice sergeants.

We were up front with the Commander because he needed men with him who knew the layout of the city and the roads that led to his battle group's destination beyond it—the Earl of Westminster's surprisingly small but reportedly splendid stone castle with its keep that towered over the old village of Westminster and the abbey next to it where the monks allegedly never stopped chanting the prayers requested by the abbey's donors except to eat or sleep. The village and it castle lay just beyond the far side of the city's walls and that was where we were headed.

Walking immediately behind the Commander and me were a handful of our men who had grown up in London before going for archers and making their marks on the Company's roll. I myself had examined each of them closely to make sure he really knew the city and how best to get from here to there within it. They had all volunteered after being informed that if they did volunteer they would be used as messengers between the two battle groups which were, for all practical purposes, operating on opposite sides of London.

Unlike the rest of our men, the volunteer messengers had all been dressed in serf's clothes in an effort to keep them from being recognized. After much discussion it had been decided that they would be unarmed except for their personal knifes so that they not attract attention when they were moving alone through the city. Captain Franklin had several similarly clothed former Londoners with him.

A ferocious looking and overly large sergeant by the name of Henry Fox walked immediately behind me and my prisoner. Sergeant Fox had tied a line around the reeve's neck and was holding it tightly in his left hand whilst carrying one of his galley's short swords in his right. It was safe to say that John Reeve was not going to run away or sound the alarm or do anything else we did not want him to do; not and live to tell about it, at least.

Chapter Thirty-nine

Westminster's castle.

We began marching for Westminster's castle about four hours before sunrise. Despite the hour and the darkness there were people and a handful of wagons moving on the river road. They saw our lantern coming towards them and were inevitably surprised at seeing the long lines of men walking silently behind it instead of the wagon they expected to meet with a lantern carrier walking in front of it.

The wagons coming toward us in the dark usually, but not always, had someone walking in front of them carrying a lantern just as we were doing. That was to help them stay on the road when the clouds covered the moonlight and to warn people that they were coming. There also seemed to be people sleeping rough everywhere on both sides of the road all the way from the river to the city wall.

Every so often we could hear the faint sound of talking or see a blur of movement when the moon was not being blocked by clouds. There were no cries of alarm or shouted questions as we passed in the night and I could sense that the men were becoming more and more relaxed with every step they took. At least I was.

As we followed our lantern carrier and walked along the river road with each man holding tight to the tunic of the man in front of him we could sense the wall of the city to our right despite the darkness and periodically see it in the moonlight looming above us as a great dark shadow. After we got past the bridge the river road split in two with the leftmost split of the road continuing on along the river and the rightmost branching off to become the road that circled around the city on the outside of the city wall. We stayed to the right and commenced walking all the way around the city to the other side wherein lay the village of Westminster and the Castle of the Earl of Westminster.

Commander Robertson had us marching two abreast and we were moving fast enough that no one overtook us. Only once did a hurried warning have to be passed from man to man.

"Heads up lads; a wagon is coming without a lantern carrier walking in front of it."

After that, the Commander had one of the archers seize the bridles of the on-coming wagon horses and hold them in place until our men finished passing. He did so even if they had a lantern carrier leading them.

Neither the startled walkers we encountered nor the wagon drivers and their lantern carriers ever protested, not once. To the contrary, they saw our lantern coming, and then the first few of the men in the two long lines of heavily armed men walking silently behind it; and wisely said not a word as they passed us going in the other direction.

A feeling of danger seemed to hang in the darkness of the night and the travelers we encountered on the road seemed to feel it; they somehow understood that any kind of loud complaint or shouted warning would get them instantly cut down and be their last. Mostly they just hurried to get out of our way, made the sign of the cross, and muttered a brief prayer or two.

****** *Captain Adams*

We left the road and walked in a wide circle around the village of Westminster to reach our destination, the construction site of an old monastic church that was being rebuilt once again by some Franciscan monks and priests from the nearby abbey. We reached the site about an hour before the sun arrived. When we finally did the lantern was extinguished, we halted our march, and our men quietly were told to sit and rest without talking. We were on the far side of a huge construction site on the grounds of a Franciscan abbey.

The abbey's church had been under reconstruction for years and there was an equally large construction site beyond it at King Henry's palace. The king was apparently paying for both of them with the idea that he would live in one and pray in the other. I had several times been in the area visiting merchants and seen them whilst carrying out my duties as the captain of the Company's shipping post. I had not, however, ever actually visited either site.

Our men went to ground behind a large barn where the reeve had told us the tools of the abbey's construction workers' were stored. We would launch most of our surprise attack on the Earl's castle from that particular spot because, according to the Earl's reeve, it was the closest place to the Earl's nearby castle where our men would be out of sight of the village, the camp where the workers lived, and the castle.

When we finally reached the construction site the men were ordered to sit down behind the barn and silently wait for the opening of the castle's gate to admit the castle's servants who lived in the village. According to the reeve, we would not be bothered or noticed if we waited there because there never were any masons or other construction workers in the vicinity until well after the sun arrived when the morning's prayers were finished. That was because the men rebuilding the old church were required to pray at the abbey each morning at daybreak before they began their day's work. Apparently the workers and their families had to show up and pray for God's guidance each morning before they began to work. If they did not pray with the monks for God to guide their hands and eyes they were not allowed to do God's work and would not be fed or paid for that day. The reeve said it had been that way for years.

Some of the archers were initially very tense and clutching their weapons as they waited in the dim moonlight, a response to their situation which was certainly understandable under the circumstances; others just stretched on the ground and napped. There was no sign that anyone knew of our arrival; everything was quiet except for the periodic barking of a couple of dogs.

According to the reeve it would only take our men one or two minutes to run from where they were waiting to the gate of the Earl's stronghold. If that turned out not to be true he was a dead man for sure.

The Earl's castle was just beyond the storage yard where the stones for the new walls were being assembled and worked on by the masons employed by the abbey's master builder. Not everyone waited for dawn: Commander Robertson immediately led eight of us, including himself and me, toward the large wooden entrance gate in the castle's wall. It was the only way in or out of the castle.

As we crept through the masons' stone yard and toward the castle's gate we could see waiting in the faint moonlight that there was, just as the reeve had said there might be on this day of the week, a horse-drawn wagon filled with firewood. It was waiting to enter the bailey of the castle and, according to the reeve, and would do so when the gate was opened at dawn to admit the castle's servants who lived in the village.

We walked quietly up to the wagon and saw no one; but we could hear the snores of its sleeping driver who was slumped over on its driver's bench and the sound of the wagon horse as it stood in its traces. It was obvious that the firewood wagon would enter the castle's bailey when the gate was opened to admit the servants. Unfortunately there was no place for any of us to hide in the wagon so it could carry us in.

Our getting into the Earl's bailey when the gate opened to admit the servants who lived in the village was just the beginning. Once we were in we would have to run across the bailey and get into the keep itself before the alarm could be sounded and its doors barred. As soon as we got through the gate one of the archers accompanying us would give a single loud shout to summon our waiting men to follow us into the bailey. They would then run to join us without shouting or saying a word.

According to the reeve, the keep's main door was sometimes left unbarred at night because the Earl and his family felt secure because they knew the castle's gate was always closed and barred as soon as the sun went down. The door that was almost always open, the reeve said, was the side door into the keep from the castle's kitchen. It was left open because that was where the servants from the village entered the keep to begin their daily chores. It was also how the cooks and servants got to and from the kitchen to bring in the recently cooked bread and other foods for the castle's morning meal. According to the map the reeve had scribed for us the always-open kitchen door was on the far side of the keep and to the right.

Commander Robertson responded to seeing the firewood wagon and its driver by instantly whispering into each man's ear that we would be sticking to our original plan—we would go for both doors. The one change he made was to order one of the men to pretend to be asleep on the ground behind the wagon and be ready to jump on to the wagon and cut the driver down to silence him if he woke up and began to sound the alarm.

I was greatly pleased that we would be continuing to follow the Commander's original plan. That was because it called for me to lead the attack on the castle's gate, and then on its keep. I had volunteered to do so in order to increase my chances of getting inside the Earl's keep so I could begin taking my revenge. Also, of course, truth be told, I saw it as a chance to distinguish myself so that I would be considered for promotion when there was next an opening for a major captain.

Three of the men had already been told off to follow me through the gate and join me in heading straight for the kitchen door. Two others would follow the Commander and try to get into the keep through the main door and the sixth man would stay at the gate to hold it until reinforcements arrived. The Commander and his men would run around and join me and my three lads in entering through the kitchen door if they could not immediately get in through the main door. All six of the men accompanying the Commander and me were thought to be among the Company's better swordsmen.

At first the idea of using only eight men in the initial assault had seemed to be far too few, but upon reflection it had been decided that eight was actually a good number because having so few would reduce the chance of our men being seen or overheard as we approached the castle such that the alarm would be sounded in time to keep us out. Moreover, and even if I do say so myself, I am rather good with a sword such that the day will never come that I could not quickly finish off two or three unprepared and poorly armed and trained gate guards—and the reeve said that only one man and never more than two opened the gate in the morning. In other words, I foresaw no trouble getting into the Earl's bailey so long as I could get my foot in the gate to prevent it from being closed.

The most serious problem, if there was to be one, was likely to be *after* we got through the castle's entrance gate. It would occur if the doors from the bailey into Westminster's keep were closed and barred by the time we reached them. If they were barred, the most we could do would be to either stay in the bailey and starve the defenders out or use fire arrows and burn them out, probably the latter.

My only personal concern was that the archers rushing from the construction yard to reinforce us would see me and the other lads carrying our swords and wearing our workers' tunics and try to cut us down. That is why we eight were each carrying a black-painted shield to identify us and had paraded ourselves and our black shields in front of every man so that he could identify us. Unfortunately, men rushing into close quarters fighting sometimes forget their orders and strike out at everyone because they are so excited. It happens more frequently than you would think.

Once inside the castle's keep we eight and the rest of our men who followed us in from the construction site would immediately begin rampaging through its rooms and cutting down every man with a weapon that did not immediately throw it down and surrender. Everyone else, however, including the Earl's family and the men who laid down their weapons, would be encouraged to flee "because we are going to burn down the keep."

Allowing the Earl's people to leave the castle and carry word of its taking to the Earl was part of the plan. They were to be freed immediately so the word of our taking or laying siege to the castle would get to the Earl in the Loyal Army's encampment as soon as possible. Hopefully, the men rushing to reinforce us would not be overbalanced by their excitement and cut the Earl's people down, or the eight of us for that matter, despite their strict orders to the contrary.

The Commander's basic plan for the Earl's keep was simple and he had gone over the details of it with both his captains and his fellow initial assaulters a number of times to make sure everyone understood what he was to do.

Basically, if we got though the gate and one or both of the doors to the keep were open we would charge in and take the place and its coins whilst simultaneously allowing the survivors to escape so they could spread the word of its capture and destruction.

On the other hand, if we did not get through the gate or if we got through the gate but cannot find an entrance into the keep, we would try to hold on to whatever ground we had taken and use fire arrows to either burn the defenders into ashes or force them to surrender. The problem of burning the defenders out, of course, was that it would take time and make the chests of coins and flower paste in the castle harder to find and recover.

What was *not* a problem even if we did not get into the keep immediately was that there was almost always at least one escape tunnel in such an old and established castle. Someone such as the Earl's wife would almost certainly to know about it and try to use it to escape or send for help. We certainly hoped she would do so because we wanted the Earl and the barons' army to know what we were doing. Hopefully, of course, we would get in, take the valuables in the Earl's treasure room, burn the place down, and sooner or later someone who escaped or watched would inform the Earl and he would hurry back. Sooner was better.

It was a good plan in one sense since the primary goal of our attack, and of our siege if our attack failed to take the keep, was to get word of our attack to the Earl so that he and his men would hurriedly return from Devon to save whatever they could of the Earl's possessions. On the other hand, we had to get into both the bailey *and* the keep if we were to also get the Earl's coins and recover what he had taken from the Company's shipping post. Getting in and then burning then place down was definitely better than the other way around.

Chapter Forty

Our move against the Tower.

Captain Franklin and his men arrived at the Tower at least three hours before the appearance of dawn's early light. He and his archers spent those hours marching all the way around the great walled fortress that was just outside London's city wall. Its four main gates and two small postern doors had all been closed and barred for the night—and they would stay that way when morning arrived because he left a substantial force at each of them with very firm orders not to let anyone out.

It did not take long before they were discovered. An alert guard on the Tower's wall noticed the lantern moving toward him on the footpath that ran all the way around the Tower. It was the only interesting thing he had seen that night so he paid attention to it. Upon looking more closely in the moonlight as the lantern passed on the path below him he was able to make out the two long lines of men walking silently behind it. He gasped in surprise and promptly began shouting for his sergeant.

A minute or so later a horn started blowing somewhere in the distance and a distant drum deep in the fortress started beating with a sense of urgency.

******

Initial contact was made with some of the Tower's garrison and servants even before the sun arrived. Slightly more than a hundred men under the command of Harold Smith, the captain of Galley Forty-eight, were in a battle formation astride the very short road that ran between the Tower Gate in the great stone wall that surrounded London to the Tower's City Gate. The archers had just finished digging little holes for the butts of their bladed pikes to keep them from slipping when charging horsemen impaled themselves on them. They were resting in their battle ranks when the gate in the city wall opened behind them. It was still dark but the first glimpses of dawn's early light were expected momentarily.

A steady stream of Tower servants and others began pouring out of the city as soon as the Tower Gate in the city wall was opened—and were astonished to find that they would not be allowed to proceed all the way down the road that ran between the gate in the city's wall to the gate in the Tower's wall. A few of them turned back and reentered the city; most of them, however, gathered off to one side in little groups and waved their hands about in the moonlight as they gobbled with each other as to what was happening and what they should do next.

One sputtering and incredulous knight with a sore head from too much wine was among the early arrivals.

From the look and smell of him he had spent the night drinking and wenching in London and was now attempting to return to his post in the Tower. He responded to being stopped after identifying himself as a knight by shouting and threatening.

Captain Smith was having none of it.

"Sergeant Edwardson, take three men and escort Sir Alfred back to the city gate and see that he goes through it. If he gives you any trouble you are to immediately kill him for the traitor he must be for refusing the orders of King Henry's army."

Sir Alfred's bloodshot eyes almost popped out of his head when he heard the Captain's order and then saw Sergeant Edwardson salute Captain Smith and repeat the order back so that Captain Smith would know that he understood the order and would obey it.

Fortunately for Sir Alfred he had sobered up enough to understand that his life depended upon him stopping his blustering and doing what he was told. The knight was not too bright but it did not take an alchemist to understand from the way the order was given and received that the sergeant and his men might really kill him if he made even the slightest bit of additional trouble. As he was being led away he consoled himself with shouting over his shoulder to Captain Smith that things would have been very different if he had been wearing his armour and carrying a sword. Captain Smith just smiled.

Contact with the Tower itself was made soon thereafter even though it was still dark. It came after a small door in the Tower's City Gate was opened and someone came out far enough to see us standing in our battle formation ranks just out of crossbow range. He ran back to the door shouting and a moment later the door was slammed shut behind him. Less than a minute later there was a call from the top of the Tower wall.

"A Hoy to whoever is out there. Who are you and what do you want?" The hoy came from the top of the wall above the Tower's city gate.

"Hoy the Tower. We are the supporters of King Henry who have come here from Cornwall" Captain Smith shouted back. "And what we want is for you and the rest of the Tower's garrison to stay there and not come out and try to protect the Earl of Westminster and the other traitors who are trying to overthrow the king."

It was what Captain Smith had been told to say.

"What is that you say? Who is trying to overthrow the king?" There was a note of surprise in the questioner's voice.

"Stop wasting your time asking questions. Go to the Tower's Constable and tell him that my commander wants to talk with him. He is waiting for him at the River Gate. And I would advise you not to try to sortie out from any of your gates and postern doors. We have men at every one of your gates and doors with orders from the commander of King Henry's army to take the head of anyone who tries to leave in order to join the traitors." *There was no commander of the king's army, at least not that we knew about, so saying that there was should help cause uncertainty and confusion amongst both the garrison and also the barons when they hear about it.*

We could not, of course, actually keep the Tower's garrison from leaving to join the barons in Devon or for any other reason. That was because there was almost certainly at least one escape tunnel in the Tower that came up somewhere in the city, and probably more than one. We had no idea where their entrances might be. Indeed, we were counting on the tunnels or some other secret exit being used so that word of our siege on the Tower and attacks on the rebels' castles and chevaucheeing in the London area would reach the Loyal Army. We *wanted* the barons to know that Cornwall's archers were out in force.

What we really wanted, of course, was for some of the barons of the Loyal Army to respond to our gambit by rushing back to the city to fight us off and save their keeps and lands. When they did we would board our galleys and return to Cornwall to finish off those who were foolish enough not to leave with them. At least that was the plan.

****** *Major Captain Franklin*

When the sun came up the men remaining under my direct command and I were astride the cart path that ran up from the road along the river to the Tower. It is always better to be safe than sorry so I had them in the Company's traditional seven-deep battle lines that were used to fight mounted knights. And we certainly attracted a lot of attention even before the Tower's river gate started to open to admit the wagons and people that had, as usual, begun gathering by that time and were waiting to enter.

Whoever in the Tower had first opened the gate to admit its usual array of servants, supplicants, and hungry paupers was surprised to find that no one was there. He stepped out to investigate, saw the dim outline of our assembled ranks, and promptly ran back to the gate and slammed it closed so hard that the noise it made could be heard all the way out to where we were waiting in our battle formation just out of crossbow range.

There were a number of wagons and people-carrying horse carts and hand carts waiting to enter the Tower along with a number of walkers coming in off the road that ran along the Thames. We attempted to send them away but many of them would not leave the area. Instead they gathered along the cart path behind us and talked excitedly amongst themselves.

My number two, Captain Stephen Weaver of Gallery Ninety-seven, dealt with the people as they arrived. He had to explain over and over again that we were archers loyal to the king who were "keeping the Tower's garrison from joining the rebel barons whilst we are taking and destroying the rebel barons' castles and conducting a chevauchee to burn their crops, and kill the animals on their lands."

As you might imagine, Captain Weaver had to repeat his explanation over and over again as more and more people and wagons arrived intending to enter the Tower and go about their normal daily business. In addition, in less than an hour worried merchants and moneylenders began coming out of the city to see for themselves and find out if the tales they were being told were true. They inevitably attempted to question Captain Weaver and worried aloud at when he told them that we intended to destroy the rebels' castles and devastate their lands with a chevauchee.

Also constantly arriving were a steady stream of the merchants whose goods had been in our warehouse awaiting shipment and the holders of the Company's money orders who were anxious to redeem them.

Captain Weaver did his best to reassure everyone. Over and over he explained that the Company, as always, fully guaranteed that everyone who had consigned their goods and coins to the Company would suffer no losses and that more than enough replacement coins to fully meet the Company's obligations were already en route from the Company's other shipping posts. The coins would, the captain told them, be made available as soon as soon as it was safe to bring them into the city.

The biggest sensation of all, however, was amongst the men in the Tower's garrison. More and more heads appeared on the wall overlooking the Tower's riverside gate and to a man they appeared to be taken aback and astonished at what they saw and heard.

"Hoy to you down there. I am Sir Hugh FitzOtho, the Constable of the Tower and what is all this about a barons' revolt?"

He shouted his question down from atop the Tower wall rather arrogantly.

"Are you a baron or an English or French knight, Sir Hugh."

"Aye; that I am. I be a knight. And who be you?"

"I be the captain from Cornwall whose archers will take your head and the heads of any of your men who try to come out from behind the Tower's walls without my permission. And you will not get that permission until we finish destroying the castles of the rebel barons and putting a chevauchee on their lands."

I said what I said with a right proper snarl so Sir Hugh and everyone listening to us would get the message—and I deliberately used the French word chevauchee, meaning a "scorched earth raid," to properly describe the total destruction of the barons' properties that our raids intended to achieve.

That is what the Commander told me to say. Even more important, at least to me, was that taking their heads was exactly what I was determined to do if the Constable was foolish enough to come out with his men and try to either fight us to help the barons or get past us to join them—either of which he might attempt to do if he was already aligned with the rebels or considering the possibility of joining them or because he was just plain stupid.

Truth be told, I enjoyed threatening Sir Hugh and rather hoped that he would try to ride out and break our siege. That was probably because my grandfather was a small franklin who got killed fighting for King John and caused our family's land to be lost to an arrogant baron just like Sir Hugh. According to my mother the local baron just took the land and there was no one to stop him because the justiciar was his brother. It was the first time I had ever had an opportunity to actually threaten a knight or baron—and it felt quite good to do it; particularly since I meant every word I said.

What we really wanted, of course, was for the Constable or some of his men to use the Tower's escape tunnels and get word to the rebel barons that we were besieging the Tower to keep its garrison inside whilst we were destroying their castles and putting a chevauchee on their lands. Our thinking was that when the barons heard what was happening to their estates and that there was no one available to defend them they might decide to hurry back to defend their estates themselves.

At least that is what we hoped would happen. If it did not it would cause a very big problem because we would have to move on to our next plan to get them to leave Cornwall alone—the big problem being that, at least so far as I knew, we had no next plan.

****** *Captain Adams at the Earl of Westminster's castle*

I listened to the Commander's whispered final orders and then moved as quietly as I could to a position about twenty feet down the castle wall on the right side of the entrance gate. It was on the right so the gate would open out towards me. When it did so, opened towards me that is, I would be behind it and unseen by whoever opened it.

As soon as I got to the wall I covered my double-bladed short sword and shield with a piece of old sail that I was carrying for that purpose and then leaned up against the wall's uneven stones and pretended to be a vagabond or supplicant sleeping rough. In the night's darkness I was not likely to be noticed unless I moved or made some noise when there was enough moonlight for someone above me on the castle's wall to look down and see me.

What I was doing was all part of the plan. Everyone else except the man under the wagon, meaning the Commander and the other five men, moved back and pretended to be sleeping rough much further back along the left side of the castle wall—so they would not appear to be threatening in the event they were seen by whoever opened the gate or by someone looking down from atop the wall. The castle had no moat.

There had been no surprises in the whispered final orders I received from the Commander; they were basically a repeat of the orders I had been given several times earlier. I immediately breathed "aye Commander" into his ear and moved to my waiting place against the castle wall on the right side of the gate. As I moved to the wall, the Commander and the other five men moved further back along the wall to the *left* of the gate so they were well behind the firewood wagon and not likely to be seen by either the arriving servants or the man who usually opened the gate each morning. The reeve had told us that the gate opener was usually just an unarmed servant, especially now that the Earl was away in the southwest with his knights and most of his guards and levies.

One thing was certain: I intended to take no chances: I would use my sword and cut the gate opener down if he was armed *or* might close the gate behind me before the others arrived. The reeve said he or they would at most be wearing sheathed swords; but one never knew for sure and even an unarmed man might be able to shut the gate behind me as I ran for the kitchen door.

******

I was leaning with my back against the wall and pretending to be asleep even though my eyes were open and I was listening intently. But I certainly opened my eyes even wider when I heard the sound of footsteps and women's voices coming up the path from the nearby village. A minute or so later in the moonlight I could see the vague outlines of three women walking towards the gate. They were almost certainly castle servants, perhaps its cooks and servers.

The three women walked straight to the castle's gate without giving any indication that they had seen either me or the man under the wagon. Then one of them startled me by loudly shouting "Hoy, Andrew. We are here. Let us in."

There was a muffled acknowledgment from behind the gate. A moment later there was the distinctive sound of its wooden bar being removed and dropped on the ground followed by the creak of the gate being pushed open from the inside and starting to swing out and towards me. In the background I heard the now-awake wagon driver say something. I took a tight grip on my sword and shield and got myself ready.

I waited to make my move until the gate was partially open and the three women were starting to walk in through it. Then I leaped to my feet and rushed to the gate to prevent it being closed behind them. It was getting light rapidly but it was still mostly dark.

The last of the three women must have heard me or perhaps she had seen me coming out of the corner of her eye. She turned her head to look towards me and started to say something. Too late. I hooked the edge of the gate with my shield-carrying left arm and used it to pull the partially open gate toward me to open it even further. I did so as I went around it with my sword at the ready in my right hand to deliver a great downward slash. The gate was surprisingly heavy as I pulled on it.

Everything seemed to happen at once as I simultaneously pulled the gate further open and came around the end of it with my sword held high and ready to chop down on anyone who look dangerous: Several of the woman screamed when they saw me in the dim light, and the nearby and newly-awakened wagon driver heard them and asked some sort of question. At the same time I heard the Commander bark out an order and the pounding of feet as he and the archers with him started running toward the gate.

Chapter Forty-one

The surprise attack.

By the dawn's early light I saw the vague shapes of three women and two men as I came around the still-opening gate with my sword held high so I would be ready to cut them down. Every one of them reacted with surprise and astonishment at seeing me suddenly come around from behind the gate and appear in front of them holding a raised sword. They all gasped out little screams and instinctively backed away from me. As I got up close to them I could see that both of the men were unarmed.

"Save yourselves. Run out of the castle and escape. Hurry," I screamed at them as I motioned frantically towards the half-open gate behind me and waved my sword at them threateningly. "It is your only chance."

All five of them just gaped at me. Then one of the women took a tentative step toward the partially open gate; and then broke into a run. That broke the spell that held them and the others started to follow her out of the bailey. They all went except one man who just stood there and continued to stare at me in shocked disbelief. I gave him a push to get him started as I ran past him and headed for the kitchen door.

Commander Robertson and the others came rushing through the partially open gate holding their shields in one hand and their swords in the other just as the first of the five servants at the gate, the quick-thinking woman, went hurrying through it heading in the other direction. I was well on my way to the kitchen door as the Commander and the men following him came running through the gate and entered the bailey. Some of the men followed the Commander as he headed straight for the keep's main entrance door; the others followed me except for one of my men who stayed to hold the gate until our main force arrived from the construction site. So far so good; we were inside the castle's curtain wall.

* * * * * *

I ran around the corner of the keep and reached the door to the kitchen just as a rather large grey-haired woman was starting to come out of the castle's dark interior carrying a lighted candle. She gasped when she saw me. By the dawn's early light I could see a man poking at the kitchen fire with something in his hands, probably a stick of wood that would soon be burning. He was cooking flatbreads with cheese on them by the smell of it.

The cook had heard the sound of my running and spun around to gape at me in disbelief and surprise just before I reached the door and the woman saw me. I could see clearly enough in the rapidly improving pre-dawn light to make out the grey in his hair and beard.

Behind me I could hear the sound of running feet as two of the three men assigned to enter through the kitchen door with me came pounding around the corner of the keep with their short swords and galley shields in their hands. My third man was similar armed and waiting at the gate to keep it open until our main force arrived. We were all wearing chain shirts and so were the Commander and the men with him.

The woman stopped in the doorway at the sight of me, speechless and stunned at the sight of me, and then she screeched in surprise and pain as I instantly reached out and grabbed a big handful of the hair on her head with my galley shield hand and literally pulled her all the out of the doorway before I let go of her. The galley shield being held on my arm by its arm sling banged her on the head as I did.

For a brief moment we looked each other in the eye as I stood in the doorway in order to hold the door for my on-coming men. She could see that I was tremendously excited and I could see that she was shocked and surprised. Later I learned that she was the baroness.

"Run," I shouted at the woman and the astonished cook in my loudest command voice as I let go of the woman's hair. "Save yourselves. This is one of the castles we have been ordered to sack because its lord is a traitor to the king and also a robber." *That there would be more attacks like this one was the message we wanted the rebel barons to get.*

The cook started to back away; the somewhat disheveled woman, however, just stared at me with a most disbelieving look on her face and did not move an inch. Neither did I for a second or so. We just looked at each other. But then two of the men assigned to me arrived and I turned and rushed on into the darkness of the keep. One of the men, a sergeant by the name of Jack Cooper who was well known for his ability to fight, followed right behind me. The second man followed his orders and stayed behind to hold the door until the rest of the archers arrived from the construction site. So far so good. *I never did hear what happened to the baroness.*

I entered Westminster's keep hoping that the reinforcements who had been waiting at the construction site were already on their way to reinforce us and running hard. When they reached the castle some of them were to join us inside the keep; the rest were under the command of Adam Jenkins of Galley Eighty-one and assigned to eliminate any of the castle's guards who were in their hovels in the lines behind the keep where some of the Earl's men lived with their families. Without the successful arrival of our main force we eight would be up shite river without an oar if Westminster had left enough fighting men inside the keep or the bailey.

We knew all about the location of the castle's lines behind the keep where some of the guards lived because that is where John the Earl's reeve lived with his wife. What we did *not* know for sure was how many of the castle's knights and guards were still in the castle now that most of them had marched off to Devon and Cornwall with the Earl. And, of course, we did not know how many of those remaining in the castle we could disarm or cut down before they picked up their weapons and started trying to fight us off.

I began hearing screams and shouts and other of the familiar sounds of intense close quarters fighting as soon as I rushed into the night-darkened keep. The Commander and his men had obviously gotten in through the main door that opened into a room next to the castle's great hall. The hall was where the Westminster fed his knights and guests and where some of them probably had been sleeping.

Many of the Earl's knights and guests, according to John the reeve, slept in a nearby room filled with little rounded privacy chambers made of bricks that they could crawl into to sleep by themselves or with a woman. The reeve said they looked like short upside down aqueduct pipes or horse troughs that had one or both ends open so people could crawl into them and sleep in privacy. He said they stood about as high as a man's dingle when he was standing to piss. Apparently it was the latest thing in comfortably housing a castle's visitors and the Earl was quite proud of them.

Where we thought we were most likely to encounter resistance when the castle was just waking up was in and around the great hall and in the stall-like lines which housed his guards and important servants. According to John reeve the latter were against the castle wall behind the keep. And from the sounds we could hear as we rushed into the keep through the kitchen door it seemed likely the Commander and his men was meeting resistance.

According to the Earl's reeve, there was only the one knight who was serving as the castle's constable and six or seven armed guards now in the castle. That was because most of them had followed the Earl to western Devon. But the reeve had been our prisoner for several weeks and things may have changed since he was last here.

****** *Captain Adams*

I ran down a dark hallway towards the sound of the fighting with Sergeant Cooper close behind. He was one of the veteran archers who had been asked to volunteer to accompany me because they were considered to be among the Company's better swordsmen. The men with the Commander were chosen because they were thought to be similarly good.

Sergeant Cooper and I ran down the dimly lit hallway towards the increasingly loud sounds of fighting. There was woman coming the other way carrying something that turned out to be a chamber pot. I did not slow down at all; I knocked her aside with my shield and she went sprawling against the wall and fell. Sergeant Cooper was running right behind me jumped over her without missing a step and kept coming too. We were anxious to get into the fight because we were both veterans with enough experience to understand that the best and safest time to fight is when you are armed and ready to fight and the men you are fighting are not. Besides, it sounded as though the Commander and his men needed help.

And they certainly did need help. We found the castle's unlighted and still extremely dim great hall to be a hotbed of fighting and angry shouting. It was almost totally dark because the wooden shutters over the halls window openings had not yet been opened and its candle, if there had been one, had been knocked over and gone out.

"Archers. Archers" I heard men shouting and began constantly shouting myself as I joined the fray. And so did my men and the Commander and his men. It was the only way we could identify ourselves in the dark. Anyone not shouting "archers" was fair game as my men and I moved forward in the darkness with our shields held out in front of us and making great outward slices and stabbing thrusts with our swords. I did not hit anyone.

From the sound of it, the Commander and at least one of his men seemed to be in one corner of the hall as we entered the room. They had likely been elsewhere because I promptly tripped over a still-live man and almost went down. I hope he was not one of ours because I reached backwards as I tripped over him and gave him a great slicing slash as I steadied myself with my shield against the rush covered stone floor.

A moment later I had regained my balance and moved toward some vague shapes that had begun responding to our shouts by shouting "Westminster. Westminster." That was a bad sign because it meant we were probably going up against experienced fighting men.

Suddenly, at least seemed to happen all of a sudden, the shouting stopped and everything became silent for a moment. "Who are you?" someone shouted out with a London accent. My eyes had adjusted to the dark and I could see the shape of the man who asked standing nearby. I turned my shield toward him and got ready to go for him.

"We are the king's men from Cornwall," the Commander answered from a corner of the room. I recognized his voice and could see a shape in the very dim light that was probably him. "We have been sent by the king to destroy this keep because it belongs to a traitor and a murdering robber baron."

"Impossible," someone shouted. "That is impossible." This one had the accent of a man from the midlands.

"No it is not," I shouted back towards the voice. "I know the Earl is in Devon with the other rebel barons because I saw him there. And I watched with my own eyes as his men fought their way into the London shipping post of Cornwall's Company of Archers and robbed it of its coins. King Henry is right; the Earl of Westminster is a traitor and a robber. He has broken the King's law for sure. He is a traitor."

"And so is everyone who fights for him," the Commander shouted. "Throw down your arms and save yourselves by swearing in the name of Jesus that you are loyal to your king. If you do, we will let you go free since you are not in the west with the King's enemies. It is only the keeps of traitorous barons such Westminster that we are destroying for the king."

There was a long pause. Then a man's voice asked a question from the other side of the hall near where the Commander was standing.

"Will you swear in the name of Jesus that what you said about the Earl is true and that you will let us go free if we swear our loyalty to the king?"

"Aye, I do," the Commander said loudly, I swear it is true in the name of Jesus. Now drop your weapons. We have no quarrel with you so long as you are prepared to stand with King Henry. If you will swear that you are loyal to the king and drop your swords, we will let you leave and take your wounded with you." *Did we care if they were loyal to the king? Of course not; but it was a good story and we wanted to take the castle without any of our men being hurt.*

A moment later there was a great sigh of resignation and a loud clang as a sword was thrown down on to the hall's stone floor. Then there were muttered words and several more clangs, four or five in all. That was when I suddenly felt like trembling and could feel my arms begin to prickle—because one of the swords hit the floor only a foot or so behind me.

Chapter Forty-two

We recover our coins and paste.

No one in the room spoke or moved for several seconds after the defenders' swords and knives were thrown down on to the stone floor of Westminster's hall. All that could be heard for a few seconds was heavy breathing. Then a man on the floor groaned in obvious pain and pleaded for help.

"That sounds like Robert Green," a new voice said anxiously from the other end of the hall. "Can we go to help him?"

"Yes," said the Commander. "It does sound as though he needs a bit of barbering and sewing. You can go to him now and take him and your other wounded with you when you leave."

Someone began pulling open the wooden shutters that covered the hall's wall openings. The light quickly improved so that everyone's once-dim shape could now be seen more clearly. And yes one of the Earl's men had been right behind me with a sword; I was lucky he did not cut me down. Thank you Jesus and all the saints.

A moment later a great horde of archers began storming into the hall. Despite the increased visibility I actually had to hold up my shield to protect one of the baroness's relatives from an over-excited archer.

****** *Captain Adams*

   I was anxious to begin searching the keep for my shipping post's missing coin and flower paste chests but Commander Robertson's first order had been to open the shutters covering the halls wall openings so more light could get in. There was a sliver of light coming through a nearby wooden shutter so I moved to it and reached up to pull it open. Others started doing the same thing with the other shutters and in a few moments it was possible to clearly see the results of the fighting.

   What we saw when the light improved was a dead man lying in a pool of blood and another poor soul in the Earl's livery who would almost certainly need a mercy. There were also three other wounded men including one of our archers. Four of the prisoners were uninjured of whom two, a father and his young son, turned out to be relatives of the baroness who were visiting the castle. They apparently had had no particular interest in fighting for the Earl and had the wit to hide themselves under the hall's long table when the fighting started.

   Fortunately, all of the dead and seriously wounded men were men of the castle who had tried to defend it. Our only wounded man was one of the men who had accompanied the Commander.   He would be alright if the deep slice in his arm did not turn black and begin to smell. Arrangements were immediately made to have him escorted back to the galleys so one of the sailors who had expertise in repairing sails could sew him up. The prisoners were held for questioning and subsequently released.

Some of our men had stormed up the stairs and were no doubt already tromping around in the Earl's sleeping room and, God forbid, in his treasury. "I am going to the Earl's rooms to protect the coins," I shouted towards the Commander as I rushed out of the hall past archers who were still coming in. I did not wait for his agreement or to help with the prisoners and wounded. Day had arrived and the rest of the wooden shutters over the keep's wall openings were being opened to let in even more light.

I went up the stairs two at a time along with some of the archers from the construction site that were still pouring into the keep through its open main door. Sergeant Cooper was right behind me and so was the chosen man who had held the kitchen door until our main party arrived. As I ran up the stairs I tried to struggle out of my tunic in order that my rank could be seen—and got so tangled up that I almost tripped and fell. I began swearing and calling out curses as I did; it is no easy thing to take off a tunic and put it back on whilst you are running up dimly lit stairs carrying a sword and shield.

Finally I stopped at the top of the stairs, put my sword and shield down on the floor of the hallway at the top of the stairs, and turned my tunic inside out so my stripes would show. Then I began moving to the left along the crowded hallway to search for the Earl's sleeping room and his treasury which was almost certainly adjacent to it. As I did I began ordering the crowd of archers who had gotten up the stairs ahead of me to go back down to the stairs and wait outside in the bailey. Two of my archers stayed with me; the third man who had waited at the gate until the main body of archers arrived was nowhere to be seen.

Less than a minute later I had finished clearing everyone out of the Earl's sleeping room, opened the wooden shutters over its wall openings so there was enough light to see, and was trying to light one of the candles in the room so I could see to search the Earl's treasury which, as was inevitably the case in a castle, had no wall openings to admit light.

"Does anyone have a fire stone and a striker?" I shouted; and then cursed because I had just sent everyone down the stairs except my two men and I knew that they did not have fire starters in their personal pouches.

While I waited for a fire stone and a striker I entered into the Earl's dark treasure room.   By the light coming in through the doorway from the sleeping room now that its wall openings had been thrown open I could make out that there were chests on the floor and on a small wooden table

I tried to pick up the chest that was closest to the door with the intention of carrying it into the Earl's sleeping room to see what might be in it, but it was too heavy for one man to carry. Coins for sure.

"Yes!" I said under my breath so no one could hear me. I thought about recruiting some of the men to help me carry it out into the light for viewing but decided to wait for fear that the chest might be dropped or spilled in the darkness. Instead I went back into the sleeping room, threw the last two of its wooden shutters open, and prowled around to see what I could see. But there was nothing special; just the usual smelly sleeping skins, some hooks with tunics and dresses hanging on them, and a stool on which the baroness could sit and look at herself in a piece of polished glass.

It took a while but an archer finally arrived who had had the wit to carry a fire stone and striker in his personal pouch. I watched his efforts impatiently until he got a flame on to one of the candles. Lieutenant White hurried into the room just as he did. My friend was still breathing hard as a result of running from the construction site.

"Light the other candles and bring them in too. Then stay with me up here in case the damn things go out," I told the archer with the fire starter. As soon as he had another one lit I carried the first candle into the Earl's treasury. Sergeant Cooper had appointed himself my bodyguard and followed me in with his sword still unsheathed.

It was about then I realized I could have just given the unlit candle to one of the archers and told him to take it to the kitchen and use the kitchen fire to light it. I really felt stupid but I certainly did not mention it either then or later to Thomas or anyone else.

******

I walked into the Earl's treasure room with the candle held high over my head in to light it up. Thomas White joined me a moment later carrying another. In the flickering light we could see that the rumours amongst the merchants and moneylenders in the city that the Earl was very rich were true. There was no half way about it; owning land in and around London and renting it out was a good way to earn coins. We saw a number of chests full of coins and other valuables including three chests of coins and four chests of flower paste that I recognized as having come from my shipping post.

"Get all these chests carried down the stairs and stack them outside by the keep's front door," I ordered the archers who were waiting at the door. Then I turned to a Sergeant Major who had come into the Earl's sleeping room as I was giving my orders. I did not remember his name but I could see his rank.

"Ah, there you are Sergeant Major. I want you to take charge of the chests and their guards. There is a wagon outside with firewood in it. Gather up all the men you can lay your hands on to help unload the firewood and load the chests. Hurry, Sergeant Major. Run. We will be setting this place on fire in a few minutes and those chests must go with us. If the wagon is gone sent some men back to the construction site and have them seize another. Have the men pull it by hand if necessary."

The Sergeant Major sheathed his sword and left in a hurry, and rightly so. I was anxious to get the chests out of the treasure room and into a wagon because I knew Commander Robertson planned to burn down Westminster's keep as soon as possible and then move on to the nearby keep of another of the Loyal Army's important nobles, Lord Cadeby.

Cadeby was a member of the barons' Great Council and with the Loyal Army in Devon. Whether we would actually be able to get into Lord Cadeby's castle on Haverstock hill was uncertain because sooner or later the word would reach its constable that the archers were out. But perhaps it was possible. But if we could not get in, we would at the very least lay a siege on his castle in order to encourage him to return to London with his men.

"Is everything out of here?" the Commander asked. He came hurrying into the treasure room to join us just as the Sergeant Major was running out of it. The Commander seemed to be very excited. So was everyone else including me.

"It will be in a few minutes, Commander," I said as I came to attention and saluted.

"Move fast Richard. You are to take the twenty of Charles Tomson's men and make sure that this place is set on fire. Do it as soon as everything valuable is out of here and on its way to our galleys. Captain Jenkins' and the men of his galley have been ordered to accompany the chests there and then stay with them to guard them. You are to stay here until the fire you set is strong enough to destroy Westminster's keep and then you and your lads are to follow me to Cadeby's.

"I am going to take the rest of the men, all but the twenty I am leaving with you. When you are sure the fire cannot be put out I want you to march your lads quick-time to Lord Cadeby's castle to rejoin us. Catch up with us as soon as you can. I am leaving immediately; if we hurry we might be able to get there before Cadeby's constable learns we are out and bars his castle's gate."

****** *Captain Tomson, Galley Eighty-six*

When we looked back we could see the first puffs of black smoke coming from Westminster's keep began billowing into the air. At the time we were marching as fast as possible to Lord Cadeby's keep with about three hundred and fifty of the five hundred or so archers we had brought to London. A wagon had been obtain from the abbey and our wounded man and Westminster's coins and flower paste chests had already been loaded into it and dispatched under heavy guard to our waiting galleys.

Twenty or so of my men were temporarily remaining behind under the command of Richard Adams to make sure Westminster's keep kept burning until there was nothing left but an empty shell with scorched stone walls. They would follow us to Cadeby's as soon as they were sure Westminster's keep had been totally destroyed.

Lord Cadeby's keep was similar to Westminster's in that it too was just outside of London and within easy walking distance of the great stone wall that surrounded the city. But London was even bigger than I thought; according to the London-birthed archers guiding us it would take more than an hour of fast marching to reach it.

Not everyone was going to Cadebys. The men of one of the galley companies in our original column had returned to the quay as additional guards for the wagon load of chests we had taken from the Earl of Westminster's treasury. It was sent with a very strong force consisting of about a hundred men under the command of Moses Jenkins, one of my fellow captains. He and they would stay on the galleys to guard them now that the cat was out of the sack that we were raiding in the vicinity of London.

Our galleys were to be heavily guarded because they would be holding the treasure we could accumulated whilst also serving as our headquarters and barbering hospital for the Company's forces. The captains of our various forces were told to be at all time instantly ready to run for our galleys and to hot foot it back to the galleys if they ever thought they were about to be seriously challenged. Trying to stand our ground against a force that was likely to inflict substantial casualties on our men was forbidden.

In addition, according to the Commander, there was no need to take serious casualties by fighting a mostly meaningless battle to take the castle of an absent baron. We were to either leave a few men under a dependable lieutenant to besiege a castle we could not gull our way into or just ignore it entirely and go on to the next one on the list.

Treasure from looting a castle was fine, the Commander periodically reminded us as we marched, but our main goal was to draw the barons away from Cornwall. Even so, treasure and the prize money it would yield were not to be ignored. Accordingly, to further increase the safety of any valuables we captured they were to be distributed amongst the six galleys so that only some of them would be lost if one of our galleys went down or was taken.

As Captain Jenkins was leaving to convoy the treasure to the quay the Commander called after him to remind him that special care had to be taken when loading the chests so their weight would not cause them to break through the hull in a storm and be lost along with the galley. I heard him issue his warning and immediately became quite concerned about my galley because I would not be there to see its share of the chests properly stowed.

Other efforts also were being undertaken to safeguard our men. For example, there were several fortified keeps and towers *inside* the city walls that belonged to one or another of the rebel lords along with the London homes that a good number of the wealthier barons maintained in the city. For better or worse, the Commander had decided to leave them alone, at least initially.

Our not going inside London's walls was a good decision so far as my men and I were concerned. That was because there was a good chance that burning down the barons' strongholds in the city would cause the fire to spread and cause the city's merchants and moneylenders to turn against the Company. Besides, if a counterattack was somehow organized by the barons' supporters and we had to run it was better for us to be out in the open countryside instead of hemmed in by London's buildings and the great stone wall that surrounded the city.

We were in luck; we reached Cadeby's castle before anyone in it had a chance to be informed that we were coming and might be a threat. Once again our main force of archers was held back out of sight whilst a small assault force took the gate by surprise and held it until our main force arrived. This time we used a covered goods wagon hired from Westminster Abbey's church construction site to gain entrance.

The abbot himself had initially bustled out and demanded we pay him directly for the use of a couple of the abbey's covered construction wagons. He ended up agreeing, however, to the Commander's counter-offer—that the abbey's monks and servants mine the stones of Westminster's now-burning castle and use them in the new church in exchange for his monks' prayers for the king and the use of a couple of three of the abbey's wagons. It seems the Company was able to turn the ownership of Westminster's stones over to the abbey because we had acquired them "by right of conquest" as was allowed by an obscure passage somewhere in the bible.

This time archers hidden in one of the abbey's wagons led the assault. It all happened very quickly and quietly. The horse pulling the abbey's covered wagon just trotted right up to the open gate and went on through it without stopping at the gate to ask permission.

As soon as the wagon was inside Cadeby's bailey its covers were thrown back and the archers hiding in it jumped out. Some ran back to hold the gate until our main force could arrive whilst the others entered the main door into Cadeby's keep and captured it. Not a drop of blood was spilled on either side and thirty minutes later another stream of black smoke began pouring into the sky.

In less than an hour we were already marching hard on our way to yet another lord's nearby holding. This time we did not leave anyone behind to tend to the fire. What was unfortunate was that no one had to be sent to help guard the treasure from Cadeby's keep that was on its way to our galleys—because the only thing we found in Cadeby's treasure room was a dead mouse.

Chapter Forty-three

Unexpected Visitors.

Three exhausting days and five burned castle keeps later we finally reached a castle on the far outskirts of London with a garrison that was waiting on high alert and ready to fight to defend it. At least it seemed that way since its constable had barred the castle's entrance gate and his men were on its walls with their weapons. Word of our burning and pillaging had obviously reached them.

We backed off and laid a siege with about twenty archers under the command of one of our galley lieutenants. Then we moved on to the castle of the next London-area baron on our list. It too was on the far side of the city but further out from the city's wall.

I did not accompany the men who were marching to the next castle; I had been slightly wounded in the leg and was sent back with some recently captured coins and weapons to take command of our galleys and keep them in a high state of readiness. We were in a hurry and rightly so; by now a relay of fast-moving gallopers was likely to have reached the Loyal Army and reported what was happening in and around London. One thing was for sure; word of the fighting had reached the king and his court at Windsor Castle.

My wounded leg was still hurting and puffed up from being sewed up and I had no more than reached the Thames and our raft of moored galleys than we had visitors. A middle-aged knight who identified himself as Sir Albert Ridge and a ferret-faced bishop with a scraggly beard by the name of Cuomo rode up on to the quay where our heavily-guarded galleys were moored. They were accompanied by about a dozen of the king's guards under the command of a tough-looking sergeant. I was the senior man present because I had just brought in some coins we had taken out of Lord George of Islington's keep before we burned it.

The somewhat winded and sweating men of the king's guard had walked all the way from Windsor and were veterans enough that they immediately sat down on the quay and rested. They did so whilst the knight rather pompously dismounted from his horse, haughtily announced his name and title, and demanded "in the name of the king" to speak to "whomever is the captain of the men conducting an unauthorized chevauchee and raiding castles in the London area and also blocking access to the king's Tower."

The ferret-faced bishop, on the other hand, remained aboard his horse and looked somewhat fearful. But he did lean over and hold out his hand so I could kiss his ring. From the look of him he was not happy at being present and was more than ready to kick his horse in the ribs and bolt on a moment's notice if danger threatened.

I ignored the bishop's outstretched ring and looked at the self-important knight with suspicious eyes. When he finished announcing himself and telling us what he wanted I told him that the Company's commander, Commander Robertson, was unavailable because he was out destroying the castles of the rebel barons who had risen against the king. Then I began forthrightly telling a combination of truth and lies to fill the two men's heads with the Company's version of what we were doing and why.

What I did *not* do was inquire about the bishop or acknowledge him. I ignored him because I do not like arrogant priests even more than I do not like arrogant knights—probably because I had been ordained as an Angelovian priest as an afterthought when I passed out of the Company school and knew how little it meant to be a priest, except for the ability to extract coins and other donations from the faithful, and that bishoprics were mostly bought by useless idlers from wealthy families.

Although I did not know it at the time, it was the bishop's self-centered concern for his own Islington estates and his reputation in the eyes of King Henry that explained why he had overcome his fear of bodily harm and volunteered to accompany Sir Albert. He was accompanying Sir Albert, Bishop Cuomo told me after the knight finally introduced him, "to add the Church's concern for what you are doing to the concerns expressed by King Henry."

What he said infuriated me. Or, truth be told, I pretended that it did.

"The Church has a concern, does it? Why that is indeed strange. Because it is almost certainly the will of God that has delivered you to us," I thundered, "because we are concerned about *you* and why *you* and Sir Albert are here." Then I dropped my voice to almost a whisper and hissed very menacingly "and now you will have a chance to come aboard and tell us."

All I knew from Sir Albert's initial introduction was that Cuomo was the Bishop of London. As such I knew he had the revenues from the Church's estates in and around Islington. What I did not know at the time was that he had been in the barons' encampment in front of Okehampton and was a compulsive liar who would say or do anything to increase his influence and enrich himself.

Some people claim it is the drinking too much of the waters of drawn from Islington's foul pond that jumbles up the thinking of a man like Cuomo such that he constantly promotes himself by telling stories that are not true; others that it is drinking too much of the particularly foul ale that is brewed by the local alewives with the pond's waters. I myself tend to go with the latter explanation.

I turned back to face Sir Albert after I finished scaring the bishop

"We are *not* blocking access to the Tower, Sir Albert," I said rather sternly after he introduced the bishop and I pointedly declined to kiss his ring. I said it rather loudly so the archers standing on the quay and on the deck of the nearest galley could hear me.

"To the contrary. Everyone is free to *enter* the Tower; what they cannot do after they enter it is *leave* to join the barons who have rebelled against King Henry and are presently attempting to conduct a chevauchee against the king's supporters in Cornwall and Devon. What we do not want, and will not permit, is for anyone to leave the Tower and interfere with the chevauchee *we* are conducting against the rebel barons who have stronghold in the London area.

"As I am sure you know, we are raiding the rebel barons' lands and burning their keeps in response to the chevauchee the barons are conducting in Devon and Cornwall. The difference being, of course, is that *we* have been very successful whereas *they* have failed miserably and suffered great losses."

Sir Albert started to say something. But I cut him off with a dismissive lift of my hand and again spoke loudly so the archers could hear me. As I did I sensed that a number of archers were beginning to come off the galleys to join me and their mates who were already on the quay.

"My name is Adams, *Captain* Adams to you two, and I find your concerns for the men we have bottled up in the Tower to be very interesting. It sounds as though you both want the garrison to be able to leave so they can join the rebels or protect their holds. If so, you and your priest should be arrested and your necks chopped or stretched at the end of a rope; and my friends and I are just the men to do it.

"So tell me again and be clear about it: Do you two really want us to let the men of the Tower garrison go free so they can go off to join the rebels in Devon and fight against the king?"

I asked my question of Sir Albert with a loud and very serious and accusing tone to my voice.

"No of course not. Bishop Cuomo and I are .. er .. uh.. loyal to the king; very loyal, actually. Er. Umm,"

Sir Albert mumbled his response to my threat. He was clearly taken aback; people obviously did not usually speak to him in such a threatening manner. The bishop was wide-eyed with astonishment and concern. This was obviously the reception that the bishop had feared and neither of them had expected.

"We have heard there might be some sort of trouble in Devon and Cornwall. But what is this about London?" the knight finally asked with much less arrogance in his voice.

"Trouble in Devon and Cornwall?" I exclaimed with an even greater amount of anger and incredulity in my voice. "There is a lot more going on in the southwest and around London than just trouble. The lands and holds of the Company of Archers have been attacked in Devon and

Cornwall. And with my own eyes I have seen the Earl of Westminster's men attack merchants in London and carry off their coins and goods."

"I have also with my own eyes seen Westminster and his fellow traitors try to force their way into Cornwall so they can forage—and be soundly defeated for their efforts I am happy to report. I am also aware of the fighting on the road as the rebels marched on Devon and Cornwall and the barons' heavy losses when they tried to take Okehampton Castle on the approaches to Cornwall and then, later, tried to fight their way across the ford."

Then I leaned forward spoke loudly toward the knight with a great deal of venom in my voice.

"During the fighting my men and I had the pleasure of killing many of the traitorous knights and nobles who attacked us along with a large number of their men. We would be happy to add another knight and one of Rome's priests to the list."

And then after a pause I added to my threat.

"And that will happen as sure as God made green apples if I ever think that either of you are supporting the rebel barons who want to replace our king and his rightful heir—so you would be well advised to watch your tongues." *I had not been at Okehampton, of course, but I had heard all about it from the prisoners we had taken, including the captured knight we had carried to London for just such an opportunity as this to get our side of the story told.*

There was menace in my voice as I leaned forward and gave the two of them a hard look and made a stabbing motion with my pointing finger toward Sir Albert. As I did I sensed that the backs of the archers gathering around us on the quay were beginning to stiffen in response to my anger and accusations. There was tension in the air.

"In fact," I said softly with a hiss of anger in my voice, "I rather doubt the king would barely notice your absence if *you* and your priest were to somehow get caught up in the fighting and *never* returned to your duties."

Sir Albert looked aghast when he heard my threat and the bishop's face turned white under his scraggly beard. The knight struggled a bit to find the right response. But then he did.

"Oh right you are, Captain Adams, right you are. Well then. Of course there is more than just a few troubles happening at the moment; of course there is. That is why we are here, to make inquiries and try to find out what is happening so we can inform the king, is that not so, Bishop Cuomo?"

Sir Albert had been looking at me and listening intently as I spoke. Now he looked around for the first time as he gestured toward Bishop Cuomo. His eyes widened. Seeing yourself surrounded by fifty or sixty ferocious-looking archers who are staring at you with anger in their eyes and their arrows nocked will have that effect every time.

The guardsmen accompanying Sir Albert and the bishop had been resting on the quay within earshot of us. My threatening words had reached them and they had seen the archers become more and more resolute and move into killing positions around them. They understood the rapidly growing and very real signs of danger coming from the archers and were beginning to get to their feet. There were enough veterans amongst them such that they knew that very few of their company would escape alive if our arrows started being pushed at them. They desperately wanted to run or, at least, have someone tell them what to do.

"Perhaps you two illustrious gentlemen would like to come aboard and enjoy our hospitality whilst you wait for our Company's commander to return. In fact, I insist on it."

I issued my invitation rather firmly as I gestured with a mocking bow towards the boarding plank with a little welcoming bow. It was presented as an offer they could not refuse. I could feel the tension in the air continue to increase; things were becoming dangerous.

"Sailing Sergeant," I shouted to the roof of the forward deck castle where he was standing with a small group of watchers, "It is overly warm up here in the sun and the king's men on quay are our friends and have not been properly welcomed. Break out a copper coin for each of them so he can buy a bowl of tavern ale and something to eat whilst he waits for Sir Albert and the bishop, and then point them to the nearest tavern where they can find a cool place to wait until they are needed. And have the three prisoners and some cheese and ale brought to the forward deck castle."

My words somehow seemed to calm things down. I could sense the tension begin to dissipate and the archers and the guardsmen start to relax. *They would fight some other time*. Then I turned back to Sir Albert.

"You do not mind your men receiving our largess, do you Sir Albert? It is a tradition of a Papal order such as ours to welcome friends just as it is our tradition to kill our enemies. Our company's commander, Commander Robertson, will be along sooner or later. But you might find the delay helpful because, fortunately, there are some prisoners on board with us. I think it likely they can help you and Bishop Cuomo with your inquiries whilst you are waiting for our company's Commander to return."

Papal order? Bishop Cuomo's mouth dropped open in surprise and Sir Albert looked confused. But they began dutifully moving towards the boarding plank.

Our visitors reluctantly, very reluctantly, come aboard just as the king's greatly relieved guards were leaving with their newly acquired coins to find someplace to eat and drink. I promised to send a runner to fetch them when Sir Albert and the bishop were ready to leave.

I had no idea when Commander Robertson would return from his chevauchee and castle attacks. It could be days, but I knew he would want any representatives of the king or queen who showed up to meet Westminster's reeve and a couple of the knights we had captured at Okehampton and at the ford. And for some reason I began thinking about my wife and daughter and could not get them out of my mind; I suddenly became so desperate to see them that I thought about walking down the river road to the Company's safe house.

****** Captain Adams*

I shook my head to clear it of thinking about my family as I led Sir Albert and the bishop to the nearest galley's forward deck cabin. I took them there to meet with the three prisoners we had brought to London: John the Earl's reeve, one of the wounded knights we captured at Okehampton, and the wounded son of one of the barons who had been taken at the ford when he crawled ashore on the Cornwall side of the ford.

Our prisoners did as they were told to do under the threat of being summarily executed if they did not—they spoke the truth and did so in a believable manner. As they spoke I could see the eyes of my two guests widen in surprise at what they were hearing, both when the prisoners described what they had been trying to do when they were captured and when they described the serious casualties inflicted on the barons by the archers each time they met.

I was struck by a thought as I listened: By the time the fighting is over all of England will know how dangerous it is to attack the Company or attempt to diddle us. It gave me a great deal of satisfaction when I thought about it; my fellow captains and our men had been unrecognized and unrespected in England for too long as far as I was concerned. It was time for the gentry to know what much of the rest of the Christian world already knew about the Company—and not be surprised when we did not obey them when they told us to do something or step out of the way when we saw them coming.

The knight and the bishop stayed with the prisoners for more than an hour and professed to be taken aback and amazed, or so they claimed, at what they heard from our prisoners. Commander Robertson never did appear. Finally I pretended to receive a message from him regretting that he was unable to return to meet with them but would be willing to do so in the near future when he finished burning the next rebel keep.

As they were leaving I told Sir Albert and the bishop the "good news for the Church and the King" about the castles we had been destroying.

"We have given the stones from the Earl of Westminster's castle and the others whose holds we have been torching in the London area to the church being rebuilt by the abbey located next to Westminster village. The abbey's monks and servants will mine the stones from the ruins and put them to God's work. We are doing so in the king's name, of course, on the condition that the abbey's monks say ten prayers for King Henry and the safety of his realm for each stone they mine from the ruins of the traitors' castles."

What I did not tell the two men or even hint at, of course, was the real reason we were destroying the barons' castles—to encourage some of the nobles now in Devon to hurry back to London with their men to protect their properties and, in so doing, reduce the Loyal Army.

Actually I was not sure the Commander had had time to approach the monastery's abbot or that the abbot had agreed that he and his monks would take the stones and chant the required prayers for the king. But I was so confident that they would sooner or later agree to do so that I announced it as fact—so far as I was concerned it was certain the abbot would do so because the Commander had said he intended to make an offer of the stones to him that it would be impossible for him to refuse. Besides, if the current abbot did not agree to mine the stones and chant the required prayers to pay for them his replacement surely would. It was, in other words, a done deal so far as I was concerned even though the abbot and his monks may not have yet have heard about it.

Chapter Forty-four

Things change.

Sir Albert and the bishop talked with the prisoners for more than an hour. Moses Jenson and I were there in the forward deck castle with them and listened intently whilst they talked. We even asked a few questions of our own to make sure the prisoners' tales got properly told. Everything was much more relaxed by the time the talking ended and the foul-smelling prisoners were returned to where they were imprisoned—the cargo hold where they sat in the darkness with an armed guard always sitting on the deck next to the wooden plank that served as the cargo hold's hatch cover.

It was too late in the day for Sir Albert and the bishop to ride to Windsor by the time the meeting with our prisoners ended and their guardsmen were recalled. As a result of the lateness of the day, and in response to my inquiry as they were leaving, Sir Albert and Bishop Cuomo told us that they were going to spend the night at the bishop's London residence and then return to Windsor in the morning. They would, they said, report what they had heard to the king and queen as soon as they arrived.

But would they accurately tell what they heard or would they say something different in order to mislead them? I was uneasy as I bade them farewell. I had the strong feeling that one or both of them were actively supporting the rebel barons.

It was about then that it struck me that it really did not matter what King Henry and the Queen and their courtiers heard or thought or were arrogant enough to attempt to order: We were attacking castles and chevaucheeing on the outskirts of London as a gambit to draw the barons and their armies away from Cornwall—and we would continue to do so until the barons left Devon and Cornwall no matter whether the king and queen and their courtiers liked it or not. Moreover, as soon as the barons' men were out of Devon most of our men would sail for east, or at least so we would claim.

The only thing that was certain, or so we thought at the time, was that we would not continue to fight with the barons once they left Devon or go to war against the French or anyone else even if the king ordered us to do so.

******

A wet and bedraggled Commander Robertson walked over the boarding plank and on to our raft of galleys two days later. He was accompanied by several hundred of the men who had been out with him including a wagon load of wounded men and the bodies of a couple of archers whose luck had run out. There was immediately much running around getting food and drink for everyone. And when not enough was instantly available the Commander ordered that every returning man be given some liberty coins and told to take the rest of the day off and come back no later than two hours after dark. They were ecstatic; he was not.

"I am getting too old for this shite," was what I heard the exhausted Commander mutter as we followed him to the forward castle so he could meet in private with his captains. He muttered it to himself but I was walking immediately behind him and distinctly heard what he said.

The first thing the Commander did was sit down and call for a bowl of ale. Then he tried to catch up on all the latest news and information.

"Any word about the barons?" was the first thing he had asked when we reached the privacy of the deck castle which he had taken for himself when we arrived.

When he was told that there was nothing new to report, the Commander sighed and began giving orders. The first and most important was to order all the archers on the galleys, every single one of them who was fit, into the field to replace the men he had brought back to be rested and resupplied. They were to leave first thing in the morning immediately after they had something to eat to break their overnight fasts.

I was honoured by being given command of the men going out as replacements with Captain Jenson of Galley Ninety-one as my number two. That was fine and so was where I was to lead them and what I was to have them do when we got there—either help Captain Tomson and the men with him burn down the castle of one of the deMontfort cousins or lay a siege on it and then go on to the next castle on the list.

What was not fine was that when we reached the castle I was to report to Captain Tomson of Galley Eighty-six and be under his command as his number two until the castle was taken or under siege. This upset me greatly but I said not a word and tried to hide my disappointment.

Of course I was upset. Tomson was junior to me; the command should have been mine. On the other hand perhaps Tomson and his men had already taken the castle or laid a siege on it. As soon as they had done either the Commander wanted him to return to the galleys with the men who had not yet been rested. Then, I would be the commander of the men in the field with Moses Jenson as my number two.

I was looking forward to having another chance to draw favourable attention to myself. But I was concerned—even though I had never before served with Moses and his reputation, what little I knew of it, was that of a likeable do-nothing who never should have been promoted. It was worrisome to me that he had been the first of the captains to be sent back to the galleys. Why was that? I did not know and for some reason it greatly concerned me.

We had been in London for six days when I set out first thing on rainy morning with Moses Jenson and all the fully rested men from our galleys. Our destination was one of the de Montfort family's castles to the northeast of London. Moses and his men were totally bored with sitting about as guards and more than ready to go for a long walk around to the other side of the city and then out to the de Montfort castle. Their enthusiasm was understandable; their only time in the field so far had been to run from the abbey's construction site to the Earl of Westminster's castle after it had already been taken.

I was the only archer not walking as we set out from the quay. Commander Robertson ordered me to ride in one of Westminster Abbey's horse-drawn covered wagons because my leg had been stitched up as a result of being wounded and he was afraid the stitches would pull out and I would have to be sewed up again by one of the sail makers. It was a kindly gesture because the damn sewing inevitably hurts even if you swallow some flower paste before it happens. We would use the wagon to bring back our dead and wounded and any coins or loot we took.

My isolation as the only passenger in the wagon soon ended as footsore archers began being loaded aboard so they would not have to be abandoned along the way.

In any event, I spent most of the day in a wagon bouncing along on my arse and most of my time thinking about how we could take the castle. The problem, of course, was that none of us had ever seen it and I had not a clue as to how we might get through its gate and take it by surprise. Perhaps with archers hidden in the wagon I decided early on. It was the only thing I could think to do. And that meant I would need Moses' best swordsmen and fastest runners.

"Hoy Moses, come aboard and ride with me. There are things we need to talk about and decisions to be made."

******

Taking the de Montfort castle was not to be. Before we reached it we were recalled by a hard-riding a galloper from the Company's stable in London. James, one of the hostlers from the Company's London stable, caught up with us on the road to deliver a short parchment from Commander Robertson containing our recall orders. After a brief stop with us to deliver the parchment and have a piss and a drink of water, James rode on to carry a similar message Captain Samson and his men. Other couriers, James had reported, were being sent to recall the relatively small forces of archers who were besieging a couple of castles we had not been able to gull our way into.

James the courier did not know what was in the message or why he was delivering it. The only thing he could tell me was that a galley had come in from Cornwall with news that seemed to please everyone. I was sure that only one thing could have had such an effect—some or all of the rebel barons had broken camp and were marching for London.

I immediately called a halt to the march, paraded the men, and informed them that some good news had apparently come in to the Commander from Cornwall and that we would immediately begin marching back to the galleys. The men understood what the message meant and there was much cheering, handshaking, and back slapping even though I cautioned them that we did not yet know the details, only that we were being recalled.

And, as is almost always the case when there is good news in England, the rain started up once again just as we turned around and began marching back to the river and the relative safety of our galleys. It was a warm rain, however, and only lasted an hour or so. Everyone's spirits were high despite it and the men marched jauntily with our marching drum beating the step and the men shouting out many bawdy marching chants.

The men's high spirits were contagious. Travelers on the road cheerfully stepped aside to let us pass and smiled with us even though they did not know why. Sometimes they would call out to ask who we were and why we were in such good spirits, but all I would shout back from the wagon was that "We are archers from Cornwall and have received good news."

The question Moses and I spent the rest of the day in the wagon discussing was whether we should wait in London for the barons to return and once again blood them, or should we sail for Cornwall to clean up anyone the barons left behind? Moses and I talked about it constantly. It was clear to both of us that we should avoid the barons whilst we were on foot without our horse archers to scout and harass them. The decision, of course, would be up to Commander Robertson; but we talked non-stop about it and some of our personal experiences all the way back to the Thames.

By the time we arrived we knew a great deal about each other and I was greatly reassured about Captain Jenson. He was just unlucky.

Chapter Forty-five

Are we homeward bound or not.

We returned to the quay before the sun went down. It had been a very long day with only a few dropouts with sore feet needing a ride in the wagon. There had been a great deal of talking and speculation amongst our men in between their marching songs and chants. Some of the men were sure we were going to visit the king to put him right; others that we would be sailing straight to Cyprus or various other ports; and a couple of men were sure they had overheard Moses and I talking about sailing to the north where the Vikings lived. Returning to Cornwall or Cyprus, however, were the most frequent destinations mentioned and the ones I thought most likely.

The talking in the column also dealt with even more important matters so far as most of the men were concerned—such as whether there would be any liberty coins paid out when they reached the quay and, if so, would there be enough so they could afford to dip their dingles in addition to drinking. And throughout it all there was much talk about, and claims to know, how much prize money would come from the loot we took out of the castles we seized. It was one of the loudest and liveliest marches I had ever witnessed.

And all of us were wrong as to what would happen next.

****** *Captain Adams*

Commander Robertson was standing on the quay waiting for us as we marched in with our drum booming and the marching sergeant calling chants and the men responding. I was marching in my rightful place at the very front of the column and could see that the Commander was not alone. A small group of gentry-dressed men including a couple of men who appeared to be wearing priests' robes were waiting with him. One of them was wearing a bishop's mitre - Sir Albert and Bishop Cuomo had returned and they had brought some gentry with them.

Waiting further along the quay were what were obviously the carriages and horses that had carried the gentry to us. Next to them was a grounded litter that had obviously been carried to the quay by the gang of laborers, probably serfs or slaves, who were sitting at rest around it. Also sitting and waiting amongst the various conveyances were the guards and litter carriers who had accompanied our visitors. They all got to their feet and watched as we marched in.

There was no doubt about it; it was an impressive arrival with the men putting their feet down to the beat of the drum. It also turned out to be a bad mistake because it alerted the watchers to our abilities.

In the little crowd of six or seven men standing around the Commander were Sir Albert and Bishop Cuomo. I saw them as I raised my hand and then dropped it to signal the marching sergeant to halt the men and the drum.

Commander Robertson moved away from the little crowd and towards me as we stopped. Several of the men standing around him started to move forward with him, but he gestured with his open hand to hold them and then said something that stopped them in their tracks with a look of surprise on their faces.

I approached him, stood to attention, and knuckled my brow in salute. He returned the salute and in a soft voice whispered an explanation as to why he had come out to meet me and gave me an order. As he did I recognized Major Captain Franklin standing amongst our visitors. He and his men from the galley companies assigned to seal off the Tower did not have far to walk and were already on board.

"This lot just arrived a few minutes ago and I did not have time to send a messenger to warn you. If anyone asks, and they will, you and your men are under a mercenary contract to fight in the east and will be sailing for Lisbon and Cyprus as soon as the rest of our men arrive. Do not mention Cornwall."

I must have looked confused because the Commander told me more.

"This gaggle of gentry who have suddenly come out of nowhere and honoured us with their presence includes the king's chancellor, Bishop Cuomo who is the bishop of London, and the Nuncio as well as Sir Alfred and couple of courtiers. They are all saying that King Henry wants us to stop our attacks and, instead, place ourselves under the command of the Earl of Westminster and help the barons repel the French.

"But that is not the half of it. They also want me to accompany them back to Windsor because the king wants to give me his orders personally and knight me for my services. Unfortunately for them, I do not believe a word they say about the king wanting us to serve under Westminster or that King Henry wants me to go to Windsor to meet him and be knighted.

"To the contrary, I think they are trying to get me alone so they can kill me. That is probably because they think the force we have brought to London will fall apart the way a baron's army usually does when a baron is killed and an adequate heir is not nearby to immediately take over. One of them even asked me if any of my sons were with me and seemed to be pleased when I said I only had daughters. And even if what they say about the king wanting to talk to me turns out to be true I would never go to Windsor or put myself or a single one of our men under Westminster's command. What do you think, Richard?"

"I agree with you Commander. None of them can be trusted." *What else could I say, eh?* "I also think we should invite the worthies on board to talk about how our armies would be combined with Westminster's—and once they are on board take them for a cruise down the river and question them rather rigorously. But perhaps whilst you are bringing them aboard I should walk over and talk to the sergeants of their guards to see if I can learn anything that might be useful."

"Great minds think alike, Richard, yes they do. Because bringing them aboard and questioning them rather rigorously is exactly what I have in mind as soon as your men are back aboard their galleys. And I like your idea of talking to their guards. So please order your men to return to their galleys and then go visit the guards whilst I bring the gentry aboard."

As I walked over to visit with the guards I realized I had not seen my friend, Lieutenant Cooper. How strange. But then it struck me. One of the worthies visiting us was the king's chancellor. Peter had been living in his household as one of his clerics and must have recognized him as we marched up. Which meant Peter was probably staying out of sight until he knew if it was alright to reveal himself. *Hmm. I wonder where he is hiding.*

****** *Captain Adams*

My visit to the guards was well worth the walk. They had heard how friendly we treated their mates a few days earlier and were obviously hoping for the same. In any event, I learnt a lot and I found myself humming a popular tavern sing along tune when I boarded the galley raft about ten minutes later to join the Commander and our illustrious guests. They were standing in the shade of the sail of the down river galley farthest out into the Thames in order "to better catch the cooling airs."

By the time I returned from the quay almost all of the men we had brought to London had re-boarded their galleys. The only exceptions were the fifty or sixty men who had been left behind at a couple of castles as besiegers. So far as I knew the missing men had been recalled were on their way back.

The Commander saw me returning from my meeting with the gentry's guards and nodded to Captain Jeffers and his sailing sergeant as soon as I came aboard. A sailor let go of the line he was holding and moments later we began drifting away from the galley raft. As soon as we were clear the rest of our galleys cast off their lines one after another and began drifting down the river behind us.

Our "guests" suddenly realized what was happening and began getting very excited. So did their guards on shore when they saw us begin moving down the river; they shouted and began running down the road to follow us. One of our galleys, Number Fifty-seven carrying our dead and wounded, remained behind to wait for the last of our men; the five on the river were fully manned and then some.

"It is alright, lads. No worries." I shouted across the water to the now-anxious guards who had begun running along riverbank and shouting for us to stop. "We are just going for a cruise to better catch a cooling breeze for the gentry. We will be back after the sun goes down."

It was a lie, of course, but it might confuse them and give us a few more hours to do whatever it was that the Commander wanted to do. He smiled appreciatively and gave me a nod.

Our "guests" were left alone and under a very loose guard whilst we talked to one of the priests in the stern deck castle. He was our spy Thomas White. I had not recognized him at first because we had never met. But I certainly learned more about him and was impressed as I listened to his report.

Interestingly enough, in the course of listening to Sergeant White, or Father White the Chancellor's cleric as he was known to our guests, we learnt quite a bit about both the barons' plans and, in particular, Bishop Cuomo whom the others, to a man according to Sergeant White, smiled at to his face and disparaged behind his back.

The bishop was an Italian who had been appointed by the previous French Pope as a reconciliation gesture because Cuomo was thought, rightly as it turned out, to be uniquely weak and pliable despite his efforts to project himself as a man of strength and his attempts to be charming. It was not until much later that we learned he lied to everyone all the time and was supporting the rebels only for what he could get for himself. It was a family trait according to Sergeant White who had apparently met his brother.

We also learned that there were now two men claiming to be the Bishop of London and two men claiming to be the Papal Nuncio, the Pope's ambassador to King Henry. They had been appointed by rival claimants to the papacy, one Frenchman and one Italian, and each had the backing of some of the city's priests and England's nobles.

At first as I listened it bothered me greatly that I had not known about there being two men claiming to be the Archbishop of London; probably because I did not understand their insignificance. But then I realized what it meant that there were two of them—that their titles were somewhat meaningless and their powers limited.

What counted was *not* just which of the claimants for each position had the ear of the king and the leaders of barons and what they told them. It was *also* what the somewhat isolated and feeble-minded king and his ambitious barons would do with whatever information and advice they were given. It was a revelation that at first I thought I should bring to the attention of Commander Robertson and my fellow captains. The king and the barons could, after all, respond to our efforts by attempting to once again do something stupid because they did not understand the Company.

But then again, why should I bother to bring it up; having two claimants for each of the Church's main sinecures in England was a religious conflict pure and simple and need not involve the Company in any way—the Company would almost certainly deal with both bishops if it became necessary and "contribute" to the personal purses of both Popes if there ended up being two.

******

What we learned from the priestly Sergeant Thomas White, who had immediately been promoted to become Lieutenant Thomas White and donned an archer's tunic, was stunning. He had read all the parchment messages received by the Chancellor, scribed the responses, and listened quietly to everything at the Chancellor's meetings.

There was no doubt about it according to Lieutenant White. The Chancellor, the Nuncio, and Bishop Cuomo were at the very center of the plot to make Westminster the next king. The two priests were doing so in return for his promise of enough coins to buy a cardinal's position for each of them in Rome or wherever the next Pope reigned; the Chancellor for promises of coins, a great swath of land in the midlands, and titles for his two sons. The De Montforts' priest was to become the Bishop of London and get the diocese's revenues.

Of immediate importance in the new lieutenant's report was that the Earl of Westminster had learned of our attacks and was returning to London with as much of the Loyal Army as were willing to follow him. He was expected to arrive sometime late tomorrow afternoon or the next day.

What we learned that was equally important was that all of our visitors, according to Lieutenant White, were beholden to Westminster in one way or another, every one of them. According to the new lieutenant, they had been ordered by Westminster to contact us and make whatever promises of payment and of recognition and advancement as might be necessary to get us to "change sides" and support him. *Ordered?*

According to the new lieutenant, the Earl and the others expected us to be willing to do so because they apparently thought we were just another free company of mercenaries who would, as mercenary companies often did in these modern times, change sides if offered enough coins.

"They do not understand that we are primarily a merchant company and need to honour our agreements and commitments in order to retain our customers and be able to fetch high prices for our services," explained Lieutenant White.

"And the king?" asked the Commander. "What is his part in all this?"

"None. He is poxed and apparently knows very little about what has been happening. The Nuncio and the Bishop have been keeping his head too filled with fears of purgatory and hopes for salvation for him to think of anything else."

"So the king did not send our visitors to us as they claim; are you sure of that, Lieutenant?"

"Aye, Commander. I am sure. King Henry does not know they are here. They were laughing about it as we arrived."

But then I remembered something about the old Roman road and the narrow bridge over the Thames at Oxford. An hour later we had a plan.

Chapter Forty-six

Four big surprises.

We turned around and rowed back up the river until we reached the London Bridge and could go no further because of the height of our Galleys' masts. Along the way we met Number Fifty-six coming down the river after boarding the returnees from our two besieging forces. It turned around and followed us. We also waved cheerfully to the still-anxious and pleading guards as we rowed past them.

When we reached the bridge over the Thames each of the galleys launched its four-oared dinghy with nine of its best fighting men crammed into it along with their weapons including swords and shields for every man. We also offered so many coins to a couple of fishermen in fishing boats near the bridge that we were able to board ten more men, five in each of the little two-oared boats.

Rowing up the river to Oxford in our dinghies to intercept the returning barons' army was all that we could do. It would have been easier to ride to Oxford on horses, of course, but we had no horses and, besides, all our riders were still in Cornwall. Walking to Oxford was out because we probably could not have reached the next bridge over the Thames, the bridge at Oxford, before Westminster and his army reached it. Besides, it would have been much too dangerous for our men to be both afoot and heavily outnumbered so far from our galleys.

In any event, it was not the barons' army that we were after; it was its commander, the Earl of Westminster. If we could trap him and kill him on the narrow bridge that crossed the Thames at Oxford the Loyal Army would fall apart, or so we hoped and told each other. Afterwards we would escape from the risk of a counterattack by making our way down the river in our dinghies. That was the plan and what we hoped to do.

******

Our eight little boats were so heavily overloaded that they might have sunk had there been any significant waves on the river or a heavy wind. The Commander was in one boat and I was in another. Each of the other six was commanded by one of the galley captains and carried his best fighting men.

It was, as you might expect, time-consuming and tiring to row all the way up the river from London to Oxford. It took many hours and my arms were tired and my hands raw from taking my turn at rowing. But the men were all experienced rowers with strong arms. Even so, we only made it to Oxford after rowing hard and continually all that long day and the following night. Even so, it was well into the next morning by the time we tied up just below the bridge on the Oxford side of the river. It would have taken even longer if the archers in the dinghies had not all been experienced rowers with particularly strong arms.

But had we gotten to the bridge in time? I went ashore with Commander Robertson to find out; and I was so stiff from sitting in the dinghy for so many hours that I damn near fell into the water when I was climbing out of it to go ashore. Everyone else stayed aboard and was soon trying to get a few minutes of sleep. Some of the towns' people and the travelers on the road saw us arrive but our weapons were carefully kept out of sight and no one paid much attention.

A few minutes later and we knew we had reached Oxford in time. At least we had done so if the toll collector stationed at the Oxford end of the bridge was to be believed when we told him that we had an important message for the Earl of Westminster and inquired if he had recently crossed the bridge with his army.

According to the Toll Collector, a few riders and messengers from the barons' army had come over the bridge into Oxford in the last forty-eight hours, but not any parties of gentry or soldiers. More importantly, the collector did not think the Earl of Westminster was one of the few.

"Mostly couriers going to and from the army they was; no gentry coming this way from the army. The word from people traveling on the road is that the gentry and their army will begin arriving sometime today. And I will not be here when they do—I am going to go home to my wife and bar the door. Aye, you heard me right. I am going to bar the door; the word is that many of the poor sods are starving and have no coins to buy food—and we all know what that means."

****** *Several surprises*

We walked down the riverbank to where our dinghies were waiting and Commander Robertson immediately began giving the orders necessary to implement his plan. Half of dinghies were pulled ashore at the foot of the bridge near where he and I had come ashore; the other half were rowed to the other side of the river and similarly pulled ashore close to the bridge. The dinghies at both ends of the bridge were immediately turned over and our weapons concealed under them.

The men had long ago turned their tunics inside out to conceal their archer stripes. Now we merely looked like unarmed workmen who were idling about waiting for work, at least that is how we hoped we looked. But that might not be enough to allay suspicion. So Commander Robertson moved the archers some distance away from the bridge and separated them according to their dinghies into little groups of seven or eight men each.

Our plan was simple as all good plans must be: When the Earl of Westminster was on the bridge almost everyone in our force would rush to the bridge and try to kill everyone on it. The only exceptions were a couple of men who remained with our dinghies to guard them and me and Sergeant Fox. I was to walk up the road about five hundred paces towards Cornwall and place John the reeve and Sergeant Fox where I wanted them to sit so they could watch the travelers on the road without drawing attention to themselves. The reeve would once again have a rope around his neck attaching him to Sergeant Fox.

John Reeve was with us because he knew the Earl by sight. If he identified the Earl to me and did not try to warn him the reeve would immediately be cut loose and receive the pouch of coins Sergeant Fox was carrying that would make him wealthy enough that he would never have to return to the Earl's service. On the other hand, if the reeve tried to warn the Earl his throat would be cut on the spot by Sergeant Fox. We had long ago taken the measure of the reeve and were rather certain as to which option he would choose.

Our plan began to unfold as soon as the Commander Robertson returned to where our dinghies were nosed into the shore next to the bridge. I took Sergeant Fox and the reeve to where I wanted them to wait and then walked back to get myself closer to the bridge. We were downstream side of the road and I was in a position where I could see Sergeant Fox and the reeve and be seen by our various groups of attackers.

My task when John and Sergeant Fox signaled that Westminster was coming was to raise my hands over my head and stretch. That was the signal to our men who were scattered about in little innocent-appearing groups that Westminster was coming and it was time to move into position.

I would then walk along the side of the road slightly behind the Earl as he moved toward the bridge. I would make a second signal to our attackers by twirling my arm above my head when the Earl was well on to the bridge and somewhat blocked from turning back by the men and wagons who were coming along behind him.

When the reeve reported Westminster approaching on the road to the bridge my signal would send the men drifting back towards their weapons. And when I saw him actually riding or walking far enough on to the bridge my second signal would cause our men to seize their weapons and within seconds block off both ends of the bridge—thus trapping Westminster and whomever else was on the bridge with him.

As soon as they had their weapons in hand the thirty or so veteran swordsmen at each end of the bridge would begin working their way through the unsuspecting barons' men on the bridge and use their short swords to kill them all whilst protecting themselves with their galley shields.

If everything went according to plan the killing of the Earl and the other men on the bridge would happen before the barons' men had a chance to seize their weapons and fight back. Afterwards our men would rush to their dinghies, row down the river to our galleys, and we would immediately set our sails for Cornwall for the purpose of finishing off any of the barons' men who were still there.

That was our plan to kill the commander of the so-called Loyal Army and it came very close to succeeding.

We watched and waited as the barons' men and their wagons began to reach the bridge and cross over it into Oxford. Their column seemed endless and they looked hungry, bedraggled, and disheartened. Or perhaps that was what I wanted to see. In any event, very few of them were carrying weapons. They had either been abandoned or, more likely, were being carried in the wagons. It was very encouraging.

Several hours later the reeve and Sergeant Fox suddenly stood up. The Earl is coming. As soon as they did I stood up and raised my arms in a great stretch. As I did the little groups of archers who had been intently watching me immediately began moving towards their weapons.

The archers at both ends of the bridge had reached their weapons and were standing ready to turn over their dinghies and grab them when, two or three minutes later, I saw the Earl enter the bridge and begin riding over it. I waited until he was well on to the bridge. Then I raised my right hand and twirled it over my head to give the second signal.

Everything suddenly began moving fast: The archers turned over their dinghies to reveal their weapons, snatched them up, ran to the entrances to the bridge, and began cutting down everyone on it.

There was great shouting and screaming as our men reached the two entrance to the bridge and began cutting down the unsuspecting soldiers and camp followers of Westminster's army who were jammed on to the narrow bridge with him—and then, to our great shock and surprise, within seconds people began jumping off the bridge into the river to escape.

I had marked the Earl and watched him as he began slowly riding his horse across the bridge towards Oxford which started at the end of the bridge. He was in the midst of the men and wagons of his army who were crossing the bridge at the same time. He was easy to track because he was riding his horse, wearing fine clothes, and had several similarly well-dressed men on horseback around him who were clearly deferential.

The attack caused the Earl and the horsemen with him to stand in their saddles and look back and forth at both ends of the bridge as the archers coming from either end of the bridge closed in on them. I watched as he and the other horsemen drew their swords and prepared to fight off the on-coming archers. Then, to my great distress, I clearly saw him slide off his horse and a moment later jump off the bridge into the river with a great splash. That was when I lost sight of him.

Did he swim to safety or join some of the others and wade ashore with the water up to his neck or did he drown? We had no way of knowing. There was, however, no doubt about it at the time—Westminster surprised us by attempting to escape in a way we had not considered.

****** Richard Adams

Our attack caught the Loyal Army totally by surprise. There was still no organized resistance by the time the Earl jumped to safety and I began blowing the withdrawal whistle. The archers on the bridge began withdrawing immediately. Even so, four of our men were wounded, one was killed by a knight on horseback who was himself immediately unhorsed and killed, and quite a few of ours had bumps and bruises earned whilst climbing over the dead and wounded to get at the Earl and his soldiers and camp followers who were still alive on the bridge.

I began blowing my recall whistle as soon as I saw the Earl jump off the bridge. The archers promptly began withdrawing to our dinghies with our casualties. They left behind a bridge covered with dead and seriously wounded barons' men and their camp followers.

Neither Sergeant Fox nor I participated in the surprise attack. Once I gave the signal that Westminster was on the bridge we ran to the dinghies at our end of the bridge and commenced to load and dispatch our men as fast they returned from the fighting. John the reeve was turned loose with the rope still tied around his neck and a pouch of coins in his hand.

Sergeant Fox and I stood knee deep in the water and waited with the last dinghy for what seemed like hours in case the ensuing chaos and confusion had caused us to miscount the number of archers who had returned. We stayed there until a gang of the barons' men brandishing weapons began coming down the path to get to us. Indeed Sergeant Fox and I waited so long to push off the last dinghy and be pulled aboard that several of our dinghies began rowing back up the river to see if we needed assistance.

The archers in the dinghy I was holding back were clearly quite anxious to leave; but they also understood and totally approved of why I refused to leave until the last moment. They even laughed when I said "we are going to wait a bit in case some of our lads stopped at yonder tavern for a bowl." Even so, their sighs and looks of relief when I finally did shout "push off" to Sergeant Fox would have made me laugh if the situation had not been so dangerous.

****** *Richard Adams*

It was a lot easier to float down the Thames than to row up it. We soon joined up with the rest of the Company dinghies and spent the rest of the day floating down the Thames with a bit of rowing now and then to keep us in the swiftest part of the current and pointed downstream. It was a jovial trip for most of us. The one exception was the unlucky chosen man who had somehow fallen to the sword of a now-deceased knight who did not have the wit of the Earl to try to escape. We would bury him at sea.

The traffic on the river was not particularly heavy because we were above London. Even so, we constantly saw boats and barges moving in both directions and we periodically could see fishermen along the riverbank. We did not get close enough to most of them to exchange hoys. That was because those that were rowing their way upstream avoided the swiftest parts of the river in which we were sailing, and those coming downstream were mostly drifting and rowing easy as we were doing so that we rarely passed anyone and were rarely passed ourselves.

We reached the bridge and re-boarded our moored galleys the next morning just as the sun was coming up. Our men were not allowed to go ashore so I could not. The only people allowed to go ashore were the wounded knight and the baron's son. They had been promised their freedom if they told the truth whenever they were questioned and as far as we could tell they had done so. How they would get back to their homes was up to them; they were happy to go and it freed up additional space in our cargo hold for the gentry.

It had been two long days and nights and I was still tired despite napping on and off as we floated down the Thames. Our galleys had cast off their moorings and continued down the river as soon as we climbed aboard and were replaced on the dinghies' oars by the fresh arms of some of the archers who had remained behind.

Most of the day was spent moving down the Thames to the sea and periodically rowing as each galley's dinghy pulled its bow this way and that to avoid colliding with the other traffic on the river.

When we finally reached the sea the dinghies and their five-man crews came aboard their galleys and we set our sails for Cornwall. I felt very low and out of sorts as we cleared the Thames; once again I had travelled on the river past my family and shipping post without being able to stop to make sure they were alright.

I spent a mostly sleepless night that night despite feeling so sad and tired that even my bones seemed to ache.

******

The lookout's hail came when we were three days out of London and had just finished putting the bishop, the Nuncio, and the rest of their party over the side so they could swim off and join Jesus. It was inevitable; we no longer had a need for them and too many archers had been killed and wounded by the barons for a lesser revenge to suffice.

Because of my rank I was standing on the roof of the forward castle with Commander Robertson and Captain Stone, the galley's captain, when the hail came. It was a partially cloudy day and we had a quartering wind.

"A hoy to the deck. There be sails to the southwest." And then a few moments later he added "There be many of them."

"My God," Captain Stone said a minute or so later with disbelief in his voice as the sails came over the horizon and into view. "The French are out and they are heading towards Exeter."

The appearance of the French fleet was a great surprise. What should we do? All eyes turned to the Commander. After a brief pause he told us.

"We will send them a "go away" message with our longbows and then wait off Cornwall until we see where the French intend to land," he said. "Then we will decide what to do next, if anything.

As we approached the first of the French transports a few minutes later Commander Robertson turned towards me and the other men standing with him on the castle roof and asked "What do you think Westminster will do now?"

The Commander asked his question just as we had begun rowing our way through the French fleet and showering the unsuspecting men on their decks with arrows as we did.

"Raise his rents most likely," someone behind me said with a grunt as he pushed out his first arrow.

End of the story

* * * * * *

* * * * * *

* * * * * *

Be of good cheer. At this very moment additional manuscripts from the chest discovered under the rubble in the basement of the Bodleian Library are being translated from Latin into English. That is encouraging because it means that more of the action-packed saga of Britain's first great merchant company can be told. The next book in the series is *The Paris Gambit*.

And there are other books by Martin Archer that you can read while you wait for it – a hilarious comedy entitled *The Wonderful New ERA Conspiracy* that Mel Brooks of *Blazing Saddles* fame was about to do as a movie before he passed away; a crime story *Cage's Crew* wherein the "hero" is a hard man who is a professional thief and robber; and five books in an action-packed military saga *Soldiers and Marines.*

Martin has also helped bring the wonderful books of the late Jacqueline Lindauer to Amazon and recommends them highly, particularly if you enjoy books such as Antoine de Saint-Exupery's *The Little Prince.*

Martin Archer's books in order in the exciting and action-packed *The Company of Archers* saga:

The Archers

The Archers' Castle

The Archers' Return

The Archers' War

Rescuing the Hostages

Kings *and Crusaders*

The Archers' Gold

The Missing Treasure

Castling the King

Amazon eBooks in Martin Archer's epic *Soldiers and Marines* saga:

Soldiers and Marines

Peace and Conflict

War Breaks Out

War in the East

Israel's Next War (A prescient book much hated by Islamic reviewers)

eBook Collections on Amazon

The Archers Stories I - complete books I, II, III, IV, V, VI.

The Archers Stories II - complete books VII, VIII, IX, X.

The Archers Stories III - complete books XI, XII, XIII.

The Archers Stories IV – complete books XIV, XV, XVI, and XVII.

The Archers Stories V – complete books XVIII, XIX, and XX.

The Archers Stories VI – complete books XXI, XXII, and XXIII.

The Soldiers and Marines Saga - complete books I, II, and III.

Other books you might enjoy:

The Great New ERA Conspiracy by Martin Archer. (hilarious comedy)

Cage's Crew by Martin Archer writing as Raymond Casey. (action-packed story of a robbery gone wrong.)

America's Next War by Michael Cameron and Martin Archer– an adaption of Martin Archer's *War Breaks Out* to set it in the immediate future when Eastern and Western Europe go to war over another wave of Islamic refugees.

AND, all the books of the late Jacqueline Lindauer and Antoine de Saint-Exupery that are now available on Amazon.

How it all started: Sample Pages from Book One of the Archers saga

.... We sometimes had to shoulder our way through the crowded streets and push people away as we walked towards the church. Beggars and desperate women and young boys began pulling on our clothes and crying out to us. In the distance black smoke was rising from somewhere in the city, probably from looters torching somebody's house or a merchant's stall.

The doors to the front of the old stone church were closed. Through the cracks in the wooden doors we could see the heavy wooden bar holding them shut.

"Come on. There must be a side door for the priests to use. There always is."

We walked around to the side of the church and there it was. I began banging on the door. After a while, a muffled voice on the other side told us to go away.

"The church is not open." The voice said.

"We have come from Lord Edmund to see the Bishop of Damascus. Let us in. We know he is in there."

We could hear something being moved and then an eye appeared at the peep hole in the door. A few seconds later, the door swung open and we hurried in.

The light inside the room was dim because the windows were shuttered.

Our greeter was a slender fellow with alert eyes who could not be much more than an inch or two over five feet tall. He studied us intently as he bowed us in and then quickly shut and barred the door behind us. He seemed quite anxious.

"We have come from Lord Edmund's castle in the Bekka Valley to see the Bishop," I said in the bastardised French dialect some people are now calling English. And then Thomas repeated my words in Latin. *Which is what I should have done in the first place.*

"I shall tell him you are here and ask if he will receive you," the man replied in Latin. "I am Yoram, the Bishop's scrivener; may I tell him who you are and why you are here?"

"I am William, the captain of the men who are left of the Company of English archers who fought in the Bekka with Lord Edmund, and this is Father Thomas, our priest. We are here to collect our Company's pay for helping to defend Lord Edmund's fief these past two years."

"I shall inform His Eminence of your arrival. Please wait here."

The Bishop's scrivener had a strange accent; I wonder how he came to be here?

Some time passed before the anxious little man returned. While he was gone we looked around the room. It was quite luxurious with a floor of stones instead of the mud floors one usually finds in a church.

The room was quite dark. The windows were covered with heavy wooden shutters and sealed shut with wooden bars; the light in the room, such as it was, came from cracks in the shutters and smaller windows high on the walls above the shuttered windows. There was a somewhat tattered tribal carpet on the floor.

The anxious little man returned and gave us a most courteous nod and bow.

"His Grace will see you now. Please follow me."

The Bishop's clerk led us into a narrow, dimly lit passage with stone walls and a low ceiling. He went first and then Thomas and then me. We had taken but a few steps when he turned back toward us and in a low voice issued a cryptic warning.

"Protect yourselves. The Bishop does not want to pay you. You are in mortal danger."

The little man nodded in silent agreement when I held up my hand. Thomas and I needed to take a moment to get ourselves ready.

He watched closely, and his eyes opened in surprise as we prepared ourselves. Then, when I gave a nod to let him know we were ready, he rewarded us with a tight smile and another nod—and began walking again with a determined look on his face.

A few seconds later we turned another corner and came to an open door. It opened into a large room with beamed ceilings more than six feet high. I knew the height because I could stand upright after I bent my head to get through the entrance door.

A portly older man in a bishop's robes was sitting behind a rough wooden table, and there was a heavily bearded and rather formidable-looking guard with a sword in a wooden scabbard standing in front of the table. There was a closed chest on the table and a jumble of tools and chests in the corner covered by another old tribal rug and a broken chair.

The Bishop smiled to show us his bad teeth and beckoned us in. We could see him clearly despite the dim light coming in from the small window openings near the ceiling of the room.

After a moment he stood and extended his hand over the table so we could kiss his ring. First Thomas and then I approached and half kneeled to kiss it. Then I stepped back and towards the guard to make room for Thomas so he could re-approach the table and stand next to me as the Bishop re-seated himself.

"What is it you want to see me about?" the Bishop asked in Latin.

He said it with a sincere smile and leaned forward expectantly.

"I am William, captain of the late Lord Edmund's English archers, and this is Father Thomas, our priest and confessor." *And my older brother, although I do not intend to mention it at the moment.*

"How can that be? Another man was commanding the archers when I visited Lord Edmund earlier this year, and we made our arrangements to pay you."

"He is dead. He took an arrow in the arm and it turned purple and rotted until he died. Another took his place and he is dead also. Now I am the captain of the Company."

The Bishop crossed himself and mumbled a brief prayer under his breath. Then he looked at me expectantly and listened intently.

"We have come to get the money Lord Edmund entrusted to you to pay us. We looked for you before we left the valley, but Beaufort Castle was about to fall and you had already fled. So we followed you here; we have come to collect our Company's pay."

"Of course. Of course. I have it right here in the chest.

"Aran," he said, nodding to the burly soldier standing next to me, "tells me there are eighteen of you. Is that correct?" *And how would he be knowing that?*

"Yes, Eminence, that is correct."

"Well then, four gold Constantinople coins for each man is seventy-two; and you shall have them here and now."

"No, Eminence, that is not correct."

I reached inside my tunic and pulled out the Company's copy of the contract with Lord Edmund, and laid the parchment on the desk in front of him.

As I placed it on the table, I tapped it with my finger and casually stepped further to the side, and even closer to his swordsman, so Thomas could once again step into my place in front of the Bishop and nod his agreement confirming it was indeed in our contract.

"The contract calls for the Company to be paid four gold bezant coins from Constantinople for each of eighty-seven men and six more coins to the Company for each man who is killed or loses both of his eyes, arms, legs, or his ballocks.

"It sums to one thousand and twenty-six bezants in all—and I know you have them because I was present when Lord Edmund gave you more than enough coins for our contract and you agreed to pay them to us. So here we are. We want our bezants."

"Oh yes. So you are. So you are. Of course. Well, you shall certainly get what is due you. God wills it."

I sensed the swordsman stiffen as the Bishop said the words and opened the lid of the chest. The Bishop reached in with both hands and took a big handful of gold bezants in his left hand and placed them on the table.

He spread the gold coins out on the table and motioned Thomas forward to help him count as he reached back in to fetch another handful. I stepped further to the left and even closer to the guard so Thomas would have plenty of room to step forward to help the Bishop count.

Everything happened at once when Thomas leaned forward to start counting the coins. The Bishop reached again into his money chest as if to get another handful. This time he came out with a dagger—and lunged across the coins on the table to drive it into Thomas's chest with a grunt of satisfaction.

The swordsman next to me simultaneously began pulling his sword from its wooden scabbard. Killing us had all been prearranged. .....

**** End of the Sample Pages ****

Printed in Great Britain
by Amazon

78684526R00363